Be Happy with My Life.

By

Summerset Downs

Dedicated to Katies all over the world.
And Rachel.

Other works by Terence F. Moss.
Stage Musicals
London Town the Musical
Angels and Kings
Soul Traders (Edinburgh Festival)

Television pilots
The Inglish Civil War
Closing Time
Dave

Stage plays
Better by Far. 2015
Ali's Bar 2017
Old 2021
Petroleum 2021

Novels
The Prospect of Redemption
The Killing Plan
The Tusitala
Charlie Christmas and the Nancy Stanley Mystery
Death of a Sparrow

Contacts.
Terence F. Moss
Also writes under the name of
Summerset Downs.
Summerset Downs can be contacted at
summersetdowns@hotmail.com

CONTENTS

Be Happy with My Life

By

Summerset Downs

Trinity Farrier.

So, small, so very small, traversing the journey from the darkness to the light for just a few short weeks, then suddenly drawn back toward dark canyons forever, to rest with so many others – never to see the sands on faraway shores or feel one delicious moment of apricity.

CHAPTER 1
Katie.
December 2006

Death! That was the first thing that popped into my head while I sat in the waiting room, gazing up at the sculptured pattern of the suspended ceiling tiles. Don't get me wrong, it wasn't the tiles that made me think of death; they weren't that bad. They were inanimate objects designed not to arouse intense feelings - apart from mediocrity. In that respect, they had succeeded admirably. I found the tiles to be curiously attractive, but that was it. They were not something I would have at home, but they were strangely pleasing to the eye. The moon's surface probably looked remarkably similar when seen through a telescope. But then most things, when viewed from a distance, take on an entirely unfamiliar perspective when seen up close.

I had always viewed death much the same as the moon; it was so far away that it was not worth wasting too much time thinking about it. Now and then, we are obliged to confront the existential reality of life - we are born, we live, and then... But not me; I had never actually given it any real consideration. When you are young, you don't; it usually happens to other people. Mainly old people, well older than me anyway.

Why precisely are we here? What does it all mean? I only ask myself those questions when someone I know dies, or the funeral service drags on. All that nonsense stays firmly locked away in a cupboard under the stairs the rest of the time. Best not to dwell on it too much, I thought. Nothing ever came from dwelling too much on anything, especially something I didn't understand.

But this time, it was different. I might die, and suddenly, for the first time, I had to confront the stark fragility of my mortality and how precarious life is. The harsh reality was;was I just wasn't young anymore; I was nearly twenty-eight.

I was probably being a tiny bit melodramatic. Getting it out of proportion to what it really was is what I do - when I don't know something.

I remember seeing a play a few years ago, and for the first ten minutes, one of the characters flipped a coin in the air, and it

4

always landed the same way up. With each flip, I could feel the tension grow more intense as I waited for the coin to fall the other way up... it never did - till it did. Maybe life is like that, just a toss of a coin. Fear and anxiety lie in the unknown, the maybe's and the what ifs - not in certainty. You can prepare for what you know will happen but not for what you don't know will happen. I guess it's all to do with the black swan theory.

Would it be a slow, lingering, painful death, I wondered? I always assumed the worse - but then I guess that's what everybody thinks when something unexpected pops up on your body. I was trying my best not to think about it - flooding my brain with The Dark Side of the Moon and wondering what happened to Syd Barrett after he was kicked out of the band. That took my mind off other things for a while... then I remembered he'd died, the final toss....

Surely not me. I must be too young for breast cancer – it must be something else. I googled the possible alternatives. Then another shot of reality bit my arse. Come on, get real – twenty-eight! Of course, I wasn't too young. Anybody can get cancer at any time. It had become very cosmopolitan and not remotely ageist. A multi-cultural disease for a modern society...

Could it be a boil? I wondered. Now there was a lovely thought. No! It wasn't a boil; I knew that much. Had lots of them as I wandered through puberty, they were enormous and horrible, and my mum squeezed them out ahhh. That was a hormone problem, and I always got them on my bum. There was no squeezing this one out. I have hormone problems now, but that's because I'm pregnant, so I eat coal - and sardines in tomato sauce - from the tin, which helps - a bit,

It was at the end of my first trimester when I first noticed the 'little lump.' Well, strictly speaking, it wasn't me but John. He stumbled on it while on an explorational meander over my body during a late-night preamble to sex. He loved to do that from time to time. Sometimes spending hours gently running his fingertips over and kissing every inch of my skin. He probably knew my body better than I did. Up to that moment, I had been quietly enjoying myself, well – maybe not too quietly.

'You've got a lump,' he mumbled. The words didn't quite register at first.

Innocuous? Yes, of course. I didn't think it was anything at all to start.

Unobtrusive? Well, it wasn't another nipple or anything like that, but then my nipples had always been the sticky-out variety. They had always fascinated John, so it would have taken a concerted effort to have outshone one of those bad boys.

Inoffensive? Yes, absolutely, and of no relevance whatsoever, among all the other changes my body was going through and went through every time I fell pregnant. It was just a tiny blemish in what had once been a perfect body. In my dreams, many moons ago. But we thought it was worth checking out. This is why I am sitting in the surgery waiting room today, wondering whether it could be something after all.

The buzzer sounded for number 43… 43? That was me, I thought - I wasn't sure, then I checked my disc: yes, it was me. I looked around to see if anybody else would jump up and take my place… but there were no takers. Everybody was looking at me, waiting to see what I would do… well, that's how it felt. In fact, nobody took any notice of me at all.

I pulled out my earphone, and the flood of Floyd that had stopped me from thinking too intensely ended abruptly. I walked over to face the panel on the wall and placed my token 43 on token 42. Then I glanced around the room again at all the other patients, each with their own problem. Each one expecting some redemption or relief from what ailed them or, more prosaically, a magical potion that would enable them to carry on as they had before...

In millions of subtle combinations, chemicals now dictated and controlled how we lived our lives. Unknowingly, we had all slowly relinquished our bodies to pharmaceutical companies and scientists. Deep down, way, way down, I wondered whether I, too, was about to be asked to surrender my body and soul to the harlequins of the apothecary. I did not come here under any illusions; most of us don't, to be honest. We arrive, fearing the worst. Praying for salvation while grasping tenaciously to any slender thread of hope. That is all there is left when the carpet of contentment is about to be ripped from under your feet.

I remember strolling down the corridor towards Doctor Emanuel Sawyer's room - experiencing a resigned acceptance as I paused to read each poster Blu-Tacked to the wall.

**DON'T SMOKE OR DRINK
IF YOU ARE PREGNANT!**

DON'T HAVE UNPROTECTED SEX!

**EXERCISE MORE, EAT LESS,
LIVE LONGER!**

(I am sure they nicked part of that from Star Trek, but they'd forgotten the bit about prosper.)

**DON'T USE RECREATIONAL DRUGS –
DRUGS AREN'T FUN.
DRUGS ARE SERIOUS!**

**GET SOMEONE TO CHECK YOUR NUTS OUT,
EVERY DAY!**

(No, I made that one in case any men are reading this).

I carefully read each one in the vain hope that it might give me some tiny morsel of respite from the fear that had been troubling me over the last couple of weeks.

**IF YOU FIND A SUSPICIOUS LUMP –
SEE A DOCTOR!**

At last, that was it—my poster. I had, and I was.

I stood outside the door for a moment, still pondering. I could have just turned around and walked out, and nothing would change; everything would have stayed the same as it was. But would it? I wondered. I could go home, just put it out of my mind and carry on, and never think of it again, and the lump would disappear in a couple of weeks... But I couldn't, and it probably wouldn't.

I was committed to moving forward, as are we all. To seek out our destiny, whatever it might be. To journey down the inevitable path that, one day, most of us must take. Today was my day; it was my turn. I always get a bit like this, all worldly-wise and philosophical, when I am scared shitless. I knocked gently on Manni's door.

'Come in,' his soft, lilting voice so calm, firm, in control and reassuring.

I stuck my head around the door and smiled. But then I always did when I saw Manni. He was one of those people who somehow managed to charm you into smiling whenever you met him. That was the thing about him that I would never forget.

'Hi Manni, it's me.' He was a friend and my doctor and we had known each other for nearly ten years, socially and professionally. In a village the size of Baddesley-Minton, it was hard not to know almost everybody to one degree or another. Manni would come to dinner three, possibly four times a year. He was pleasant company, and our children loved him. Apart from the odd disparaging comment about the practice computer system, which he loathed, he never spoke about his work.

I had wondered whether seeing Manni over something like this was such a good idea. Would it change our relationship? But then I reasoned that he knew everything else about my body intimately, probably more so than John. No, maybe not that much: so one more little lump would hardly amount to a hill of beans in the overall scheme of things. It was probably something harmless anyway - a cyst or a blocked milk duct; I had read about those on google.

Manni stood up and embraced me. 'Hi, Katie.' Manni had been my doctor throughout all my pregnancies, and a strong bond had developed between us. Something beyond the normal patient-physician relationship, but then maybe not. Maybe it was something that happened between all pregnant women and their doctors.

He gestured to the chair next to his desk. I sat down, and he sat down to face me. His passion for his profession always shone through, despite all the trials and tribulations that now beset the N.H.S. He was old school, not interested in the management issues of running a surgery. His only concern was keeping his patients as healthy as he could. To hell with budgetary controls and practice target schedules; this was all that mattered to him. He couldn't perform miracles. And he couldn't return you to what you once were. Time was remorseless, relentless, and unforgiving. But he could make you well enough to carry on from where you were - well enough to carry on to the next crossroad.

'You're looking well,' he said, glancing at his computer screen. His computer's technological wizardry lay before him, but I knew he despised the intrusion and secretly yearned for the unfussy days of doctor's notes and files. He had already become an anachronism in his own lifetime, a remnant from another age. Soon he would be retiring after nearly forty years in practice. To some, he had administered good advice and wise counsel. To others, when necessary, he had prescribed pills and potions. Most of all, he had been there when many of our lives had begun, to help us as we entered this daunting new world – but more importantly, he was also there when it was time to depart. Such was the life of a small village doctor. Manni's wife died a few years earlier, and they never had children. So there wasn't much for him to look forward to in retirement. But he would always have the memories of all the people he had helped along the way, something to give him comfort in the years ahead.

'Thank you,' I replied. It was always a good start. Some doctors might ask, 'How are you today?' to which the serio-comedic reply should be - in a Groucho Marks drawl - "Well, doctor, I don't know – that's why I'm here - ba-boom!' but we never say it, do we?

'So how are things coming along with baby? I wasn't expecting to see you for another month or two,' asked Manni.

'The pregnancy is fine… I've actually come to see you about something else…'

'Oh, right,' Manni replied, looking at me quizzically while leaning his head very slightly to one side.

I was reluctant to continue. Acutely aware that once I had opened Pandora's box of tricks, there was never any going back – unless, of course, there was nothing in there in the first place…

'I've found a lump…' I whispered. Self-assurance slowly drained away, giving way to nervous apprehension.

'Where exactly,' he enquired, affecting an almost casual indifference while scribbling a few notes on his pad? Manni had started this conversation many times before but was far from complacent. He just needed to appear that way, having grown fearful and ambivalent with age. While having a healthy respect for the incredibly efficient killing machine to which I was alluding, he refused to acknowledge just how competent and resourceful it was. To him, it was a body within a body, each growing simultaneously, one slowly growing older and weaker, one growing stronger. The only difference was that one had a soul, a heart, and a destiny - a purpose for its very existence. In contrast, the other only had a destination. As he saw it, his calling, his raison d'etre, was to help redirect the latter down a much longer highway before it eventually arrived at journey's end. Better still, encourage it to turn left at the next roundabout and end its journey down some dusty road in the middle of nowhere, preferably dead. At a dinner party, he had propounded this scathing and strangely animated denunciation of cancer on one of the exceedingly rare occasions when he had drunk a little too much. The venomous nature of his outcry surprised us all, clearly displaying his utter contempt for the disease which literally ate you alive. In no small part, this was undoubtedly due to Manni's wife succumbing to cancer just a few years earlier. In a way, I found it strangely comforting having someone who felt that impassioned listening to me now. He would understand exactly how I was feeling.

Manni scribbled a few more notes as we spoke, glancing down occasionally as he wrote. He would retype them into his computer later. Manni had mentioned his reservations about computers on many occasions. Vehemently despising this contrivance's incursion into the archetypal relationship he had always tried to maintain with patients. He felt it implied a subliminal disregard – disrespecting the patient as a human being - if he did not engage with them face to face when they spoke. Whatever the gravity of the ailment - whether life-threatening or not – it was unquestionably something of concern to them at that moment. Head down, typing away with two fingers was not the ideal way to inspire confidence and respect.

I pointed to my left breast. 'My boob.' I thought about joking about it, probably at John's expense, but decided against it. We were past that stage.

'When did you first notice it?'

'About a couple of weeks ago. I thought it might be a… well, a cyst or something, with my hormones changing, and it seems to grow larger by the day.'

'Right. I had better have a look. Can you go behind the...'? He nodded to the curtains. I knew the routine.

'Please remove your blouse and bra and lie on the examination table. Let me know when you are ready.'

'Right,' I said, standing up and walking to the screen. I removed my coat, blouse, and bra and lay on the bed, gazing at the ceiling, contemplating what was to follow. I noticed the tiles were the same design here as they were in the waiting room. It's funny what you see when your mind is somewhere else.

'I'm ready,' I said after a few moments.

Manni looked at both breasts' overall shape first, signifying, with an open hand gesture, that there was nothing significant he could see.

'Where exactly is this little bugger then?' Manni asked, looking straight into my eyes. There was just a tiny hint of a reassuring smile; he could already sense the spectre of angst in my demeanour. I knew he would do his utmost to ease my anxiety, but even he couldn't get inside my head to ward off the dancing demons.

I moved my finger slowly to the lump just above my left nipple.

'There,' I added unnecessarily.

Manni touched it gently, probing all around to better understand its size.

'I need to squeeze it gently to gauge how hard and large it is. Is that okay?'

'Fine,' I replied. 'I've had a lot worse.'

He gently squeezed the lump a couple of times.

'Did that hurt?'

'No.'

'Right, that's fine. You can get dressed now.' Manni closed the curtain behind him. When I returned from behind the screen, he was seated at his desk, making more notes.

'Well, what do you think?'

'It's hard to tell.' We both smiled briefly at his unintended pun, but I could see that Manni regretted the levity. That was not his way. He did have a lovely smile, I thought. What a shame he didn't have someone at home with whom to share it.

11

'It could be a blocked milk duct or a cyst, as you suggested, but I think it would be best to have a biopsy and an ultrasound scan to be certain. I can arrange that in the next few days, but I shouldn't think there is anything to worry about.' He smiled reassuringly, but I couldn't smile back this time. He now had my undivided attention. The word biopsy had been surreptitiously dropped into the conversation. It was like lobbing in a live hand grenade... the seconds ticked by.

'Is it bad?' I eventually asked. I thought I had detected the tiniest hint of concern in Manni's voice, but I wasn't a hundred per cent sure. I would probably have felt just the same even if he had suddenly produced a Kiss-Me-Quick hat, performed an impromptu dance routine, and cracked a few jokes before mentioning the biopsy.

'As I said, probably a blocked milk duct. That's not unusual at this stage of pregnancy. Probably an agalactoceles – that's a milk-filled cyst – or even fibroadenomas. That's a fibrous lump. They're both completely harmless...' Manni scrunched his nose up indifferently as if to say they were both of no concern. I was now listening intently for any subtle inflexion in his voice, searching for the tiniest hint of an as-yet unmentioned agenda.

Harmless, right... I can do harmless. Panic over, I thought. It was all beginning to sound more reassuring, but then I suppose that was his intention.

'... but to be safe, we'll do the tests first, and then we'll know for certain. The biopsy and the scan will be done at St Mary's, so I'll make the appointment and let you know when. It will probably be early next week if that's okay?'

'Yes, that's fine. Sooner, the better, hey?' That was my token, if somewhat hollow gesture, to an upbeat frame of mind.

Manni smiled. 'So, are there any other issues?'

'No, I think that's enough to be going on with,' I replied, feeling less agitated than when I came in.

'And how are Jamie, Julia and Poppy?'

'They're fine.' I was surprised he remembered their names, as he hadn't needed to see them for a while.

'You remembered their names?' I replied, trying desperately not to sound condescending or disingenuous, which I just about managed.

'Oh, my memory's not that good,' he mumbled self-deprecatingly. 'It's all there.' He pointed at the screen and grinned, but I could see no mention of their names.

'It does have a few redeeming qualities, but I still hate the damn things.'

I stood up to leave.

'I'll be in touch as soon as I have the appointment for the hospital.' He smiled again, and I embraced and kissed him on the cheek to thank him. I realised this was inappropriate, but I didn't care; he was primarily a friend, which was all that mattered.

As the door closed, a tiny tear ran down Manni's cheek. He would be glad when the last day came, and he didn't have to do this anymore, then he wouldn't have to suffer the feeling he now felt deep down in the pit of his stomach.

The surgery rang seven days later to ask if I could pop in to discuss my test results. The secretary sounded upbeat on the phone, relieving some of the anxiety I'd harboured over the last few weeks. But then, I suppose that's how they are supposed to sound on the phone.

'Come in, Katie. Please sit down.' Manni rustled around on his desk for my file. Having located it, he opened it and glanced at it momentarily as if to double-check the information. But I'm sure he did not need to; he had probably already read the results before I came in.

I looked at him like a judge about to pronounce a verdict. Something told me it wasn't going to be a suspended sentence.

'There's good news… and some not-so-good news. I'll explain the not-so-good first.' I was eternally grateful that he didn't take the clichéd route of asking me which one I wanted first; that phrase always got right up my nose.

'The biopsy indicates the lump is malignant, an aggressive form of invasive lobular breast carcinoma. But there is no evidence of HER-2 oncogene, which is a big long-term plus. It's at stage two, so we must operate as soon as possible and begin a course of chemotherapy immediately to tidy up any possible spread of cancer cells. Fortunately, there is no evidence *at the moment,'* Manni added this in a softer tone, 'of any invasion into other areas or the lymph nodes. For a few seconds, the words floated listlessly in the air - pieces of confetti thrown up at a wedding – temporarily pixelating the imagery. But the blurriness soon cleared as the confetti quickly fell back to earth.

It all sounded so very clinical, precise and to the point. I was utterly overwhelmed by all the medical terms that had suddenly become specific to me and nobody else; it was my very own unique variation on an extraordinarily complex theme. But I understood most of what he said, and for that, I was thankful. There is never any point in dancing around the handbags; it just annoys people, and he knew it would have infuriated me.

I didn't say anything immediately – I had to take a deep breath. It wasn't as if I wasn't half expecting it. I am a realist and a pragmatist. I have never laboured under any illusions about my mortality, but it still came as a shock. For the first time in my life, I could not see the light at the end of the tunnel.

'Does that mean a mastectomy?' I mumbled. I love my body and my boobs; I've had them all my life, nearly – well, since I was eleven. How could I get by without them? Would I still be a woman? What would John think? Would he still love me if I was deformed?

These were my first thoughts, ridiculously absurd as they might be. The question of whether I would die never entered my mind... until it did.

'No, not necessarily,' said Manni. His warm smile and soft, soothing tone brought some comfort, and I was eternally grateful for this. 'More a lumpectomy, but obviously, that depends on what the surgeons find when they... we have found it early, and that's good. The reconstructive surgeons are excellent these days.'

So, what were they like in the past? I wondered sardonically.

'Chemo, you mentioned chemo. Will that affect my baby?'

'That's the good news. It shouldn't, as you have just passed into the second trimester. In the first three months, it's quite different, so it's the good and not-so-good news thing once again - if you can call any of it good.' Manni paused momentarily to let me absorb what he had said. He was naturally cautious with his wording, but "*Shouldn't*" was one of those semi-reassuring words that promises much. But tucked away, out of sight, just behind the letters, was just the tiniest hint of uncertainty - if you looked close enough. And I did.

Some people probably react quite badly to this sort of news once it sinks in, and he was obviously waiting to see if I would be one of them. I wasn't.

'So, what happens now?' I asked coolly. I was still not feeling any real emotion about the test results. The diagnosis had sunk in, but the prognosis was yet to come.

'I've scheduled you for next Thursday for the surgery, and the chemo will start a few days later.'

'That fast?' I gasped. That took my breath away.

'Yes. We don't want to waste any time. It is aggressive. We couldn't wait six months if that's what you were thinking.'

'No, I understand... And the prognosis?'

'If we start next week, there is every chance of a full recovery with no long-term problems. Statistically, the survival rate is around eighty-five per cent.'

'You haven't mentioned radiation therapy yet.' I had looked that up on google as well. Where would we be without it? I wondered. Christ, we would have to start rereading medical books again.

'No, I haven't. That would be more effective, but it could seriously affect the pregnancy. That's why we are taking this route. We would have to end the pregnancy if we took the radiation route, so on balance...'

'That's fair enough. I understand.' That was a definite non-starter.

'The surgeon will advise you much better than I can, but I believe this is the route he will take unless something changes. You should get the admission letter in a day or two, and I will pop into the hospital on the day.'

'Thank you.'

'So how is John taking all this?' asked Manni.

'Philosophically. You know John, but that may change. He doesn't know about the diagnosis yet, but...'

Manni smiled. 'He's not here today?'

'He wanted to come, but I told him I wanted to do this on my own so I could come to terms with it... whatever the outcome - before I got back. I don't know how he will react, so I wanted to prepare myself first... if you see what I mean?'

'Yes, I understand.'

We stood up simultaneously, and I kissed Manni on the cheek, as always. He held me tightly for a moment and whispered, 'We will get through this, I promise.'

I could have kissed him again for saying that, but I didn't; I smiled and began to leave. Then something made me turn back and ask the question I knew I had to ask.

'You will save me, Manni, won't you, please? I can't die yet. I need a little more time, enough time to get everything organised.'

Manni looked stunned momentarily before answering, 'We will do everything we can, and I am sure it will be all right. You won't die, not yet.' He was steadfast and reassuring but not surprised by my outburst.

'I'm sorry to ask, but it's John and the children. I haven't made any plans for them if... well, I don't know how they would cope if I suddenly weren't here anymore. I...'

'You won't be leaving them just yet,' replied Manni with another reassuring smile. 'I can promise you that much.'

It felt so good just to hear the words I nearly... 'Good, that's good, but I'll still prepare a plan or something anyway... just in case.'

'It won't be necessary, Katie, believe me,' whispered Manni, trying his level best to reassure me.

But he didn't know I was a bit of a control freak. The kid's birthday parties, holidays, weekends, Christmas, the washing and ironing. I had to have them all planned out. They were perfectly organised, and every possible eventuality was catered for, even... I stopped there.

'Thank you,' I replied. I believed what Manni said, but I would prepare another plan anyway... just in case.

I wandered back to the car in a daze, past St Peter's Church. I hadn't been there for ages since John and I were married. Apart from a few christenings - ours and some friends, three or four weddings and the odd Sunday service in summer. I stopped and looked up and noticed the main door was open. It was a part-time church these days after amalgamation with St Jude's in Baddesley-Minton. It now only opened on alternate Sundays and Wednesdays. I walked up the nave towards the cross, the sound of my footsteps tumbling around the aisles, and I sat down on a pew near the front. It was incredibly quiet and strangely tranquil; I appeared to be alone. I had not prayed for a long time and felt guilty about turning up out of the blue and asking for a huge favour. I thought the worst he could say was no, so what did I have to lose? For no reason, Pascal's wager about the probability of the existence of God suddenly sprang to mind. It was an article in one of the Sunday papers a few weeks ago.

I noticed that woody, waxy smell mixed with something flowery and sweet that you always seemed to find in old churches, and it made me feel good. It put me in the right frame of mind to ask the question. I actually knelt down, which I don't usually do. Normally, I would just perch my bum on the edge of the seat, which seems to be what most people do these days. But today, I knelt, closed my eyes, and prayed.

God, will you just let me stay long enough to get things organised for John and our children? I'm not asking for me, you understand. If it is my time, then fair enough, I know how it works, but they don't, not really, so if you could let me stay... just a little bit longer, it would be really appreciated. I'm not going to lie to you. I don't come to church much, well, you know that, and I don't suppose that will change much, but I will try if it helps my case, so there you are. If you could just see your way clear to help me out here, I'll do my best in the future.

I looked at the stained-glass window and thought about their pretty colours and how wonderful God was. But no beam of divine celestial light suddenly struck me from heaven. So I said thank you, scrambled to my feet and left, saying goodbye to the verger as I walked past him, gently pressing a two-pound coin into his hand as I went. He looked a little surprised and watched me in wonderment as I walked away.

CHAPTER 2

John and the Easter Rabbit.

Easter 2006.

'Don't eat my rabbit!' shouted Poppy, glaring at Jamie with the maddened passion and loitering malevolence of a self-possessed gorgon.

Jamie, her eighteen-month-old brother, was sitting in the middle of the lounge floor holding Poppy's Easter chocolate rabbit - focusing intently on its one remaining ear. He had already consumed the other. The evidence – if it became necessary to present proof of his felonious act of thievery in a court of law – was clear to see. It was smeared all over his face.

Jamie flinched at this unexpected and surprisingly vociferous interruption. His proposed intention was to consume the rest of the resurrection treat in the relative peace and solitude of the lounge. But he was old enough to understand that Poppy was directing her comments at him. Glancing briefly up at her with a mischievously dismayed expression, he swiftly started to nibble off the left ear before she could take another step towards him.

It was gone in an instant, lost forever in Jamie's mouth, where it instantly began to melt. He smiled with the ecstatic glow only experienced when consuming chocolate – delicious chocolate, the panacea for all ills and chariot of wondrous enjoyment.

Not for one moment did Jamie avert his eyes from his sister's as he slowly consumed the treat, so transfixed was he by her squinty expression. He was carefully watching her every movement. Just in case, she should make a sudden desperate lunge for the remains of the chocolate rabbit she had so carelessly left within his reach.

Her malevolent expression conveyed a mixture of emotions, some worse than others, but that was not her real intention. She was not vindictive, just saddened by the sudden and unexpected loss of part of her Easter rabbit. She had fantasised about the instant gratification she would experience while consuming the chocolate treat, but that dream had been cruelly snatched away.

Jamie's only concern was the imminent fear of losing that which he had purloined and which, with steely determination, he intended to hold on to at all costs. He cautiously observed Poppy while furiously nibbling away at the rabbit, looking for any sign that she might be about to launch a retaliatory incursion to retrieve said rabbit. But she did not.

'Mummy!' shouted Poppy, now directing her despairing protestations towards her mother, who was in the kitchen. 'Jamie's eating my Easter rabbit. Can you stop him?' Poppy glared back at Jamie, her face horribly contorted by the scowl she had adopted. It was proving to be a wholly unsuccessful attempt at intimidation.

Julia sat quietly in her highchair, reviewing the dramatic events unfolding around her, possibly wondering why she could not enjoy some of the spoils of Jamie's good fortune. The squabbling siblings' animated protestations were fascinating, but Julia didn't fully understand their argument. Until now, she had taken little notice of what was happening before her. A neutral observer, you might say. However, she was increasingly becoming intrigued by Poppy's remarkable ability to perform grotesque facial transmogrifications. The possibility of a chocolate feast now appeared to be of less interest.

For some misguided reason, Poppy appeared to be labouring under the misapprehension that the monstrous image she was affecting might deter Jamie from his goal of devouring another large piece of the rabbit. She was wrong; it did not, and he would, given enough time.

'Jamie's doing what,' queried Katie, sounding slightly confused? She was still in the kitchen preparing lunch and couldn't quite make out what Poppy was saying. She stopped what she was doing momentarily and popped her head around the door just as Poppy ran back into the kitchen. Jamie's momentary distraction at Poppy's frightful manifestation had now passed, and his attention quickly returned to his original plan – the consumption of the remains of the chocolate bunny.

'Jamie's eating my favourite Easter rabbit,' repeated Poppy forlornly. As if being favoured would make a difference. Her outcry suggested Jamie had devoured the last piece of chocolate rabbit left on earth. He had not. But he had, in all the confusion,

19

successfully nibbled off the rabbit's other ear and was now passionately grasping the rabbit's remains in both hands. Jamie smiled contentedly while quietly contemplating the consumption of the rabbit's head.

'I'll be there in a moment,' replied Katie. 'I'm just making lunch.' She had prepared some marmite sandwiches and was cutting them into little triangles. For some inexplicable reason, Poppy and Jamie preferred their sandwiches cut into triangles, not squares.

'You like triangular sandwiches, don't you? Have one of these.' asked Katie, subtly trying to subvert Poppy's attention, but Poppy was having none of it.

'No!' she replied, mumbling a quiet 'thank you.' She wasn't going to be palmed off with a marmite sandwich in place of a chocolate rabbit – her chocolate rabbit.

Poppy scowled for a moment, then sauntered back into the lounge. 'Mummy!' exclaimed Poppy sounding thoroughly downhearted, 'Now Jamie's eaten half my rabbit's head.' Poppy had executed at least half a dozen facial expressions over less than five minutes, each signifying bitter disappointment. Maybe she'll become a Shakespearian actor, thought Katie whimsically. Anyway, how could it be her favourite rabbit if all she wanted to do was eat it? Carrying the plate of sandwiches, she walked back into the lounge to see what was happening. Sure enough, Jamie had nibbled off both ears, his face now smothered in melted chocolate. He looked delighted without a care in the world. Poppy, however, did not.

'You must have left it somewhere where he could reach it,' remarked Katie, gently removing the rabbit's remains from Jamie's hands and passing it back to Poppy. Jamie looked up at his mother with a dismayed expression. His lips began to turn down at the corners and quiver. He was about to start crying when Katie smiled at him, picked up one of the triangular sandwiches off the plate and offered it to him.

'Have a marmite sandwich; they are your favourite,' she suggested. It was a ruse to divert his attention. And Jamie did consider the offer for a few moments before scrunching up his face and pushing it away in a token gesture of defiant rejection. The triangular sandwiches were not going down too well. Perhaps

I should have cut them into squares, after all, pondered Katie a little despairingly.

She wiped some of the chocolate from Jamie's face with her finger and popped it into his mouth. As he licked it off, he smiled benignly, the remains of the uneaten part of the rabbit now a distant memory. Poppy, looking very disheartened, gazed mournfully at what was left. She had now lost interest in the severely disfigured rabbit and placed it to one side.

'You do still have a large chocolate egg as well, so a few ears don't really matter much, do they?' asked Katie, endeavouring to mollify Poppy.

'They were enormous ears,' she replied grudgingly, 'but I suppose not.'

'Where did you leave it?'

'On the table.'

'Well, I don't know how Jamie managed to get hold of it,' said Katie. 'It's a bit of a mystery. I'm sure he can't reach the table yet.' Katie said it in a way that hinted that maybe, she had left it somewhere more accessible to Jamie. Poppy didn't notice the subtle inflexion.

Julia sat quietly and patiently in her chair, wondering if any chocolate would ever come her way.

'Sandwich, Julia,' asked Katie, offering her one of the marmite sandwiches? Julia smiled and reluctantly took the sandwich and began eating it. There seemed little likelihood of a chocolate bunny appearing any time soon.

Success, at last, thought Katie. Somebody likes my sandwiches. It was a minor triumph, but a triumph nevertheless.

'Sandwich, Poppy?' asked Katie once again,

Poppy mumbled something incoherent, then broke off a piece of what was left of the rabbit, which she had now started eating.

'Sorry?' said Katie, waiting for an audible reply.

'No, thank you, Mummy,' replied Poppy apologetically.

'Right.'

John came in from the garden and surveyed the situation.

'You look a bit glum,' he said, looking at Poppy. Poppy looked up at her father and mumbled something else incoherent. She obviously wasn't in the mood for idle chitchat, so John glanced towards Katie for an explanation.

'Jamie managed to find Poppy's rabbit and ate the ears!'

'Oh, I'm so sorry,' said John, glancing back at Poppy, attempting a vacuous stab at empathy while dropping the ends of his mouth into a clown-like expression...

Poppy still didn't say anything but continued to work on her sullen, seriously disgruntled look. Body language was already becoming one of her primary means of communication.

'Still, ear today, gone tomorrow – or today in this case,' remarked John jovially.

Poppy gave him a disparaging glare, clearly indicating his pathetic stab at a pun was unappreciated and that this was, in fact, a very grave matter. John could see that Poppy was still clearly distraught, so he gently bit his lip in an effort not to smile.

'I had big plans for my rabbit.'

'I bet you did,' replied John, desperately trying to suppress a grin - he failed miserably.

'It's not funny, Dad. I was looking forward to eating his ears.'

'I agree, stealing chocolate is not funny. In fact, it's an extremely serious matter in my book.' John tried to adopt a stern, reproachful expression of empathy, but it didn't work; it lacked conviction. Poppy realised she would not be receiving much sympathy here, so she wandered off towards her bedroom to finish the rabbit alone.

'Poppy?' said John.

Poppy turned back to her father. 'Yes, Dad.'

'Can I ask you a question?'

Poppy looked at her dad with cautious curiosity. 'Yes?' she warily replied.

'What if Alfie had eaten your chocolate and became ill?'

'Why would he become ill?' asked Poppy with a puzzled expression.

'Dogs can't eat our chocolate. It's not good for them, but they don't know that, so Alfie would eat it if he found it.'

Poppy didn't answer immediately - she was having a problem following John's strange logic.

'So, whose fault would it be... if Alfie became ill because he had eaten your chocolate, which you had left somewhere where he or Jamie could find it?'

Poppy was now beginning to see where John's questions were leading. 'I suppose it would be my fault.'

'We're not trying to apportion blame here because Alfie didn't eat your chocolate. But you see, Jamie does not know the rules about eating other people's chocolate either, so a little bit of this problem comes down to you accepting responsibility for where you put your rabbit. Jamie didn't know it was wrong, did he?'

'No, I suppose not.'

'So, do you feel a little better about it now?'

'Yes, Dad, I suppose,' she replied reluctantly.

John smiled, and Poppy half-smiled back, then wandered off to her bedroom to finish her rabbit alone.

I smiled at John. 'How is it going?'

'Should be finished in a couple of hours.' He was referring to the latest batch of ceramic vases that he was firing in his workshop kiln.

John had inherited the house and the pottery business from his father, who died prematurely in 2001, aged forty-seven. John's mother died suddenly when he was fifteen. It had taken him years to come to terms with that unexpected loss, but his father's death had changed his life profoundly. From an early age, he had never intended to work in the family business, firmly setting his sights on becoming an infant schoolteacher. But after his mother died, he found himself surreptitiously encouraged by his father to help in the pottery workshop at weekends and evenings. It was a ruse to distract him from his grief. He was young and receptive and enjoyed working with his father, a man with remarkable patience who never once raised his voice in anger. This was some achievement in the working environment of a business that handled intrinsically delicate and fragile creations. Some of which were broken through simple carelessness. That memory had left a deep impression that had guided John for most of his life.

Slowly, he became increasingly fascinated by how a handful of clay or kaolin could be magically transformed into a magnificent ceramic pot or porcelain vase. His father, always inspirational in his counselling and uncannily prescient in his intuition, infused a sense of wonderment in the ancient craft. John could not help but be swept up and captivated by his beguiling enthusiasm. It was as if the tide of uncertainty, the vision of a life of unrelenting, drear predictability, had somehow morphed into one malevolent form. This recurring nightmare had secretly haunted John since his mother died. But this manifestation, which had constantly threatened to overwhelm and consume him, had slowly faded into the shadows. It left behind a wraithlike vision of perfectly formed swirls of spiritual creation - once hidden - but now revealed in the tall vases he crafted. It was as if he were being prepared for something far more significant in life, but he didn't know what.

John had always felt that he could not communicate with his contemporaries conventionally for reasons he could not explain. It was as if he were assailed continuously by an inexplicable audio interference that muddled the messages he received. For this reason, he preferred his own company or the company of his father, never wholly understanding the pervading declension of reality until much later. This possibly explained his earlier preference for teaching infants rather than older children. In their presence, he felt better able to manage and develop the delicate communication thread necessary to allow him to form a bond between himself and the children.

Working with clay and forming pots helped him face his demons, so his father's ruse worked. Despite qualifying as a teacher, he had begun working full-time in the pottery from twenty-four, just after his father's death. John's one enduring memory of the days when he worked with his father was his love of classical music, which he listened to all day while in the pottery. John maintained this ritual whenever he was in the workshop, using the same old Roberts radio that his father had used.

The mellifluous melodies of Debussy, Mendelssohn, and Satie could always be heard floating wistfully in the air. It was as if they were loitering in the workshop, waiting for something to be created into which they could immerse themselves for the rest of eternity. Somehow, as if by magical astral infusion, the music would permeate the raw clay and eventually rise to the surface of the final glaze, now transformed into sentient radiation. They seemed to emanate stillness, tranquillity, calm... and sometimes a little sadness. It was possibly a vicarious reflection of the environment in which they had been created and now inhabited. Some tall black opalescent pieces were painted with an ethereally gold filigree pattern. This may have been why they appeared so captivatingly tactile and attractive to potential customers.

Becoming a potter was not a particularly hard decision to make. Deep down in his soul, John knew that he was morally and spiritually, albeit on an existential level, obliged to carry on where his father had stopped. In a meaningless world where everything eventually ends, the perpetuation of the craft and the responsibility for taking the business forward seemed to give life a specific meaning and rationale. A reason to exist and a reason to believe. Somehow the pottery appeared to exert an otherworldly force that inexplicably drew him in.

The desire to mould these sublimely decorative objects was now embedded in his very being. He knew that he would always be a potter and nothing else for the rest of his life as long as he was able.

He hoped to emulate his father's easy-mannered, thoughtful, and considerate nature and pass this on to his children as they grew older. Hopefully, he would have more luck seeing his grandchildren grow up than his father. The latter had held Poppy on just three occasions in the brief period before his death.

John was happy and contented with the way things had turned out. Somehow, working in the pottery business had the effect of tempering the grief he thought he would experience. Working with clay daily kept him in contact… it was a conduit through which John could convey his feelings to somewhere unknown. A place where he knew his father now dwelt.

Bearing in mind the vagaries of the business, some people considered his decision to give up his career as a teacher to be a mistake, but he did not. He knew a career as a potter was a financially precarious choice, but it didn't matter. He started teaching pottery at the local school once a week, which satisfied his vocational pedagogical aspirations and his passion "to pot." To pot! It was an unusual verb, but the only one he could think of that correctly described what he did.

Only as John grew older did he realise that his father must also have been grieving after his wife had died. But he had never allowed his anguish and despair to show or affect how he was with John. He held his father in high esteem, even more so as the years passed after his death – and he realised just what a modest and moral man he had been and how important that was.

The pottery business produced a reasonable living for John and Katie. They sold pots, porcelain vases, dishes, plates, and other items to many shops in Lavendon and Godalming and from their shop next to their pottery works behind their home in Baddesley-Minton.

By far, the most popular items were those depicting images of Shelbury Bridge and the tragic story of two local lovers jumping to their deaths from the bridge. This undoubtedly aided sales. As long as the bridge remained, customers would always want to buy a memento of their visit.

When John wasn't working in pottery, he also enjoyed oil painting and charcoal drawing. His favourite subject was his wife, Katie, the girl with golden hair who had bewitched and beguiled him as a teenager. She would eventually yield to his relentless marriage proposals. Faint heart never won fair maiden – never more so than in this partnership.

She, too, had never considered the possibility of marrying anybody else. But nevertheless, had decided to bide her time and play a waiting game, teasing John a little on the journey to the altar. She enjoyed the thrill of the chase. This was partly due to a streak of obstinate wilfulness, the spirit of the wild gipsy in her soul. She believed that once she had succumbed to his request, that frisson of anticipation that excited her would be gone, but she was wrong. Even after they were married and had started a family, that magical ingredient which had existed between them right from the beginning never diminished. It was there in the sparkle of an eye or a glancing touch as they passed each other. That was until…

CHAPTER 3

Katie and her Alluginations.
January 2007

As the anaesthetic began wearing off, I could just make out some shadowy figures in the room. Ghostly apparitions were slowly drifting around my bed, nomadic clouds of fog deftly defying the natural laws of gravity. There were some pretty coloured lights, and far away, I could hear ticking sounds like tiny animals moving cautiously through the forest. I remember something similar at Glasto in '97.

'Howa dadit goerrara goma bre, bre stits.' I knew exactly what I meant to say – it just refused to come out the way I intended, turning into gibberish as it left my mouth - so nothing new there.

Mr Reynolds moved closer to my bed, coming into sharper focus.

'Hi, Katie, how are you feeling?'

'Prissed! Berwains gone powidgey. Am I... am I drabling?'

'That will pass. Your neurotransmitters have just gone a bit wonky – they often do that afterwards. You might even experience some hallucinations before the anaesthetic is completely out of your system, but it's nothing to worry about. I'll come back later to discuss how the procedure went.'

'Bwing on the alluginations,' I muttered, 'wappy days.' I could clearly understand what Mr Reynolds was saying, but I just couldn't string the right syllables together in the correct order to reply. I knew I sounded a little demented and wasn't making any sense. That made me smile. Now I understand how smackheads must feel after jacking-up on cocaine... possibly.

While glancing over my notes, Mr Reynolds looked up at me several times, smiled charmingly, as doctors do, and then left. He came back just over an hour later, by which time I had almost fully recovered from the anaesthesia and was assessing the collateral damage as best I could. Everything still appeared to be as I remembered it, which wasn't what I had expected. But then I couldn't see under the bandages.

Mr Reynolds sat down on the edge of the bed and smiled again.

'Hi, Katie, so how do you feel now?'

'I'm good. Not talking Welsh anymore.' (Apologies to the Welsh.)

Mr Reynolds smiled. 'Well, the good news is…' That clichéd phrase inevitably presupposes some unwelcome news is also about to follow, so I prepared myself for the worst. Today, I would draw a heavy line under fiction and accept that this was now strictly non-fiction territory. But for some reason - maybe it was the last remaining traces of the anaesthetic - I was having difficulty differentiating between them. They were intermingling - morphing into each other and creating a strange illusion… it was all a little surreal.

'… the surgery went well, and fortunately, very little tissue had to be removed. I have completed some minor reconstructive work after the lumpectomy. I can also confirm that there has been no invasion into the lymph nodes. We did another biopsy while you were out, and it's all good. We can talk about that later.' I listened intently, taking in everything he said, and smiled, waiting tentatively for the punch line.

'So, what's the bad news?' I asked a little cagily. 'The suspense is killing me.' He cracked a tiny grin at my crude attempt at gallows humour.

'There is none. That's it for now.'

'Oh!' I replied, obviously looking a little surprised.

'I'll write all this down, so you have something to refer to later. So don't worry about forgetting something.'

'Thank you. So, what happens next?'

'I'll go over the boring stuff before we discharge you – that will probably be tomorrow.' He smiled reassuringly once again. It really did make a difference.

'Is John here?' I asked after a few seconds spent carefully digesting his summation of the situation.

'Your husband, yes, he's outside. I'll ask him to come in if you're ready.'

'Yes, I would like that.' Mr Reynolds left, and John came in a few minutes later, holding a bunch of flowers.

'Hi, darling.' John kissed me on the forehead and touched my cheek with his fingertips, caressing me as if I were one of his delicate porcelain vases. 'I've just spoken with Mr Reynolds, and he...'

'I hope you will still love me, John,' I interrupted abruptly; I just needed to get the words out, 'now that I'm a bit ugly. I am so sorry I did this to my body, but I will always love you – that's if you still want me. Please say you won't leave me?' I was rambling, and then I burst into tears. I don't know where it all came from, but for some reason, I was suddenly overwhelmed with a sense of useless desperation and loss of control. Despite everything the surgeon had said, I completely lost the plot momentarily. The sudden realisation of a personal disfigurement, one that had been sort of self-inflicted, was all I could see.

All I could think of was how it might affect John and how he would see me in the future. This had suddenly hit home. That and the last remnants of the anaesthesia made me feel over-emotional and vulnerable. Getting pissed also made me feel this way.

I'd rushed the words – I do tend to waffle on a bit in this sort of situation. But it would be much easier if I didn't allow John to break the rhythm while I was in full flow. I would have lost the thread and felt I needed to say what I wanted before he could interrupt me. My heartfelt pleading words seem to fill the room with a wretched mistiness. Even bringing a tear to the eye of the case-hardened nurse who had come in to adjust the bedside monitors. As for John, he couldn't believe what I had said. I wanted to be as strong as usual but couldn't do it today. I was so scared, and he could see it – and that worried him. I could see him welling up inside from the unintended pain I inflicted on him; that was never my intention.

'Oh, please don't cry darling and don't be silly. You haven't done anything. This just happened, it could happen to anybody, and you're not ugly; you could never be that... even without makeup.' He had taken a bit of a flyer on the last quip, but it had worked. It brought a smile to my face. 'And I'm not going to leave you-you, silly girl... who would do my washing? I can't work the damn machine,' he added with perfect timing. John carefully embraced me and kissed me again, and at once, I felt better.

'The surgeon says everything went to plan, and there were no problems... everything is going to be fine.'

29

'Yes, it all seems good. It's just...' I didn't finish what I was going to say. I was feeling a little better now. Melodrama was back under control. 'So, how are the children?'

'They're fine,' John looked slightly surprised at the question. 'It's only been a few hours, well six since breakfast, and they were all okay then.' He flashed me a curiously quizzical expression that made me smile again. That was when I realised just how much I loved him and how I couldn't bear to ever be without him.

'Of course, of course. I've just lost track of time a bit. Have you not been home?'

'No, I sat in the waiting room.'

'You didn't have to.'

John didn't answer. He didn't need to tell me that he would never have left me while I was being operated on; I knew that.

'Do you want me to bring the children in?'

I thought about that for a few moments. 'Are they here?'

'No, they are still at home with your mum.'

'No, I don't want them to see me like this. I'll be home tomorrow.' I laid back on my pillow and smiled again. I was beginning to come to terms with the first part of my journey.

'I'll leave you to sleep now,' said John, 'but I'll be back in the morning to take you home, okay?'

'Are you going home?'

'Yes, I'll have to give the pub a miss tonight.' *John never goes to the pub.*

'Good. Kiss the children for me.'

'I will.'

John kissed me again and left.

I fell asleep most of the afternoon, but not before lifting my head skywards, opening my eyes and whispering, 'Thank you.'

In the early evening, Mr Reynolds returned and sat on the edge of the bed.

'So, Katie, are you still feeling okay?'

'A little bruised, but I'm good.'

'Great. As you may or may not know, you're going home tomorrow, probably glad to escape from here, no doubt.'

I smiled. I was looking forward to seeing the children, even though it had only been one day, but then I'd never been away from home overnight, not since the twins were born. I looked at him, someone I had grown to know and like over the last two days and wondered what it must feel like to have this fantastic ability to prolong life.

'Now we need to discuss what happens next, so do you want me to wait for John to come back, or shall I...'

'Let's do it now,' I interjected a little abruptly.

'Right. Okay.' He paused for a moment to gather his thoughts. 'The post-surgery biopsy confirms what we already knew about the nature of this kind of cancer. I am not going to frustrate you with all the terminology, but as I originally told you, it is aggressive and invasive - but we have arrested the development for now. It is rare for someone to develop breast cancer when pregnant, which means we have certain limitations on the post-op treatments we can adopt at this point in time. I would like to have started radiation therapy at once to reduce the possibility of any spread or recurrence. That would have been the best choice, but there are, as you may know, considerable risks to your baby with this treatment. Your doctor has probably explained that to you.'

'Yes, he did, but could you explain again?' I asked.

'Well, to the unborn foetus, it could cause birth defects, possible miscarriage, even a risk of childhood cancer, which is a little bizarre...' He paused for a moment to allow me time to absorb that. I slowly nodded, acknowledging I understood what he had said even if some of it had not completely sunk in.

'We might even have to terminate the pregnancy,' he continued, 'and we don't want to do that, so I am proposing a course of adjuvant therapy...'

I wrinkled up my eyes and nose almost playfully at that one - in the vain hope of expressing visually that I was not sure what adjuvant therapy actually was.

'I am sorry,' he shook his head as if scolding himself and continued. 'I mean chemotherapy. I propose a course of drugs, tamoxifen and letrozole, over eight cycles. That's one per month for the next eight months. You only take the drugs for around five days, and then you have a three-week break to allow the blood count levels to recover. However, even with chemo, we must stop at around thirty-six weeks as that could also harm your baby. A three to four-week suspension would protect your baby from infection in the last few weeks without affecting the treatment's integrity. After your baby is born, we can finish the course of chemotherapy and consider radiation therapy if necessary. That will depend, to a large degree, on your body's response to the drugs.

'So, it would be better if I didn't take any drugs at all until after I give birth?'

'I couldn't advise that; your chances of survival would be profoundly reduced if you didn't have the therapy now. We've started with the surgery but must finish the whole procedure; otherwise, we may have wasted our...' he paused momentarily, 'your time. If we don't neutralise alien cells quickly, you will probably die within a year.' It was tough, unemotional, and abrupt; the message was remarkably unambiguous. He did his best to drive this point home... as hard as possible.

I must have looked a little startled at his ominous pronouncement. The word 'alien' bounced around in my head for a few seconds, conjuring up all sorts of dreadful manifestations. He was definitely not coating this prognosis with honey; that much was for sure. But, deep down, I knew I preferred it that way.

'Oh, I see,' I was quiet for a few moments absorbing his deliberations, 'but my baby will be okay with the chemo, and I might survive?' I asked.

'Yes, there's an eighty to eighty-five per cent chance you will both be fine afterwards, which is why I believe it's the route we must take. You must finish this... You don't really have a choice.'

'And that's as good as it gets?' I asked. I've always loved that line since Jack Nicholson said it in a film. I had waited for years to reuse it at precisely the right moment, and this was it.

'I'm afraid so.'

He sounded harsh in his summation, but I knew he only wanted us to live, my baby and me. It would have been idiotic to make any other choice.

'Okay then, chemo it is. When do we start?' I sounded strangely jubilant about the decision, which, I think, surprised him a little.

'Next week. Monday morning.'

'Monday morning, it is then.'

We smiled at each other for distinctly different reasons, and then he left.

I fell into a restful sleep for the rest of the night, and the following day, John came in, and we made the journey home together, back to our children and to prepare for what lay ahead.

Over the next six months, I completed five chemo cycles, each a little more debilitating than before, each sapping a little more of my strength. It was a constant battle to stay positive and try to eat for the baby while feeling sick and nauseous simultaneously, but I managed. You do, don't you?

During the one week in four that I received the chemo, I couldn't take Poppy to school, so John would drive her in by the back-road route through the country lanes. But the back road had no pavements or pathways, so I always walked the long way to school over Shelbury Bridge when I took Poppy in. They stopped the chemo in May, I had Trinity in June, and I finished the chemo treatment in early July. Then I started to think about a plan… just in case.

CHAPTER 4

The First Encounter

June 2007

'Leja, have you seen my laptop bag? I can't find it anywhere.' Lauren's plea appeared to emanate from somewhere beyond the other side of the lounge.

Daisy glanced around the kitchen but couldn't see the bag. So, she said nothing and continued nibbling her toast while watching the tiny TV suspended under one of the kitchen wall cabinets.

'I thought I saw it on hallway table,' came Leja's reply from the other end of the house. 'I come through and look.' The absence of flowing articulation still made Lauren wince, especially when stressed. Her brain would never become fully aligned to Leja's casual slaughter of the English language. Maybe slaughter was a little harsh, but Lauren still found herself plaintively whispering the missing words into the air. Possibly in vain expectation that they might somehow move into the correct position - and that time would suddenly flip back a few seconds and repeat the corrected phrase, but it never did.

Sometimes, she wished she were a director making a film about her life. Then she could stop filming at the moment of the offensive omission and have a quiet avuncular chat with the actor concerned. She could explain the quaint subtleties of the English language, then reshoot the scene, this time perfectly articulated. But of course, she never did... maybe that was all a bit fanciful anyway. She had enough on her plate without getting involved in a Hollywood epic. For that's what it would be... with Leja as the star.

A simple 'the' or a 'will' was all that was required to alleviate the stab of syntactic pain that shot through her brain like a tiny bolt of lightning, but the words never came. No matter how much she prayed, they remained absent strangers from Leja's vocabulary. After nearly five years, Lauren had now become resigned to it – almost. It was the compromise she had to make – a small price for reliable help.

Could it be infectious? This had been her only genuine concern in the beginning. Would Daisy start to drop the odd determiner or verb out of familiarity? After all, they were together for a couple of hours each night before Lauren or her husband, Michael, arrived home. She had wondered whether continued exposure could have a long-term detrimental effect. But, so far, thank God, that had not happened. Daisy appeared to be immune. Michael still found the verbal desecration quintessentially amusing. This was something which Lauren could never understand. Occasionally he would torment Leja by asking her something with the same linguistic corruption; he did this just to amuse himself if he became bored. But Lauren never found it funny, and neither did Leja.

'Didn't daddy use it yesterday,' suggested Daisy as Lauren returned to the kitchen? Her eyes never strayed from the TV.

'Ah!' thought Lauren aloud, 'yes, yes, he did,' but Michael had already left for the office, so she couldn't ask him.

Leja came into the kitchen but without the laptop. Lauren was beginning to look a little bit fraught.

'Leja, could you have a look in Michael's study for me?'

'I think it is in hall,' replied Leja. 'I look.' She crossed the kitchen and went through the lounge and into the hallway.

'It is here,' Leja shouted back towards the kitchen, hoping Lauren could hear her, but there was no reply. She walked back into the kitchen with the laptop.

Lauren reappeared in the kitchen with a coffee cup in one hand and a buttered toast in the other.

'Thank you, Leja, you're an absolute godsend.' Leja smiled.

'Are you ready, darling?' asked Lauren.

Poppy glanced across. 'Yes, Mummy. Just need to put my coat on.'

'Have you done your homework?'

'Yes, mother,' replied Daisy, nodding with a curious squinty-eyed expression.

'Good... thank you again, Leja. All a bit chaotic this morning, sorry.' She smiled briefly.

'Yes,' mumbled Leja, never one to waste words.

'Right...' said Lauren, looking at Daisy. 'We're off to school then, darling.'

'Yes, Mummy.' Daisy jumped down from the table, put on her coat, and wrapped a long pink scarf around her neck. 'I'm ready.'

'Let's go,' said Lauren grabbing her handbag and lifting the laptop case as she flew through the lounge into the hall and out of the front door.

'See you at teatime, Daisy,' said Leja, standing at the front door. 'Have a lovely day, Lauren,' she added as an afterthought. Lauren didn't respond.

Daisy smiled back and then jumped into the back seat.

'Seatbelt on, darling, please,' said Lauren.

'Yes, Mummy, all done.'

Lauren drove off, and Leja wandered back inside, kicking the door shut behind her. She went into the lounge, flopped down on the sofa, flicked on the television, and gazed up at the ceiling, deep in thought.

So comprehensive was the social indoctrination instilled by Lauren's mother, Rosemary, that many houses – in particular, stone-clad - ex-council terraces, of which, fortunately, there weren't many in Baddesley-Minton; Ford motor cars; discount furniture shops; loud, uneducated men; fish and chips on Friday night and Tesco's One Stop shops were an absolute anathema to her. It was as if these abominations were from another planet and most definitely did not belong in what Rosemary lovingly preferred to call 'a hamlet'. She thought it sounded lovelier, less common, and more picturesque than a village. As far as Rosemary was concerned, 'village' had the unsavoury whiff of medieval inbreeding. It smacked of serfs, idiots and presbyterianism. She never held back from expressing this opinion whenever the opportunity arose. Not for one moment did she ever realise what she had become.

These social travesties did exist; of course, they did, but Lauren and Michael neither noticed nor experienced them very often. They usually shopped at Fenwick's and M & S in Guildford. Michael drove a Range Rover Sport, and Lauren had a Mercedes estate. Michael also had a Porsche plaything for weekends, but there were no Fords - and they never had fish and chips on Friday. However, Michael did occasionally pop into Tesco's on the way home - if he ran out of scotch. This, of course, unbeknown to Lauren.

Lauren, her husband Michael, a merchant banker in the City, and daughter Daisy had lived in Baddesley-Minton for seven years. Not actually in the "village," but on the outskirts where it was more secluded, which meant she did not have to mix too often with the locals. Leja, their twenty-three-year-old Lithuanian au pair cum general skivvy, had worked for them for nearly five years and lived in a three-room apartment on the ground floor at the rear of the house.

Set on high ground in a woodland setting, this was the sort of house you would typically only find in fairy tales. But then, life had been one long fairy tale for Lauren for as long as she could remember. It was the house she had always dreamed of since she was five years old; it was almost an exact replica of her dolls' house. Now she and Michael owned the full-scale version - along with Barclays bank, that is.

Lauren was indeed fortunate; she had always known precisely how her life would be from the start. Her mother, Rosemary Louise Chilcott, chairperson of the Lavendon Women's Institute for the last seven years (three unopposed); chairperson of the Lavendon District Horticultural Society (this included Baddesley-Minton); and leading light in the Lavendon Choral Society; had meticulously schooled her daughter in what she should expect from life – all from the moment she uttered her first word. Lauren had never considered, nor could she comprehend, the possibility of having anything other than what she had been promised and now possessed.

'Did you finish your homework?' enquired Lauren, glancing briefly at her mobile phone lying on the passenger seat.

'Yes, Daddy helped me. I told you that earlier when you last asked.'

'So, you did, darling, so you did. I'm sorry.'

Lauren had been sitting in the lounge on Sunday while Michael helped Daisy, but it hadn't registered. She had so many work-related things running around in her head, and she was finding it extremely hard to switch off these days, even at weekends.

'I hope you did some of it,' asked Lauren with a questioning tone - momentarily glancing at Daisy in the rear-view mirror?

'Yes, I did, most of it, actually,' replied Daisy, smiling smugly.

'Good…good. We must do something together this weekend,' suggested Lauren, 'go out somewhere… as a family.

'A walk in the woods would be fun,' replied Daisy, 'I like walking in the woods.'

'Yes, that would be nice….' Lauren hesitated; she didn't actually like walking in the woods very much, Michael did, but Lauren preferred walking around the town.

'We could go shopping in Godalming?' suggested Lauren.

'Yes, that sounds like a great idea, too,' replied Daisy sounding less enthused.

Lauren made a mental note to go for a walk in the woods with Daisy on another weekend. Almost instantly, she felt a tiny pang of guilt at suggesting something that Daisy had readily agreed to, then immediately changing the suggestion to suit herself. The problem was Lauren was worn out by Friday night. She desperately needed a weekend of peace and tranquillity to recover sufficiently and prepare for the week ahead. Hence, she seldom did anything bar shopping on Saturdays. Lauren had many friends at the advertising agency where she worked as senior marketing manager, and in the past, on odd occasions, she had asked one or two of them to come and stay for the weekend. But she was glad none of them had ever taken up her offer.

Lauren and Michael met during their first week at university, and he proposed on the day they graduated. It was all as Rosemary had predicted – as if she had somehow arranged it. But then she always did say she had it all planned from the start. They were married exactly one year later at St Peter's Church in Lavendon. Six months later, they moved out of their two-bedroom bijou flat in Godalming into the house where they would probably spend the rest of their lives together. It had cost them far more than they could afford at the time, and the mortgage was enormous. But Lauren's parents liked it so much they'd stumped up the deposit, so another one of Lauren's dreams and Rosemary's predictions had come true. Daisy Grace was born one year later.

Before Leja started working for them, they had another nanny. Tania looked after Daisy from when she was six months old till Lauren returned to work. Unfortunately, Tania left unexpectedly and went back to Lithuania. Apparently, she was pregnant. The agency promptly replaced her with Leja, who looked virtually identical. Michael wondered if there was a factory deep in the heart of Lithuania churning out stunningly attractive au-pairs. He never mentioned this observation to Lauren.

Leja looked after the house, did some food shopping, washed all the clothes, and collected Daisy from her school. She also prepared breakfast and evening meals and, in her spare time, endeavoured to learn the subtler aspects of the English language. Leja did not work the weekends unless Lauren had arranged something special - but that didn't happen often. Apparently, she hoped to become an airline pilot, but she would more likely marry one instead; it was easier. Michael made jokes about that all the time. But oddly, nobody ever laughed.

Lauren and Michael seldom returned home before 7.30 pm on weekdays. So apart from saying goodnight to Daisy – if she was still awake – and good morning at breakfast, they didn't see much of her during the week. Weekends were precious moments when they were all together.

It must have been around the middle of June. Lauren was making her usual morning journey dropping Daisy off at the primary school in Lavendon on her way to Godalming station, where she caught the 8.52 to Waterloo. If the gods were with her, she could just make it into the office by 10.30, ready for the day. Michael left much earlier, so he tended not to see Daisy in the mornings.

Every day she passed over Shelbury Bridge, crossing the River Wey at its narrowest point where it made an impressively picturesque setting, perfect for painters or photographers. During the summer months, the riverbank downstream of the bridge would seldom be without a dozen or so aspiring artists. Each one gazing thoughtfully at the structure. Each one attempting to capture the mysterious tranquillity of the buff stone arches that carried the bridge. Mostly in oil on canvas, sometimes in charcoal or watercolours. Lauren never really noticed the painters. She thought it was a hobby that most people took up in their autumnal years when they had time on their hands. She didn't have the time for such idle pursuits and wouldn't have for many years.

On this particular day, as she approached the bend just before the bridge, she slowed down, as she always did. The road narrowed at this point. It was then, for the first time, that Lauren noticed a stunningly beautiful woman with shoulder-length blonde curly hair. She appeared to be of a similar age to herself. The woman was pushing a double buggy with one hand, and the other was holding the hand of a young girl. Lauren presumed she must be the woman's eldest daughter. Clinging to her chest was a fourth child, no more than a few weeks old, swaddled in an Indian papoose carrier. The woman's crazy, golden-blonde curls were occasionally lifted by an autumnal gust of wind. The movement of the woman's hair seemed to emulate the rhythm of the undulating mane of the Afghan hound tethered by an extended lead to her waist.

The ensemble gently flounced its way over the bridge, carefully navigating the narrow footpath as it made its way towards the school. The lady was smiling and conversing with her daughter while simultaneously muttering something to her babies in the buggy. The Afghan ambled on behind as if it were a sheepdog rounding up wayward family dawdlers, but there didn't appear to be any today. As the traffic often moved slower over the bridge, sometimes coming to a standstill just for a few seconds, Lauren had the opportunity to glance at the face of the woman with the golden hair. She was surprised to see no hint of turmoil, confusion, or anguish, just an expression of calm serenity. This was someone who tremendously enjoyed and embraced her role as a mother. A woman at ease with and without a care in the world - loving and relishing life and all it had to give.

The moment quickly passed, and Lauren began edging forward with the traffic as it started to move again. She continued her journey to the school and pulled up near the entrance.

'Have a lovely day, darling,' said Lauren as Daisy leaned over to kiss her.

'Yes, mummy, I will. See you tonight.'

'Hope so,' replied Lauren, smiling.

They kissed, and Daisy jumped out of the car, laughing and skipping her way towards the school gates without a care in the world. Lauren watched her, contemplating how fortunate she was.

A few minutes after Lauren drove away, her mind inexplicably flashed back to the fleeting moment on the bridge when she first noticed the blonde lady and her family. She was unexpectedly overcome with a strange sense of awe, admiration, and envy at the thought of this other mother managing to do something so very ordinary. Something that, for financial reasons, she had chosen not to do. Instead, Lauren had assigned the role indefinitely to other people. That was the moment when she suddenly realised that she had missed all the special school occasions and other pivotal moments in her daughter's life so far. The memory of all those treasures was being enjoyed and would continue to be enjoyed by Leja and her mother-in-law Rosemary. And it would be held and remembered by them for eternity to her total exclusion.

Lauren would never have access to those moments. Never be able to glance back at those memories in years to come… but Leja and Rosemary would. Yes, she occasionally saw Daisy for a few minutes each evening before she went to bed, a few minutes at breakfast and on the school run drop off, and they spent time together on the weekends. But Lauren was never there for the memorable occasions.

Lauren had never experienced maternal thoughts of this nature before and found herself, for the very first time, questioning the very life she was living. She had never harboured any reservations about her shortcomings as a mother. But now, for reasons she did not clearly understand, she was experiencing an overwhelming sense of confusion and uncertainty about where her true allegiance should lay.

This lapse into the strange realm of uncertainty and self-doubt seemed to stem from just a few seconds spent studying the blonde-haired lady on the bridge. But that didn't make any sense, none at all. Lauren wondered if the wine she had drunk the night before could have generated this hallucinatory vision. It did taste a little off, but she put it out of her mind as something of no consequence.

Lauren parked her car at the station, just making it onto the platform before her train drew in. Once settled in her seat, she opened her laptop to check her diary for the day. Slowly, unescapably, she began descending into her other all-consuming world.

Driving Daisy to school the following day, she looked out for the lady and her family - but she didn't appear today, so Lauren thought no more about it and carried on as usual.

CHAPTER 5

Hairline Fractures
June 2007

'Do we have any more coffee, Leja?' asked Michael, lowering his newspaper to catch Leja's attention. He half-smiled instead of adding a "please" to the end of his question as if that were sufficient. Leja returned the gesture, half-smiling back but with just a tinge of superficial grovelling servitude. It was a harmless game they played from time to time. A meaningless exchange but, in Michael's mind, one that clearly displayed the existence of a servant-master relationship. How wrong could he be?

'I make some, Michael,' replied Leja, in the familiar tormented English he associated with many of his banking colleagues in the city. They had migrated from one of the Eastern European countries to work in the UK banking finance industry but still hadn't perfected the subtle refinements of the English language.

'Where did Daisy go?' asked Michael, turning to Lauren, who was checking her mobile, 'we usually have breakfast together at the weekends.'

'She had hers earlier. I think she's outside – dancing. I'm taking her to ballet lessons in half an hour,' said Lauren, placing her mobile on the breakfast table.

'Oh, right.' Michael lifted his paper and resumed reading. Daisy flitted past the French windows as if on cue, twirling around and waving her hands in the air. Michael didn't notice her, and Lauren had her back to the window.

'I saw something rather remarkable this week,' said Lauren wistfully while cradling her coffee. Intimate breakfast chats during the week were virtually non-existent. Michael left home well before Lauren, so catching up at the weekends was essential to them both. What conversations they did have over dinner in the evening tended towards work-related matters; at weekends, business was strictly off-limits… most of the time.

Michael lowered his paper and smiled at Lauren, half expecting a glib witticism. 'Go on.'

'No, it's not a joke,' replied Lauren reproachfully. She scrunched up her eyebrows disapprovingly at his less-than-interested tone; he dropped the smile. 'It was something that made me feel good to be alive, and for some reason, I found it remarkably uplifting and inspiring.'

Michael, now intrigued, placed his newspaper on the table, picked up a piece of toast and nibbled at the corner while adopting a cautionary expression in expectation of what she was about to say. Whatever it was, it was important to her, and she wanted to share it with him. So the least he could do was listen with a modicum of interest.

Theirs was a relationship founded, as so many are, in the beginning, on love, trust, and a mutual understanding. Most of all, it was a relationship that created a sense of iridescent pleasure whenever they were in each other's company. Occasionally it was abrasive - even confrontational, but never too extreme, merely sound checks to ensure the other party was still paying attention. A gentle prod to induce comment of one sort or another - as one might prod a pig with a stick to provoke a positive reaction. It could sometimes be amusing to watch – even endearing. Without this interactive element, everything else would still exist - but it would have little meaning without the grounding of a sense of inner contentment and well-being. However, Lauren was beginning to have tiny niggling doubts about whether they still had this innate, vital and unique quality.

Lauren and Michael had always embraced a~~ passionate~~an enthusiastic belief that a relationship's spirituality was essential in a marriage. An intangible, a thread of commonality and purpose connecting them. They could discuss thoughts they could not, would not, want to talk about with almost anybody else on the planet. For this reason, today, she had his undivided attention.

'I thought *we* made you feel good to be alive and inspired you,' clipped Michael, but he wasn't adding anything.

'Of course, you do. That's not what I meant, and you know that. This was something entirely different. It was as if something had touched me, somewhere inside, in a place I didn't realise hadn't been touched in a long while.'

'Tell me more,' replied Michael by a hairsbreadth, narrowly avoiding patronising condescension by not making a pathetic stab at sexual innuendo. 'I'm intrigued; I can see it has affected you.'

Lauren paused for a moment before recalling the incident. 'I saw this stunningly beautiful woman with crazy blonde curly hair walking over Shelbury Bridge. I've never seen her before - but they changed the train timetable a couple of weeks ago - and now I drive past a little earlier, which is probably why I haven't seen her till now.' She paused once more while carefully assembling all the words she wanted to say in her head. For some inexplicable reason, she knew it was vital to recall the moment precisely as she had experienced it without embellishment or melodrama before sharing it with Michael.

'It wasn't some dazzling road to Damascus moment,' continued Lauren, 'or anything like that. It was something very ordinary that captured my attention for maybe no more than a few seconds. But for some reason, I felt it was important, crucially important, almost a pivotal moment in my life - but I haven't a clue why.'

Michael chose not to interrupt, something he would have under different circumstances, but oddly not on this occasion. He picked up the fresh coffee Leja had just poured him, took a sip and said nothing. Not for a moment did Michael take his eyes off Lauren. He could feel the intensity in her tone, something that usually portended some significant issue for imminent discussion. A few things shot through his mind, but nothing lingered for more than a few milliseconds.

Leja glanced at Lauren to see if she wanted her cup refilled, but Lauren just waved her hand over the top and smiled. Michael could see that whatever she was about to say meant a great deal to her.

'This woman... was walking her daughter to school and pushing one of those double buggies with two children in it, with another child, who I presume could only be a few weeks old, clinging to her chest in a baby carrier. And to finish it off, this gorgeous golden-haired Afghan hound was lolloping along behind her. And do you know what?'

Michael still said nothing; it wasn't necessary. Instead, he just shook his head nonchalantly. This was not the moment for crass flippancy or blithe asides.

Lauren continued, 'she looked so unruffled...- so totally unfazed by all that was happening around her. So sublimely calm despite walking four children and a dog to school, which must be over a mile from where she lives... I don't remember seeing any houses on that side of the road until you reach the pub.' She took another sip of her coffee. 'How does she do that?' asked Lauren looking wistfully to the heavens with an expression of wonderment and bewilderment, as if searching for some divine revelation.

Michael thought that now was the opportune moment to comment. 'What, walk to school?' he asked blankly, sounding slightly underwhelmed after the emotional outpour.

'No, not walk to school,' responded Lauren sharply, 'Well, yes, she was walking to school, but what I'm referring to is how in control and unfazed she seemed. All that responsibility. It would have been absolute pandemonium if it had been me.'

'Oh, I see what you mean... Well, that's easy... Mother's Little Helper,' replied Michael curtly, without a second thought. He picked up his newspaper and continued reading. Lauren's recollection of the event had not been what he was expecting, but then he didn't know what he had expected.

'Mother's little helper?' enquired Lauren, intrigued by his cryptic comment - swiftly refocusing her attention back on Michael.

'You missed the Sixties, didn't you?' asked Michael with just a hint of tongue-in-cheek superciliousness.

'So, did you by about twenty-five years, unless you've been lying to me about your age all these years,' replied Lauren smirking. She knew exactly how old he was and that he had missed the Sixties by many miles. 'Mind you, your hair is thinning a bit on top, so maybe you have knocked a few years off...' She smiled.

'It's by the Rolling Stones – "Mother's Little Helper."- Great song – an ode to anxious mothers unable to cope with everyday life until they discovered Valium....'

'Valium,' repeated Lauren?

Michael realised that Lauren was still confused over his reference. 'Valium, that's what the song is all about. It was a drug created to combat anxiety; it kept stressed-out mothers going in the nineteen-sixties.'

'I see, and you think that's what she's on?' asked Lauren with a curious expression of disbelief.

'Looks amazing, walks to school with four screaming kids and a lolloping mountain dog surrounded by chaos and yet doesn't appear to have a care in the world... Has to be stoned out of her brain on Benzos. That or weed... or crack.'

Lauren was taken aback by Michael's condescending dismissal, and for a few moments, she found herself lost for words. 'It was an Afghan hound, actually, not a mountain dog. The children weren't screaming, and there was no chaos, as you so nicely put it...' Lauren paused for a moment before continuing, 'I can't believe you can be so dismissive about someone you don't even know or have ever met.' It was a mild rebuke, but Michael could see that Lauren did not appreciate his off-hand brutal annihilation of the idyllic vision of genteel innocence she had been trying so hard to convey. Sadly, the milk of human kindness had run dry years ago in Michael's world.

Although Lauren worked in a highly-pressurised and stressful environment, one, paradoxically, she enjoyed immensely - her humanity always shone through. She was the one who would always find time to talk to a member of her staff quietly and in confidence if they had a problem. But some days, even she craved a less complicated life, like the other world the lady on the bridge inhabited.

'Afghan hound, then. Same difference. Still, a big unruly monster of a dog, as I remember,' mumbled Michael in a semi-conciliatory manner.

'That's what you'd think,' replied Lauren, 'but that wasn't how it was. As I said, she was completely in control, and I don't think she was stoned, as you so quaintly put it.'

For some reason - one which she couldn't easily explain - Lauren found herself feeling overly protective: driven by an intangible moral obligation to defend someone she had never spoken to and had only seen once.

'Maybe she was just very well organised,' suggested Michael in a vain attempt to appease Lauren. His wife was displaying profound respect and admiration for the woman. He had misjudged that entirely and would not easily dislodge it from Lauren's mindset.

'Maybe,' pondered Lauren. Facetious cynicism can be such a disagreeable trait, she thought to herself.

'I am sure if we had another three children and bought a gangly dog, you would cope just as well. Women do that. It's in the genes.' Michael smiled at Lauren, and Lauren smiled back appreciatively, but she wasn't convinced it was a genuine compliment. There was still a tiny lingering trace of derision tucked away somewhere – hiding in the corner.

'I don't think so. I have to admit I am completely in awe of that lady.'

'You run an office with what – nearly forty people in it. Do you have any problems doing that?' asked Michael adopting a slightly different tack.

'Well, no,' replied Lauren contemplatively.

'Exactly, that's my point. You have to put things into perspective.'

'Maybe I'm a little jealous?'

'Of what?' said Michael, sounding surprised.

'She does what mothers should do, something very ordinary but vitally important; she is being a mother!'

'You are a mother, and you are doing what a mother is supposed to do, and you hold down a demanding job as well. That's important.'

'But we only have Daisy Grace,' replied Lauren.

'You're not getting all broody just because you've seen this woman out walking with her tribe of sprogs?'

'That sounds horrible.'

'I didn't mean it to be, it's just that....'

'I know what you mean, and no, I'm not. I don't want more children, yet – we don't want any more, do we?' It was a loaded question, and Lauren subtly gauged his expression as he replied.

'No, not right now, we don't. We're both heavily committed career-wise, aren't we? That's what we agreed, yes?' ventured

Michael tentatively, unsure what the real agenda was or where this was leading.

'Yes, yes we are,' said Lauren reflectively.

'Right,' concluded Michael authoritively.

'They're not just a tribe of sprogs; they are a family,' qualified Lauren with a hint of contemptuous incredulity. 'An incredibly happy family from what I could make out.' She glared at Michael, trying to appear stern and reproachful, but didn't quite manage to pull it off.

'Yes, you're right; I apologise for my choice of words. It's just that this momentary glimpse of this woman seems to have had a profoundly odd effect on you.'

'No, not really. It just made me wonder about the other road.'

'The other road?' queried Michael.

'Less trodden…'

'Ah, that road. Well…' But Michael did not finish. He knew some sentences were better left unfinished. Sometimes, they lead you to places you don't want to visit.

Michael finished his breakfast and moved into the lounge while Leja cleared the kitchen table, and Lauren prepared to leave.

'I'm ready, Mummy,' said Daisy, suddenly appearing from nowhere and pirouetting in the middle of the kitchen.

'I'll be a few minutes,' replied Lauren. 'Go and talk to Daddy. He hasn't seen you this morning.'

'Okay,' said Daisy curtly, in an annoyingly descending dual tone that she adopted occasionally. She smiled and skipped off to the lounge.

'Mummy says I should come and talk to you for five minutes before I go to ballet lessons.'

'And I would like to talk to you,' replied Michael, putting his paper on the table. 'So, tell me, what have you been doing at school this week?'

'Oh, nothing really, just silly, boring things.'

'Oh, well, maybe we should get you a job if you're bored with school. Would you like that?'

'And become a wage slave like you and Mummy? I don't think so, Daddy. I wouldn't have time for all my other social activities.'

'Like what,' asked Michael, a little surprised at her answer? He obviously hadn't been paying attention lately. Daisy's conversational skills had improved remarkably since their last proper talk. Even if they had become lightly peppered with the odd radical indoctrination, which Michael could only attribute to Rosemary - Lauren's mother. *'Marry well, and you will never have to soil your hands with common labour,'* was one of Rosemary's favourite mantras. One that he found particularly irksome and profoundly exasperating at times. She had never forgiven Michael for allowing Lauren to return to work, which deprived her of the possibility of having more grandchildren. Not that Michael had any say in the matter. Lauren was her own woman.

'Well, each day I like to read and play with my friends, and I like spending time with Timothy.'

'Timothy?' enquired Michael sounding a little intrigued, 'who is Timothy?'

'Timothy, my hamster. Silly Daddy,' replied Daisy, scowling playfully at her father.

'Oh, of course... I thought Timothy's name was Henrietta?' he added as an afterthought. Daisy looked at Michael with a curious grin.

'It was - when he was a she, but she died, and you and Mummy bought me Timothy, and he's a he.' Daisy looked at him carefully, weighing up his response.

'Oh, of course. I just haven't seen him recently,' said Michael.

'Don't you remember the After Eight mints,' enquired Daisy?

'What?' replied Michael appearing confused.

'The After Eight Mints, you always buy me mints when a hamster dies.'

'Do I?' replied Michael scrunching his eyebrows.

'Yes. And I eat all the mints, and then we bury the hamster in the box. Hamsters fit in the box quite nicely.'

'Do they? asked Michael, now even more bewildered by the conversation.

'Maybe mummy bought the After Eight mints,' suggested Daisy curiously.

'Yes, maybe it was. I must have forgotten.'

'That's perfectly normal Daddy. I would ascribe that failure to the inherent psychological pressure of senior managerial commitment. Occasionally, it can contribute towards a state of absentmindedness and decaying peripheral awareness as you grow older, especially when you switch off for a few hours.'

Daisy stood gazing at Michael with her head tilted to one side, waiting for a reply. Michael briefly glanced around the room to assure himself that it was Daisy who had just uttered this stunningly eloquent and insightful appraisal of his observational shortcomings. Having overheard Daisy's cutting assessment, Lauren popped her head around the kitchen door and grinned at Michael, lifting her eyebrows and smirking with a clownish expression.

'Yes, you are right....' Michael was flabbergasted but tried not to show it. However, he managed to shut his mouth, which had fallen half-open. 'So, Daddy, what are you doing today while I am at ballet lessons?' It wasn't exactly the Spanish Inquisition, but Michael was acutely aware that on his present form, a whimsical reply just wouldn't cut it. Not without provoking further searching and highly demoralising questions.

'I will read the paper. Carefully consider what is happening in the world, form my own opinions on how to solve the problems and then maybe have a little nap till you return. And then I think we will all go shopping in Godalming and maybe go to Costa for coffee. I know you like that.' He hoped that his answer would satisfy Daisy's probing inquiry.

'That sounds most satisfactory, Daddy. I am most happy to acquiesce to your suggestion,' replied Daisy with a tiny grin.

'Come on, Daisy, I'm leaving,' called Lauren from the kitchen.

'Coming, Mother,' replied Daisy, tilting her head to the other side while still smiling at Michael. 'I have just sorted Daddy out for the day.' She gave him another beguiling smile that nearly broke his heart and skipped joyfully back to the kitchen. He sat back in his chair, feeling a little shell-shocked and proud thinking about what she had said – or, more accurately, how she had so eloquently expressed it. Daisy was growing up so fast – seven going on seventeen – and he had hardly noticed the subtle changes. They seemed to have happened when he wasn't there. He could remember the first things she did, like when she began moving around on her back like an upturned crab. And scrabbling to make headway over shiny floors, always searching for the carpeted areas where she would have better traction. She had no place she wanted to go, just a desire to embrace the sensation of moving for the sheer unadulterated pleasure of doing so. It was the same when she began to crawl, direction unknown, unimportant. Her goal was merely to gain speed and continue the exploration of her small but fast-expanding world. One day she found the strength to pull herself upright and stand unaided for a second or two, albeit with the aid of some item of furniture or the helping hand of either Lauren or Michael. She would tenaciously grasp whatever was available to enable her to make it to the next stage of her journey through life.

He could remember the first day she began toddling around unaided and the first day she started to form words. But between then and now, there had been a quantum leap. She had ceased to be a dependent child. She had become a self-determining free-thinking individual with the ability to respond to and justify any action she or anybody else undertook. Those were the times that, somehow, he had missed, and to a similar degree, unfortunately, so had Lauren.

'Do you want a lift into town, Leja?' asked Lauren.

'If there is nothing else to do - yes, please,' replied Leja.

'No, we can let you escape for the weekend.'

'See you Monday, Leja,' said Michael from the lounge.

Michael came out to kiss Lauren and Daisy goodbye. He watched them climb into the car and then went back into the lounge to continue reading the newspaper and think about the morning's conversations.

CHAPTER 6

Lauren
Early July 2007

'I wonder if we will see her today,' asked Daisy, whimsically peering out of the car window.

'See who?' queried Lauren.

'You know. The lady with the blonde hair, the one you look at most days as we drive past her.' Lauren was slightly surprised because she had never mentioned anything to Daisy about the woman she saw on the bridge. Obviously, Daisy had been covertly monitoring her and taking notes. Children intuitively watch what adults do and store it away. It's part of the learning process. She should have remembered that.

'Maybe we'll see her in a minute,' replied Lauren. No point in denying it, she thought. She had nothing to hide. 'Shelbury Bridge is just around the corner, so...' The traffic started slowing down as it always did before the bend. Just as they rounded the corner and the bridge came into view, and as luck would have it, the lady with the blonde hair appeared on the other side of the road with her children and the trailing Afghan hound. Lauren didn't see them immediately; she was focused on the car in front, which was moving a little erratically.

'There she is, Mummy!' exclaimed Daisy, excitedly pointing out the window.

It was, without a doubt, a charming and arresting image. As always, the lady looked immaculate, radiant and serene. Today, her daughter appeared animatedly enthralled in a conversation with her mother while happily skipping from one foot to the other. She was possibly discussing what she would be doing today or what they would do after school. Or maybe there was some special event coming up that she wanted her mother to attend. There could be any number of reasons for her cheerful disposition.

Neither Lauren nor Michael had ever attended any of Daisy's school events. But fortunately, Leja or Rosemary would generally step in to act as a substitute parent if it were something important, so Daisy was never left feeling neglected. It wasn't the same as having her parents there, but it was the only option available.

Daisy and Leja got on well, and Leja, being only twenty-three, was much closer in years to Daisy than Lauren or Rosemary, so the au pair arrangement worked well on the popular culture communication level. Even though Lauren was only thirty, there was a discernible gap in how they communicated and what they communicated about, and it was becoming wider every day. At times Leja almost felt like an elder sister to Daisy, not just the hired help, but only in Lauren's eyes...

Lauren watched as the lady on the bridge stopped walking and knelt to say something to her two children in the buggy. She smiled, then kissed the baby she was carrying in the papoose. A moment later, she turned to her elder daughter, who was holding onto the buggy and kissed her too. The girl threw her arms around her mother to give her a hug. Then the lady stood up and continued walking, but not before turning around and saying a few words of encouragement to the Afghan hound. He had been faithfully trailing someway behind but had suddenly decided to catch up and join in the happy throng.

For some inexplicable reason, Lauren was suddenly overwhelmed by this ordinary yet seminally *mitfreude* moment. The whole inspiringly pivotal gesture had conveyed a profoundly gratifying sensation, and she could feel a lump beginning to well up in her throat. *What was happening,* she wondered? *This isn't me.* For some unfathomable reason, Lauren thought she would burst out crying. She was so overcome by the experience of seeing something so profoundly joyous and yet completely familiar. And it had just happened to somebody she didn't even know. It felt like she was in one of those mawkishly over-sentimentalised scenes cynically depicted in romantic films. With the right music, it was guaranteed to ring the last ounce of sappiness out of a vulnerable audience, but this was not a film. This was real life, and it was happening right now. Somehow, Lauren held back her feelings, just enough so Daisy didn't notice...

The effortless way this lady viscerally connected with her children and their dog left Lauren awestruck with admiration. It was not an epiphany, nor was it remotely unusual. It was just one of those moments millions of mothers worldwide experience daily - mothers performing the same routine ritual. And yet, despite this valiant attempt at normalisation and simplification of the event she had just witnessed, Lauren knew, somewhere, deep down inside, this was a defining moment in her life. What she did not know, nor would she realise for the next few years - was what this defining moment really meant. Nor would she know what it was trying to tell her. All sorts of thoughts swirled around in her head. It was all a chaotic whirlwind of confusion. Then the traffic started to move, and she and the moment were gone.

'Do you know that girl?' enquired Lauren once she had regained her composure.

'No, she's not in my class, but we are in the same year. I see her at playtime occasionally. Do you want me to find out who she is?' asked Daisy quizzically, but with a speculative cadence, as if there might be a hidden agenda tucked away somewhere in the question. Daisy was becoming annoyingly intuitive.

'No, it's not important. I just wondered, that's all,' replied Lauren indifferently.

During the day, Lauren didn't have much opportunity to dwell on the moment on the bridge. She was totally engaged with all the many managerial decisions that invariably seemed to keep her mind fully occupied until early evening.

On her way home on the train, however, as she slowly segued back into a more tranquil state of mind, she began reflecting deeply on the incident that morning. She wondered why such an innocuous and seemingly unimportant event had made such a profound impression on her.

They did not pass the lady again on the way to school that week.

The following Tuesday, Lauren and Daisy had breakfast as usual. They left the house a little earlier than usual as it was raining. As they approached the bend just before the bridge, Lauren, for some reason, had an inkling that she would see the lady today. Sure enough, a few moments later, on the other side of the road, under a huge multi-coloured umbrella, she could see the lady slowly walking towards the bridge as usual, with her four children and their dog.

'Her name's Poppy, by the way,' said Daisy, suddenly, 'And her mummy's name is Katie.' The sudden production of this unsolicited information caught Lauren unaware.

'I thought you said you didn't know her?' asked Lauren.

'I don't. I just spoke to a few friends at school, and one mentioned that she lives on the other side of the village.'

'Katie,' murmured Lauren. I suppose that's better than just calling her the lady or the lady on the bridge. That sounded so impersonal and detached. She did not want to be disconnected - she wanted to share a little of the joy that the lady – Katie – experienced each day. 'Katie and Poppy,' she rolled the names over in her mind. She thought it suited them so perfectly. As Lauren drove past Katie on the bridge, she looked at her, and something inside made her feel good. A visceral sensation of synergy and commonality flashed between them, yet she still did not know Katie… She never would.

'So, Katie and Poppy,' reiterated Lauren after a few moments.

'Yes.'

'That's nicer and friendlier.' She sounded pleased that she now had names to attach to the faces.

'Yes,' repeated Daisy, 'much nicer.'

They arrived at the school gates, and Daisy undid her seat belt and jumped out of the car.

'You have a lovely day, darling,' said Lauren, kissing her through the open window.

'Yes, Mummy,' replied Daisy smiling. 'You too, and don't work too hard.' She gave her mother a castigatory smile, waving her forefinger at her menacingly. Lauren felt a warm glow. Just for a moment, she forgot who the mother was and who the child was, and it made her feel happy. It was a good feeling, and she liked it.

Lauren drove off to the station, parked, walked onto the platform, and bought herself a latte before boarding the train to London. Once she had settled down, she opened her diary for the day. As usual, it was full of appointments, meetings, and all the other things that filled her day. Just for a few moments, her mind drifted back to the memory of Katie with her family on the bridge. It made her feel a little happier in herself to know that she had been able to share – albeit at a distance – a tiny part of Katie's life today, if only for a few seconds.

The day passed much quicker than usual for the first time in a long time. She had a sense of there being a new purpose in her life. She had no idea what it was, but somehow it made the day seem a little shorter. She could not remember when that was last the case. She always had Daisy and Michael to go home to. They filled some of the boxes in her life, but Katie filled one more, one that had lain empty for a long time. But not any longer. On the journey home, she wondered again how it was that just catching sight of Katie and her family, maybe twice a week for just a few fleeting moments, could make such a difference to her life, but somehow it did.

She arrived back home just before seven o'clock. Michael came in half an hour later.

'How was your day?' asked Michael as he did almost every day.

'Good, in fact, really good.' Michael looked at Lauren with a curious expression.

'Have you something to tell me?' he asked.

'No. Why?' replied Lauren smiling, looking bemused and a little intrigued.

'Well… you just look… different, cheerier, dare I say, but please don't take that as meaning I don't think you look happy every other night because you do. It's just you look a little more so tonight. Almost serene.' He had neatly closed off the possible rebuttal to a compliment that could be misinterpreted by a sharp mind, and hers was razor sharp. Michael had learned to be careful with the words he used.

'You're right, actually,' replied Lauren, with an overwhelming sense of euphoria and well-being that she couldn't hide. 'I do feel good. I saw Katie and Poppy today, and it made me feel… good, really good.' She smiled at Michael.

'Katie and Poppy, do I know them,' asked Michael with a strained expression? As if he thought he should know them but had somehow forgotten. He gazed skywards, searching his memory, looking a little confused.

'Sorry,' said Lauren. 'No, you don't. It's the lady on the bridge walking her daughter to school that I see most mornings. I'm sure I mentioned her a few weeks ago.'

'Oh, yes, I do remember. We had a slight disagreement over Valium, as I remember. You told me off.'

'So, I did,' she smiled, but only to herself.

'So, you know their names now. Have you met them?'

'No, I haven't. Daisy told me. She spoke to one of her school friends who lives near them.'

'Oh, I see. So, are you going to meet up with them?'

'Meet them?' queried Lauren, a little surprised. 'I don't know. I hadn't thought about it.' She went quiet for a few moments, carefully pondering Michael's question. 'Do you know what?' she said. 'I don't think I should.'

'Why not?' asked Michael. 'She obviously fascinates you. She may be good company, a new friend even, and she obviously makes you feel good.'

'I have all the friends I need; I don't want a new friend. All I need is what she already gives me.'

'Which is what, precisely?' asked Michael, now sounding curiously intrigued and a little confused.

'Tranquillity, serenity... and calm, that is what she instils in me every time I see her, and that might change if I got to know her, and I could lose it forever.'

'You derive all that from just a glance once, maybe twice a week?' asked Michael, his curiosity now morphed into bewilderment.

'Yes, I do, but I don't know why. Somehow just seeing that lady,'

'Katie,' qualified, Michael?

'Yes, Katie...' replied Lauren smiling, 'seeing her and her children and the dog does something. It's as if she somehow replenishes part of my soul, enough to make it whole again and get me through the day. I need that sometimes.'

'It's all starting to sound a little like transcendental hogwash, like some quirky epiphany on the road-to-Damascus moment. You're not going all spiritually weird on me, are you,' asked Michael, teasing her with just the tiniest hint of measured cynicism? He had never been particularly moved by any piece of art, ballet, or song, but Lauren had been deeply affected by this fleeting glimpse of an absolute stranger. This was not something Michael had ever experienced with Lauren before. He suddenly realised he was beginning to see a side to her that he had never known existed. He found it strangely enchanting.

'No, it's not anything like that,' mumbled Lauren. 'Just seeing her touched a spot in me somewhere, that's all, and it made me think about my own mortality and what's really important in life.'

Michael did not say anything more; it felt inappropriate.

They all sat down and had dinner together. Michael had returned a little earlier than usual; Daisy was still up. It was a rarity during the week, and they enjoyed it even more for that reason. Lauren wondered what it must be like to have dinner with a large family every night, and her mind wandered briefly to a different place.

'Dinner, Poppy. Can you go tell your father,' asked Katie? She put Jamie and Julia into their high chairs and gave them a squash beaker. Baby Trinity had already been fed and was asleep in the carrycot in the corner. John came in from the garden and kissed Katie.

'What's that for?' asked Katie, smiling and looking slightly surprised.

'Because... because you are gorgeous, and I love you, Katie Rose Farrier.' He loved to use her full name whenever circumstances allowed because he enjoyed its beautifully resolved sound. It was part of who she was, what she had once been, and what she was now, his wife, lover, and mother of their children, but more than anything else, his best friend. As his school science teacher had incessantly endeavoured to explain, the whole was always more significant than the sum of the constituent parts.

'Well, you're not wrong there,' she replied, tongue in cheek.

John washed his hands and sat down while Poppy moved the vegetables to the table.

'So, how was your day?' asked Katie.

'It was good. I had some new orders, which should keep us going for two or three months.'

'It's good to be busy,' said Katie.

'Not too busy, though. I'm happy, just "pottering" along.' He looked up at Katie, and she smiled at his silly pun. At the very beginning of their relationship, they had agreed that a simple life would be most agreeable to them and that neither wished to become part of the rat race that had consumed so many of their friends. They had decided to have a family first rather than Katie starting her career. That way, they could enjoy the simple pleasures of parenthood and have a decent family life. Katie had been to university and trained as a solicitor but only practised for a year before meeting John and deciding almost immediately to give up work and start a family.

Maybe after they had all grown up, she might do something if she was still minded to do so. However, she loved the family life they had created. And it was becoming increasingly unlikely that she would consider any notable change in her life for at least fifteen years, if not longer. By which time, it would probably be too late, but that was the choice she had made, and she was happy with it. The maternal spirit burned brightly and with a burning passion in Katie's heart.

'Hi there,' said Michael, gently waving his hand to attract Lauren's attention while moving his head closer across the table towards her. She appeared to be gazing trance-like into space. 'Wine, darling?'

'Oh,' said Lauren, suddenly returning. 'I'm sorry. I don't know what happened there, a... yes, please.'

'You were miles away,' said Michael, smiling. 'Not pressure of work, I hope.' He poured her a glass of wine.

'No, no, it wasn't. Mind you, it has been hectic these last couple of weeks. We have just signed a contract for a major new chocolate promotion, so I will be swamped right through to May next year. They've asked me to head up the whole campaign, and if it works out as I think it should, I could be in line for a promotion.'

'That is good, really good,' said Michael, 'but does that mean we will see less of you?' he added with some reservation.

'No, not at all. In fact, I'm hoping to get back a little earlier each day. I'll have more staff now, and some work can be done at home.' It sounded ideal, but it seldom worked out that way.

CHAPTER 7

Alfie, the Afghan poet.
July 2007

The sun rose early, or at least it seemed to, probably because there were no clouds. It must have been just after five in the morning when the light started creeping under the curtains into their bedroom. In winter, Michael woke earlier than Lauren and was gone by seven. But in summer, they would rise together and wander around the bathroom, washing their teeth and showering before going downstairs at around six. Usually, they would have a coffee on the little table by the rear patio doors in the kitchen. The house faced east, so by six, they had the full splendour of the rising sun - the bringer of life - to gaze at as they drank their coffee and ate croissants. It was truly glorious – the pure joy of just watching the day begin and wondering what it might bring.

As they moved into July, Lauren and Michael would sit outside on the patio for breakfast. They were fortunate insomuch that the Victorian walled garden that surrounded the area just outside the kitchen seemed to catch and hold the sun's warmth like an old jumper. A typical early morning for France or Italy, but not England, not usually anyway. Michael poured himself another cup of coffee and sighed quietly to himself.

'What?' asked Lauren, smiling as she sipped her coffee.

'Nothing,' replied Michael, looking surprised.

'You sighed, yearningly, I think.'

'How can you tell if I sighed yearningly,' asked Michael? Intrigued by Lauren's question, glancing at her with a puzzled expression.

'All sighs are yearning for something... aren't they,' replied Lauren?

'Are they?'

'Of course.'

'It's just so gloriously wonderful, isn't it?' Michael gestured to the garden and the sun in an all-encompassing majestic motion. In his mind, the feeling was not dissimilar to that a vicar might experience when fondly gazing down on his flock of faithful parishioners. He had often wondered why churchgoers were commonly referred to with the same collective noun as sheep; the unspoken conclusion always made him snigger. This only further enhanced his nihilistic opinions.

'Yes, but then everything is, isn't it?' replied Lauren, sounding a little curious at Michael's tone, unsure of what exactly he was alluding to.

'Well, yes, but wouldn't it be nice if it were like this every day instead of....' He didn't finish what he was thinking but quietly sighed. This was the first time Michael had even mildly hinted that the city's cut and thrust might be supplanted by a simple country life. 'Mind you, I couldn't sit around here all day, gazing at the flowers and twiddling my thumbs. I would go barmy in a week.' He laughed, then adopted a demented country yokel-type facial expression with his tongue dangling out of the corner of his mouth. This swiftly dispelled any tenuous suggestion he may have inadvertently conveyed about a sudden career change. Not that he could change career even if he wanted to; Michael wasn't qualified for anything other than what he did. While still at university, he joined a rock band, a decision inspired by the then prime minister Tony Blair. Having no discernible talent or musical ability whatsoever, he gave up after two years, not realising that talent was never an essential prerequisite for a music career.

Lauren smiled, but behind the smile, she also wondered about their chosen life. They had both taken the devil's purse, working twelve-hour days, and they did make a lot of money. Although they had not exactly sold their souls, they had sacrificed something else far more valuable. And that was precious time – and a great deal of it. Something they could never recoup.

Apart from the first few months after Daisy was born, Lauren only saw her for an hour a day at most, including the drive to school. Most nights, Daisy would be asleep long before Lauren or Michael returned home. Weekends were the one redeeming factor that made everything worthwhile.

Michael's sighed; it was small, insignificant, inconsequential, no more than a gentle whisper. But it triggered thoughts that had always quietly lain in the back of Lauren's mind. But there they would lay, and there they would have to stay for a little longer...

Leja came through from her bedroom and started making breakfast; Daisy came down just after seven. After eating, Lauren and Daisy said their goodbyes, climbed into the Mercedes and drove away.

As Lauren turned into the bend just before Shelbury Bridge, she began to slow down with the traffic. As she did so, Katie came into view, making her way towards the bridge on the other side of the road. Katie was not wearing a coat today; maybe she hadn't worn one for a while, wondered Lauren; it had been warm, even at that time of the morning, and Lauren had not seen her for the last few days. Katie was wearing a flouncy floral-design dress. It was similar to something Lauren had seen Bridget Bardot wearing in a nineteen-fifties film she had recently watched. The dress, tied tightly at the waist with a broad white belt, billowed out as Katie walked, putting Lauren in mind of a shimmering but infinitely less erratic Dervish dancer. The dress majestically rose and fell in perfect rhythm to her gait as she and her family slowly made their way over the bridge.

Summer was here at last, and Katie didn't seem to have a worry in the world, lost in another eternity. She honestly did not have a care, and that thought somehow lifted Lauren's heart for a few fleeting moments. This vicarious embodiment concerned her at first. The very nature of enjoyment was subjective; if you liked something and it gave you pleasure, that was simple enough. If you could share that joy with friends, even better. But she was deriving pleasure from watching somebody else enjoy themselves, and somehow that seemed wrong, almost furtively voyeuristic. Or was it, she wondered. *What right had she to piggyback on someone else's contentment and enjoyment with life? But then why not? What could be wrong? Who could that hurt? Nobody...* So many questions – and never any answers. She felt confused by the sense of cinema verité she was experiencing: the honesty, truth, all there for anyone to see, for anyone to enjoy if only they knew how.

The more she thought about it, the more she felt at ease. People are not selfish when happy; they are generous and charitable and want to share their feelings. That was the simple truth of the matter.

She was taking nothing away, yet she was the recipient of something intangible, some glorious elation. Undoubtedly that was the ultimate panacea for all ills – to enjoy life. It cost Katie nothing, yet Lauren was acquiring something beyond price from the experience and would continue to do so for as long as possible. With the calm stillness now instilled by watching Katie, maybe she could capture some of the benefits for herself.

Lauren noticed something was a little different today. Katie had replaced the buggy with a larger model. This version had an ingenious arrangement for her baby to be carried in a jockey seat on top. However, one of the twins had decided that she wanted to walk despite having the option to ride in the buggy. She was restrained from wandering too far by a set of reins held by Katie. But she still held on to her mother's hand while trying to emulate her gently undulating gait. This was the first time Lauren had seen either of Katie's younger children. And this one, another girl, a sister for Poppy, also appeared to have inherited her mother's carefree joie de vivre. This exuberant sense of joyous merriment and innocent bewilderment seemed to percolate all the way through the family and then infuse the air around them. It was as if the river of trials and tribulations that darkened the rest of the world had never reached their front door, held back by an invisible barrier of consciousness.

Poppy trailed behind Katie with the Afghan hound, flouncing majestically last of all at the back – as usual. Bringing up the rear guard to the resplendent entourage.

Lauren would have to give the dog a name! She could not keep thinking of it as just 'the dog' or Afghan hound. It was an integral part of the family, an essential part of the imagery, so it is vital to give it a name.

'What shall we call Katie's dog,' mumbled Lauren unconsciously?

'Pardon,' replied Daisy, deeply ensconced in something she was reading. She glanced up at Lauren's reflection in the rear-view mirror, and it just caught her eye.

Lauren at once realised what she had done, so she continued. 'Katie's dog. What shall we call it?'

'Alfie already has a name,' replied Daisy matter-of-factly, as if everybody knew its name except Lauren. 'He's called Alfie.'

Daisy smiled at the sassiness of her reply.

Lauren giggled with pride at how quick Daisy was becoming at the cheeky reply. Maybe, a little too clever for her own good.

'Alfie – it's called Alfie?' asked Lauren, slightly surprised.

'Yes.'

'Who told you?'

'Poppy – sort of.'

'Sort of?' enquired Lauren.

'Well, Miss Samuels asked the class which of us had a pet, and if we did, could we put our hands up.'

'And?'

'I put my hand up, and Miss Samuels asked me to tell the whole class about my pet Hamster, Timothy.

'And what did you say?'

'Well, there wasn't much to say, really. I said it sits in a cage for most of the day, eats hamster food and poos and wees a bit, and that's about it, oh and I have to clean it out regularly... It's not really a pet, is it? It doesn't do anything. It just exists - put on earth to procreate more hamsters and make poo.' This sudden digression into borderline nihilism, something she had probably picked up from Michael, caught Lauren a little off guard. Especially at that time of the morning when her mind was on less radical doctrines and directed more specifically at the pure joy of living. But then maybe it wasn't so vastly different after all.

She pursed her lips together, tentatively agreeing with Daisy's comprehensive, somewhat ruthlessly dismissive, summation of the meaning of life. But, having no desire at that moment to explore that avenue of thought any further, she curtly redirected the conversation to the matter of Miss Samuels' initial enquiry to the class.

'Then what happened?' asked Lauren.

'Miss Samuels asked the rest of the class, who put their hands up to tell us about their pets.' Daisy went quiet and started reading again.

'And?' said Lauren, expecting Daisy to elaborate. It was that thing about nature abhorring a vacuum.

'Oh,' said Daisy, looking up again, surprised. 'Some of the girls have ponies or dogs. One girl, Ophelia, even has a llama.' Lauren's mouth fell open for a second, but she said nothing. There wasn't much she could say.

'Poppy stood up and told the class they had an Afghan hound and that they had named it Lord Tennyson, but they called him Alfie for short because he likes poetry...

Lauren half-smiled at the explanation, although slightly confused by the final comment. Alfie sounded profoundly more interesting as a pet than Timothy.

'Alfie likes poetry,' queried Lauren casually, not wishing to delve too deep into what appeared to be an unfathomably unique canine characteristic?

'That's what she said,' replied Daisy with an air of naïve innocence, apparently unaware of the ridiculous nature of her statement. 'I know it sounds preposterous for a dog to like poetry. I did mention the preternatural aspect of her declaration at the time, but Poppy seemed convinced that Alfie does.'

Lauren was occasionally awestruck at some of the words Daisy casually dropped into conversations. Some of which she would have wagered good money on Daisy, not knowing the meaning. And yet, she had used them articulately and in the correct context, and Lauren would have lost her money. Deep down, it gave her a gratifying feeling to hear her daughter talking so eloquently, a sensation she couldn't easily define. *Maybe she should ask Daisy what word would describe how she was feeling,* she thought to herself. But not just yet. That might be asking too much.

'So, is Poppy in your class now?'

'No, not normally. But one of the teachers was indisposed, so they amalgamated two classes into one for some lessons.'

Lauren smiled to herself again. 'So, you're mingling with some new friends now?'

'I don't know, Mummy... What is mingling?'

Lauren almost burst out laughing at the question, feeling totally ambushed. Having heard her daughter using several words, she thought she could not possibly understand and then pleading unfamiliarity with another that Lauren felt sure she would have known. Then she glanced into the rear-view mirror and, seeing Daisy smiling broadly, realised she had been well and truly suckered.

They arrived at school, and Daisy jumped out.

'See you later, Mummy,' she said, kissing Lauren through the open window. 'We can do some mingling tonight if you like.'

Daisy smirked endearingly and gambolled away, happy in the knowledge that she had befuddled her mother.

Lauren smiled, but she would not be early tonight- and they would not be doing any 'mingling.' As Daisy entered the playground, Lauren could feel a watery sensation in the corner of her eye and quickly wiped it away. She drove off to the railway station, thinking about what Daisy had said and of Katie's family, complete with Alfie, the poetry lover. They would all still be making their way to school on foot. For some inexplicable reason, she felt the conversation with Daisy was heralding a change of direction in the wind - but in which direction she could not tell.

CHAPTER 8

The Polka-Dot Dress.
Late July 2007

It was another gloriously sunny day. In fact, it had been warm and dry for most of June and July. This was one of the better years. Lauren had some fearful memories of past winters that had bypassed Spring altogether, stretching into late June, but not this year. The summer had started early and promised to continue unabated into late autumn. When the weather was right, this part of the world transformed into one of the most beautiful parts of the county, and it was times like this that made her thankful for being able to live where she did. Everything was as near to perfect as she could have ever hoped for.

Sadly, the summer days were already growing shorter and passing far too quickly for Lauren - she was becoming a little impatient. Fortunately, they were fast approaching the beginning of the school summer holidays - and she would soon be having a few weeks off. Hopefully, she could spend some time with Michael and Daisy and enjoy the latter part of the summer. She was looking forward to that.

Today, as on most weekdays, she took Daisy on the short journey to Lavendon Primary; it was the last week of school. The morning traffic was becoming busier with the influx of tourists as the days grew warmer. Many were drawn not just by the village's bucolic beauty but by the enchanting legend of the lovers.

As they approached Shelbury Bridge, Lauren could see the artists had already begun to arrive. They were eagerly setting themselves up on the banks on both sides of the river in front of the bridge. Preparing to capture the glorious moment when the sun began to splutter dappled specks of razored light through the gangly tops of the silver birches and golden oaks on the east side of the bridge. Eventually, bursting over the trees' heads, gently flooding the landscape with a goldeny-yellow shimmering light.

The four or five hours while the sun slowly rose to its zenith – always exceeding all expectations. Before slowing beginning its descent, eventually settling behind the trees on the west side.

These were moments of worldly perfection. These were the visions, the record of nature's creation the artists had come to capture forever as best they could on canvas and film, in their hearts and minds. Only the memory was left behind when the moment was gone, but even memories fade to shadows over time. They enthusiastically painted, sketched, clicked, and scribbled until the light faded. Then they were gone for another day.

Watching this transformation must have been similar to how the villagers felt when Brigadoon briefly rose through the mist before disappearing forever and taking the two lovers with it. Maybe lovers came to view the bridge in summer. Perhaps, they hoped that in one glorious moment, they would be swept away to another world where they would be happy forever. This was the ethereally charismatic effect the panorama of Shelbury Bridge could have on you.

Lauren had seen many paintings of the scene for sale in local art galleries in Lavendon and Guildford. It was a ubiquitous image, almost iconic in some interpretations. Often depicted by some of the more avant-garde artists as a transitional stage. Something between the past and what had been, on the right-hand side of the bridge – and the future, and what was to come, on the left-hand side - from where the interlopers and invaders would appear.

In some quarters, it was considered a pictorial analogy of life. By others, a metaphorical allegory of something, but of what no one was really quite sure, but that was more to do with local myth and a touch of slick marketing. The bridge had been in its present form for over two hundred and fifty years. Before that, as a medieval wooden bridge so, it had seen many changes during its lifetime. Lauren often wondered what had happened to all the people depicted in the paintings and how their lives would have been. Undoubtedly less satisfying than hers was the conclusion.

Her house was once four cottages. So four separate families, probably large families, had once lived in the same footprint that the four of them now occupied. They did not consider the house to be unusually excessive in its dimensions, but such were the changing demands of modern family life.

Amid all these thoughts, Lauren suddenly spotted Katie and her family slowly making their way over Shelbury Bridge on the far side of the road. Katie wore a red and white polka-dot dress today, and her crazy golden blonde hair seemed livelier than ever. One of the twins walked beside her holding her hand as always. Presumably, the other twin - (*Lauren had always assumed they were twins*) - had decided not to walk to the school and was still in the buggy. The baby was in the jockey seat on top. The twin that was walking twin wore a dress identical to Katie's. A near-perfect mini version of her mother, but without so much crazy hair.

Poppy, trailing a few steps behind, was dressed in her school uniform but without the jacket today. Dangling from her hand was the lead back to Alfie, the last of all. He must have had a bath recently because his golden coat seemed to be bouncing more than usual to the rhythm of their pace. The whole procession set in the misty early morning sunshine brought a small lump to Lauren's throat. Such unrestrained contentment and joy at just being there, watching them wandering with carefree abandonment over the bridge, was almost too much for Lauren to absorb.

Lauren wondered why Katie had made so much effort to dress and coordinate the three-year-old for such a short journey. Maybe intentionally or unintentionally completing this wonderfully picturesque image. This tableau of tranquillity – colour – beauty, a fleeting moment in time that would be forever burnt into the memory of casual observers and then Lauren understood…

'I like Katie's dress, Mummy,' commented Daisy.

'Yes, it is pretty.'

'Maybe you should buy one like that… you might like it.'

Lauren dwelt on Daisy's reply for a few seconds, wondering whether something more profound was being conveyed in the context - something she was obviously missing.

'Why do you think I would like a dress like that?' Katie asked warily.

'Well, you like Katie.'

'I don't know Katie.'

'You know what I mean, Mummy.'

You know what I mean, thought Lauren. *I wonder what that means.* She was going to ask Daisy but thought better of it. She may have been only seven years old but at times exhibited the insight of somebody much older, wiser, and undeniably erudite.

'It is a pretty dress, but not for me,' said Lauren.

'Why not?'

'You have to be a special sort of person to wear a dress like that. It wouldn't look right on me.'

'Yes, it would,' contradicted Daisy, 'You would look stunning.'

'Thank you, darling,' replied Lauren, completely taken aback by the unsolicited compliment. 'I might think about it in that case.'

'Good.'

Across the road, Katie smiled at something, and Poppy began jumping up and down and laughing. Lauren wondered what they were laughing at, then the traffic started moving again, and they were gone for today.

Over dinner that night, Lauren mentioned what Daisy had said earlier that day.

'Daisy thinks I should buy a red-and-white polka-dot dress.'

'Does she?' replied Michael quizzically. 'What inspired her to suggest something like that?'

'Why should something inspire her to make the suggestion?' Lauren asked guardedly.

'Well, it sounds as if she's seen somebody wearing one and that's where she got the idea. It smacks of some crafty plan,' replied Michael, grinning cynically at Lauren.

'That is a little disingenuous – even a little unkind,' replied Lauren, gently remonstrating with Michael. 'Are we Mister Grumpy today?'

'No, I am not,' replied Michael indignantly while spearing a new potato and popping it into his mouth.

'Well, it sounds like it to me.'

'Maybe it was a little unkind. I apologise.' He smiled again at Lauren.

'Apology accepted,' said Lauren, smiling back. She paused for a few moments before continuing.

'We have, actually.'

'What?'

'Seen one.'

'One what?'

'Dress.'

'There you go. I knew I was right. Who was it?' asked Michael smugly.

'You're so bloody arrogant at times.'

'I did guess right though, didn't I?' said Michael, spearing another potato and wrinkling up his nose.

'Katie.'

'Katie… Do we know a Katie?'

'Yes, I mentioned her before on various occasions. She's the lady I see most mornings crossing Shelbury Bridge.'

'Ah, that Katie. Yes, I remember now,' *but he hadn't,* 'and was she wearing one today?'

'Yes.'

'And I guess it looked good?'

'Yes, it did.'

'Well, go and buy yourself one if you like it.'

'I wanted to know if you thought I would look good in it.'

'Ah, well, I don't know about that… I would have to see it on first before I could give you a definite yea or nay.'

'I'll think about it,' replied Lauren quietly.

'I wonder why she walks to school daily,' asked Michael?

'Maybe she likes to. With all the palaver of getting four children into a car, maybe it's easier.'

'But it must take her more than half an hour to get to school?'

'She not in a hurry to get anywhere else. Maybe she enjoys the walk.'

'You don't think she works?'

'With three children under three, I wouldn't think so. Anyway, that's when you enjoy them the most.'

'Is it?' asked Michael a little cagily.

'I did, with Daisy.'

'Did you?' replied Michael, looking up at Lauren. 'So, do you regret going back to work so quickly?'

That was an uncharacteristically searching question, thought Lauren. 'No, why should I?' she replied with firm assurance.

'Well… do you think you've missed out?'

'No, not really, and anyway, Daisy's at school all day now, so it's only for a few years anyway.'

'But maybe those few years are important?' suggested Michael.

'So is my job. I would go mad trapped at home all day. I'm not made that way,' Lauren felt an odd pang of conscience as she said the words, knowing they weren't strictly true.

'I thought you were.' Michael smiled.

'Well, maybe a little, maybe next time.'

'Next time?' exclaimed Michael. 'Is there going to be a next time?'

'Maybe there already is,' replied Lauren glancing up at Michael to gauge his reaction.

Michael put his wine glass down on the table. 'Maybe?'

'I missed last month.'

Michael's jaw dropped as if he were going to say something, but nothing came out.

'I do, sometimes. It all depends on what happens this month.'

'So, you could be..?'

'Possibly. What do you think,' Lauren asked tentatively?

'I don't know. I'm not a doctor. I'm a merchant banker.' Michael appeared profoundly confused. Unfortunately, Lauren grinned every time he mentioned he was a banker because of the ingrained cockney rhyming connotation. She had mentioned it to Michael many times, so he now tended to phrase it differently, if possible. That was to avoid the embarrassment of watching Lauren burst into uncontrollable fits of laughter, especially when she'd had a few drinks…

'No,' replied Lauren. 'What I meant was, what do you think about having more children?'

'Oh, I see, well… yes… but what about your job?'

'There is maternity leave. We are allowed time off for good behaviour and to have babies, like last time. We don't have to drop them in the paddy fields and continue picking rice these days.'

Michael smiled. 'Of course. I'd forgotten.' He continued eating his dinner.

'Do you think we should get Daisy a pet?' asked Lauren, suddenly changing the subject.

Michael looked up from the table. 'She has a pet – a hamster.'

'I was thinking of something a little more substantial. A hamster in a cage is not really a pet. You can't interact with it –

it's more like something you just look after, like an elderly parent.'

'We don't keep your mother in a cage,' replied Michael. 'Unfortunately,' he added with a tiny smirk. 'But it's an interesting thought.'

'I'll mention that next time she comes around,' replied Lauren.

'No, please don't. I was only joking.'

Lauren smiled,

'Has she asked for something?' continued Michael.

'No, not exactly, but something happened at school, and I think she feels a little left out. I thought maybe a pony possibly, or a dog?'

'Well, I don't mind, but maybe you should ask her first. She may not be that interested - she has never mentioned it to me.' Lauren nodded and took a sip of her wine.

A few weeks later, Lauren told Michael she was having a period. All whimsical thoughts of another child gracefully withdrew to where they would quietly mark time until another day. She was disappointed, but she didn't show it. It was not planned, so it was probably for the best.

'There will be other times,' said Michael reassuringly. 'There's no rush right now.' He meant it as an empathetic gesture, but it didn't quite come over that way.

CHAPTER 9

Something changed.
September 2007

It must have been on the Friday of the first week in September. Daisy had just started the autumn term back at school. Lauren hadn't noticed Katie while making the school run, but then she hadn't given it much thought; her mind was on other things. She had just been assigned to run another significant advertising promotion at Barrington-Marsh. All her time, thoughts and energy at work and home, awake and asleep and in between, were once again going to be confiscated. Her life – her time – was determined by factors beyond her control, but she was willing to pay this price for success in her career. It was important to her. It instilled a sense of self-worth and helped support the lifestyle she and Michael had become accustomed to.

It was a day like almost every other day, except it wasn't raining, which was always a good start. In fact, it was a glorious day. The sun was already shining, and the air was crisp and clean, unlike London's acrid, bittersweet humidity into which she would soon be immersed. She opened one of the kitchen doors, wandered onto the patio, and carefully surveyed the garden. It was still looking glorious. She could feel the first regular injection of caffeine coursing through her veins and invigorating her senses. The same black adrenalin that kept the city alive. The fading hues of autumn had not yet begun to take hold. It was only at this time of day – when no other sound could be heard except for birdsong. Only when her mind was still relatively uncluttered by the city's self-indulgent hubris – did she fully appreciate how beautiful life really was. Very soon, she would be swept up by her masters. Unceremoniously deposited back amid the pompous pandemonium of the city. Daisy called out - she turned and re-entered the kitchen, closing the patio door behind her. She picked up her coat and laptop bag and headed towards the front door, where they said goodbye to Leja.

As she turned left out of the drive, Lauren lowered the window just enough to feel one more breath of country air for that morning.

It was after she started to turn into the last bend just before the bridge that she saw Katie, Poppy, the twins, and Alfie making their way as usual on the other side of the road. This was something Lauren had missed over the past seven weeks. The traffic came to a stop for some reason. For a few moments, she didn't need to concentrate on the road ahead and took the opportunity to watch Katie's family slowly making their passage, this daily ritual. As usual, Daisy was reading in the back, probably doing the homework she had been set the previous day. These were precious moments to Lauren, rare windows of tranquillity in a life of organised chaos.

She suddenly realised just how much she had missed this routine. The daily anchor to reality that seeing Katie gave her. For a few seconds, her mind vacated thoughts of work and gathered in this tiny caravan of life, this theatre of being, playing out before her. There was a stillness about the imagery that evoked thoughts of the pure humility of living and the honesty of existence. This was the opposite of the materialistic life she led. She had no choice but to choose the life she had. For her, life had no meaning unless she gave it meaning. No existence without material substance, but watching Katie engendered niggling doubts about the harsh materialism of her life.

But today, there was something different. The carefree spring in Katie's walk was suppressed, almost languidly indifferent. It was as if she were tired, but not so tired that she could not walk to school. Maybe Lauren had just simply forgotten the usual rhythm of Katie's gait. She had always paid particular attention to it when watching people.

It was surprising how much she could gauge a person's true character from how they walked. So much could be gleaned from pace, rhythm and tempo. The canter of the businessman urgently making his way to an important meeting is brisk, focused, sharp and precise. The swagger of confidence and the arrogant inner belief of someone successful and prosperous. The market trader, cheeky, self-assured, confident of his identity as a man serving his community, always ready with a kind word for the elderly lady as he helps her cross the road and risqué, harmless innuendo for the not-so-elderly lady. The lawyer – and there seemed to be many in London near where she worked. Slick, smart, economical - almost as if walking from the knees and not the hips to conserve all his energy for more important matters. Barristers, however, were something entirely different. They managed to glide magisterially over the ground having no desire to soil the soles of their expensive shoes with the streets' detritus.

But none of this was relevant today. It was a trivial detail of no importance whatever, and yet… Lauren had not seen Katie for some time, so why had she noticed the change. These tiny characteristics are usually quickly forgotten, but they troubled her for some inexplicable reason. The traffic in front had now come to a standstill, so she applied the handbrake. Up ahead, a caravan was arguing with the corner pillar on the far side of the bridge and having to back up - always a complicated manoeuvre, especially on a bridge, with traffic piled up behind.

Lauren took the opportunity to observe Katie and Poppy, and the twins. Still, only one walking – surely the other would be walking soon, she wondered… Then she noticed that the jockey seat that usually sat on the buggy wasn't there. Odd, thought Lauren; maybe Daddy was looking after the baby, giving Katie a break. The caravan eventually disentangled itself from the bridge and was back on its way, closely followed by the long queue of traffic that had built up. Lauren finally dropped Daisy off at school, kissed her goodbye, and drove to Godalming station.

The following week Lauren saw Katie and her family on three more occasions. The tiny procession dawdled over the bridge slower than they used to walk, and the jockey seat was still missing.

'Do you still see Poppy at school?' asked Lauren casually one morning.

'Yes, I do sometimes,' replied Daisy, glancing up from the book she was reading. 'We're in the same class now.'

'Oh, I didn't realise.'

Daisy did not say anything more, leaving Lauren to reopen the conversation.

'Do you get on well with her?'

'Yes, she's nice.'

'You must invite her round for tea one day.'

'Yes, that would be nice… Poppy's father is a potter, you know.'

'A potter? No, I didn't know that. Did Poppy tell you?'

'Well, no, not really. Miss Samuels told us that a Mr Farrier was coming to the school to give us a pottery demonstration. I knew that was Poppy's surname, so I asked her if that was her father, and she said yes, it was.'

'That sounds like it could be fun,' suggested Lauren.

'I don't know,' replied Daisy, with just the tiniest hesitancy.

Daisy's tentative reply was enough to prompt a further enquiry from Lauren. 'What don't you know,' asked Lauren, naively venturing into the precarious territory of negative narrative?

'Well... Poppy has been incredibly sad since she came back to school, much sadder than anybody else, so I don't think she will enjoy it that much, even if it is her dad.'

'Why so?' asked Lauren, venturing further into the unknown.

'Well, I think she is still upset about her baby sister Trinity dying during the summer holiday.'

Bang! It was all so matter-of-fact. This devastating piece of information conveyed with not a hint of emotional inflexion. The cold, dispassionate delivery - so uncharacteristic of Daisy. It was almost impossible for Lauren to process what she had just heard. Her brain wanted to instantly reject the content as profoundly flawed in some way – unsuitable for absorption into the cerebral cortex without further clarification. She eased her foot off the accelerator; she needed to switch priorities momentarily.

Did she just say that? Did she really just say what she thought she said? Or had she imagined it... No, she did say it. I did not imagine it... It was almost incomprehensible. Daisy had uttered the words as if they had somehow been encapsulated within a water-filled balloon of blasé nonchalance, within which they could just bounce around harmlessly inside the car. But it had exploded, inflicting a catastrophic blow on Lauren. She was being repaid in battalions of anguish for her innocent enquiry.

Daisy probably didn't understand the profound significance of what she had said. Her bluntness, the pure innocence of a child, somebody unable, as yet, to appreciate the occasional necessity for tact and sensitivity. But even allowing for that dispensation - it could not lessen the shock to Lauren's sensibilities.

Lauren's mind began to race, backtracking over the past few days. She thought about the missing jockey seat and the languid atmosphere that seemed to have enveloped and consumed the family of late. Suddenly everything began to fall into place.

'What happened?' asked Lauren, realising almost at once that maybe she should not have asked, but it was too late.

'Trinity caught something called....' Daisy paused for a second, scuffling around in her head for the right word. 'Menge.... itis?'

'Meningitis!' corrected Lauren. A shiver ran down her back.

'Yes, that was it, then something else, I think... Then Trinity died.' Daisy resumed reading her book.

Lauren found herself suddenly fighting back the tears that had instantly welled up from nowhere. Her stomach suddenly felt painful and hollow, as if she had been sick and then not eaten for days. She tried to imagine how desolate Katie must be feeling right now. But she just couldn't envisage the full extent of the anguish she must have been suffering.

She quickly wiped the dampness from her eyes with the back of one hand, the other still holding the steering wheel, just managing to keep the car in a straight line as she continued her journey. She searched her pockets for a handkerchief, found one, and used it to dab away a few more tears. She thought about the deathly word that had invaded her brain and completely overwhelmed her. But try as she might, she could not stop it from gently banging around inside her head. Bouncing off her skull like some delinquent ping-pong ball.

It was a disease that had concerned her more than any other when Daisy was younger. It was always the battle that took few prisoners. The haunting darkness lurking in the corner, the arbitrary and capricious infection that swept in from nowhere and could so quickly and mercilessly deprive a child of limbs at best but, more often than not, of life itself. It had taken Katie's daughter without a moment's hesitation. Chance had taken dominion over life.

Daisy appeared almost unaffected by the mention of the word. Lauren wondered whether she really did fully comprehend what the finality of death meant. It could not be easily explained without resorting to banal platitudes and humdrum analogies. And that was something which she had always promised she would never engage.

But then most children initially appear impervious to this emotional pain, so maybe they just see it differently from adults. Perhaps part of being a child is this inbuilt perception of immortality, a safety barrier from behind which they were invincible. The enormity and finality of death just didn't register. Maybe that was how they were wired today, wondered Lauren, a mechanism to protect them when they could be most vulnerable to a devastating assault on their senses. Maybe susceptibility to emotional pain was something they grew into as they entered their teens. It was the time when hormones and pheromones began taking control of their minds and bodies.

'That is so terribly sad,' said Lauren. 'I must send her some flowers or something.' Daisy didn't reply.

'So, when is Mr Farrier coming to the school?' asked Lauren after a few more moments, now partially recovered from Daisy's shattering revelation.

'I think in a couple of weeks,' replied Daisy.

'Something to look forward to, then?'

'Yes.'

It went strangely quiet in the car for a couple of minutes. Lauren tried to restart the conversation, but she couldn't find the right words to say – her mind was still spinning – so she said nothing.

They arrived at school, and Daisy jumped out of the car, kissed Lauren, and trotted off through the gates. Lauren watched as she walked away. She said a little prayer, then drove on to the railway station with oddly disparate thoughts running around her head.

She saw Katie on three more occasions over the following two weeks. She noted that she was beginning to walk with a noticeably less ponderous pace. But still, the smile had not returned. Always a distant gaze, the slight detachment from her surroundings. But never so much as to affect how she cosseted the twins, Poppy or Alfie. Life was moving on again, and winter was drawing ever closer again.

'I am so sorry,' said the doctor, 'but Trinity's natural defence mechanism is not working properly. The chemotherapy should not have affected her any more than we were expecting. Having that break for the last few weeks of pregnancy usually works fine - but this time, for some reason, it didn't.'

'So, me having the chemo killed my daughter!' exclaimed Katie.

'No, not at all. Any child can contract meningitis, but it moved so fast, it was unlikely we could have saved her under any circumstances.'

'But she would have been stronger and more naturally resistant to infection if I hadn't had the chemo?'

'We don't know that for certain; there's no way of telling. It just happens. I am so deeply sorry…'

'A perfectly healthy child could just as easily have contracted the virus, but….'

The words just drifted away.

CHAPTER 10

The Divine Potter.

October 2007

'Mr Farrier is coming to our school today,' announced Daisy. Lauren glanced in the rear-view mirror and saw Daisy making a pot-spinning gesture with her hands.

'Mr Farrier – the potter?'

'Yes, Poppy's dad,' replied Daisy.

'I remember you mentioned this a few weeks ago. You must tell me all about it tonight. I would like to know more about Mr Farrier and his pottery.'

'I may bring you a pot,' said Poppy.

'That would be nice,' said Lauren, wondering what it could possibly look like and whether it would be any better than her miserable attempts. 'I went to pottery classes once, just after you were born, but I wasn't particularly good.'

'Why did you stop,' enquired Daisy?

'Time, or more accurately, the lack of it and anyway, I was going back to work in a few months, so I wouldn't have been able to keep it up for much longer. It was just something I'd fancied doing. But I soon realised I wasn't really cut out for working with my hands...' Lauren smiled as she remembered some of the objects she had made, all of which had long since been discarded, '...just my brain. My pots were really awful.'

'I bet they weren't. I can't believe anything you do is bad.'

Lauren didn't reply straight away but mused thoughtfully over Daisy's comment.

That night she arrived home a little earlier than usual. She sat down with Daisy and Leja for dinner but didn't eat anything, preferring to wait until Michael came home.

'So how was the pottery lesson,' enquired Lauren?

Daisy hesitated for a moment, carefully considering her reply. 'It was... interesting.' The last word left floating in mid-air with a nuance of restraint – as if she were about to utter something of further enlightenment but had changed her mind at the last moment.

'Oh,' said Lauren, sounding slightly surprised - for some reason believing that Daisy might have found it dull.

'Not boring, then?'

'No, not at all. Mr Farrier...' she paused as she marshalled the words together in her head, 'likes to refer to everything he does as a metaphorical analogy. It made the whole lesson very thought-provoking.'

Yes, I suppose it would, thought Lauren. That fitted in perfectly with the image of Mr Farrier that she was beginning to assemble in her mind. He was evidently a philosophical partisan - an evangelical potter on a journey who had decided to suspend the mundane expositional element of his craft. The part that would undoubtedly have been of little interest to curious seven-year-olds. Instead, had chosen to promote a continuing interest in the art form by introducing an element of spiritual comparison. Not only was Lauren beginning to understand Mr Farrier – but she was becoming increasingly intrigued by him.

'And.... you actually know what that means?' Lauren found herself asking. It was patronising and arrogant, virtually insulting her daughter's intelligence. Fortunately, she managed to articulate the question so that the emphasis was subtly transferred to the last word. So the words left her lips sounding more like a glowing compliment than a derisory insult – although this was more by luck than intent.

'Yes, of course!' replied Daisy a little indignantly, having glimpsed a tiny hint of the alternative interpretation. 'Miss Samuels, who teaches us English...' she emphasised the last word as if to make a point, 'told us never to use a word unless we fully understand the meaning.'

'Absolutely,' replied Lauren, quickly moving on. One admonishment a day was quite enough to be going on with.

'So, what did Mr Farrier do?'

Daisy paused for a moment to carefully consider the question. 'He showed us how to make a pot,' replied Daisy. She spoke with a gently scathing hint of condescension, disbelief, and pained expression that clearly indicated there must have been a profound breakdown in communications. 'He doesn't make cakes,' she added lightly as an afterthought.

Lauren almost burst out laughing at Daisy's astringent retort. She deserved that and only just managed to contain herself sufficiently to hold on to a remnant of dignity.

Leja did not understand the quip and looked slightly confused. 'The potter doesn't make cakes?' she questioned innocently, emphasising the word 'doesn't.' It would be some time before she fully understood the intricacies of dry English humour and acerbic wit, thought Lauren.

'That's right,' replied Daisy, looking bemused. 'He makes pots.' She smiled again. Leja still looked confused.

At times like this, Lauren quietly said a prayer to thank God for His gift of motherhood – moments like this that made it all worthwhile.

'Mr Farrier…' continued Daisy, totally unaware of the effect her comment had on Lauren, 'said that to start making anything, first a lump of clay must be taken from the earth and placed in the middle of the wheel head. Then it is carefully shaped with the hands while spinning the wheel and applying water.

Khnum, the Egyptian god of the river Nile, was thought to be the creator of all children. He made them with clay from the banks of the River Nile. He then placed them in their mothers' wombs. He was known as the Divine Potter. Out of almost nothing, he created life. We thought that was funny and utterly ridiculous because we all know where babies really come from. But Mr Farrier didn't mind. In fact, he thought it was a bit silly too.

'Then he opened his arms as if to embrace the whole class and said,' "We, us potters, take muddy clay from the ground and make it into something exquisite, something that should last a lifetime, sometimes even longer. But then, one day… suddenly… it is gone forever, like life!"

'He looked sad when he told us that part,' said Daisy.

'Did he?' replied Lauren, pondering over what inner strength and courage he must have to be able to draw that kind of parallel at that moment in time.

Daisy continued. 'We all made a little pot or something on his wheel, and he took them away to be fired at his workshop. He will bring them back to school to be painted in a few weeks.'

'It sounds like Mr Farrier is a fascinating person.'

'Yes, yes, he is remarkably interesting,' said Daisy. 'I am so sorry about his baby.' It was a simple declaration of her feelings, not loaded with false sentiment or mawkishness - but it left Lauren trying desperately to hold back another tear. She had seriously underestimated Daisy's ability to understand the significance of what had happened to the Farrier family, curtly reminded how instinctively insightful Daisy was once again. She remonstrated with herself about prejudging everything. Only Leja asking if they wanted more tea before she went to her room averted a potentially embarrassing moment.

Later that night, while watching television, Lauren's thoughts drifted off to how life must have been at the Farriers' house over the past few months. She wondered how they would have dealt with their baby's death. Lauren could only imagine what pain they must have suffered and were still suffering. She pulled Daisy a little closer to her on the sofa for a moment and held her very tightly.

'You're crushing me, Mummy,' Daisy cried out.

'That's because I love you, darling.'

'And I love you too, Mummy, but I don't stop you breathing.' Lauren laughed.

'I think it's time for your bed now, missy,' she whispered.

'Okay, Mummy,' and off she skipped without a care in the world.

Lauren did not see Katie again for nearly a week. She only had to be a minute or two early arriving at the bridge or Katie a minute or two late, and her daily fix of the other life, the one she peered into for just a few seconds, would be lost until the next occasion.

When she did next see her, it was late October, and summer had started to become a distant memory for another year. The flowers had begun to disappear from the hedgerows and gardens. The occasional sunflowers that brought such joy during the summer months had dipped their weary heads. But autumn's beautiful golden yellow colours had begun to arrive and were starting to tinge the oaks, maples, and beeches. Everything was preparing for the long haul through autumn and into winter. On days when the sun shone brightly early in the morning, it quickly burnt off the river mist. The painters and photographers would occasionally return for maybe a day or two to capture the magnificence of the autumnal shades. The sparkle of sunlight dancing off the dew on the leaves and flickering through the tall trees brought a new perspective to Shelbury Bridge, a whole new range of visions to be captured on canvas and camera.

CHAPTER 11

The Winter Dormouse.
November 2007

'You will need your big coat and the armbands today,' suggested Katie. 'It's very misty and cold out there.'

'Okay Mum,' replied Poppy, rummaging through the cupboard in the hall. It was a vast cupboard. In fact, it was almost a room. It was full of coats, umbrellas, boots and shoes, toilet rolls, dog leads and boxes of apples. Each apple had been carefully wrapped in newspaper. There were also two long thin tree branches that John had fashioned into walking sticks, but he had never used them as such. There was also something unidentifiable in a plastic container without a lid, which nobody would accept responsibility for. It emanated a strange odour. Poppy was sure she once saw it move.

'Can you also find James and Julia's coats, please?'

'Yes, mummy,' replied Poppy grudgingly.

Katie wore a large imitation astrakhan fur coat that John had bought her for Christmas, and the twins, now both walking, had matching pink and blue coats with hoods. Poppy wore a functional, all-weather school coat and a bright pink scarf. Even Alfie's hair was a little thicker now in preparation for winter. Once everybody was dressed and had been checked by Katie, they began the daily trek to school.

They all kissed John goodbye before leaving, except for Alfie, who just waggled his tail in anticipation of his daily walk.

The bridge artists came much later now, if at all. It was too cold and damp at 8.30 in the morning to mix up oils. A resilient painter or photographer might occasionally appear if the sun was shining, but they would not stay for long.

As autumn slowly transitioned into winter, the days started darker. Katie's family were now easily recognised by the array of fluorescent yellow armbands on the twins and Poppy and a few stickers on the buggy, which Katie still pushed to school. She did this in case she needed to pick up some odd groceries from the convenience store opposite the school or carry the twins back home if they became tired. Viewed from a distance, the ensemble created the appearance of a large swarm of fireflies. As usual, wandering behind was Alfie, now adorned with his winter outfit of fluorescent collar and flashes on his lead, strung out all the way to the buggy.

Watching the entourage winding its way slowly across the bridge gave rise to a plethora of rambling thoughts in Lauren's mind. It may have been a little inhospitable, even difficult, not to use a car in the depths of winter, but somehow she knew there was an extra special family bond being formed. Something for life, something they would never forget. The sound of the river rushing over the rocks beneath the bridge, the strange murky haze rising from the river on cold days, sometimes completely enveloping parts of the bridge. The trickle of low early sunlight peeking through the tall oaks, the damp mist of a faraway woody bonfire with a hint of mouldy leaves, and so many other woodland aromas associated with winter in the country. All this was lost to Lauren and Daisy, breathing air that had been comprehensively purified and stripped of all physical impurities by the car's air-filtration system.

'It must be freezing having to walk to school every day,' remarked Lauren one morning while driving over the bridge.

'It would be lovely to walk with them,' replied Daisy wistfully. 'I love the damp, cold, woody smell of winter. It's so real, so alive, so full of life.'

Lauren did not reply straight away, carefully contemplating Daisy's prescient observation. *So, real, so alive, so full of life.* As she rolled the words over and over in her mind, she felt a tiny lump appear in her throat. She hadn't thought about the pure pleasure of living for ages. It was left to Daisy to remind her of other, less complicated ways of enjoying life. Ways that she had forgotten about many years ago.

They lived in the country because Lauren had always aspired to that kind of life, but had she ever truly embraced what it really meant? In the office, her colleagues were very envious of her lifestyle. But did anybody really want to live in the country because it was the country? Or because the trappings of success dictated that that is where you had to live to prove you were successful and that you had "*arrived...*"

Her mind drifted off briefly, recalling a dormouse that regularly appeared in late autumn or early winter, scampering across her kitchen. It still managed to alarm her the first time she saw it each year. But it could not have been the same mouse – she was sure they didn't live that long. And yet, with immaculate timing, it reappeared, making the identical journey along the same prescribed route from behind the fridge to the larder cupboard before darting behind the Aga. Lauren and Michael (*Daisy refused to become involved in the mouse hunt*) had searched everywhere for the point of entry but never found it. Michael suggested it may have come through the back door when Lauren wasn't looking, searching for somewhere warm and cosy where it and a few close relatives could spend the winter.

Michael would place humane mousetraps in the usual places, and every year he eventually caught the dormouse (*which was no more than the size of a small strawberry*) and deposited him into the compost bin. But three weeks later, the dormouse would be back... or maybe it wasn't the same mouse after all? Perhaps the route to the Aga had been genetically implanted at birth in each new generation, a sort of familial rite of passage.

'Are you sure about that?' asked Lauren, interrupting her own meandering thoughts about the dormouse. 'I could ask Katie if I could drop you off here each day if you like. I am sure she wouldn't mind one more.'

'You don't know Katie,' replied Daisy, sounding surprisingly pedantic. 'You only watch her walking to school - from a distance,' the last three words were added after an uncomfortable pause - and in a slightly different tone.

'I don't watch her,' replied Lauren, a little disturbed by how it sounded. 'You make me sound like a weird stalker or a psychopath.'

'Is that like a nutter?' enquired Daisy with just a hint of mischief.

'I am not a nutter,' replied Lauren a little indignantly.

'No, I didn't say you were, but I don't know what a psychopath is.'

'Well, a psychopath is a nutter, in a manner of speaking, but that's a misleading generalisation.' Daisy smiled. Lauren wondered if she should have made that comparison, knowing how quickly children latch on to an unusual or indelicate turn of phrase.

Daisy glazed over for a moment with a semi-serious expression. 'So, what are you doing if you are not watching Katie?'

'I'm just enjoying, or should I say participating in the shared altruistic experience of seeing somebody happy, and she always seems so, despite...' Lauren didn't finish.

'I see,' said Daisy, appearing reasonably satisfied with the answer. But it was all starting to sound like the office-speak advertising jargon Lauren occasionally used at home. Her mother could have been describing the joy of eating a bar of chocolate for all she knew.

'So, would you like me to speak to Katie about you walking to school with them?' asked Lauren. Swiftly trying to move the conversation away from the uncomfortable voyeuristic avenue down which it now appeared to be travelling.

'I'll think about it,' replied Daisy, cautiously weighing up the pros and cons of what could be a long-term commitment from which it would be tough to withdraw from at some later stage.

'You'll let me know, then?' said Lauren.

'I will.'

That Friday night, Daisy returned from school holding something wrapped up in brown paper, which she placed in the centre of the kitchen table.

'What is that?' asked Leja.

'It's a surprise for Mummy and Daddy.'

'Oh, and can you tell me what it is?'

'No, it's a surprise. You can see it when they come home.' Daisy was very secretive about the parcel.

'Okay,' said Leja, 'so would you like dinner now?'

'Yes, please. I'm starving.'

'Right, I make you dinner then. I call you when it's ready.'

'Thank you,' said Daisy, wandering off to the lounge.

At just after half-past seven, Michael and Lauren arrived within a few minutes of each other. Daisy had finished dinner but was still up as she was allowed an extension to her bedtime on Fridays.

'Hello, Mummy and Daddy. I have a surprise for you.' She appeared overly excited, having contained herself for the last three hours, patiently waiting for her parents' return.

'And what is it?' asked Lauren, taking her coat off.

'It's on the kitchen table.'

Lauren unwrapped the gift. A hideously coloured dark green vase with splodged yellow flowers. It stood nine inches high, big enough to hold one small flower stem.

'It's lovely,' said Lauren. 'Did you paint it?'

'Yes, I did.'

'We will put it on the shelf in the lounge,' said Lauren. And that is where it stayed for the next three years.

CHAPTER 12

Daisy's Nativity.
December 2007

It was a cold and bleak December morning, and Lauren was driving Daisy to school as usual.

'I am playing Mary in the Nativity play at school. Are you coming, Mummy,' asked Daisy, a little unexpectedly? It was one of those defining moments in a parent-child relationship. She was dammed to eternal hell as a pariah for the heinous crime of child neglect if she did not go, especially after missing Daisy's earlier theatrical outing the previous year. Invariably the play fell on one of the last two days before the office Christmas closure when inter-office social intercourse peaked. Not attending the office party meant missing subtle, throwaway hints about what might be happening the following year. Non-attendance was akin to professional suicide. Acceptance of one invitation meant declining the other, so neither option was desirable, but for entirely different reasons.

Lauren thought very carefully before answering. The ground was liberally littered with booby traps and bottomless potholes, surreptitiously concealed by a misty layer of swirling fairy dust. One wrong footing and she would be consigned to instant ignominy.

'You haven't mentioned that before,' replied Lauren a little cautiously.

Daisy looked at Lauren's reflection in the rear-view mirror to gauge her reaction, but Lauren kept looking straight ahead.

'I must have forgotten – but I'm mentioning it now. It is the best part of the show, you know... apart from Joseph and I am much better than Joseph – Jonathan Enright is a terrible actor. He has the stage presence of a bucket. I should have had his part.'

An astonishingly cruel and revealing statement, although possibly a tad narcissistic, thought Lauren. An insightfully harsh critic and potential child prodigy all wrapped up in one neat little package. But then, didn't all parents feel the same way? Somewhat unexpectedly, sexual equality and female emancipation had now invaded the sacred echelons of the traditional school nativity play.

Lauren had never really seen eye to eye with God. They were nodding acquaintances on a 'needs must' basis – i.e. weddings, funerals and christenings, things of that ilk. They had mutually parted company after an embarrassing incident with one of the nuns at her convent school. An episode that she had tried to erase from her memory ever since.

'When is it?'

'Thursday the fifteenth. I did give you a letter from the school. It's on the last day before we break up for the Christmas holiday.'

'I'm sure I would have remembered if you'd given me a letter. When did you give it to me?'

'Weeks ago, I think.' It sounded suspiciously vague.

Lauren searched her memory for some sort of recollection but couldn't remember Daisy giving her any letters recently or mentioning the school play.

'Are you sure you didn't give it to Daddy or Leja?'

'No, I definitely gave it to you.'

Daisy threw Lauren a curious expression but said nothing. She was carefully choosing her moment after a suitable period of silence had passed. This subtle tactic would generate a further emotional burden on her mother.

'So, can you and Daddy come and see me?' asked Daisy. 'I am particularly good,' she added, somewhat immodestly.

'Of course, we will try. I will speak to Daddy tonight.' That Thursday afternoon was not going to be easy, not with the added pressure of the new campaign at work. It was still relatively early in the program, and many staff were already working Saturdays to ensure they hit the floor running when everything kicked off in January. Hopefully, Michael might return home a little earlier from work, and possibly Leja could go with him. That would be some small compensation for her not attending. Hopefully, that would extricate her from a disagreeable predicament.

They passed over Shelbury Bridge but did not see Katie today, which was probably fortunate for Lauren in some respects. The last thing she needed right now was to be reminded that she was a little wanting in the Good Mother department.

That night Lauren spoke to Michael about Daisy's request.

'Do you think you could be back early on the fifteenth? Daisy is starring in the Christmas Nativity and wants us to go.'

'That is going to be almost impossible. We're in the middle of a merger at the moment, so it's all hands to the pump. In fact, it will be a bit touch and go even for Christmas Eve.'

'She will be terribly disappointed; we've missed every Christmas play in which she has ever performed,' replied Lauren.

'I know, I know, but what can I say?'

'Yes, that would be good. I am also trying, but I am up against it right now. There's a hint of promotion in the air, and I don't want to jeopardise my chances, not right now.'

'I'll check it out and let you know. Can't Leja and your mother go?' suggested Michael as an afterthought.

'Yes, they could, but that is not the point. Daisy wants us to see her.'

'Em,' muttered Michael under his breath.

The following day as Lauren drove over Shelbury bridge. She saw Katie and her family or "tribe," as Michael had once derisorily referred to them. Lauren thought it was a disparaging word to use about any family and tried to put it from her mind. She would never allow it to be used again in reference to Katie's family without strenuous and vociferous opposition. That was the least she could do for her *friend* – and then she thought about the resolution she had just made. It explicitly referenced Katie as a friend, but they were not friends. They were not even acquaintances – in fact, they had never met. Lauren felt slightly confused, unsure why her mind was playing these paradoxical games. She was not a friend, but she thought she was. S- she didn't know Katie but thought she did. She had no connection with her, yet she was beginning to feel inextricably connected to her by some tenuous invisible thread.

She wondered whether Katie would be going to the Nativity play. But of course, she would; what a stupid question, she told herself. How could Lauren ever consider that Katie would not be going? In a way, knowing Katie would be there to watch the play was comforting. It was a peculiar psychological juxtaposition of parental responsibility, knowing she would be there watching Poppy and Daisy on her behalf. Someone who meant something important to Lauren would be there. But was that just a self-centred cop-out? She wondered. Was she just comforting her conscious with a clever yet unforgivably lame excuse? Lauren knew Leja and Rosemary would be there, but that didn't feel the same for some reason. She tried to imagine what Katie would be thinking as she watched the play and how Katie would feel. If she could succeed in that, she might be able to channel the same feeling herself without being there. It was a very peculiar train of thought, trying to predict a sequence of events that might happen through a third party. But it helped relieve the remorse she was already beginning to suffer for being too busy to attend.

One day things would change, and she would be the one who walked to school with her children interacting with life and nature without a care in the world, but not just yet.

As expected, Lauren and Michael did not get back in time to see the nativity play. It was staged at 3.00pm, so there was never any realistic possibility of them being there. But Leja and Rosemary did go, and when Lauren and Michael returned home late on Friday evening, they were regaled with the highlights of Daisy's performance.

'The play was enormous success. All the children were absolutely wonderful, especially Daisy,' announced Leja when Lauren arrived home later that night. Leja had obviously derived immense enjoyment from the performance. This made Lauren feel even worse than she already did.

Aren't they always, thought Lauren, when you can't be there?

The school had also permitted video cameras, so Rosemary recorded the whole production. This was something that Lauren and Michael would no doubt replay many times at their leisure in the future. But nothing could make up for the disappointment that Daisy harboured and would remember for many years.

In a quiet moment, sometime later, Lauren asked Daisy if Katie had been at the play. Daisy told her she had been sitting in the front row with a man who Daisy said was her husband, Mr Farrier.

'I think I saw them holding hands, Mummy ... the lights were very bright, so it was hard to see the audience clearly.'

Inexplicably, for reasons she couldn't explain, that seemed to ease some of the guilt - the sin of absence that Lauren was now experiencing.

Lauren and Michael did manage to get five days off for Christmas. Unhindered by any commitment before, they were both unceremoniously hawed back into the infernal fray of the Big City. Lauren with her chocolate marketing campaign and Michael with the merger. Both had been bought and sold by the mandarins of finance. Both were inexorably tethered to the silver towers of Canary Wharf.

Leja had returned to see her parents in Lithuania over Christmas and would return the same day Lauren and Michael returned to the carnival. So, Lauren and Michael did spend some quality time at home with Daisy over Christmas after all, if only for a few days.

CHAPTER 13

Decline and Fall.
June 2008

The banking industry's sudden and utterly unexpected collapse in mid-2008 brought a bitter blow to Michael and Lauren. She had planned their future, or at least as far ahead as she could reasonably predict, on the assumption that Michael's salary would continue indefinitely. This was something which she had always been led to believe was not an unreasonable basis on which to map out her life. Her salary was always the cream on the top of the cake to finance the little luxuries. The Porsche sports car for nights out. The four-berth cabin cruiser they kept moored down on the river Itchen for weekends in summer. The skiing holidays in January at Val d'Isère in the lodge they co-owned with three other couples... The list went on, but now something unpredictable, something not included within their algorithm of life, something which they had therefore not made any contingency for happened. She had no control over it, and it had thrown her plans into total confusion and disarray.

Without prior planning, she became the family's sole breadwinner almost overnight. Their very existence now depended almost entirely on her career. But Lauren had never intended to work permanently, possibly another five years at most. Now that plan, if it could still be called a plan, was severely jeopardised to one degree or another. The slender thread of unity that binds all families was stretched thin, if not entirely broken. The saccharin-saturated existence they had lived for so long would slowly dissolve and re-crystallise into a brittle, bitter reality, but still... life went on.

'So, what happened at school today, Daisy Grace?' asked Lauren. She would pop into Daisy's room most nights and sit on her bed if she got in early enough – and if Daisy were still awake – just to talk about her day.

'Mr Farrier came back to school again.'

'Ah, the Divine Potter,' said Lauren wistfully.

Daisy smiled with an expression of amazement. 'You remembered my story? But that was ages ago.' She appeared genuinely surprised that her mother could remember such a trivial detail with everything else that was going on in her life.

'Last October, I believe, that's when you told me about Mr Farrier.'

Daisy was lost for words. 'But how did you remember that?'

'Not just a pretty face,' replied Lauren, tapping her nose.

Daisy smiled.

'So, what did he come for this time,' asked Lauren?

'To tell us more stories about pottery and how to make a few different things.'

'Oh, I see, and what did you make this time?'

'Well, I made something a few weeks ago and painted it, and I will bring it home next week for you to see.

'I look forward to that,' said Lauren. 'Is it like the last "pot" you made,' she asked? She could not help but smile at the thought of Daisy's last creation. It still stood in pride of place in the lounge. A peculiar dark green vase with yellow splodges that leaned badly to one side. Strangely reminiscent of something Salvador Dali might have made if he had been drunk and in a bad mood.

'No, much better than the wonky pot, and it is very shiny. Mr Farrier will fire it this week, but not like Daddy.'

'Not like Daddy?' enquired Lauren, intrigued by Daisy's odd comment.

'I heard you say that Daddy was fired, but my clay pot will be made extremely hot. They also call that firing, but that's different, right?'

'Yes, it is, in a manner of speaking, but losing your job can make you hot as well... Daddy was definitely very hot when he was fired.' Lauren half smiled at her caustic quip, but Daisy did not appreciate the subtleties of Lauren's acerbic witticism, not just yet.

'Why was Daddy fired?' asked Daisy.

'Well, I know you must have heard me say that, but it's a little different in Daddy's line of work. It's not really being fired. It's... when there's not enough work to do, the company has to let some people go on a long holiday. So they can find more work somewhere else, and that's what Daddy is doing.'

'In the garden,' asked Daisy with an odd expression?

'Sorry,' said Lauren? Not sure she heard that correctly.

'Is Daddy looking for another job in the garden?'

'No, darling. in London.'

'But he is always happy in the garden,' said Daisy.

'That's because he enjoys gardening, but he's not looking for a job out there. Nobody would pay him.'

'You could pay him. Then he could stay at home all the time and be happy,' replied Daisy, a curious expression flashing across her face.

'I wouldn't be able to pay him very much,' replied Lauren with some caution; she could sense a message coming.

'Money is not important; it shouldn't be your only goal. Contentment in your soul and deliverance is all that matters.'

'Who told you that?' asked Lauren, but she need not have bothered; she instinctively knew the answer.

'Mr Farrier. He said that working with his hands was the most important and rewarding thing in his life, apart from being with his family... except that is for coming to school and showing us how to make pots.'

'He sounds like a very wise man.'

'He is.'

'Right, well, I think it's sleep time for you now, missy.' Lauren leaned over and kissed Daisy on the head. 'Love you, darling.'

'Love you too, Mummy. Goodnight.' Lauren got up, turned off the light and left the room.

For no reason at all, or possibly for no reason she was aware of at that moment, thoughts of Katie and her family sprang to mind. Her surrogate self - for that was how she was beginning to see Katie: in the other quixotically parallel existence she passively peered into. Or voyeured, which was probably more accurate – for a few minutes each week.

Was that even a word, she wondered? Possibly not, but it somehow described how she felt, so it was good enough. In her daydreams, she was beginning to secretly aspire to this life that intoxicated her for reasons she did not understand. It was a narcotic - her own particular mind candy, and she was becoming addicted. But why, Lauren wondered – why when she had everything she had always desired – did she now want to live someone else's life.

Would Katie ever be confronted with such a game-changing seminal moment in her uncomplicated life, she asked herself? Not likely, she reasoned, but then she remembered something that had happened to Katie not so very long ago. She had managed to overcome that trial, a defining ordeal and a pivotal moment in any woman's life, and she had survived. That was infinitely worse than dealing with what was probably nothing more than a temporary blip in Lauren's state of being and her increasing awareness of her true consciousness.

We are what we become, and we become what we aspire to – Christ! Thought Lauren, where did that piece of bumper-sticker claptrap philosophy come from? Sounded suspiciously like the hippie-Hari-Hindi mantras she was constantly bombarded with by Banora Breanoora. Banora was one of her colleagues in the office - employed by the company as a creative copywriter Monday to Friday. But she would while away her weekends meditating and reciting banal tuneless intonations in a tented forest commune on the outskirts of the Watford Gap. She said it gave her inspiration and generated internal karma. But Lauren had serious doubts about whether camping in a muddy field in the rain and smoking pot could conjure up the same mystical allure as an ashram in the upper reaches of Kathmandu. Something to which Lauren was far more attracted.

Initially, Michael did not appear unduly concerned about the sudden change in their financial circumstances. He genuinely believed there was every possibility he would secure a similar position with another merchant bank very soon.

'There is nothing to worry about,' Michael had reassured her. 'I am just going to take a break for a month or two to regroup, and then I'll start looking for a new position once the current financial upheaval has settled down.'

It all sounded very positive, but Lauren was not quite so confident. Unfortunately, Michael had seriously misread the gravity of the situation. The Northern Rock meltdown problem was endemic, more so than anybody had realised at first. In a surprisingly short period, it began to rampage mercilessly and devastatingly through every tier of management in every bank. Not just the Northern Rock, where Michael once worked.

The problem became exponentially larger, not smaller. There were no jobs, not now, not for the foreseeable future. And as Michael knew nothing of any other profession, it became abundantly clear that the likelihood of him finding employment anytime soon had all but disappeared overnight.

After four months of being unemployed, the last two enthusiastically trying to find another job, he realised his situation was far worse than he had initially imagined. It was catastrophically grim, as one of his former colleagues had colourfully described it. Michael began drinking whiskey in the evenings, something he had never done before. They usually drank a bottle of chardonnay together at dinner. Now he had started drinking whiskey after they had eaten - sometimes alone in his study.

By October, Michael had stopped getting up in the mornings with Lauren. Previously they arose together at around six-thirty. He would leave home at about seven-thirty, with Lauren going at around eight-thirty to take Daisy to school before driving to the station. But now, he didn't even bother to get up until after eleven o'clock when the house was relatively quiet.

'You could take Daisy to school if you like - that would get you up each day,' suggested Lauren one day.

'That is bloody ridiculous,' he replied. 'You drive past Daisy's school on your way to the station, so what is the point of me getting up early, getting dressed and making the same journey?' It made perfect sense. There was no arguing with the logic, but that wasn't the point.

So, Lauren carried on as before, preparing for work and driving Daisy to school. She preferred it this anyway because she enjoyed their little chats in the morning on the way in - and of course, she would occasionally see Katie and her family. This was a welcome distraction from the problems at home, if only for a few minutes each day. The real benefit was derived from the odd way that occasionally catching sight of Katie and her family reminded her of how different things were in other people's lives. It also left an enduring image that would invariably come back to her in quieter moments during the day and somehow bring her moments of serenity and composure. It was as if it were a form of meditation, but without the drugs, mud, or whale music. She wondered whether her colleague Banora, who went to Watford at the weekends, would approve of her unorthodox meditative process.

Lauren worked with many people in her office, many of whom she liked and admired. But she had never formed a spiritual connection with any of them as compelling as the one she had created with Katie. On her return home each evening, she would find, somewhat frustratingly, that Michael had done little, if anything, during the day. Most of the household chores were done by Leja anyway, so he had nothing left to do anyway. Unfortunately, even the most trivial things she had asked him to do were left unattended.

'Your study is a bit of a mess,' said Lauren one Saturday morning.

'Is it?' he replied casually while continuing to read the newspaper, not fully comprehending the subtext of her observation.

'I could ask Leja to clean it up for you?'

'I'd rather you didn't,' he replied, which effectively meant, I like it as it is. I know where I can find everything.

'But you are not actually using it right now, are you?'

'Well, I am, for research purposes,' he replied indignantly.

Lauren could have asked him what he was researching, but there didn't seem to be any point. He was probably checking that week's best supermarket deals on Jack Daniels.

'Did you put all the sun loungers away and cover the swing yet? We need to clear up the garden, ready for winter.'

'I'll do it next week, first thing.' But it wouldn't be done, and she would have to ask him again the following Saturday. She envisioned snow piling up on the parasols and foxes building winter homes under the sun loungers.

This, more than anything else, was beginning to annoy Lauren intensely. The lack of application to minor tasks was causing damage to their relationship, especially as time was no longer an issue for Michael

It displayed a complete lack of consideration and respect for her insomuch as she was doing her best in a dire situation, but he was not. The destructive seeds of uncertainty and exasperation had been sown.

She now passionately believed that tomorrow was a new day, a chance to start again, no matter what happened today. Life still carried on, so there was no time for retrospective regrets. That was the mystical influence of Banora once again.

She also knew allowing despair to creep in and take hold would be fatal. So she fought desperately to keep that corrosive element, that subversive and seditious invader, at bay, but was she succeeding? She began to wonder whether she was already losing that battle.

Fortunately, they did have some savings. So there was enough money to continue with a reasonable lifestyle for at least nine months to a year if they were prudent. But it would still mean making sacrifices.

'I will definitely get another job within six months,' Michael had reassured Lauren several times, but she wasn't so confident. She still worked in the city and heard the mutterings and rumours on the street. Being stuck at home, Michael was isolated from the raw reality of their situation – and way outside of the social media loop.

'We could sell the Porsche,' suggested Lauren one day. 'We would still have my car' (*Michael's Range Rover had gone back when the bank went broke)* 'and the run-around.' It seemed a reasonable suggestion to Lauren as they hardly ever used the car. Michael had stopped attending the golf club because he could no longer afford the membership and green fees. There was no point in him trying to impress his fellow members when they were all perfectly aware of his situation.

'No way,' said Michael, looking deeply wounded by that suggestion. You would have thought she'd suggested chopping three inches off his penis by how he reacted.

'I worked hard for that. It was *our* reward...' he'd emphasised the possessive adjective in that suspiciously annoying way that always got right up Lauren's nose...

Our reward? I don't ever remember driving it, she thought.

'...for being successful,' continued Michael, 'and anyway, I need to see it to incentivise me and remind me of the good times.'

Sounds like office psyche banker bullshit to me, thought Lauren. She sensed it would be a long while before the good times returned. And as for the incentivising defence argument, that obviously wasn't working. So her suggestion fell on deaf ears, and the Porsche continued its lonely vigil in the garage. She did wonder about the disingenuous use of the phrase "our reward." When they both earned good salaries, Michael decided Lauren might just as well hang on to her old Mercedes estate. It was dependable. He bought the Porsche for the two of them...

'I'm bound to get a new job soon. They will be screaming out for people with my experience before long. I'll need the Porsche then,' as Michael frequently reminded her. This was despite nearly six months having passed. But Lauren now passionately believed that to be just another extremely large cartload of delusional horseshit. Of course, she did not say anything to Michael – how could she?

'We could let Leja go,' he had suggested half-heartedly on one occasion. 'She costs us a fortune.' This was quite different from the day when he had fervently insisted they take her on full-time rather than use the services of Lauren's mother. Rosemary had offered to help around the house at no cost, but Michael had vehemently vetoed that suggestion.

'Absolutely not!' replied Lauren vociferously. 'She is a godsend around the house. This would look like a rubbish tip in a week if it weren't for Leja.'

'Recycling centre,' corrected Michael glibly with an irritating smirk.

'What?'

'They don't call them rubbish tips anymore. They're recycling centres,' replied Michael. It was an ill-timed shot at light-hearted facetiousness but missed the goal by a mile.

Lauren just glared at him. 'Our recycling centre looks clean and tidy. This wouldn't – hence my use of the word's rubbish tip.' She emphasised the words with air quotes.

'How do you know that?' asked Michael, sounding slightly wounded.

'Because I know you and I have to take your rubbish there in my Mercedes as it won't fit in the Porsche.' Lauren threw him a wry expression.

'Oh…' Michael paused to reflect on what she had said. 'I'm sure the house wouldn't get that bad,' he replied defensively.

'I'm sure it would,' Lauren replied. 'There is no such thing as a cleaning fairy, you know. It's all done by real people. Mainly Leja and me.'

'I am sure I could do something,' challenged Michael. Lauren looked at him despairingly. 'Apart from the cleaning, Leja also cooks the meals, does the washing, ironing, shopping, and many other things, not forgetting that she picks Daisy up from school. Are you going to do all those or any of them, for that matter?' Michael quietly shook his head.

'We could ask Rosemary to come around. She would love to help. Probably desperate for something to do,' suggested Michael cagily.

Lauren was almost at a loss for words, not because it smacked of a total lack of sincerity, but because he had dispelled that suggestion out of hand when Lauren had suggested it a few years earlier. She did not even have to reply to his proposition; the look of utter disdain on her face said more than words could ever convey.

'Maybe not,' mumbled Michael, quickly withdrawing that suggestion, having considered the further problems and responsibilities it would create.

Not surprisingly, the state of their relationship began to deteriorate much faster from that point. Lauren was surprised at how quickly he had changed. From a man she had always respected and admired to a man, she was beginning to despise. Sex was becoming an exceedingly rare occurrence, not helped by Michael coming to bed drunk most nights. Although not a significant consideration, she still believed it was essential to their relationship. It helped in some small way to mend little fences broken during the day. It was also something she was beginning to miss.

Distasteful as it was to admit it, for the first time in her life, she had been forced to face the harsh reality that life, in general, was changing. Ultimately, everything was governed, to one degree or another - by a constant flow of money, or at least hers had been. Now the river of plenty had dried up or, to be more accurate, had been reduced to a trickling stream.

CHAPTER 14

Jeff
June 2008

A few days later, Lauren was going to the station as usual – it was late November. They were in the opening stages of a harsh winter, and blustery winds and rain were battering the bridge as they crossed over. She could see Katie and her children on the other side, still endeavouring to make their usual journey to school. Scarves wavering like tethered kites in the wind. Poppy, hanging on for dear life to the buggy. The twins safely ensconced inside the buggy. Finally, a somewhat bewildered Alfie trailed behind, his hair buffeted by the winds. And yet, despite the apparent struggle they had to endure, Katie and Poppy looked happy, and Alfie appeared in his element, facing the climatic onslaught. *I bet even the twins were smiling,* thought Lauren. They may have been windswept and wet and blown to kingdom come, but they would be happy. Poppy had grown considerably over the last eighteen months and was only a head below Katie now.

'I bet you wouldn't want to be out in that damn weather today,' said Lauren, not realising she had said it aloud. She'd had words with Michael that morning about not getting up again, which put her into an agitated frame of mind.

'No, Mum, I wouldn't,' replied Daisy. 'It looks damn horrible.' Lauren winced, then smiled, rebuking herself under her breath for using the word. *She must not take things too seriously,* she told herself, *and not let her feelings come out in her conversations with Daisy.* At all costs, she should not let herself be affected by what was happening at home. 'Is Daddy ill now, Mummy?' enquired Daisy innocently.

'Ill? No, he's just taking a short break from work to spend more time home with us.'

'Oh, I see. So why does daddy stay in bed all day?'

'He doesn't stay in bed all day,' replied Lauren defensively. 'He just gets up a little later than us.'

'Leja says she takes him a cup of tea at lunchtime, and he's still in bed then.'

'Does she?' replied Lauren curiously. She was unaware of that arrangement.

'I would love to stay in bed all day,' said Daisy

'You do on Saturdays,' replied Lauren chiding her a little.

'I meant during the week.'

'But you have to go to school, so you couldn't, and anyway, it's no good lazing around in bed all day - it softens the brain.' Lauren smiled discreetly to herself at her sarcastic quip. She found herself doing that more often these days. She didn't think Daisy would notice the indirect inference.

'Is Daddy's brain going soft then?' countered Daisy, quick as lightning.

'No, it isn't,' replied Lauren, 'Daddy's just resting.'

'Oh, I see.' Lauren could almost hear Daisy's brain whirling.

'What if...'

'No what if's,' interrupted Lauren. 'Monday to Friday, you go to school, so you must get up with me.'

'Right.' Daisy resumed gazing out the car window and pondered what they had chatted about.

Lauren thought about Daisy's comments as they continued their journey to the school and afterwards on the way to the station. Once she was settled on the train, other more prosaic matters filled her mind. She sat back and prepared for whatever outrageous fortunes awaited her at Barrington Marsh Associates. Interspersed with her concerns over matters at home, issues that were now beginning to weigh heavily on her mind.

She arrived at the office just as Jeff, the managing director, arrived. They exchanged the usual morning pleasantries.

'So how are things progressing on the Banbury contract,' asked Jeff, pressing the lift button. This was the television marketing contract the company had won two months earlier, which Jeff had placed under her complete control.

'It's good. Should be finished editing the preliminary video shoots in a few days. They look good. I'll give you a call when they're ready to view.'

'I look forward to that,' replied Jeff, but his expression said he did not appear overly concerned by the campaign she was running. His mind was somewhere else. They both stared at the closed lift door.

'I think you'll like them,' she added after a few moments of silence, trying to fill the awkward space.

'I probably will,' replied Jeff smiling. There was another awkward silence as they continued gazing at the lift doors. 'Look,' said Jeff turning to Lauren, 'I don't want to stick my nose in where it's not wanted, but is everything okay with you?'

Lauren looked surprised. 'Okay? Why yes, of course.' She turned to face Jeff. 'Have you heard something I haven't?' She suddenly became defensive and tried to control her immediate inclination to clam up.

'Is it something to do with the campaign?'

The lift doors opened, and they both stepped in. The doors closed, and it began ascending.

'No,' Jeff continued, 'nothing like that. That's all fine as far as I know. I was more concerned about you.'

'Me? Why me?'

'I've heard that Michael got chopped – with quite a few others, I hasten to add, in this banking meltdown thing, I just wondered if you were all right... if there was anything I could do to help.'

'Oh, I see... I'm sorry, I was a little sharp just now, but....'

'No problem,' interrupted Jeff. 'It's just that quite a few of my friends at the golf club have been affected, and it has meant quite a change of circumstances for some of them....'

'It was actually back in June,' muttered Lauren, looking slightly ashamed.

'Oh, I didn't realise it was that long ago. So, are you all right?' The hidden agenda behind the question was obvious, neatly encapsulated within the delicate way he had expressed the last words. It was all to do with the cadence; so many things are.

'I think so – at the moment, anyway. I mean, I'm still working, and that makes a tremendous difference. We have some reserves, so nothing is too desperate. I am sure something will turn up soon. We've just had to cut down on the champagne and caviar for breakfast.' Lauren quipped demurely.

The lift arrived at their floor, the doors opened, and they both stepped out. It went quiet again for a few moments.

'You have champagne and caviar for breakfast?' exclaimed Jeff, his eyes lighting up with delayed surprise. 'Wow! That sounds amazing. A fantastic way to start the day.'

Lauren stopped momentarily and turned to look up at him. She had a tiny hint of mischievousness in her eyes. 'Yes, of course we do. We must maintain standards. One of our Filipino maids brings it up to our bedroom every morning. Doesn't yours?'

'No, I don't have one,' replied Jeff with a flat expression that conveyed nothing.

'Oh, your wife then. Doesn't she bring you some early morning treats?' suggested Lauren with the tiniest hint of a smirk at the corners of her mouth.

'I'm not married,' replied Jeff, still holding the deadpan expression, 'so no wife and no Filipino maid.'

'I am sorry, I should have said partner,' Lauren hastily corrected herself. 'I didn't mean to...' For a moment, she thought she might have completely misread the situation. Being politically correct could be a real bitch at times, she mused.

'Not gay either,' said Jeff, looking a little dismayed. He moved a little closer. 'I don't look gay - do I - for Christ's sake?' He whispered this with a dubiously suspect expression of acute concern. Placing his hand tartly on his waist and dropping a hip. Fortunately, nobody else in the hallway saw his outrageously stereotypical, homophobic pose. Lauren creased up with laughter and nearly fell off her heels. She had not laughed so much in a long time but had wanted to, at something, anything. He had simply pressed all the right buttons at the right moment. It was unexpected and completely out of character.

Jeff caught her tottering and, pursing his lips together muttered, 'Oops,' in an appallingly camp fashion before fluttering his eyes outrageously.

Lauren almost collapsed again, unable to contain herself, and Jeff caught her again. She straightened up and looked at the man holding both her arms to support her. The man she had known and worked with for nearly five years. In that split second, she suddenly realised she didn't know him at all. He was much, much funnier than Lauren ever remembered from the office parties. And he was much stronger than she imagined; he was like a different person. Lauren straightened out her jacket, endeavouring to regain some composure, when she suddenly realised she had wet herself just a little. She couldn't believe it; Jeff had made her laugh so much. This was the effect he had had on her. She was stunned.

'I'll have to go to the bathroom to sort my makeup. You've made me laugh too much,' blurted Lauren.

'Yes, Mrs Penfold, I understand.' He smiled drily as one of his other employees walked past.

'It's Lauren,' said Lauren smiling back.

'Yes, yes, I know. I just thought….'

Lauren turned away to walk to the bathroom, then turned back momentarily to glance at Jeff, who was walking up the hallway to his office. He put his hand on his waist for a few seconds and minced for a few steps. Somehow, he knew Lauren was watching him – well, he hoped to God she was anyway. Lauren cracked up again and walked a little faster towards the bathroom. When she arrived, Lauren realised she did not have a spare pair of knickers, so she took the damp ones off, washed them, and dried them as best she could under the hand dryer. Lauren didn't put them back on but stuffed them into her handbag, wrapped in some tissue. She would dry them off on the radiator in her office later.

Lauren could not get the incident entirely out of her mind for days. It made her smile every time she thought about it or saw him. But there was something else, some tiny niggling detail within the episode she had missed, something that she knew was significant. But she couldn't figure out precisely what it was, not right now, but it would come to her…. eventually.

CHAPTER 15

The First Sign.

Christmas 2008

It must have been about a week later, one of the last days of school before the Christmas holiday. Lauren was driving to the railway station as usual. It was surprisingly dry and sunny, the kind of day she loved in winter. As Lauren crossed the bridge, she could see Katie and the twins. They were both walking today, Jamie and Julia holding hands and Katie holding on to Julia's. Poppy walked alone, just behind, holding on to Alfie's lead. She had adopted an air of liberated individuality as she followed her mother. Now free of the constraint of holding on to the buggy, she relished her newfound freedom. Poppy had grown noticeably taller over the two years since Lauren first noticed the family crossing the bridge. Her head was now above the level of the parapet wall.

Now nine, Poppy was already gaining confidence with her increased stature. The fiery streak of independence that had always been clearly evident, if contained, was becoming more apparent. She was moving inexorably towards the rebellious adolescent breakout stage. She stood just three inches shorter than her mother. She would probably be the same height as Katie, possibly taller in another year.

Daisy was no different. Self-assured, but not excessively so, and noticeably confident, Lauren hadn't noticed the changes. They weren't so obvious, maybe because they appeared so gradually. A few millimetres each week, perhaps a centimetre a month. It was hard to tell precisely when; one day, she just seemed taller.

It was at this moment, in one fleeting glimpse, that Lauren noticed something that Katie did. A tiny gesture with her hand. Almost indiscernible unless subconsciously you were looking for it. Katie touched her abdomen almost as if for reassurance. In that split second, Lauren knew that Katie must be pregnant again. Her heart skipped a beat with joy for some reason - she didn't know why. Lauren still didn't know Katie, still never having spoken to her. And yet this tenuous gossamer thread of communication spiralled out between them. Something intangible connected mothers and their babies; she did not know what it was - she just knew it existed.

'Did you see that Daisy?' asked Lauren as if needing confirmation.

'What?' said Daisy, looking up from her book.

'Katie. Did you see Katie?'

Daisy looked out of the window. 'I can see her, yes.'

'No, did you see her just now?'

'No, I was reading. Why?'

'Oh, nothing, it's not important.' But it was to Lauren. For some reason, she chose not to elaborate or expand on her thoughts. Lauren was sure she saw what she thought she saw, which was enough for now.

Lauren wondered again - as she had done many times before - whether they might become friends one day. She felt sure that if they did, they would be good friends forever. She did not know why she felt that way - she just did.

She could see that Katie was, at last, nearly back to her former self after the previous summer's events. But she knew that could only be on the outside, a cosmetic artifice for the rest of the world. On the inside, the pain would still be there for many years, possibly forever. But a new baby would help make that transition from past sadness to future happiness and make it easier to bear.

Today they were all smiling, laughing, and enjoying life – for life was moving on, and there was a lesson to be learnt. Lauren had often wondered whether she envied Katie's lifestyle. Unassuming, unpretentious, uncomplicated, almost uninhibited in some ways. In the height of summer, - her crazy blonde curly hair, vibrant, visceral evidence of a free spirit encapsulated within a terpsichorean soul, and that had to be saying something about her. *I am free – I am alive – I am living – I am happy.*' But never unconscionably so. Always the perfect balance of responsibility, trust, reason and measured caution – always caution, the impiety of overconfidence always contained, never allowed to roam free without licence.

But then Lauren knew nothing of Katie's home life. For all she knew, Katie's could be as complicated, even more so than hers. Katie had to contend with something Lauren could only imagine in her worst nightmare. But somehow, despite that devastating episode, she did not think Katie's life was too bad. There was an overpowering sense of ease, contentment, stillness, and humility about her that could neither be artificial nor pretence. Katie had come to terms with her existence and appeared genuinely happy. She had also come to a settlement with life. Lauren felt a pang of jealousy - for this tangible panacea for all ills was attainable. The incontrovertible evidence was there to be seen almost every day. And yet, although only a few yards away, it might as well have been on the dark side of the moon. For all the likelihood there was of her arriving on the same Karmic plateau anytime soon. She had Daisy, and she felt blessed for that, but there were now some tiny niggling doubts about so many other things.

CHAPTER 16

Lunch at Zeferelli's.

Late January 2009

Christmas passed quietly that year. Michael's situation had not improved, and he was becoming more taciturn and withdrawn as the weeks slowly drifted by. Yes, he still made the daily effort to inquire about possible vacancies. But he was losing traction with every rejection - drifting further into despair and despondency. It was now the midst of deepest winter once more, and Michael was even denied the opportunity to carry out rudimentary garden maintenance.

Over the past few months, he had begun drinking wine or whiskey at lunchtime and in the evenings. Not enormous quantities, and he never became drunk, but it was enough to dull the sense of failure that was never far from his mind. Some days he would wander down to the village pub and sit in a corner, quietly reading the newspapers and drinking ale. He even got to know some of the locals, mostly farmers. Some days he spent hours listening to things he knew nothing about. But then they knew nothing about futures trading, stocks, bonds, or commodity one-day options. So rather than bore them, he allowed them to bore him. It was an equitable arrangement, an act of reciprocity to which he happily consented. He also learned something about farming processes, livestock husbandry and seasonal cultivation techniques in the bargain.

He could secure a job feeding pigs and cattle if all else failed. Apparently, there was a severe problem encouraging new people into the farming industry. The thought trundled around in his head for several days before being summarily dismissed.

Things at work were going well for Lauren in what could only be loosely described as a paradoxical whirlwind. Jeff had asked her out for lunch today to discuss the contract she was working on, and although lunchtime meetings were the norm with her team, he had never invited her to lunch before. She somehow felt that it might be leading to something else. She did not know what exactly, but in the back of her mind, she was becoming a little uncertain about a few things, not least the developing relationship with Jeff.

Lauren had never been to Zeferelli's before. She had heard about it from colleagues at work but had never eaten there. She had also been told it was extravagantly expensive. Borderline decadent and exquisitely chic in an understated retro nineteen twenties Italian style. From what little she could see when she entered the restaurant lobby, it was undeniably as stylish as she had been informed.

The maître d' materialised in front of her. A veritable pantomime genie appearing, as if by magic out of a bottle – in a puff of smoke; she never saw him arrive.

'Good afternoon, madam, welcome to our restaurant; you 'ave a booking?' He spoke with an overcooked Italian accent, which left a tiny suggestion of uncertainty over its authenticity. But then you could never tell ~~for sure~~ with any Italian waiter working in an Italian restaurant in London.

'I think so,' replied Lauren gingerly, 'my name is Lauren Penfold.'

The Maître d' was ~~a little reluctant initially~~initially reluctant to let her continue her journey into the dining area as her name ~~did not appear to be~~was not on his reservation list. Lauren considered the possibility that she might have the wrong day or time – even the wrong restaurant. All these thoughts shot through her mind as the embarrassment cloud loomed overhead.

He did, however, with extraordinary skill and panache, somehow successfully perform the remarkably virtuous and delicate deception of preventing her from continuing beyond the lobby without appearing offensive, obstructive, or inhospitable. He smiled at Lauren while insisting on fastidiously rechecking the booking list -:

'I am supposed to be meeting somebody - the booking is probably in his name,' Lauren added with a fleeting air of desperation.

'And what is the gentleman's name?' asked the maître d' with the tiniest hint of a smile.

'Jeff, Jeffery Marsh,' replied Lauren, at which point his demeanour made a sudden U-turn to apologetic sycophancy.

'I am so sorry, madam, I did not realise ~~that~~you were....'

'Please don't apologise; it's my fault. I should have mentioned it when I arrived.' Lauren felt instantly obliged to exonerate him from all blame and for the embarrassment he had inadvertently visited on her. His initial reluctance to allow her to ~~pass through into~~enter the restaurant was now forgiven. But she was not really sure whether he had caused her any embarrassment at all. Such was his adroit professionalism and impeccable manners when doing ~~so well what he was employed to do~~what he was employed to do so well.

'Signor Marsh,' he muttered under his breath, gently rebuking himself while throwing his arms up in the air with a highly exaggerated air of theatricality. 'Mamma mia,' he muttered quietly ~~to himself~~, his face lighting up and his eyes suddenly becoming much more prominent. She could see at once that there was someone else behind the façade she had first encountered, 'Of course, he *isa oneovour mosta favourite customars.*' He turned and gestured for her to follow him as he minced his way into the inner sanctum. Lauren was still trying to decide whether the accent was genuine or not.

After a few paces, he turned back to Lauren, his expression a master class in obsequiousness. 'I must *apologisea* once again for not realising at once that such a beautiful woman would only be here to dine with....' *Yes. It was undeniably a very suspect Italian accent.*

'It's okay - I understand what you have to do. It's for...'

'Hi Lauren, over here,' interrupted Jeff in a slightly raised yet restrained voice. He, obviously, did not wish to intrude on the other diner's conversations. It was more of a private club atmosphere than a restaurant, sedate communication in regal opulence. Lovers and friends in various combinations and business people probably escaping from the office for a few hours – just as they were.

The Maître d' smiled, his task now completed. He returned to the lobby to continue his screening duties.

She could see Jeff standing at the bar talking to someone she presumed was a waiter, so she made her way over.

'What would you like to drink? I'm on the Long Island iced tea?' asked Jeff, animatedly waving ~~the cocktail he was drinking~~his cocktail.

'Tea, that sounds lovely,' said Lauren.

'It's not exactly tea,' replied Jeff with some hesitation.

'Oh, well, let me think,' she picked up the drink's menu.

'I've booked us a quiet table in the corner if that's okay – oh, sorry, I haven't introduced you to Zefe.' He turned to the man beside him, who looked like a waiter.

'Zefe is an old friend. He owns this dump.' So, the man she thought was a waiter was, in fact, the owner. He stood up, took hold of her hand, and kissed it regally without touching her skin - the whole gesture conducted with remarkable aplomb.

Zefe was thirtyish, with shoulder-length, jet-black hair and shiny dark olive skin. Greek god was possibly over-egging it a bit, but that was the category she was edging towards. He smiled, and for a moment, she was sure the room became a little brighter.

'I'll have still water, please,' said Lauren.

'Ice and lemon?' asked the bartender, who had patiently awaited the order.

'Yes, please. Thank you.'

'The bartender smiled and turned around.'

Lauren looked at Jeff with a surprised expression, 'Is that nice to call this lovely restaurant a dump?'

'It's a joke,' replied Jeff, 'we play football together sometimes, and he always says I play like a big girl's blouse, so I always insult his restaurant.' He made a san-fairy-ann gesture with his hands.

Zefe smiled. 'It is true.' He held his hands up, 'He still plays like a girl - present company excluded, of course.' The blatantly sexist remark careered into outer space. Lauren decided to let it go for now. 'I am sure you would make a wonderful footballer,' added Zefe as a sort of apology… I think.

'I don't play football.'

'No, somehow I didn't think you would, but if you did, you would probably still be better than Jesse Jeff,' replied Zefe.

'Jesse Jeff,' enquired Lauren, obviously amused by the reference.

Jeff screwed his face up, looking at Zefe, 'back into the kitchen pot-boy,' he muttered.

Zefe bowed his head and smiled discreetly, 'Madam.' Lauren laughed at their schoolboy banter.

'I will leave you two to your lunch. I have other people who desperately need my services,' said Zefe, smiling and lighting up the restaurant again.

'Would you like me to show you to your table before I leave?' asked Zefe.

'No, we're okay,' replied Jeff.

Zefe politely withdrew from the conversation, not wishing to intrude any further. He knew his presence was no longer required.

'Still water, ice and lemon. Would you like me to take it to your table?' asked the bartender.

'No, that is fine,' replied Lauren. 'Thank you.' She sipped her drink and turned to Jeff, 'He's extremely handsome, isn't he?' She did not know why she commented on his stunning appearance. Maybe it was some sort of defence mechanism as if to say, *'I'm neutral here because I am happily married and secure, so I can speak openly about how or what I feel about someone or something.'*

'Who, Zefe?' asked Jeff curiously.

'Yes.'

'Such a shame,' replied Jeff with a mournful expression.

'A shame?' enquired Lauren, now intrigued.

'All the ladies fall in love with him the moment they see him.'

'Do they?'

'Yes.'

Lauren paused for a moment… 'Why a shame?'

'Well, he's gay.' Jeff half-smiled, so ladies just aren't his thing.'

'Oh, I see. Well, I didn't fancy him anyway.' She looked a little surprised and slightly embarrassed.

'I hope not. You're married,' replied Jeff, his expression left little doubt over what he meant.

'You're joking about him being gay, aren't you?'

'No, actually, not on that.'

'Oh… Shall we sit down?' asked Lauren, changing the subject. 'I have a lot to go through, and I have….'

'Yes, of course.' Jeff picked up their two drinks from the bar. He led Lauren to a table in the corner of the restaurant. This slightly elevated position partially obscured them from the rest of the diners.

121

'Is this okay? We don't want to be interrupted.'

'It's fine,' said Lauren. She started to take some papers out of her case.

'Leave that for now.' He shook his hand with his index finger, gesturing that she should return the documents to the case. 'We can get to the work thing a little later.'

'Oh right, whatever you say,' replied Lauren, slightly surprised, before sliding the papers back and closing the case.

'Look, I'm going to be perfectly honest here. I asked you to come out to dinner under a false pretence.'

'Oh, so what is the reason,' asked Lauren?'

'Well, it's this new campaign you're looking after....'

'Yes,' replied Lauren a little prematurely. A tiny element of concern had now taken hold. With Michael out of work, she felt naturally vulnerable to anything jeopardising her position. Both she and Michael being unemployed could quickly become a significant problem.

Jeff saw that she looked a little uneasy and quickly tried to reassure her. He waved his hand in a conciliatory fashion to put her mind at rest.

'There's no problem. Nothing to worry about, in fact, just the opposite.' He smiled disarmingly again, and she could feel the warmth of his eyes, which for some reason, she thought a little odd – not unpleasant, just unusual. *He couldn't sack me, not with eyes like that,* she thought. *Christ! How ridiculously naïve was that? Panic had not settled in yet, but it was on the sidelines - standing on tippy-toes, ready to pounce.*

'Right,' Lauren was still apprehensive, unsure where this was going. To some small degree, Jeff's expression assuaged the nuance of anxiety that was now bouncing around in her head. She took a small sip of the water and held the glass tightly in her hand; Jeff took a large gulp of his iced tea. He smiled reassuringly. Jeff was rather nice, she thought. She had never actually looked at him before as a person, just as the head of the company, his company, in fact. Although he had always been accessible and approachable, there was still the invisible barrier between employer and employee. The Rubicon, which you never crossed or if you did decide to attempt, you did so at your own peril, for once you had reached the other side, there was never any going back.

He had lovely teeth, not quite as bright as Zefe's, but then Zefe's just didn't seem real, though no doubt they were. Michael had excellent teeth as well. Lauren always found herself checking out people's teeth for some obscure reason. Maybe, she thought, people who look after their teeth also look after their bodies. Then she began to wonder where all this was heading – beautiful teeth – beautiful bodies? Her brain was all over the place. Maybe her true vocation was as a dentist and not in television marketing after all.

The one thing about Jeff that did make him stand out was his azure blue eyes. This close to him, she could almost see through them into his soul, even his heart. It was an illusion, of course, for they weren't blue at all. They just seemed to be reflecting the blueness from somewhere deep inside. It must have been like this in *Alice Through the Looking Glass*, she thought when Alice stepped into the looking glass and found another world. Was there another world behind Jeff's eyes, she wondered? She knew very little about him. Nobody knew a great deal, only what he allowed them to know.

'The menu,' repeated the waiter.

'Oh, I'm sorry, I was miles away,' said Lauren. Returning from her cerebral ramblings, she took the menu and looked at Jeff.

'I'll return in a few minutes,' said the waiter.

'Thank you,' said Lauren.

'Penny for them,' said Jeff.

'Sorry,' replied Lauren, sounding a little confused.

'Penny, for your thoughts. You seemed miles away there for a few moments.'

'Oh… I was just thinking about some things I must do on the Banbury job when I return to the office. I…'

Jeff interrupted, 'relax, it will wait till you get back. You have a talented team; you've trained them well. They won't let you down, not in a few hours anyway, if at all.'

'Yes, yes, you're right,' she replied, acknowledging his reassuring compliment. He was right. Of course, he was.

'I think I'll have the soup and the sea bass. What about you?'

'I'll have the same,' said Lauren. She didn't look at the menu, just glanced at it cursorily, then closed it.

'Good,'

'So, how long have you known Zefe?' asked Lauren.

'Must be over ten years now, I suppose. I used to visit his last restaurant with my ex-wife.'

'You were married?' exclaimed Lauren, a little surprised.

'Divorced about...' he looked up for a few seconds working out the number, 'eight years ago, yes, eight years.'

'How long were you married?'

'Five years.'

'Not long then, really.'

'No, it was a mistake.'

'Aren't all marriages that end in divorce,' asked Lauren with sardonic erudition? Jeff smiled wryly at her quick-witted reply.

'That is a little brutal, isn't it,' replied Jeff?

'A simple observation, I thought. A divorce is an end, isn't it?'

'No, not at all. People divorce for many reasons, not always the right reasons. My marriage was a mistake, and it ended, but many marriages that don't end are a mistake.'

'That is a little cynical,' suggested Lauren, 'you sound have if you were hurt badly before and after.'

'You could say that, but enough of this maudlin talk. We are here to talk about you, not me....' He turned to the waiter who had just returned.

'Two soups and two sea basses, thank you.'

The waiter made a note, 'and to drink?'

'I was going to have a bottle of the sparkling rose; would you like that?' Jeff asked, looking at Lauren. 'It's from the Bordeaux region just outside of Bergerac, as I remember.... you'll love it.'

'Yes, that would be lovely, but I don't know if I'll be any use in the office when I get back if I do?'

Jeff smiled, 'I shouldn't think a couple of glasses of wine will have that much effect.'

'Maybe not, as long as we don't drift into a second bottle.'

'Why should we?' asked Jeff curiously

'Well, it depends on what you want to ask me... the real reason for us being here is....'

'Ah, I see; well, that's simple.' He took another sip of his iced tea. 'It's really nice. You should try it.' He offered Lauren the glass, and as their hands touched, she felt a warm shiver of pleasure burst through her body and wiz around her brain. Just for a second, she became a tiny bit light-headed, almost intoxicated. *This is so stupid,* she said to herself. *I cannot possibly be pissed on water.* She hadn't felt that deliciously overwhelming sensation in a long while, not with Michael. It was just sex now, and even that was rare. She used to feel it with him, but not anymore. There was only one other person she had experienced that sensation with, Brian Harvey from East 17 at the Brixton Academy in 1992. But she was only fifteen and very pissed when he touched her hand while singing. She thought she'd had a massive orgasm, but she'd just peed her knickers - again.

She took a sip of the iced tea. 'That is nice... really nice. I have never had anything quite like that before. What's in it?'

'Well, it's Tequila, Vodka, Bacardi, Triple-sec, Gin and coke and a few other bits and pieces.'

'That's almost everything except the kitchen sink.'

'Yes, I suppose it is.'

'Wow, you would never know,' replied Lauren taking another sip.

'No, that is the point, it looks perfectly harmless, but it can blow your knickers out of the window.'

'Oh,' said Lauren, 'I hope not,' gently rebuking him with a half-hearted squint of fixed astonishment.

Were they flirting, she asked herself? She wasn't sure. It had been so long since she had done anything like that, and she wasn't sure what it was anymore. Social attitudes seem to change so quickly, especially when you are 'out of play,' so to speak. Once considered, risqué was now de rigueur; once thought promiscuous and tarty was now the norm. Lauren's mother, Rosemary, had warned Lauren at a very early age that she should not allow a boy to kiss her until the second date for reasons of propriety. Now, total strangers fucked within twenty minutes of meeting each other - and flirting had almost been relegated to a bygone age. Yet here she was doing it, or so she thought, but she wasn't a hundred per cent certain... yet.

'Oh no, please don't misunderstand me,' pleaded Jeff sounding a little embarrassed. 'I haven't brought you here with the sole intention of getting you drunk and banging your brains out in the bog. It's for something else entirely.' That clarification only served to confuse Lauren even further. She took a deep breath before taking another sip of his iced tea.

'That didn't quite come out the way I intended either,' continued Jeff sheepishly. He sounded genuinely apologetic. Apparently concerned that he may have unintentionally offended her or overstepped the mark. He glanced briefly at the floor to see how big the hole he was sinking into was.

'Just lunch then?' asked Lauren

'Yes... just lunch.'

His eyes took on the appearance of a scolded puppy. Lauren could have stopped it right there, but something inside her told her to play on; she was ahead, play the advantage rule, so she did.

'Something else entirely?' queried Lauren pursing her lips together. She shot Jeff a stern expression of reproachful fury that narrowly missed its target as it was utterly devoid of the essential quality of venom.

'Please go on. I'm intrigued.' She was enjoying this; she had not had so much fun with a man for ages; it was almost like...

'Oh... no... what I meant was it's to do with work.' He still looked a little embarrassed; he, too, had been out of play for quite some time.

'I hope so,' replied Lauren, still holding her expressionless glare. She took a long hard look at Jeff while sipping his iced tea. 'I'll have one of these.'

'Right,' said Jeff. Then Lauren laughed, 'I am so sorry, I am just winding you up, I have no idea why I am here, and I really don't think anything untoward is going on.'

'So, you don't think this is some sordid attempt to....'

'No, I don't - I trust you explicitly.'

'Oh, I see,' Jeff still looked a little confused, but he was beginning to understand how she worked.

'This is really nice,' said Lauren referring to the iced tea again. You need to get another couple. I've nearly drunk yours?'

Jeff smiled at Lauren and beckoned the waiter over, and ordered another two Long Island Teas.

'So why have you brought me here?'

'I have been in discussions with Banbury, and… well, they will be rolling out a new product. They are certain it will take their customer base by storm if we can develop the right promotional concept. That is - if you can come up with a great idea, which I am sure you can.'

'But I'm already tied up full-time on their other chocolate bar promotion,' replied Lauren.

'They want us to do it. They are offering an enormous budget for the campaign.'

'But I haven't the time….'

'I want to promote you.'

'To what?' she was a little intrigued because she was already head of the department.

'I want to make you the creative director for the whole company. You'll oversee all five sectors.'

'Oh,' replied Lauren looking like a rabbit caught in the headlights.

The waiter returned with the two Long Island Iced Teas, and she grabbed one and swallowed half of it in one gulp.

Jeff looked surprised, 'you really do like it, don't you?'

'I need it after that proposition,' she smiled playfully. 'But how will promoting me help?'

'You will just have to come up with the basic concepts. The various departments will do all the structural creative work for you; just let them run with it. All you have to do is devise the idea and oversee implementation. It's easy.' There was a naughty glint in his eye as if he were giving away a closely guarded secret.

'But you do most of that.'

'Except for what you do, and what you do is better than what I do now. I can see that, even if you can't.'

'But you have come up with some fantastic things in the past. Other agencies look to us for inspiration. They even pinch some of our ideas.

'I'm not as good as I was. I just don't have the edge any longer, and to be perfectly honest - I am losing interest.'

'But why?'

'There's only so many years you can do this before you have to move on to something real. Something that actually means something, not just how to entice people into buying bloody Easter eggs at Easter, for Christ's sake.' He smirked at the unintended biblical connotation of his blasphemy.

'I like Easter eggs,' replied Lauren with the tiniest hint of flippancy.

'We all like 'em and buy them, so why do we need to try and sell them?'

Lauren shrugged.

'You know Salman Rushdie?' asked Jeff.

'Of course, not personally, though.'

'Naughty but Nice! Irresistibubble'

Lauren thought for a few moments, 'Cakes and Chocolate.'

'Correct on both counts, but who were the manufacturers?'

'Oh, I don't know.'

'That is my point. It's all for nothing. All that effort has been forgotten in a few years, but not for Salman. He could see it wouldn't last, so he switched to writing books, they last forever, and people remember his name now.'

'He wrote those slogans?' Lauren sounded surprised.

'He did indeed. In fact, we both worked for the same agency at the same time. He was a bit older than me, but look where he is now, and look at me still doing the same old thing, pushing chocolate and cakes.'

'So, what exactly are you saying?'

'I would like you to take over my position to run the company more or less. I want to try something else, maybe even write a book.'

Lauren sat back in her chair, trying to process what he was saying and what it would mean. It had all been a bit too much all at the same time. Now she was drowning in a sea of dreams.

'So, you fancy yourself as another Salman Rushdie, do you?'

'I'll never know if I don't try.'

Lauren thought about his proposition a little more. 'From when exactly?'

'Whenever it is good for you, we need to talk about money, share options and all those sorts of things, but I'm sure you'll find them all agreeable.'

'You do realise you have me at a distinct advantage?' said Lauren. She knew it was poor tactics to give anything away during negotiations, but she felt obliged to be completely honest with him.

'Do I? I wasn't aware of it?'

'Things have changed. Michael's been unemployed for nearly eight months. We've lost two-thirds of our income, you do know that.' Jeff nodded nonchalantly.

'Yes, I do, but I made this offer based on proven ability, not out of charity or misplaced compassion.'

'Oh,' replied Lauren, not sounding entirely convinced.

Jeff adopted a stern, commanding expression, bringing his eyebrows closer together in a half-hearted attempt at an austere and resolute appearance. Lauren thought it looked rather cute, but she would never be able to take him too seriously again. Not after the incident at the lift doors six months previously. That was something she would never forget. Moments like that change your perception of somebody forever.

'Lauren, you can do this job, and you are worth the money I will offer you, probably more, but we have to start somewhere. I need you to do it. Nobody else in the company can.'

Lauren didn't say anything for a moment but just gazed down into her glass thoughtfully. 'Do you know what my plan was?'

'Your plan?' asked Jeff, suddenly realising he wasn't the only one with a plan.

'My life plan.'

'Oh... no, I don't think you ever mentioned it.'

'Michael was going to become a director or something in his bank and retire at maybe fifty-five; that's another twenty-five years. I would retire in a year or two, have two more children, maybe take up horse riding and live a quiet life in the country. Maybe come to London once a week for some shopping and go to the theatre, whatever - you get the picture?'

'I see, so you're not going to consider my offer then?' replied Jeff, now looking a little despondent.

'Well, no, I didn't say that. As I said, things have changed.'

'And?'

'Well, it's beginning to look like Michael's skill set isn't going to be in great demand for a while. Maybe a long while, so maybe I'll have to rewrite part of my plan, reconfigure the timing.'

'Reconfigure it,' queried Jeff?

'To fit the current situation.'

'Which means what exactly?' said Jeff, still unsure where this was going.

Lauren looked him straight in the eyes... 'I could give you three years, but no more.'

'Three years!' exclaimed Jeff,

'Three years of my life, you get the freedom to write your book, but after that, I'm out, no matter what.'

'That's all I need; you could make a lot of money in that time and hopefully find someone as good as you to take over from you when you go.'

'I could do that.'

'Good. It's a deal, then?' asked Jeff.

'Possibly, but I need two or three days to think about it and discuss it with Michael.'

'Fair enough, but there is one condition?' said Jeff.

'What?' said Lauren cautiously.

'Well, what if Michael gets another job? Will you leave before the...

'No! A deal's a deal,' interrupted Lauren. 'If I promise three years, I will keep my promise no matter what happens.' There was, however, one very remote possibility she had not considered when making that promise...

'Good,' said Jeff.

'To our deal,' said Lauren raising her glass.

'To our deal,' replied Jeff, gently touching glasses.

'Two Carrot and Coriander soups?' asked the waiter with perfect timing.

Jeff nodded, and the waiter placed them on the table. 'Would you like the wine now?'

'Yes, please,' said Jeff, 'I think we have something to celebrate.' He looked enquiringly at Lauren.

'I will still have to think about it,' said Lauren, but she smiled as she said it. There really wasn't very much to think about.

CHAPTER 17

New Shoes and Old Words.

February 2009

It is part of the rich tapestry of life that just as one door closes, another smaller door opens, tucked away in the corner of the same room. But, if you are not careful, the opportunity which has suddenly presented itself can just as quickly disappear while you are still looking at the door that just closed. The trick is to be bold and grab the opportunity with both hands while you can. You must hold on tightly as the winds of confusion and procrastination swirl around. When they have subsided, you may find the prospect no longer exists, and the door has been closed forever.

Lauren arrived home just after eight o'clock to be greeted by Michael at the front door, which was a little surprising. He was radiant with joy, which unsettled her momentarily. He was also stone-cold sober, shaved, and dressed, which surprised her even more.

'Hello darling,' said Lauren with a hint of wariness and surprise, but he didn't seem to hear her.

'I have some great news,' said Michael.

'Good, I guess,' replied Lauren with an almost untraceable hint of reservation... 'going by your face?'

'I have an interview for a job!' He exclaimed, sounding both enthusiastic and relieved. Oddly, he also appeared a little taller than Lauren remembered. It was as if a heavy load, which he had been carrying for a long time, had suddenly been lifted from his shoulders, and now he could stand upright again. Lauren made a mental note, never allowing herself to fall into the pit of despair he had stumbled into, no matter what happened.

She kissed him benignly on the cheek. For some reason, she didn't feel overly affectionate tonight.

'That's wonderful news, darling.' She hung up her coat and put her laptop bag on the hall table.

'Who with?'

'Barclays Investments. It's not the same situation as before, but I fit the general criteria, so....'

'Did the agency contact you, or did you contact them?'

'The agency called me.'

'That's good. The salary offered is always better if they need you more than you need them.' Such is the way of the world, she thought. That was why Jeff had offered her such a significant salary increase.

'When are you going for the interview,' queried Lauren? For some reason, her mind drifted back to her lunchtime conversation with Jeff and the offer he had made only a few hours earlier. She had virtually made up her mind on the train journey back to Godalming to accept and was preparing to tell Michael, but he had managed to hijack the situation with his news. She wondered whether now would be a good time to mention it or if it would be better to leave it until after his interview. If his meeting went badly, then nothing would be lost. However, if it did go well, she might have to reconsider how to deal with Jeff's proposal.

'Tuesday morning,' replied Michael.

'Well, let's hope it goes well,' said Lauren smiling encouragingly. But her mixed feelings about the situation did not sit comfortably over the weekend, and she had problems sleeping. She had set her heart on accepting Jeff's offer. Now, the opportunity of a lifetime could be snatched away from her at the very last moment.

Fortunately, the two days passed quickly and relatively quietly. On Monday, Lauren drove to Lavendon as usual. It was a cold and blustery morning, and the traffic was quieter today. As she approached the bend on Shelbury Bridge, she noticed Alfie, the fluffy tail-ender bouncing along the footpath on the other side of the road. Lauren purposely slowed to watch Katie and her family for a few moments. Lauren wondered how Katie's new baby was coming along. She didn't seem to be showing much yet, but she was well wrapped up against the Northwind, which was understandable.

'April!' she muttered. *She would probably have the baby in April or May*, which was her best guess if her first observation was the correct interpretation of the chronology. Of course, she could have it completely wrong, but she knew she hadn't. It should happen, life is fair most of the time, and Katie and John deserved this.

'Pardon,' said Daisy.

'Pardon?' replied Lauren sounding a little confused.

'You said April.'

'Did I?' replied Lauren sounding a little surprised, as she wasn't aware she had said anything.

'Yes.'

'Oh, sorry, must have been thinking out loud.'

'About what?'

'Well, April, obviously.'

Daisy realised this obtuse conversation was going nowhere, so she returned to gazing out of the car window and looking at Poppy.

Lauren noticed that Poppy appeared even taller today. It had only been a few months since her head was peeking above the parapet wall. Now she seemed to be head and shoulders above it. Then she noticed that poppy appeared to be wearing elevated platform shoes. At the age of nine, she fully embraced height's distinct psychological advantage. She also had a somewhat wayward demeanour about her, newfound confidence not unlike Daisy, who had, up to that moment, been sitting quietly in the back of the car.

'Poppy's wearing heels, Mummy. Can I have some?' Daisy suddenly exclaimed. She never missed a trick.

'They're not heels. They're just platforms,' corrected Lauren. 'And anyway, I didn't think you could wear them to school.'

'Poppy is!'

'That's Katie's decision, not mine.'

'Whatever,' mumbled Daisy contemptuously.

'Whatever!' exclaimed Lauren sharply. She despised the inappropriate annexation of the word, the nature and context of which had been transformed into an annoyingly abrupt conversation killer.

'I'm sorry,' said Daisy. She knew her mother disapproved of words being arbitrarily sequestrated to street slang. Becoming a part of the new bastardised English language. In her opinion, 'Whatever' was one of the worst serial offenders.

'Could I just have some platforms, then? I don't want to look like a midget.'

'Aaaah,' mumbled Lauren through gritted teeth. That was another word she hated being arbitrarily bandied about.

'You won't look like a… smaller person just because you're not wearing platforms.' She disliked sounding censorial. It had the unsavoury whiff of militant Presbyterianism about it. Fortunately, she worked in an environment where she had to be constantly vigilant of unintentionally offending anybody on so many diverse levels. Lauren knew what was coming and was preparing herself, but nothing happened.

'They do look nice, though, don't they?' asked Daisy.

Ah, thought Lauren, the subtle backdoor approach. That was commendable if a little wily. 'Yes, they do.' She replied cautiously.

'They make Poppy look elegant yet demure, don't you think?'

'Demure! Where did you get that from?' asked Lauren. It wasn't a word she would have expected Daisy to employ in everyday conversation. But then Daisy continually surprised her with her ever-widening vocabulary.

'Miss Samuels told us the word. She said it's one of the many words to describe how young ladies should be. Demure, fascinating, mysterious, charming, and slightly aloof… and many other old words.'

'Did she,' replied Lauren? Mulling thoughtfully over the "Old words" turn of phrase.

Miss Samuels was a fascinating teacher. That much was beyond any doubt, thought Lauren. One day she would have to have a quiet tête-à-tête with this woman and thank her.

'So, can I have some?'

'We'll see. I'll speak to your father first…but I suppose so. We'll go out on Saturday and have a look if we have time.'

'Oh good, I'm so happy.' She returned to the book she had been reading… mission accomplished.

'But not for school,' added Lauren after a few seconds.

Daisy glanced up. 'Okay… fair enough.' Then she continued reading without further comment. Lauren realised she had been well and truly bushwhacked on the shoes and spent the next five minutes trying to work out how that had happened.

Lauren's thoughts then shifted back to her own situation. Jeff would be looking for some indication today as to whether she would be accepting his proposal. She would have to stall him - at least until after Michael's interview. But the more she thought about it, the more assured she became that she could make a success of this opportunity. If nothing else, Lauren deserved her shot at the title. She had worked long and hard at Barrington Marsh Associates, and this was her reward. It was only for three years, and she could still have more children after completing the contract. I would only be thirty-five years old, coming up to thirty-six. There would still be plenty of time. Of course, Michael might think differently, but then why should she sacrifice this once-in-a-lifetime opportunity just because Michael had managed to get his career back on track. But then, maybe he wouldn't object. Perhaps he would be happy for her to take the promotion. Maybe the interview would not go so well. Possibly the vacancy wouldn't be what Michael was after. These were the imponderables she would have to contend with. Her mind drifted back to Katie and her new baby, and she remembered all the fun she'd had when Daisy was born. It was the kind of enjoyment and self-fulfilment you can't buy; In one lifetime, you only get a few chances to grab hold of something like that.

Deep inside, she felt a tiny pang of yearning. It lingered for a few moments - just long enough to catch her attention. Possibly some sort of subconscious poke from her bank of happy memories, but no sooner had it caught her attention than it was gone.

She dropped Daisy off at school and carried on to Godalming. The train arrived at Waterloo, and she disembarked and started to prepare to descend into the work mindset that she had so meticulously cultivated over the last six years. Today was like any other day, but it was one day closer to what she had been working towards for so long.

CHAPTER 18

The False Horizon.

Late February 2009

Michael rose early for the first time in months and was showered, shaved, and dressed before Lauren awoke. It was still dark outside. He went downstairs to the kitchen and switched on the Delonghi to make himself a cup of freshly ground coffee. Michael loved the coffee aroma in the morning - when he was alone. Standing by the french windows, he drank the coffee, staring out into the woodland beyond the garden, watching the mist that rolled over the garden most mornings in winter. Soon the sun would rise and burn it away. It was almost an analogy for something happening in his life, but try as he may, he couldn't think what that might be.

It was too early to leave, so he thought he would browse yesterday's papers and catch up on the news. Since he had been out of work, he had lost touch with current affairs and only took cursory notice of the news on television. Keeping abreast of world events didn't seem so essential when you no longer rode on the crazy carousel in the City of London.

Nobody would ask your opinion on the oil price or how it might affect world economics at the job centre. Not on one of his twice-monthly visits to that wonderfully erudite, if ever so sanctimonious bastion of faceless deconstructers of the soul. Once, he used to despise the people who frequented these establishments, if only because he had never been out of work and had no recollection of his father being unemployed. Somehow the whole concept had always been alien to him, but no longer. Waiting for his name to be called was a levelling and humbling experience.

Concept! He thought to himself, taking another sip of coffee. How so, typically, bourgeoisie to think of unemployment as a lifestyle. Christ! He thought, when did I become a snob? Somehow, his good fortune had severely tainted his perspective on the misfortune of others. But at least he could review and revise his off-kilter opinion of the unemployed based on something more than staid rhetoric. Today, hopefully, everything will get back on track. It was always good to have a little *me* time to reflect on life and what really mattered. He hadn't done much of that in a while. Maybe he should try it more often and ease back a little on the self-pity that had almost completely enveloped and consumed him over the last nine months.

At just after seven, Lauren came down to find Michael had already prepared breakfast for everybody. Despite being out of work for over eight months, this was the first time he had bothered to make an effort. He usually left it to Leja to prepare it during the week or Lauren over the weekend.

'Good morning, darling,' said Michael in the chirpiest tone she had heard from him for some time. He gestured to the table.

'Breakfast is ready.' His smile, the smile of someone for whom hope, however tenuous and slender, had returned after disappearing without a trace in the aftermath of the storm still raging in the city. Lauren felt something stirring inside – she had had a lot of disparate feelings just lately. Maybe something was going on with her hormones that she was unaware of. Was it a sense of relief, she wondered, possibly related to the temporary reprieve from the burden she had carried for so long – not of financial support, things hadn't become that desperate, but of keeping everything moving forward despite the setback? Now, just possibly that load, that burden would be eased a little.

'Toast – Tea – coffee – croissants – orange juice.'

'Wonderful,' remarked Lauren, still slightly surprised and oddly ill at ease. Then she realised what it was she could sense… the unsavoury vestige of clawing desperation. It was the English way. It was pitiful, demeaning, and sad…and she hated it. She felt ashamed for feeling this way, but that was how it was. Nothing was going to change that – well, not today, anyway.

'Where's Leja?' asked Lauren, suddenly realising she had not seen her that morning.

'I popped in and told her she could have a lie-in as I was doing breakfast.'

'That must have worried her?'

'No, I reassured her it was a one-off as I was going into the city today.'

Lauren sat down and slowly drank her first coffee of the day. It tasted delicious. *There was hope yet,* she thought. *Decent baristas were always in demand at Costa.* She smiled at her droll witticism before realising how facetious and contemptuous it sounded. Perfectly acceptable employment for someone younger but hardly the occupation of an ex-merchant banker. *God!* she thought, *am I turning into the stereotypical cynical business bitch already?* Michael smiled back at her, unaware of her thoughts or why she was smiling. He assumed…

But self-confidence on its own would not cut the ice. Michael was out of the loop and virtually off the radar, so he would have to make up a lot of ground quickly if he were to break back into the inner sanctum of the banking fraternity.

'So, what time is your interview?'

'One o'clock.'

'So, aren't you up a little early? You could have had another couple of hours in bed.'

'Thought I would start as I intend to go on.'

'I see. Well, that's good.' Lauren finished her coffee and called up the stairs, 'Daisy!'

'Two minutes, Mum,' replied Daisy.

'You won't have time for breakfast.'

'No prob.'

'Good morning,' said Leja, popping her head around the kitchen door.

'Coffee?' asked Michael.

'Thank you,' said Leja, looking a little surprised.

'I thought you were having a lie-in,' asked Lauren?

'I was, but I thought I should get up.' Leja picked up the coffee that Michael had poured and took a sip. 'Is there anything special you want me to do today, Mrs Penfold?'

Lauren wondered why Leja still referred to her so formally but didn't bother mentioning it. It was probably better that way.

'No, just the same as usual, but could you call the electrician? The power to the garage seems to have gone again.'

'I will do,' said Leja.

'I could have a look at that,' said Michael.

'I did ask you to check why it wasn't working a few weeks ago,' replied Lauren.

Michael muttered something and continued nibbling his toast.

Daisy appeared in the kitchen, plopped down on her chair and poured some orange juice.

'Morning, Mummy, Daddy, Leja.' She smiled at Leja.

'Did you have any homework,' asked Lauren?

'Done.'

'Good.'

Lauren stood up, 'right, missy, are you ready?'

'I haven't eaten my toast yet,'

'I did call you in plenty of time,' remarked Lauren nodding her head imperceptibly.

Daisy frowned and quickly ate her toast. Then jumped up to wash her hands at the sink.

'I presume you will be back before me?' asked Lauren.

'Probably,' replied Michael, 'unless I'm out celebrating.'

Lauren flashed him a piercing glance.

'Maybe not, then. I'll save the celebrating till I get back.'

Lauren smiled and kissed Michael on the lips, she could see he was happy for the first time in a long time, and she was glad. Maybe everything could be slowly getting back on track per their 'life plan.'

Lauren and Daisy put their coats on, said goodbye, and left. Watched as they drove off down the driveway by Michael and Leja. As Lauren's car turned into the main road, Michael whispered, 'I need you for something, Leja.' He gently pulled Leja towards his body, held her tightly by the cheeks of her bum in one hand and her head in the other and kissed her.

Leja giggled. 'Naughty Mr Penfold, what could you possibly want from me?'

'I need to check something.'

'What,' she asked coquettishly?

'Your electrics. I need to check everything is working.'

'Mine is fine; it's the garage that...

Michael kissed her again.

'Oh, Mr Penfold, I am sure everything is working perfectly okay,' replied Leja playfully.

'Well, we'll see about that in a minute.' They made their way hastily back to Leja's bedroom, kissing and removing their clothes as they went, and spent the next hour in bed fucking each other.

Michael arrived a little early for the interview. Although he had done some research at home on his computer, he took the opportunity to read up a little more about the company from the brochure in reception. Unfortunately, it didn't go well. Although he was perfectly qualified to do the job, several other candidates were equally qualified but much younger than him. And, of course, they did not have to contend with the onerous baggage of being connected to a significant banking industry failure.

'How did interview go?' asked Leja when Michael arrived home just after five o'clock. He was a little drunk and had apparently driven home from the station in that condition. He was not in the mood for idle conversation.

'Bloody disaster,' replied Michael, collapsing on the sofa. He still hadn't come to terms with the dismissive way he had been treated. 'I thought the other interviewees looked younger than me, but the interview panel looked about fourteen.' He went quiet for a few seconds. 'Christ!' he mumbled aloud, 'they must be recruiting trainee bankers as they pop out of the womb to save time.'

'I can just see it in the delivery room – "congratulations, Mr and Mrs Ponsenby-Jones, you have a healthy nine-pound baby boy. Hang on a minute - something has just been pushed under the door. Oh! It's a note from Goldman Sachs. *Dear Aloysius, We are delighted you have arrived safe and well. See you Monday morning. 8am sharp.* – Bastards!'

'Sorry?' enquired Leja. 'I don't understand.' She had only been half listening to his rant.

'Oh nothing,' replied Michael, realising it was too much of a business in-joke for Leja to understand, 'it was just a bloody disaster.'

'Oh, I am sorry. Would you like something?' She smiled accommodatingly and started to undo her top to reveal her naked breasts. He had noticed that she had taken to not wearing a bra during the day when they were alone, only putting it back on in the evenings when Lauren returned home.

'That is an extremely nice offer,' replied Michael, half-smiling for the first time in three hours, 'but I could do with a cup of tea actually... and a hobnob.'

Leja looked a little confused for a few moments. She still hadn't quite got her head around his vague and flippant attitude towards their on-off-the-cuff sex arrangement. Before he had left that morning, he was all over her banging her brains out, and she was beginning to think he might even be in love with her, but now it was as if this morning had never happened.

'You don't want fuck my body?' she asked, pushing her naked breasts together with her hands to accentuate her cleavage. 'You don't want to suck my juicy strawberries?' She pushed her large nipples towards his face. 'I could put cream on them if you like?' she asked very accommodatingly. 'You like cream?'

'No, not right now, if you don't mind, Leja.'

'You just want hobnob?' asked Leja looking a little confused and curiously perturbed.

Michael looked at Leja. The undeniably easy-on-the-eye twenty-four-year-old nanny they had employed for nearly five years and with whom he had been having a casual fling for the last two months. But it was more out of sheer lust, boredom, and base animal attraction than anything meaningful.

'And tea,' added Michael, glancing through the *Metro* newspaper he had picked up on the train. 'I have really had a crap day, Leja. I would love to fuck you, but – hey! Where is Daisy?' he exclaimed, suddenly realising that she was usually home by this time and might have overheard him.

'It's not problem. I dropped her off at a friend's house after school. I pick up at six.'

'Which friend?'

'Lotte – she live half mile up lane. Do you know who I mean?' Leja looked slightly concerned momentarily, unsure if she had done something wrong.

'Oh, the Sanderson. Yes, I know them. That's fine.'

'Good,' replied Leja looking relieved. She smiled. 'Now we make fuck?'

'Is that all you think about?' asked Michael, who was tiring a little of Leja's insistence on intercourse. 'Look, I did say it was only a casual thing.'

'But I am loving you,' she replied in the peculiar, broken English that he found so amusing… some of the time.

'No, you don't. We just screw each other when we have nothing better to do, and you obviously like it, so we do it - but that is not love.' He realised how crass and invidious that sounded. He had managed to roll dismissive and demeaning into a few words and then throw it back at her as a lecture on morality.

What a self-serving, condescending shit I am turning into, he thought as Leja stood before him, about to burst into tears. What am I becoming – what have I become? He asked himself, apart from a scumbag adulterer. An uncharacteristic pang of guilt suddenly overwhelmed him.

'Look, I'm sorry, that wasn't nice,' muttered Michael apologetically.

'No, not nice at all,' sobbed Leja. 'We make bang, and I think that is love, but you say it is not, and I am confused.' Michael looked at her, standing half-naked before him, pouring her heart out. He found himself watching her breasts bounce gently every time she sniffed.

'Look, could you…' he pointed to her open top, gesturing that she should do the buttons up, and she did so, slowly.

'I thought we both understood it was just a bit of fun?' asked Michael.

'Yes, I see. I am silly and naïve. It was just fun,' Leja smiled. 'But can we still do it sometime?'

'Don't you think you should have your own boyfriend, somebody your own age?'

'I do,' she replied. 'We have sex all over weekend, but I also like sex in week as well. I have needs…'

Now Michael was confused. 'What? You fuck somebody else when you are not here, and then you come back and fuck me?' he sounded oddly incensed by that confession. 'That's not on. That's like being unfaithful.' He didn't immediately appreciate the stunning hypocrisy of the remark, but Leja did.

'But you bang your wife during the week and the weekends, so why not bang me as well?' Asked Leja with just a hint of calibrated righteous indignation, which left Michael almost at a loss for words. He was not accustomed to a rational and reasoned argument from Leja.

'Because... because, oh, I don't know, I thought.... and anyway, I haven't had sex with Lauren for months, not since....' But he was lying. He'd had sex with Lauren the previous night.

'I'm glad to hear it,' said Leja. 'That would be utterly untenable.' She smiled at her tiny moral victory.

'Utterly untenable?' parroted Michael. Surprised at her uncharacteristic choice of words and the obvious irony.

'Your English is getting better.'

'I learn from Daisy,' said Leja.

'I see,' replied Michael.

'My fucking is better, too,' she replied with a glint of humour.

Michael smiled. He got up off the sofa and led Leja back into her bedroom. It was easier. He thought about Leja's plumber boyfriend as he slipped his underpants and socks off, but not for long.

Lauren returned home at just after eight o'clock.

'Hi, darling, how did it go,' she asked as Michael kissed her hello?

'I will tell you about it over dinner.'

'Okay,' replied Lauren cautiously, detecting a muted tone in his voice but assuming he had been successful at the interview. So maybe now was the time for her news.

'Drink first?' asked Michael.

'Wine would be good.'

'Wine it is,' replied Michael opening a bottle. 'So, how was your day?'

'Good, good. I have some news too.'

'Good news, I hope,' asked Michael.

'Oh, yes. Well, I think so.'

Michael handed Lauren a glass of wine, and they clinked glasses. 'What then?' he asked, taking a sip.

'Well, I hope you won't be too cross, but I've been offered a promotion to creative director of the company and head of the European division.

'Which means what exactly?' asked Michael, looking slightly stunned.

'Well, I will head the five campaign departments.'

'Wow, that is some promotion, and it couldn't have come at a better time.'

'Well, that's why I wanted to talk to you about it, what with your job, and I haven't decided yet....' She had, but she wasn't about to tell Michael that.

'No job.'

'No job!' repeated Lauren. Looking suitably disappointed.

'But I thought that... You seemed happy when I came in, and I assumed....'

'I think I was too old.'

'But you're only thirty-two.'

'Some of those guys were in their early twenties... just.'

'Oh, I see. So, are you disappointed?'

'Why should I be? I am obviously unemployable, so you being offered this promotion is the best thing that could happen.'

'So, you don't mind if I take it. It's for a minimum of three years.'

'Three years?'

'I would be contracted for that period before I could leave or....'

'Why would you leave a position like that?' interrupted Michael, sounding mystified.

'To have more children. I would like some more before....'

Obviously, that aspect hadn't crossed Michael's mind. 'Ah, I see, of course. But you'd only be thirty-five, still young enough to have another one or two.'

'It might run on a bit, and late thirties is a bit iffy for procreation, statistically speaking.'

'Oh, I see; can we think about it over the weekend?' asked Michael

'Of course, we can. But I will need you one hundred per cent behind me if I am to take this promotion.'

'I suppose I could become a house-husband?' ventured Michael. He quietly remonstrated with himself about not throwing ill-conceived ideas into the mix before clearly and rationally thinking them through.

'And do what, exactly,' queried Lauren.

I asked for that, thought Michael... 'Well, all the things that Leja does and all the things I normally do at the weekends.' *This was not helping,* he thought.

'What, and get rid of Leja?'

'Well, I suppose so.' He suddenly realised that he was inadvertently proposing the sacking of his casual sex partner, which would mean the end of his sex-when-you-want-how-you-like-it arrangement. Something which he wholeheartedly enjoyed most of the time. Not only that, but he had also now conversely volunteered to do a lot of household chores which he absolutely detested. *How did he talk himself into this shit position,* he asked himself? *Maybe that's why I didn't get the job, not enough forward planning.*

'Is that really you?' asked Lauren, flashing Michael a strange expression that said, '*Surely you have to be joking.*'

She looked around the room as if searching for something. 'Has someone kidnapped my husband and left you in his place?' she asked sarcastically.

Michael smiled at her comment. 'Maybe you're right... maybe I will keep looking for a job.'

'I'm sure you will find something eventually; you just need to do something in the meantime to keep your mind occupied. I think we should hang on to Leja.'

'I'm sure you're right,' replied Michael, relieved that he had just avoided what could have been a catastrophic own goal. He must say less and think more. That was going to be his new maxim for the future. He smiled quietly at the comment Lauren had made about keeping himself occupied.

They touched glasses, 'To the future and your wonderful promotion offer which has saved our bacon,' toasted Michael.

'Cheers.'

'Cheers, darling.' A warm, satisfying feeling coursed through Lauren's body. In her heart, she was happy that things had turned out the way they had. She knew she could do this job, it was what she had always wanted, a chance to prove how good she was, and now she had it with Michael's blessing. There was a slight tinge of regret about closing the door on having more children for a while, possibly forever. But she held that pang of remorseful guilt in a small corner of her mind, where she could control it, for now.

By Monday morning, they had come to a decision about Lauren's offer of promotion. Lauren would take the job for the three years she had agreed, but they would try for another baby sometime during the third, hopefully with success, so Lauren would have the baby just as the agreed term expired. If she became pregnant, there would be little chance of Jeff persuading her to stay on for a few more years. It would close that door forever. It all seemed so very cold-hearted and calculating. So very different from how things were when Daisy was conceived ten years ago. To some degree, it took away some of the excitement, working to a defined schedule, but it was necessary under the circumstances. Lauren and Daisy finished breakfast, and Leja started to clear the table. Michael kissed Lauren and Daisy goodbye as they left

Strangely, Michael never even considered the ongoing relationship with Leja. He seemed to be under the illusion that it would all eventually fizzle out. And everything would go back to how it was before he was sacked - once he had secured a new job. It was just sex, after all, he told himself. That mollified all his reservations. Anyway, sex with the au pair was de rigueur, as far as he was aware.

'Squeeze them for as much money as you can get, won't you?' directed Michael adding, 'Jeff is buying your life, so don't let him have it too cheaply.'

'No, I won't, darling,' replied Lauren. Daisy waved at her father as she jumped into the car, and they drove away.'

'I hope we see Katie today,' said Lauren.

'Why?' asked Daisy.

'Well, I like to think she is part of what we do and everything that happens to me. She makes me feel grounded when things are up in the air.'

'Are they up in the air?' asked Daisy curiously.

'Well, we have made some big decisions over the weekend that may change our lives forever, and I hope they are the right ones.'

'I'm sure they will be, Mummy; you never do anything silly.'

Lauren thought about what Daisy had said and just hoped she hadn't. As they approached Shelbury Bridge, she couldn't see anybody at first because of the early morning misty haze. The traffic queue was moving slower today. The other drivers were being cautious as they crossed the bridge. Then Lauren spotted Katie's golden hair bouncing in the breeze and reflecting what little there was of the sunshine that was trying to break through. Slowly, the entourage emerged through the mist like Brigadoon.

Katie looked a little larger today; baby Farrier was definitely making its presence known. The twins were both walking. They now looked as if they were just about ready to start school themselves. They had to be nearly five and had probably been going to preschool for a while. Poppy's hair was now quite long and curly. Before long, she would walk alongside her mother, and they would look almost like sisters. Alfie wandered behind, shaking his head from side to side as if he were listening to rap music on his headphones. Katie would probably have her baby a little later than she initially calculated, probably around May or June. As the twins would be starting full-time school in September, she would still have one child at home during the day, which had to be a comfort for her. Lauren had almost forgotten what being at home with Daisy was like. It seemed so long ago, and yet it was only a few years. Time seemed to suck in so much - like a tiny black hole in space. Everything that had happened and been condensed into a tiny speck, and that was now the past. Everything that occurred now seemed to happen slowly and then suddenly speed up. It was all Einstein's fault; he was the one with all the time theories, thought Lauren a little lackadaisically.

They looked happy today, but then they always seemed happy. That was their life – to be happy. Lauren drove past them and smiled as she carried on to the school. Just that momentary glimpse would keep her in the right frame of mind for the rest of the day, well, for the morning at least.

CHAPTER 19

'When troubles come, they come not alone but....'

December 2008

'Hello, Katie,' said Manni. 'Take a seat.' He glanced away for a second, made a note about something, and then looked back at me. 'So, pregnancy going well from what I can see,' glancing at the computer screen

'Yes, no problem there.'

'The last scan was fine.'

'Yes, yes, it was.' I felt oddly reluctant to engage in the conversation, which was unusual for me. But I knew I would have to confront this issue, no matter how much I wanted to avoid it. I didn't really have a choice.

Mani looked at the screen again.

'Your blood pressure's fine. The baby's heartbeat is good, so, Katie, what's the problem?'

I must have looked surprised for a moment but then realised I was sitting in his consulting room, so that was a reasonable assumption.

'I have a little issue I need to discuss....' I was still holding back. I had trodden this road before and knew where it might lead to...

Manni lifted his eyebrows almost imperceptibly, and his eyes became slightly more significant. He could sense something and probably wondered why I had not mentioned this at the beginning of our conversation before he had gone through the usual pre-natal preamble. He waited for me to continue...

'I've had some odd bleeds... after sex....' Oddly, I felt a little embarrassed making that admission. For some reason, admitting I was having sex when I was nearly five months pregnant did not seem quite right, although I knew it was perfectly normal. 'And it smells a little unpleasant,' I added with embarrassment.

What, the sex? I thought he might have been tempted to ask. But that would have been his droll flippancy intervening, Always a useful defence mechanism whenever a patient's problems began to overwhelm him. But not today. It would not have been appropriate.

'Does it?' he asked, sounding genuinely concerned.

I nodded. 'John noticed it first.'

'Any other symptoms?' asked Manni, who had started to make some notes which, as always, he would type into his computer after I had left.

'I've lost my appetite and feel tired in the mornings. It's not something I recall happening during the last pregnancy.'

'Em,' said Manni, digesting all the information being relayed. 'When did you last have a cervical screening?'

'About a year ago.' I thought for a few moments. 'In fact, it was March, so nearer nine months... It came back all clear.'

'Did it,' replied Manni thoughtfully? 'I think we should do another screening. There's something not quite right, and we need to find the underlying cause.'

'What about the blood problem?'

'Could be some sort of urinary infection. We'll soon find out. I will arrange for another screening on... Manni looked at his computer screen and fiddled with a few keys, 'would tomorrow at ten be okay?'

'That fast?' I asked, a little surprised.

'We don't want to waste any time, bearing in mind your condition.' I could see he was thinking about what happened last time but was choosing not to mention it... but then he didn't have to.

'Oh, no, of course.'

'So, is that okay,' he asked?

'Yes, fine.'

'I'll arrange for a colposcopy at the same time as the other two procedures.' He smiled reassuringly.

'What's a colposcopy?' I inquired. I could not recall hearing about that procedure before.

'It's where we conduct further investigations if we find significant cell changes in the screening. It's not certain yet if that will be necessary. I'm just covering all avenues as we are at a transitional stage of the pregnancy.'

'Transitional?' I enquired, unsure what he meant by that.

'Moving towards the third trimester, that's all.' It meant more than Manni was prepared to go into at this stage.

'So, when will I know the results?'

'About a week. I will contact you, but I wouldn't worry too much. I see all sorts of irregularities during pregnancy, and I am sure this will be just that. It may even clear before you return next week.'

'Okay. Well, that's something,' I replied. 'You're probably right. I am a bit of a hypochondriac on the quiet.' I felt a little less apprehensive than I did before I came in. But still lingering in my mind was what happened the last time I was pregnant. I didn't mention it because I knew Manni knew all about it, and if there was anything to worry about, he would have told me.

I got up and hugged him again, as I did every time I saw him, and then I left. I would see him again next week.

CHAPTER 20

Walter, the Polish Plumber.

April 2009

The winter was nearly over, and the days were growing longer and warmer again. Surprisingly, Michael had turned his hand to working a few hours daily in the garden. It helped him to forget all the many problems that still ailed him. He had never fully appreciated the truly therapeutic benefits that could be derived from physical labour and threw himself energetically and wholeheartedly into whatever he was doing. That, of course, was when he had not worn himself out *pumping up the maid,* which was how he chose to describe fucking Leja. Not that he ever mentioned it to anybody. (It was a middle-class thing) and had become a regular morning event. It was still delightful fun, but he had become tired of a relationship based almost entirely on sex.

Michael no longer received the intimate attention from Lauren as he did from Leja, probably because Lauren was too tired for sex most weekday nights. This was perhaps why he continued the affair. However, he was still in love with Lauren despite going seriously off-grid. He had always found Lauren intellectually stimulating. This was the defining attraction for him right from the beginning. That hadn't changed.

Leja was interesting, but only in small doses. Unfortunately, she was strictly one-dimensional and very shallow as far as he was concerned. Oddly, he never noticed the irony in that appraisal. It was a harsh, demeaning summation of her character, but that was how it was. Deep down, he had always craved multi-layered immersive relationships, and Leja was never that and never would be.

Some days, he would stand in the garden, lean on his garden fork, and contemplate his capricious nature. Sometimes he despised himself and wallowed in a bit of soul-searching and self-loathing. But Leja would always spot the signs, wander out with a cup of tea, gently caress his testicles, and then give him a blow job while he was doing the weeding. This tended to make him forget his passing attack of guilt and remorse. His morality compass was well and truly buggered and now firmly pointing south.

It was on a Monday morning in late May when things started to change. Michael could remember having a barbecue in the garden the Sunday before. It was an unusually warm day for May and hopefully a precursor to a glorious summer, which would have made working in the garden even more enjoyable.

Lauren and Daisy had just left, and Michael wandered into Leja's bedroom, as usual. He half expected she had gone back to bed after clearing up the breakfast things, but she wasn't there. He was about to leave when he heard her retching in the en-suite bathroom.

'Leja! Are you okay?' he shouted through the door.

Leja made a horrible croaking sound, then spoke.

'Yes, Mr Penfold, thank you. Just a little sickness.' Somewhat bizarrely, Leja always called him Mr Penfold, except when they were screwing, when she would call him by his given name. Michael still found that a little amusing, especially when Lauren was around.

'Oh, right... anything I can do?'

'No, nothing, thanks. I am sorry, can't do the bang-bang today.'

Well, I wasn't that bothered, thought Michael, who was always a little squeamish around vomit. It brought back some horrific memories of Daisy projectile vomiting over him on various occasions when she was much younger. On one memorable day, Daisy managed to redecorate three walls, the ceiling and the floor, and the carpet had to be destroyed. She had also ruined one of his best suits, but that was all part of the rich tapestry of being a father - he reasoned philosophically.

'Are you sure I can't get you anything?' he repeated.

'One minute,' said Leja. 'I be out in one minute.'

Michael sat on the edge of Leja's bed and glanced around the bedroom. The French doors had a magnificent view stretching all the way down to the valley in the distance. Something that he had completely forgotten about. *Room could do with redecorating soon*, he thought to himself as he whiled away the minutes idly gazing skywards. Leja retched again and made a peculiar guttural squawking noise that made him wince. He was uncomfortable around this sort of thing, so he tried to block the grunting noise by humming quietly. He realised it was a remarkably banal thing to do, but he thought, what else could he do.

Michael had spent many hours looking up at the ceiling. Or, more accurately, in that general direction while the very sexy and amiable Leja, with the medium-sized but firm breasts, bounced up and down on his cock. But he had never actually noticed the ceiling before. Not in any detail, anyway. I suppose that must be some sort of backhanded compliment, he pondered to himself again. The old oak beams lent a particular enchantment to the room that...

Leja slowly emerged from the bathroom. She appeared sheepish and noticeably worse for wear. 'Hello Mr Penfold, I am so sorry for....'

Michael interrupted her. He didn't want to talk about vomit. The sound of her guttural retching had already comprehensively destroyed any possibility of sexual activity that day.

'My name is Michael. Why are you calling me Mr Penfold?'

'I don't know,' Leja timidly replied. 'Maybe because I am not doing my duties?' She looked incredibly vulnerable, much younger, and less attractive without makeup.

'Fucking me isn't your duty, for Christ's sake. It's just a bit of fun. We can stop anytime you want to.' *He thought that sounded a bit harsh and insensitive*, but that was precisely how it was as far as he was concerned.

'I don't want to stop,' burbled Leja, wiping her face with a soiled towel.

'You still have your boyfriend,' said Michael, trying to bring balanced reality into the situation. 'Maybe it might be best if you just stuck to screwing him?'

'Maybe, I'm not sure.'

'Not sure, why not?'

'I told him about us, and he was a little upset.'

'Christ! I should think he would be. He's not going to come around here and make a scene, is he?' Michael could feel panic begin to take hold of his loins, and his throat suddenly felt parched. Visions of vociferous altercations at the front door started to assemble in his head.

'You shouldn't say that word all the time.'

'What word?' Michael was a little confused.

'Christ, you are always saying word Christ. It's not good.'

'Okay, I'll use something else, but will he?'

'Will he what?' asked Leja

'Come around here?' asked Michael again, now sounding slightly frustrated.

'No, I don't think so; he can't afford to get involved with police.'

'Why not,' queried Michael? Now becoming even more alarmed. *Maybe he was a crime lord, or perhaps a people trafficker. He could also be running his own whorehouse in Baddesley-Minton.* His imagination began to run riot with the infinite range of possibilities available. *No, maybe they were all a bit too far-fetched. Indeed, he would have heard about it down the pub if there was a brothel full of Albanian prostitutes working in the village. Mind you, they wouldn't get much trade locally. Half the residents were retired, so their wives knew precisely where they were at all times. The other half were in wife-swapping clubs because they were too tight to pay for extracurricular sex.*

'Is he a Russian drug dealer?' ventured Michael guardedly.

'No, he is not drug dealer or a pimp if that is what you are thinking, he is painter and a plumber, and he comes from Poland, but he came to England without passport, so he keep "head down" as you say.'

'Oh, a painter. That could be handy,' replied Michael, thinking about Leja's bedroom. 'He could decorate your bedroom; it does need painting.' Leja looked at him with a curious expression of disbelief.

He would probably give him a reasonable price, knowing what he knew, he mused contemplatively. No. Maybe that wasn't such a bright idea, he thought, on reflection, a few seconds later.

'No, he not that type of painter, he paint me, my body with no clothes, you understand… Art?'

'Oh, right,' replied Michael.

'Anyway, I told him it is all over between us.'

'Us!' said Michael, sounding alarmed.

'Him and me, I think it best I not bang at weekends.'

'But he is your boyfriend. That's only right.'

'I am very perplexed,' said Leja.

'Look, maybe we should stop, and you just carry on with – what's his name?' Michael began to have a niggling feeling that maybe it was about time he extricated himself from this clandestine relationship before it got seriously out of hand. Which is where it most definitely appeared to be heading.

'Walter,' said Leja.

'Walter?' repeated Michael, sounding surprised,

'That's his name, Walter.'

'Walter? Are you sure?'

'Yes, it is traditional Polish name. It means powerful warrior.'

'Does it now?' enquired Michael inquisitorially with just a hint of alarm.

'Yes.' Affirmed Leja proudly.

'Right, so maybe you should just have a relationship with Walter in future. Maybe you two could get married, have lots of powerful little Polish warriors, and live happily ever after.' He half-smiled at his cynical suggestion.

'I would like that,' replied Leja, 'but I'm thinking I have your baby, so bit complicated.'

'What! Having my baby? But how?' exclaimed Michael, turning a distinctly wan colour and wondering how everything had suddenly gone a bit toxic. He could feel his legs turning to jelly.

'We make bang-bang, now me in fuck-club.'

'But surely it must be Walter's?'

'No, I don't think so, Walter always use condom, and he carefully checks it each time... for leaks. He is plumber as well as painter. He know about leaks.'

'Ah,' said Michael. 'I didn't need to know that.'

'And he keeps meticulous record of when we have ....'

'A record! Christ, what sort of plumber is he?' Michael appeared seriously alarmed at that bit of information.

'You said that word again. You won't go to heaven if you keep blaspheming.'

'What?' said Michael, unsure what Leja was referring to. Then he realised what he had said and grunted something inaudible.

'Why does he do that? It's crassly obscene,' asked Michael, adopting an expression of utter disbelief. He was desperately trying to get his head around Leja's revelation that Walter kept a meticulous record of their sexual activity, but it wasn't easy....

'He is... just like that,' replied Leja as if it were perfectly normal.

'Is he? I suppose he also keeps all his CDs in alphabetical, genre-specific order as well.' Michael was feeling a little facetious as the baby news sank in a little further.

'Yes, he does, actually... How do you know?' Leja looked genuinely surprised. Michael did not.

'Just a wild guess.'

'When we had sex, you just....'

'Yes, I know, but I thought you were on the....'

'No, I thought maybe you had.' Leja made a scissor-closing gesture with two fingers.

'No, certainly not.'

'So, we have baby.' Leja grinned and rubbed her tummy.

'Ah... no,' exclaimed Michael.

'So, what should we do?'

'Can you have an...

Leja quickly interrupted. 'No, I don't want to have abortion. I want to have baby... Our baby.'

'But you can't. Lauren will divorce me, and I don't want a divorce.'

'You should not do bang-bang then, I good Catholic girl.'

Michael sneered at that. He didn't like the sanctimonious tone she had adopted. Neither did he appreciate her assuming the high moral ground. It was all beginning to sound just a little threatening and disconcerting.

'All right, look, have the baby, but just say it's Walter's, okay?'

'Walter may not like that,' replied Leja, slightly stunned at the suggestion.

'Walter won't like being deported either,' replied Michael with a dash of self-gratifying smugness. He didn't often get the timing right for that sort of retort, usually thinking up the perfect comeback about two days later. Today, for once, Michael had it bang on the sweet spot. He was so exhilarated by his fleetness of mind that he almost did a fist pump but just managed to hold it back.

'You don't have to tell Walter you're pregnant.'

'But I won't get maintenance money if I don't tell him.'

'You wouldn't get maintenance if he's not supposed to be here, and he might twig something is not quite right when he checks his leakage records.' Michael shot Leja a disagreeable expression as he mentioned leakage.

'Oh, I see, yes. So where will we live?'

'You can carry on living here for a while. We still need you for at least another two or three years, probably longer.' Bugger, he thought, I've done it again. Jumped straight from the pot into the fire by not giving his suggestion proper consideration before locking Lauren and himself into a significant commitment for the foreseeable future.

'That would be okay,' said Leja, smiling and wiping some vomit off her cardigan.

Michael didn't say anything. There wasn't much he could say.

'I'll break it to Lauren in a day or so,' said Michael after a few moments of reflection on what lay ahead. *Maybe, it wouldn't be so bad*, he thought.

'Thank you,' said Leja. She went to kiss him, but he lurched back; he could smell the vomit, and his stomach threatened immediate retaliation.

'I think maybe you need to shower.' He gave her an odd sideways nod to the bathroom.

'Oh, yes, I am sorry. I must still smell a bit.'

'It's no problem,' he replied with a half-smile. He left the bedroom, returned to the lounge, poured himself a whiskey, sat down, and thought about the morning's developments. He was, trying to make some sense of it, rationalising the difficulty and breaking it down into smaller, manageable segments, making it easier to deal with. This was much the same process he used when he was working. Break the problem down into its constituent parts and deal logically with each issue. But how could he limit the potential damage? That was the primary issue. He had already dealt with the first question Lauren would probably ask – "*who is the father?*" That had been comprehensively dealt with by laying the responsibility firmly at Walter's doorstep. It was unlikely Walter would say anything, especially as Leja was not going to tell him about the baby. It was also unlikely that Lauren would run into Walter in the future as he lived in Godalming, so there was not much chance of that lie being uncovered. *Terminological inexactitude.* That was the Winston Churchill phrase that always sprang to mind on these occasions. Michael would not be telling a lie when he said that Walter had dumped Leja when he found out she was pregnant. He had just conveniently forgotten to mention the minor detail of who the father really was. He loved to use that euphemism. It seemed justified in the circumstance and didn't sound so harsh. It made him feel much better about the whole matter.

Of course, at this moment, this was all hypothetical; the baby was probably only a month or two into its creation, so a lot could happen in the next seven months. If Leja did eventually give birth, then the matter of maintenance would be his next problem, and he would have to deal with that at that time. Possibly of more importance was the issue of living in the same house as one of his children and being unable to show any emotional connection. To a significant degree, he could probably get away with that. He knew Lauren would undoubtedly form a relationship with the baby if only as a spiritual substitute for the one she had decided to delay for three years. So once again, that problem was not actually a problem. In some ways, it was almost a blessing in disguise. At least Lauren would not have all the hassle of getting pregnant, growing fat, having morning sickness, changing nappies and having time off work. That had to be a bonus.... So, in most respects, he could argue it was a win-win situation for everybody.

However, after further developing that train of thought, he wondered whether he might have oversimplified the issue just slightly. Perhaps it was a little self-serving; Lauren might not look at it in quite the same light as he expected after all. On a broader scale, maybe that kind of inverted, negative thinking had been why he was one of the first employees his company had let go. Still, no point in dwelling on that now, he thought. He would just have to get on with it and go with the flow. There would undoubtedly be a few other problems along the way. But he would have to deal with them as and when they popped up.

CHAPTER 21

An Unexpected Proposal.
April 2009

Lauren's day had gone well, but then most days were going well for her now. She had taken to the new promotion like a swan to Richmond Park lake. She and Jeff had now settled into a regular routine. They went out for lunch at Zefe's restaurant most Tuesdays and Fridays to discuss the progress of the various advertising campaigns she was overseeing. Today was Tuesday, and they had settled into the usual routine at their table in the corner. Jeff now insisted they drink their favourite Long Island Iced Tea cocktails before lunch and champagne while they ate. Today they were both already on the table with a large bunch of pink roses.

'How did they know,' asked Lauren looking a little surprised.

'We are regulars,' said Jeff smiling, but with the appearance of knowing something that she did not.

'But…'

'I rang them this morning,'

'Oh, I see,'

'But the roses, why the…'

'It's to celebrate.'

'Celebrate what? It's not my birthday.'

'No, it's mine.'

'Yours! You never mentioned it.'

'It didn't seem that important – it isn't usually.'

'So why the Roses?'

'I like to give presents on my birthday, especially to someone I am very fond of …' He paused to gauge Lauren's reaction.

'Fond of?' replied Lauren, 'What exactly does that mean?'

Jeff hesitated momentarily, acutely aware that what he said next could profoundly affect their relationship, in and outside of business, no matter how she responded.

'I am falling in love with you, Lauren.' There, he'd said it. Got it out in one breath without fumbling. He was a little surprised he had managed that much.

'Oh!' said Lauren, entirely taken by surprise.

'But I know you are happily married, have a lovely daughter, and I didn't want to spoil things between us, so…' He stopped talking, and Lauren felt her heart begin to pump a little faster. She could also feel her cheeks start to flush. Maybe the restaurant was a little warmer than usual today.

'And so…?' said Lauren, prompting him to continue. She wasn't sure exactly where this was going.

'I just wanted to tell you, that is all. I can't hide it from you any longer, so if you want to tell me to stop acting like a prat and drink my tea and shut up, I will understand, and I will never mention it a….'

'I don't think that not at all,' interrupted Lauren, 'it's just that, well, I do like you a lot, but I thought that maybe you had someone else in your life.'

'Like who?' said Jeff looking surprised.

'Well, I don't know. Maybe the gorgeous Zefe.'

'Zefe! Jeff looked aghast, rendered speechless for a few seconds by Lauren's assumption. 'Zefe? I'm not gay, for Christ's sake, not even a little bit,' he swiftly replied, visibly wounded by the slight. 'I thought we'd covered this ground some time ago. Didn't you believe me then?'

'Yes, of course I did, it's just that… I don't know,' Lauren felt a little confused. She seemed to be receiving mixed messages.

Jeff was stunned and momentarily looked down at the table, trying to gather his thoughts and conjure up some reasonable defence of his heterosexual inclination.

Lauren realised she might have it wrong. 'I just thought that with you both being good friends and playing in the same football team, same dressing rooms and things, well, he is nice, and I wouldn't want to come between you so….'

'Maybe, for someone that way inclined, but I am not.' He managed to amalgamate deep hurt and wounded indignation into one injured expression.

'I am so sorry. I didn't mean to cause offence. I…' Lauren paused and stared into Jeff's eyes. Somehow, she had misread the whole situation. The body language thing was utterly wrong, anyway. Lauren should have noticed that much. She worked with gay men all day and should have known the difference by now. Most of the gay guys Lauren spoke to deliberately affected a girlie tenor when talking with her. She presumed they did this to assimilate themselves seamlessly with her, the intention being to lower the tiny barrier that still existed between the sexes, but Jeff never had - she should have noticed that much. Gays tended not to be quite so obvious when speaking to other straight men; she knew that as well.

'Why don't you kiss me?' she asked, throwing oil onto the rough seas she had inadvertently created. It was brazened and entirely out of character, apparently, some sort of kneejerk reaction over which she had little control. It was a compensatory response for making a bad call, possibly a little reckless, but she had said it. It was done. What difference could one kiss make?

'What?' said a surprised Jeff.

'Kiss me,' repeated Lauren, with a naughty glint in her eye. Jeff wondered whether she had been teasing him all along. He wasn't sure.

Lauren smiled, and Jeff leaned across the table, and as he did so, she too leaned forward, and they gently kissed at first. But once he had started, his arms reached out to take hold of the tops of her arms and pull her closer toward him. Lauren's hands shot out instinctively to hold his face, and they slowly moved closer together over the table. And as they began to stand up to get even closer together, the table fell to one side, taking the champagne, iced tea and all the cutlery with it. It was all somewhat comical for a few moments. There was a tremendous crash as everything hit the floor, and champagne erupted from the bottle, but they never heard a sound, and all Lauren could feel was this warm sensation of Jeff's tongue exploring her mouth. Lauren had been waiting a long time for a moment like this; she did not know when or whether it would ever happen, but she knew now.

They parted to a riotous round of applause and cheers from their fellow diners. A little embarrassingly, they sat back down, staring at where the table had once been. They smiled at each other, and Jeff whispered, 'Did I pass the test?'

'Oh, yes, you passed that... years ago.' She gave him an even broader grin.

'You were winding me up?' exclaimed Jeff.

'Maybe.'

'Shall I replace the table now?' asked the waiter who had suddenly appeared, another Genie moment. Lauren turned around to see Zefe picking up the table. He looked up at her and quietly whispered, 'Now you have stolen the heart of my secret love. I am so sad.' He slowly backed away, smiling.

Lauren turned to Jeff and laughed, 'You planned all this.'

'No. not really. How could I? How did I know how you would react? But I did wonder if maybe you thought that...' He didn't finish.

'I will get you later.'

'I do hope so. In Paris, hopefully.'

Another waiter appeared to finish laying the table, all managed with remarkable efficiency as if this were an everyday occurrence. Then another waiter arrived with two new Long Island Teas and a fourth with a bottle of champagne and two glasses. It was perfect.

'Shall I open this one or leave it for a while?' he asked tentatively, with just the tiniest hint of a cautionary smirk.

'Open it, please,' said Lauren turning to Jeff.

'Paris?' she repeated inquisitively.

'Banbury's have asked me to take a small team over to meet their European division's marketing team. They are having a rethink on their strategy and would like some input from you, as your UK campaign is working so well.'

'Oh, I see, but when?'

'In the next few weeks would be good.'

'That quick?'

'They are keen to understand the methodology behind what you have done here and would like to incorporate it into their European marketing program.'

'How long would it be for?'

'A few days, a week at most.'

'That should not be a problem, but I should discuss it with Michael first. We have never been apart since we married.'

That was when she realised she had forgotten; she was, in fact, married! Somehow in all the confusion, that tiny detail had slipped her mind...

'I understand,' replied Jeff.

'But he is at home now, most of the time,' reasoned Lauren, carefully considering the situation.

'Yes,' agreed Jeff.

'So, it shouldn't be a problem?' replied Lauren reassuringly.

'So, tell me about your life?' said Jeff, subtly changing the topic of conversation.

'My life, why, it's not been particularly spectacular. There's not really much to tell.'

'Well... have you achieved all you set out to do?'

'I'm only thirty-two. There's a long way to go yet.'

'Are you on the right road then?'

'I think so. What about you?'

'I'm lazy, and anyway, my father passed the company to me, so my life was sort of mapped out from the start.'

'But you didn't have to stay if you didn't want to,'

'No, I didn't, but it's enjoyable. I meet nice people, and I have interesting lunches like now...' he held his hands out palm upwards to make the point, 'and it pays well.'

'So, are you looking for something different?' asked Lauren, detecting a hint of something, but she didn't quite know what.

'I don't know, maybe; maybe that's why I am so pleased that you are... working out so well in the company.'

'So, I am part of your escape plan?'

'In a way, yes, I suppose you are.'

'But what would you do if you didn't come into the office every day – you live on your own, so...?'

'You have a point. I don't know what I would do, but I know there is more to life than just this, and there is that book I always wanted to write.

'But is there?' asked Lauren.

'Is there what?'

'Is there more than this?'

'That sounds alarmingly existentialistic,' replied Jeff. With an expression that conveyed mild surprise tempered with an element of concern.

'I've never really understood what that means,' said Lauren. She was obviously taking the opportunity to redress this tiny gap in her education.

'To be honest, neither did I until my analyst explained it to me?'

'You have an analyst?' replied Lauren. She flashed him a curious inquisitorial look.

'Oh, it's okay,' replied Jeff smiling - taking Lauren's quizzical expression look in good nature. 'I'm not a nutter with a screw loose or anything like that. It's just that sometimes it's good to talk to somebody about different things - it helps to put my mind at ease. He's a friend anyway, so his fee is reasonably decent.'

'Mates rates?'

'Not that decent,' replied Jeff smiling.

'So, what do you talk about?'

'Sometimes we just talk about things that have happened during the week and how I should adjust to changes - and sometimes we just talk about the "E" word.'

'The "E" word?' repeated Lauren quizzically?

'You mentioned it just now.'

'Oh, I see.'

'One of our two deepest fears in life ironically is the inevitability of death. The other is being alone in complete isolation. You can't do much about the first, so you learn to accept it, as most of us manage to do. The other we can do something about, and through this, we can create a reason for life when there isn't any. Existence is meaningless unless you have something or someone to fill the space. It's the empty moments filled with nothingness that cause immeasurable damage. That is when you begin to think about the precarious and vacuous nature of life. It can be a vicious circle.'

'I think he's right, I would be bored stupid if I had to stay home every day, but I still wonder about it in the quieter moments.'

'Those are the dangerous times,' said Jeff.

'Are they,' replied Lauren, but she didn't say it as a question, more in a retrospective tone.

'Does that explain it at all?' The depth of their conversation had almost blocked out every other sound in the restaurant. It seemed odd that becoming so deeply involved in a discussion could do that. It wasn't a situation that arose that often for Jeff or

Lauren. It felt strange to connect with somebody at this almost Zen-like level.

'Yes, it does, in a way, a little.'

'So, you see, it's important to talk, it's important to love, and most of all, it's important to fill our lives doing something worthwhile.'

'I think what I do is worthwhile,' volleyed Lauren.

'It is, to the company and to me, unquestionably. But do you really believe it fulfils a need, or is it something we do to fill a void that somebody else has created?'

'Two lobster salads,' interrupted the waiter with his usual, perfect timing.

'Wonderful, that should fill the void in my stomach,' said Jeff light-heartedly. The weighty tone of their conversation lifted temporarily.

'Me too,' agreed Lauren smiling. The conversation had been a little more intense than she had expected for lunchtime. But it did give her something to think about.

'Enough of the depressing, philosophical claptrap,' said Jeff, 'what about this Paris thing? Have you ever been there?' He took a large sip of his Iced Tea.

'No, I never have.'

'You will love it. Paris will fill your senses till they overflow. Then it will mesmerise, enrapture, overwhelm and consume you until you can't think anymore. I have always treasured the city where I never feel alone, no matter what the circumstances. Paris is where there is no time to ponder on the things that do not matter, only on the things that bring joy to your life at that moment.'

'Tell me more,' said Lauren. 'You make it sound like another world a million miles away from here.'

'I would rather show you than tell you.' It was a relatively obvious question but presented subtly. Lauren wasn't sure what to say.

'Let's eat dinner,' she said, 'while I give your proposal further thought.'

'Yes, excellent idea, we'll eat, and I will tell you about some of the wondrous things about Paris... but not all.'

'That sounds perfect,' said Lauren.

'To Paris and...?' said Jeff, the sentence left unfinished. He lifted his cocktail glass to toast the proposition.

Lauren looked mindfully at Jeff and lifted her wine glass. 'To Paris and...' They tapped their glasses and smiled.

CHAPTER 22

Because she is Lithuanian?

'I've been asked to go to Paris for a conference next week for three, possibly four days. Will that be okay with you?' asked Lauren casually over dinner.

'Paris, that sounds amazing,' replied Michael. 'Great company jolly?'

'No, not really. We have a meeting with the board of directors of Banbury Europe. They want us to review their current marketing strategy.'

'Sounds very important.'

'It could be. The French office liked what I did with the UK programme. They think it might work in France, conceivably better than the campaign run by the company they have been using until now.'

'So, you could be working in Paris?' replied Michael, slightly concerned.

'Well, I'm not sure how I will fit in yet, and my French isn't that good anyway.'

'It's better than mine,' replied Michael

'You don't speak Fr…. ah, I see,' she smiled.

'So how will it work exactly?' asked Michael. 'It obviously won't just be the three days?

'Jeff mentioned that it could mean spending time in Paris each month if everything goes as planned. A lot depends on whether they like me.'

'I am sure they will. What's not to like?'

'Thank you,' replied Lauren. 'That's lovely.' She smiled.

'How much time?'

'Could be three, maybe four days a month. Do you think you could cope?' It was a searching question with much more to it than just the number of days.

'Yes, I could, but being away for….'

'Nothing is for certain yet,' interrupted Lauren. 'It will all depend on how things work out next week. It could all come to nothing.'

'Well, let's keep our fingers crossed. Well done.' He held his wine glass up to toast her good news, but he wasn't sure how he felt about the proposal.

'To Paris.' They clinked glasses and smiled, but Lauren felt a slight pang of guilt prick her conscience - not something she was accustomed to. Lauren knew, deep down, that however much she tried to hide it, she could not wait to get to Paris. But more importantly, she found herself becoming exhilarated and elated at the thought of spending a few days away from home with Jeff. Even though nothing had really happened yet - but the thought of Paris had already begun to work its magic.

As Lauren was obviously in a good mood since she had arrived home that night, Michael thought he would seize the opportunity to mention Leja's change in circumstances.

'There is a less important matter I need to talk to you about....' He paused for a few seconds to take a sip of wine. For a moment, Lauren's daydream fell back as she swiftly returned to earth, unsure of what was to come. A few possibilities quickly ran through her mind.

'Leja has asked me to ask you if it would be all right if... she could stay over the weekends in future. Apparently, she has broken up with Walter, so she no longer has anywhere to sleep on Friday and Saturday nights.'

'Oh, I see; that is terribly sad news.' Lauren was relieved. 'I thought they were getting on so well, even going to be married.' Under the circumstances, Lauren thought she could afford to be flexible regarding the suggestion, especially as she might be away for a few days each month. In fact, if it became a regular thing, having Leja around a bit more could be extremely useful.

'Apparently not,' replied Michael. 'Leja mentioned something about him moving closer to London because there is more work there, but Leja didn't want to move away from the village.'

'That's a little odd.'

'Why?'

'Well, I've spoken to her several times to find out her long-term plans, and I understood they would move closer to London in the next year or two anyway.'

'Well, she's obviously changed her mind. Girls do, don't they, probably for reasons we will never understand.' He felt a severe stab of pain in the middle of his back and almost turned around to see what it was.

'I wonder why she didn't mention it to me,' asked Lauren curiously?

'Probably a little embarrassed,' suggested Michael.

'I don't see why. It's a reasonable ask, as she lives here all week anyway.'

'Maybe, it's because she's Lithuanian. Maybe they think about things differently.' It was a lame explanation without a shred of credibility, and he knew it.

Lauren stopped eating and looked at Michael in disbelief. 'Because she's Lithuanian! For God's sake, what's that to do with anything?'

'I don't know. It was just a thought.'

'Was it... well, it sounds like a very bizarre one to me. Still, having Leja around will be handy if I am away.' She continued eating, pondering quietly over Michael's strange presumption.

'More wine?' asked Michael, hovering the bottle over Lauren's glass.

'Yes, please. Thank you.'

'It means you must take Daisy to school next week while I'm away.'

'No problem. I don't have a great deal on right now.' He smiled at his self-deprecatory quip.

'I'm sure you will soon,' replied Lauren reassuringly. 'So, you'll be okay?' she added after a few moments.

'Yes, yes, of course. I am sure Leja and I can get Daisy safely to school and back.'

'Good, good,' said Lauren.

'So, I can tell her that's okay then?'

'I don't see why not, but things might change if I don't get the Paris job.'

'I'm sure you will,' replied Michael smiling supportively. *If you don't, I'm in the crap big time,* flashed through his mind.

'So, when will Leja start sleeping at weekends?'

'This weekend. She was hoping to move her belongings from their flat tomorrow.'

'Oh, that soon.'

'I understand the situation is very strained at Walter's right now, so I think the sooner, the better for her.'

'Fine, no problem.'

'I'd better go and tell her after dinner, so she can arrange things for tomorrow,' suggested Michael.

'That's okay,' said Lauren, 'I'll tell her; then we can have a little heart-to-heart over what has happened. She probably feels fragile and down in the dumps right now, so she won't want you blundering about.'

'I don't go blundering about,' replied Michael, slightly incensed at Lauren's criticism. He could have elaborated but then decided against it.

'I'm sorry, I didn't mean it like that. I meant to say Leja is probably looking for someone to talk to about what happened. She has been going out with Walter for a couple of years, so it must be very upsetting for her with it all suddenly ending for no reason.' Michael took a sip of wine, which nearly went down the wrong hole.

'Fair enough, I see what you mean,' he replied in the best conciliatory tone he could muster.

He didn't want to appear too helpful and supportive; it would be out of character for him, and he knew that much. But visions of everything coming out in their little heart-to-heart and all hell breaking loose did flash through his mind. It had all been a bit stupid – getting involved with Leja just for a fun fuck whenever he felt like it. It was only out of boredom, after all. He would probably never have thought about it had he not been at home for nine months. Rattling around all day doing nothing, with Leja flitting around the house, did not help. He would have been safer with Rosemary, but it was far too late now for recriminations over that decision. What was done was done, and he would just have to get on with it as best he could.

'Are you okay, Michael?' asked Lauren.

'Sorry, what did you say?' asked Michael, suddenly realising he was still eating dinner with Lauren. 'I was miles away.'

'You've gone quite pale. Are you feeling okay? There's nothing wrong with the chicken, is there?'

'No, no, the chicken's fine. I was just thinking about work and whether I could get back into it. It's a bit worrying sometimes, not being able to support you all.'

'You don't have to worry. If I take on this European proposal with Banbury's, they'll nearly double my salary, so there is nothing to worry about money-wise.... nothing at all.'

If only it were that simple, thought Michael. 'Yes, you're right, we will be fine,' he smiled and finished his dinner. Lauren stood up and cleared the table.

'Strawberries and cream for afters?' asked Lauren.

'What?' replied Michael. Momentarily alarmed by the offer. 'Oh yes, that would be nice, thank you.' A vision of Leja suddenly appeared behind Lauren - with cream running over her nipples.

'Are you sure you're okay? You're acting very strangely tonight.'

'Yes, fine, just a little tired.'

'Oh, right.' She placed the strawberries on the table, put a few into two bowls, poured on some cream, and passed one to Michael. They ate them in silence. Lauren wondered why Michael appeared a little odd tonight. Michael looked apprehensively at the last two intimidating strawberries in his bowl. They seemed to be looking straight back at him, somehow taunting him. He devoured them quickly before glancing briefly behind Lauren to check if Leja was still there, but she wasn't. 'Thank God!' he muttered.

'Sorry?' said Lauren, glancing up, surprised at his utterance.

'Thank God! Yes, thank God for strawberries. I love them,' he smiled oddly. 'What would we do without them?' It was a pathetic explanation for his remark, and he knew it.

Lauren gazed at Michael, speculating whether he had completely lost his mind. Maybe he was going stir-crazy being at home for so long. She let the incident pass. Ascribing it to a cerebral blip or possible early indicator of Alzheimer's... No, maybe that was going a bit too far, she reasoned. But she would keep an eye on him anyway. He had definitely been acting a little strange just lately.

'Could you tidy up the tea things and load the dishwasher while I just pop in to see Leja and have a word?'

Michael just nodded.

Lauren wandered off to Leja's part of the cottage and knocked on her bedroom door. 'Leja, could I come in for a few moments?'

Leja jumped up and opened the door. 'Yes, of course, come in. Please sit down. I turn television down.' Lauren perched herself on the corner of the bed.

'Michael has explained your predicament, and I just wanted to tell you that it is fine for you to stay here over the weekends as well.' She smiled, 'I am sorry to hear about you and Walter breaking up. I thought you two got on so well together.'

'We did, but things change. Something happened, and now we don't.'

'Is there nothing I can do to help,' asked Lauren? She knew there wasn't, but she had to ask anyway.

'No, thank you, Lauren. I think everything is done.'

'Right, I see. Anyway, just so there is no confusion, I just wanted to say that we will not expect you to do anything over the weekends just because you are here. That will still be the same as before. But boyfriends might be a problem, so if we say....'

'No problem, Lauren,' interjected Leja. 'I understand. If I have new boyfriend, we make the love at his house, not here.'

'I hope that's still okay. I know it's a bit prudish, but with Daisy at a very impressionable age. I don't want her to think that adults have sex anywhere at any time. It might set a bad example.'

'I understand...' replied Leja, biting her lip while just managing to restrain herself from bursting into laughter. She thought about Michael screwing her on the same bed that Lauren was now sitting on. Over the kitchen table where they all ate dinner - in the bath, Lauren's bedroom because it was bigger than the one in Leja's bathroom. Even on the hammock in the garden where Lauren liked to sit on warm summer days.

'...I understand completely,' repeated Leja.

'Good,' said Lauren. 'I'm glad we both understand.'

Leja smiled as Lauren left.

On Friday morning, Lauren went into the office as usual, dropping Daisy off on her way. They didn't pass Katie, which was unfortunate because Lauren hoped to see her today. Somehow, Lauren thought Katie might be able to give her spiritual guidance on the decision she would soon have to make, albeit on a subliminal level.

Over the weekend, Lauren packed her suitcase for the following week as there wouldn't be much time on Monday. Flitting through her underwear drawer, she came across a red frilly chemise and thong that she'd had for some time but had never worn. Lauren could not remember where it had come from but guessed it would have been a present from Michael. She seldom bought racy items for herself. Lauren slipped her clothes off to try it on, and it fitted, which for some reason, surprised her. She flounced around in front of the mirror, catching all angles to see if there was any aspect that might not look so flattering. There weren't. So she carefully lifted it off and packed it into her suitcase.

Michael popped his head around the door while she was still standing naked. 'Would you like a cup of tea?'

For some reason, Lauren suddenly felt guilty and strangely embarrassed. She quickly picked up her knickers and put them on, trying to not make her sudden twinge of self-consciousness look too obvious. 'Oh, yes, please, thank you, darling... no need to bring it up. I'll be down in a couple of minutes.'

'Okay, well, actually... as you are - as you are, so to speak, do you fancy a little....' his eyes were beaming with anticipation. Lauren knew exactly what was coming but didn't want to have...

'Dad!' bellowed Daisy up the staircase. 'My computer's not working. Can you fix it?'

'Bugger,' said Michael with a sigh, looking instantly deflated.

'Never mind, darling, another time,' whispered Lauren, shooting him a consolatory smile, and blowing a puckered kiss off her hand. She twirled around, safe in the knowledge that he had been commandeered for other more urgent duties. She could resume packing her 'tryst trousseau.' She carefully chose the other garments and underwear she would take and neatly laid them in the case, with some dowdier bits on top, just in case. When she finished packing, she closed the case, tied the straps, and gazed at it thoughtfully. Suddenly, she realised the significance of what she was preparing for. She had never done anything like this before. Her strict Catholic upbringing left an ineradicable caveat over the immorality of infidelity burnt indelibly into her soul. She did not entertain this lambent desire lightly. But felt inexorably drawn towards this liaison for reasons she could not readily explain. Just as Icarus was drawn closer to the sun, Lauren was being drawn to the flame. But she was only too aware of the danger of flying too close...

As Lauren drove over Shelbury Bridge on Monday morning, she saw Katie and her family on the other side of the road, as usual, walking to school. Today, she looked like she was just about ready to give birth.

Today, there was a heavy mist, which only enhanced the otherworldly image so innocently portrayed before her. She felt inspired and uplifted by what she saw. It imbued a breathtaking sense of delight and pleasure at just being alive. Lauren could feel a sense of thankfulness radiating from her body for being able to enjoy what she was experiencing. But today, she also felt another completely different feeling, a dark, shivering sensation travelling slowly down her back before it ebbed away. Katie glanced over at Lauren and smiled, and Lauren gazed back at Katie and smiled in return. It was the first time they had ever acknowledged each other. Lauren began to experience a warmth emanating from Katie's soul, reaching out across the road and touching hers. Maybe Katie was sending a message about Lauren's forthcoming journey to Paris. Perhaps a warning - perhaps something else altogether, but it was all very unusual, such was the puzzling effect that Katie had on her. Lauren wanted to stop the car, jump out, run across the road, and entreat Katie's opinion. She wanted to seek her guidance, her counsel, for she knew beyond doubt that Katie would be wise and honest with her advice. It would be untainted by circumstance or reproach.

She could ask whether going to Paris was wise when she was already attracted to her boss. The man who was going with her and with whom she had already had a serious kiss. A serious kiss! She thought to herself for a moment. What the hell is a serious kiss? I suppose one that nearly wrecks a restaurant could be considered serious. One that makes many promises is also serious, and that kiss made many. But what would Katie advise? Lauren had nobody else she could confide in, nobody to warn or tell her about the problems that could lie ahead on this other road least travelled. That, of course, depended on whether Lauren decided to take that road. But that was becoming less of a possible and more of a probable outcome the more she thought about it.

Unfortunately, she did not know Katie, so she could not seek guidance. Katie would forever remain oblivious to the questions Lauren wanted to ask. And Lauren would remain oblivious to the advice she may have received. She would have to accept that this was her destiny for now. Lauren could have spoken to Rosemary, her mother, but Rosemary always spoke from the head, not from the heart, so that would have been of little use or comfort. And anyway, she had Daisy in the back seat of the car. She could hardly leave her stranded in the middle of the bridge - as she casually wandered across the road to have a serious conversation with an absolute stranger about the pros and cons of casual adultery. That would be ridiculous. She smiled to herself, almost in despair, and drove on, dropping Daisy off at school before heading off to the station.

On Tuesday morning, leaving a little earlier than usual, Michael drove Daisy to school, dropping Lauren off at Godalming station. Fortunately, they did not pass Katie.

'Now you have a wonderful time, and don't let them intimidate you. I know what the Froggies are like – they can be right bastards. I do hope everything goes to plan.' Michael's closing words just before Lauren stepped out of the car made her smile.

'I'm sure it will. I feel extremely confident about this.' She felt confident about most aspects of her trip, but not all.

Michael knew she would have carefully planned every aspect of the week ahead, but not the precise itinerary. That was locked away in Lauren's head; he would never be privy to that.

Michael jumped out of the car at the station and lifted the suitcases out of the boot.

'Christ, that one is heavy. You sure you're only going for four days?' Michael measured holidays by the weight of the luggage; it was a surprisingly good yardstick. A twenty-kilogram hold bag usually meant three weeks in the Caribbean, not four days in Paris.

'The weather might suddenly change,' replied Lauren apologetically. 'I have to be prepared for anything.' She felt another sharp pang of guilt surge swiftly through her stomach, not dissimilar to the one she had felt in the restaurant the week before. This was the worst part of pending infidelity: the trepidation, anxiety, and angst. Dispose of those inseparable comrades of conscience, and she would be free. Anyway, she was sure the extras she had packed did not weigh much – if anything at all…

Michael smiled and gave her a kiss and a hug. 'Give me a call on Saturday when you land, and I will come and pick you up from here.'

'I will. Now, are you sure you will be okay till I return?' asked Lauren.

'Yes, absolutely,' replied Michael. 'We will struggle by.'

'Right, okay.'

Lauren wandered off, pulling her two cases behind her, and Michael jumped back into the car and drove back home.

Back indoors, Leja greeted him like she did most mornings if he had popped out for fresh croissants. Naked, apart from the tiniest G-string, a touch of perfume, a little makeup and a baseball cap perched on the top of her head.

He couldn't help but notice that her body really was terrific. Try as he might, he could not resist the temptation to indulge himself a little further, despite the problems that had already been created.

'You don't look pregnant,' said Michael, tilting his head half an inch off-centre as if that might give him a better perspective on her condition.

'Are you sure sex is okay?' he added cautiously, forgetting that he'd had sex with Lauren up to a few weeks before Daisy was born.

'Sure, I am good to go. Let's play bang fuck.'

Somewhat reluctantly, he followed Leja as she provocatively wandered back to her bedroom, waggling her arse as she went. They spent the next few hours having sex and doing various other things before coming back out to have something to eat at around two o'clock. Hopefully, the small weals on his arse would be gone in a few days. Nobody would ever see the bite marks on Leja's except Michael.

CHAPTER 23

Gatwick Games.

May 2009

Lauren and Jeff arranged to meet at Costa coffee in Gatwick at ten o'clock. Jeff had already been there nearly thirty minutes before Lauren arrived. He was beginning to feel a little concerned, thinking that maybe there had been a problem with traffic and they would miss their flight, or a problem with Michael and she wouldn't be coming after all. Then he saw her crossing the shopping concourse, pulling her cabin suitcase behind her, and any concerns he had quickly evaporated.

'I was beginning to think that maybe you'd changed your mind,' said Jeff, standing up as she arrived at his table.

Lauren smiled, stood her case up and did not say a word. She embraced him and gave him the longest kiss he could ever remember anyone giving him. Longer even than the kiss they shared in Zefe's restaurant, which had precipitated such disastrous consequences. Longer even than the kisses his mother gave him when she dropped him off at school. Something which always caused considerable embarrassment and made him the subject of constant ragging from his friends. It was a memory that had haunted him for many years.

Just for a few seconds, while they were locked in their embrace, Jeff began to experience the first tremblings of an arousal, which felt a little embarrassing in the middle of the airport lounge. The kiss quickly reassured him that she had not changed her mind because she probably also knew what was happening. But more importantly, as far as he was concerned, his equipment appeared fully functional, which could sometimes be a matter of concern. She smiled at Jeff as they parted, and he knew she knew what was happening.

'About what?' She whispered as they parted. Jeff quickly sat down. It was unlike her to be so salaciously provocative in public. She knew that, and it even surprised her. She felt liberated, overwhelmed by the urge to sever ties that had restrained her for so long. For once, she could be herself, throw all inhibitions to the wind, and grasp hold of life once again, albeit only for a few days.

But she would make the most of it, that much she had promised herself, even before she left home that morning.

'Well, nothing so it appears,' replied Jeff smiling, still recovering from the kiss and other issues. 'I thought that maybe Michael had put his foot down and....'

'Michael doesn't put his foot down when I'm the only one working.'

Right, thought Jeff, making a mental note. 'Fair enough.'

'Shall we have a drink?' suggested Lauren.

'Bit early to get pissed, isn't it?'

'I meant coffee. We can have a drink later.'

'Oh, sorry, I thought...' He wasn't really thinking at all. In fact, the only thing he could think of at that moment was whether he could persuade Lauren to have sex with him in the lady's lavatory. His body had taken control of his brain and seemed to be running amok. That was a ridiculous idea, he reasoned. *Get yourself under control,* he told himself. So he put that idea right out of his mind.

'We are really going to enjoy this little holiday,' said Jeff.

'Are we?' said Lauren teasing him a little. 'I thought it was just business,' she continued with a glazed expression of muted surprise.

'I think we can easily sort the business out during the days, hopefully in the mornings. Then we can spend the afternoons walking around Paris, seeing the sights - if that's what you would like to do,' he added with an inquisitorial tone.

'That sounds wonderful,' said Lauren, and oddly, she felt good about it inside, which was where she thought there might have been a problem, but that didn't appear to be the case so far. *Maybe the guilt would kick in later,* she thought. It wasn't a sense of betrayal that seemed to hover quietly above her head, casting a tiny shadow. That's what she was expecting. It was the sudden realisation that she had somehow wrestled back control of her life for a few days.

She had never felt underappreciated or taken for granted. But the silent matrimonial killers – despisal, pity and complacency, had stealthily begun to creep into their marriage since Michael had been made redundant. It was starting to feel like they were just going through the motions. Two people merely inhabiting the same space but not really relating to each other and not enjoying the relationship anymore. For the last couple of years, the highlight of Lauren's week — had been the occasional sighting of a woman she didn't know wandering over a bridge taking her family to school. It was the emotional apex, something that had touched her deeply inside

When she thought about that, she realised what a sad existence she had been living. And the further away she was, the clearer she could see it. Ironically, the distance was lending a paradoxical clarifying disenchantment.

Yes, she did have Daisy, who filled many voids, and she had a fantastic job. But neither of these somehow seemed to fulfil all her ambitions. But now, the challenge of running a major division of Banbury's had arisen. Coupled with the possibility of an affair with Jeff, this had revitalised her. Made her feel as if she were whole again. She shouldn't have been feeling like this; it was wrong, and she knew it, but the truth was, that was how she felt, and nothing could change that. *Above all else, to thine own self be true.* She had read the words somewhere a few years ago, and occasionally, the aphorism came into her head as if to prompt her whenever she felt indecisive.

Over coffee, they chatted about various inconsequential work-related matters, but Lauren wasn't really listening. In her head, she was trying to find the rationale for how what was happening might change her life and whether she wanted it to change.

'That's our flight,' said Jeff, interrupting her thoughts.

'Oh, right,' replied Lauren, gulping down the last of her coffee before grabbing her hand luggage.

'Is that all you have?' asked Jeff, looking curiously at her surprisingly small piece of hand luggage.

Lauren looked at Jeff quizzically. 'I thought just a pair of knickers and some shoes would be enough,' she replied coquettishly. 'This is just four days of unyieldingly remorselessly sadomasochistic sex and drunken debauchery, isn't it? Starting on the plane, I presume?' Lauren's deadpan expression did not change one iota. The lady at the next table, astonished at hearing Lauren's declaration, spilt the coffee she was holding to her lips. Lauren suddenly realised what she had said. It was completely unexpected and unplanned; somehow, it just came out that way.

She was experiencing a silent primal scream of freedom unencumbered by conventional behavioural expectations, and it felt good. She probably wouldn't do half the things she was proposing - but it felt fantastically liberating to casually lob in a grenade and watch the reaction. This was freedom…

Jeff's mouth dropped open for a second before he realised she was probably winding him up... They both laughed.

'I checked my bag,' said Lauren after a pregnant pause. 'It's much bigger than this.' They both stood up and slowly made their way towards the departure gate.

'I wouldn't mind,' replied Jeff casually. 'Bugger the business, I say. There is more to life than….'

'Oh,' said Lauren sounding surprised. 'I thought advertising was your life.'

'No, life is my life, and I want to live it now, not in the future. Work is just the means to an end… I need…' He was going to say something else but stopped realising he may have recently read those words on a car bumper sticker. *Christ! he thought, my brain is turning into a cliché.*

Nevertheless, it was a surprisingly revealing admission. Just for a moment, the words dangled listlessly in the air while Lauren carefully processed the axiom before eventually allowing it to settle between her hippocampus and prefrontal cortex. Somewhere where she would have constant access to it. She would undoubtedly revisit those words many times in the coming days and deliberate on their intent.

It was salient and resounding, and in so many ways, it summed up what Jeff was all about. He was a live-now-pay-later person, not just someone who talked about it. 'Can I tell you something?' asked Jeff.

'What?' said Lauren.

'When we kissed in the lounge….'

'Yes.'

'I wanted to drag you into the washroom, and…' he paused for a moment - a young couple rushed past them, apparently in a hurry to catch a flight.

'And do what exactly,' asked Lauren playfully? She turned briefly to glance at Jeff - puckering her lips and scrunching her eyebrows, affecting a naïve, childlike innocence. He smiled...

Audrey Hepburn, in a *Breakfast at Tiffany's* type coquettish expression, was the only way he could describe how she looked. The film was one of his all-time favourites, particularly the emotional closing scene in the rain, which always, but always brought tears to his eyes.

'Make love to you!' It was not quite how it played out in the film, but it was close enough.

'Make love to me?' repeated Lauren curiously, tilting her head slightly as if she didn't quite understand what he meant. 'Please expand a little. I'm confused. I need a little more detail?' All she really wanted was to hear were the words... That would turn it on for her.

'Fuck you,' whispered Jeff. 'I wanted to bang your brains out in the bog.'

'Oh!' Lauren casually replied, grinning at the amusing alliteration while glancing around to see if anybody else heard. But, disappointingly, there was no one close. 'I see.' She smiled demurely, gently biting her top lip - utterly unfazed by Jeff's explicit suggestion. They walked swiftly towards the departure gate without breaking a step or saying anything. The frisson of anticipation indolently perched itself on an invisible thread - strung out between them like a vacuum waiting to be filled before Lauren eventually answered. 'You should have mentioned it earlier. I was feeling a little peckish. Haven't had a decent fuck in ages.'

Jeff coughed but didn't say anything immediately, his train of thought severely disrupted by Lauren's unexpected declaration. He quietly admonished himself for not having been more forthright. It would have been fun if a little rushed, but that bird had flown. Still, there would be other birds, many other birds... hopefully.

He knew then he would have his work cut out for the next four days keeping up with Lauren, but he was also beginning to relish the thought.

'Maybe we can sort something out on the plane,' suggested Jeff, but somehow it seemed to lose something without the spontaneity. There was also a tiny hint of self-flagellating desperation in his tone.

'Have you seen the size of the toilets?' asked Lauren. 'We would have to do it in two halves.'

'Two halves?' enquired Jeff. 'How does that work?'

'Well, you pop in and get started, and when you come out, I'll pop in and finish off.'

Jeff looked a little beleaguered and profoundly confused by the suggestion. That certainly wasn't how they did it in the film he'd seen, as far as he remembered.

'Is that how they do it?' he asked in the manner of somebody who had just learnt something completely new.

Lauren looked at Jeff with her mouth half-open, amused by his endearing innocence. She was undeniably going to enjoy these few days; it would be a little different and a lot of fun. In fact, it was going to be a lot different.

They made their way through the gate and boarded the plane. It was only half full today, and they quickly settled in for the journey to Paris.

CHAPTER 24

Be Happy with My Life...

June 2009

A few weeks had passed since Lauren returned from Paris. The weather had been warm for nearly a month. Finally, summer clothing was worn without the traditional English reserve and distrust of the unpredictable elements. As usual, Lauren was driving Daisy to school and hoping she might see Katie and her children walking over Shelbury Bridge. Lauren had not seen Katie for nearly three weeks, but today she was lucky. There she was, wearing a long, floaty, almost ethereal white gipsy dress and top, which, although completely covering her bump, could no longer hide it. That's strange, thought Lauren. I thought she would have had the baby weeks ago. Her mind drifted off for a few seconds. She wondered, a little whimsically, whether girls do grow plump in the night - as they sleep, and whether one day again, she would become one of the girls who grew plump in the night. It was a peculiar notion, and she had no idea where it came from, but it amused her, and she smiled at the thought. Pregnant again. Now that was a thought.

Katie appeared so gloriously happy to be pregnant and wanted the world to know about it. She was stunningly beautiful in that uncomplicated, economical way that some confident women manage to achieve with what appears to be so little effort. It belied the considerable effort she had obviously made to appear that way. But it worked, and it added something to the moment.

For a few seconds, Katie stopped walking and turned to look at Lauren again. It was only the second time that she had ever acknowledged her. And as they gazed at each other, Lauren felt a strange tingling sensation down her spine, just as before. But it was gone in a moment, and then she began to sense this peculiar unearthly connection between them, something she had never experienced before. Katie seemed to be saying something to her, but her lips weren't moving, yet she could clearly hear the words in her head: *Be happy with my life... Please be happy with my life.* Katie smiled at Lauren, and Lauren could swear the whole bridge suddenly became brighter and more colourful for a few seconds.

Lauren felt as if she were encapsulated, lost, immersed within the moment - no longer in control of her body. She smiled back as if to say, I will. I promise. And then Katie smiled for the last time, seemingly relieved and comforted by Lauren's visual assurance. Katie turned and resumed her journey with her family, and Lauren drove on. The moment had passed. Later that day, Lauren's mind wandered back to the incident on the bridge, and she thought over what had happened and why - but it would be some time before she would have the answer.

'Are you still friends with Poppy?' asked Lauren casually a few minutes later.

'Sort of. Why?' replied Daisy curiously. Constantly wary of any questions her mother asked that fell outside the realm of regular conversational spheres. She was ever conscious of the hidden agenda in what appeared to be - on the surface - an apparently innocent enquiry. Not for one moment did she consider her mother to have any Machiavellian tendencies, but it never hurt to have a healthy enquiring nature when parents made specific enquiries such as this.

'You should invite her over to tea sometime. Maybe she could stay overnight if you would like that?'

'I will think about it, but we aren't in the same class any longer, so I don't see her quite as much as I used to,' replied Daisy, never one to make rash decisions. She had learnt the subtle art of timing and watchfulness from her parents, or so she thought. Never realising how receptive they had become to spontaneous, unreasoned, impulsive decisions, sometimes with potentially devastating consequences. Daisy did wonder why her mother had made the suggestion when she had never mentioned it before. Maybe when I grow older, I should become a detective or even a private eye, she mused. But that probably involves standing around in the rain a lot and wearing a big hat, so maybe not.

'Well, it's your birthday soon. If you like, you could invite a few of your school friends over for a party. You could even have a barbecue. Daddy would love to cook the burgers for you.' "He doesn't have anything else to do at the moment" ran through her mind, but that is where it stayed.

Daisy didn't answer straight away, giving the matter further careful consideration.

Lauren's attention was momentarily distracted by the artists and photographers who had begun to return to the valley just below the bridge. Strategically spacing themselves out along the two embankments - staking a claim to their preferred positions for their stay. Each of them earnestly believed that their chosen location was the best available for their unique perspective on the panorama opening up before them. And just a little superior to any other position on this day. Each one, possibly believing their chosen location would afford them the sui generis opportunity to create their daylight version of Van Gogh's Starry Starry Night – Twinkly Twinkly Day?

In some ways, it was a bit like life: you see it from the same perspective year after year. You become so accustomed to it that you eventually conclude it couldn't be any better than it is at that precise moment. Then one day, something unexpected happens. Some otherworldly force nudges you to move just a few inches to the left or the right, and you suddenly see everything from an entirely different perspective. That's when you suddenly realise that maybe you were completely wrong all along. This could be happening to her right now, she mused. Perhaps, she was now seeing life from just a few inches to the left... or the right.

'Look at the water, mummy,' said Daisy. 'It looks wonderful.'

Lauren glanced down towards the river. It was higher than usual for this time of year. But still, it tripped, tumbled, and fell over the rocks, creating swirling pools and gashes of white water. So much beloved by the purists ardently striving to capture the transient experience of light, shadow, and movement. The sun would rise above the woods on the far side very soon. And the whole scene would be bathed in glorious early morning sunlight. The heart, soul and spirit of the river would come alive.

Lauren drove on and eventually dropped Daisy off at school.

'Don't forget what I said about Poppy staying overnight. Any Friday to Sunday is fine. Just let me know in good time, so I can arrange things.'

'Okay, Mum,' replied Daisy, kissing her mother before skipping away down the pathway to the main gates, wondering what 'things' were and why her mother was so keen on the sleepover.

Lauren carried on to the station and parked in her usual parking place. By an unspoken arrangement, regular commuters who used the car park had selected specific spots where they would park their cars each day.

No driver would ever consider parking in any bay other than the one designated under this apocryphal arrangement. What would happen if a new driver inadvertently parked in one of these predetermined spots was anybody's guess? Fortunately, it had never happened – so far. The system relied solely on good manners and a sort of parking etiquette that had developed over time, similar in some ways to the peculiarly British habit of forming orderly queues. A quintessentially British idiosyncrasy but utterly alien to the French and most of Europe. Germany was the only other country where she had experienced anything similar. Where, for whatever reason – or one which she could not fathom – the shoppers in the larger cities always walked on the right-hand side of the pavement. It was as if it was the law, and there was a clearly defined yet invisible centre line over which you would not cross. You were in trouble if you happened to stray over this line by chance. You would either quickly reverse the direction you were travelling to avoid the crush of people marching directly at you or swiftly step back over the invisible line. If it became essential for you to walk across the flow of oncoming pedestrian traffic, you would need to be decisive and tenacious - adopting an air of firm and earnest resolve. This was essential. If not, you would immediately be subjected to a host of Wagnerian glares and mutterings - explicitly intended to intimidate the unwittingly delinquent shopper and instantly wither them to dust.

You would also be well advised to move smartly to avoid being crushed underfoot. Germans can be surprisingly aggressive when provoked.

All these mundane thoughts jostled for position in Lauren's mind as she boarded the 8.52 to Waterloo. But overwhelmingly, the memories that took precedence over everything else were the afternoons and nights of passion she had spent with Jeff in Paris just a few weeks earlier. There had been no order nor rhyme or reason for what had happened. She had half-anticipated that it would be long, dull days of business meetings and discussions. Possibly poring over marketing plans and strategies, which to no small degree, it was. Maybe, after a late lunch each day, after work had finished, she and Jeff would spend the rest of each day wandering around the left bank of the Seine, watching the boats on the river. Or they would walk through the Latin Quarter's 5th and 6th arrondissements, drinking expresso coffee and Pernod in tiny pavement cafés or looking around antique shops and small art galleries. But all that had changed profoundly after their embrace just before boarding the plane at Gatwick.

Yes, sometimes, they would still sit in restaurants drinking coffee after the meetings were finished, and they would talk about their lives. Then they would slowly wander back, arms around each other, to their hotel. There, they would spend the late afternoon and early evening hours making love to the background sound of the traffic of Paris. It was idyllic, and not since she was first in love had she felt this way. He was seventeen, a boy whose name she could no longer remember. He was an unusual boy out of his time. Who, by rotation, regularly played albums by Juliet Greco, a French singer she had never heard of, or complete operas by Puccini. Somehow the music managed to summon up the silky, warm, fragrant atmosphere of Southern France and the Mediterranean. But they were in the bedroom of his house in downtown Pinner - where it always seemed to be raining. He had created something she could not find anywhere else, and she had become intoxicated. They smoked French cigarettes and cannabis - drank cheap red wine and discussed the revolution that would change the world. She loved every moment of it until it all ended suddenly after just three months when they both went off to university. They never saw each other again.

But she had learnt a lot about sex and a little about opera and radical left-wing politics. More importantly, she had learnt something about herself, and now, nearly fifteen years later, she felt the same feelings returning. That sense of exhilaration and expectation of things to come, of moving ahead to the next chapter, but not knowing the outcome.

It was all so languidly intense back then, pervasive, invasive, and all-consuming. They were swept up in the relentless amalgam of sexual exploration - the tart tang of body juices, the erotic aroma of exotic perfumes and oils, the uninhibited joy of inebriation fused with the music and impassioned conversation - always the conversation. All this overwhelmed her. Lauren and the unnamed boy would argue and scream loudly at each other about the values and benefits of social reform before reaching a perfectly timed writhing orgasm to the climax of Puccini's aria, 'Che Gelida Manina' from *La Bohème*. They would drink to excess and discuss the pros and cons of communist regimes and dictatorships. They would sit naked opposite each other on old bent cane chairs with just a candle on the table between them. Or they would lie on the floor gazing up at the ceiling, smoking marijuana and planning world peace while listening to Juliet Greco and speaking French – which they did poorly. Lauren would remember those moments – all the days of her life.

She and Jeff had not smoked cannabis. She gave that up many years ago. Nor had they listened to much music. But they drank champagne and made love to the sounds of hooting car horns and bicycle bells. The noise floated up from the road below. And each afternoon, as they made love, they grew to know each other more, each intimate part of their bodies, minds, and souls. Lauren thought... she hoped it would never end. It was all she had ever wanted, but it would end when the week was over, and she would return to Michael and carry on with her life as before. She knew that much, or at least she thought she did; she knew the rules and how the game was played.

Despite all that Lauren wished for, deep down, she knew she would probably never get what she really wanted, whatever that was.

'Do you bring all your staff to Paris and fuck their brains out all week?' Asked Lauren, lying back on her pillow and blowing out smoke rings while channelling a passable impression of Lauren Bacall. She didn't often smoke cigarettes but had felt an insatiable craving for one today.

They had been slowly drinking champagne and making love since mid-afternoon, and it was now early evening, and they were a little drunk, but not too much.

'I love it when you talk dirty,' remarked Jeff whimsically.

'You didn't answer my question.'

189

'Only the women,' replied Jeff languidly. 'I only make love to women. The others I leave to Zefe. He, too, has needs.'

Lauren smiled. 'All of them! I thought I was something special.'

'You are. You're the only one I haven't made love to... till now.'

'Oh, I see, just your plaything for today until you tire of me and toss me away like all the others.'

Jeff leaned over and kissed her again. Fortunately, she had just exhaled.

'Maybe.' They were still playing games.

'Can we go to a restaurant near the river?' asked Lauren.

'Of course. When would you like to eat?'

'Eight would be good.'

'But do we really need food? We could just carry on making love.' But he didn't mean it.

'I need food,' replied Lauren firmly. 'Soon.'

'Right,' said Jeff.

'Good,' said Lauren.

'We had better get dressed then. That only leaves you an hour.'

'Time for another...' asked Lauren, turning to face Jeff and smiling provocatively.

'Of course. Your wish is my...'

'You can manage it, then?' whispered Lauren cheekily.

Jeff rolled over on top of Lauren and convinced her that he could. Her right hand dangled by the side of the bed with small curls of smoke spiralling skywards from the cigarette as she looked up nonchalantly into his eyes. 'Can I just...'

Jeff stopped momentarily while Lauren carefully rolled the half-smoked cigarette around her fingers before deftly flicking it out of the open French veranda doors. It sailed gracefully over the ironwork balcony, hovering momentarily in mid-air before changing direction - falling gracefully to earth. When it landed, it probably startled someone standing on the pavement directly below their window. Someone who was innocently waiting to meet a friend. Someone who would always remain utterly unaware of the circumstances surrounding the origin of the airborne Gitane dog-end.

Jeff laughed at Lauren's carefree joie-de-vivre. Lesser mortals could have been easily intimidated or insulted by her casual laissez-faire childlike complacency, but he knew precisely where he stood – or lay, as was more apt, technically speaking. Lauren knew precisely where she featured in this arrangement; she was no longer a child. In the beginning, she thought it was love, and she was temporarily infatuated - but that stage soon passed, and sanity quickly returned. They would have a wonderful time, and then it would be over, and maybe that was all Lauren really wanted. For some reason, somewhere in the darkest corner of her soul, she already knew somebody else could give her all she wanted. She just didn't know yet, who that was.

After the cigarette disappeared, they resumed the pleasures of the day for another hour or so. They showered, dressed and went for dinner just before nine o'clock. It was a little later than planned, but that was no concern to either of them. They were not that hungry as it happened. It was merely a respite from the exigencies of the day and an opportunity to take in the wondrous sights of Paris by night. They ordered salad Niçoise followed by mussels with bacon and cider in cream, and more champagne. They sat in the restaurant until nearly one o'clock before eventually retiring to their hotel room to continue making love for the next few hours. They eventually fell asleep in each other's arms around four in the morning, just as a welcome breeze began gently blowing into their room from the north. Slowly Lauren wrapped the silence of the night around her body, the silence was impenetrable, and it protected her from the things on which she did not wish to dwell.

The following Monday, the train pulled into Waterloo on time, and Lauren made her way to the office by taxi as she always did, and nothing had changed.

CHAPTER 25

Dave the Dustman
Early August 2009

It was just after eight o'clock when Lauren eventually arrived home. Michael greeted her with his customary, if uninspiring, 'Hello darling. How was your day?'

It had become a conversational habit, followed by a no-nonsense peck on the cheek, which owed more to convention than affection.

Oh, how she yearned to be unexpectedly swept off her feet again in an embrace that would take her breath away. Whisked off on a magic carpet ride to some white sandy beach in the sun. Somewhere she could indulge herself with endless love and romance, but not today.

The opening gambit never varied very much, if at all – not even by inflexion. Had Michael bothered to demonstrate just a tiny hint of sincerity, he might have significantly enhanced the sense of genuine interest he was half-heartedly trying to convey.

Fortunately, Lauren's working day had always included the drive to the station from home, which occasionally was the most inspiring part of the day. Either because of the conversations she had with Daisy, which were always very enlightening and invariably entertaining, or the occasional sighting of Katie and her family. Something she found strangely inspiring. It made her long for something different. She just didn't know what. Unfortunately, she had not seen Katie for nearly three weeks because of the school holidays, so she felt a little lacklustre and in desperate need of something inspirational.

She would have loved to have told Michael how good it made her feel when she did see Katie and how it sustained her during the rest of her day, but somehow it seldom seemed quite the right moment to talk about it, so she kept it to herself, in her heart, it pleased her to do so.

On occasions, she had watched Michael speaking to Dave – the council refuge collector who usually emptied their refuge bins. He conversed with more animated enthusiasm than he ever managed to conjure up when talking to her. But maybe she was being a tad overly sensitive with that observation. They were, after all, both cricket fans, so there would always be some light-hearted banter between them. Invariably it would be crafted from the previous week's performance by one county or another.

'Weren't Surrey crap last week? They are really going to have to find a decent fast bowler for next season.'

The usual retort would undoubtedly be highly distasteful and politically incorrect.

They would both fall about laughing before Dave would eventually trundle off with our weekly bin load of garbage. Such was the amusing repartee they would engage in every Friday morning, without fail, just before she left for the office. This odd relationship had developed during Michael's period of unemployment, but it would soon fade once he found a new job.

With some fascination, Lauren occasionally wondered at the incongruity of the subject matter. Surely most men only discussed football in public - but maybe that was just disingenuous stereotyping - and here was the unequivocal evidence to prove the opposite. She blamed Rosemary for her obliquely stilted opinion on the working classes' social-behavioural patterns and the detrimental effect they can have. But then, Rosemary had always been a devout snob. It was a genetic thing with her – like religion.

She wasn't jealous of Michael's workaday friendship with Dave, a relationship that effortlessly crossed the social divide. How could she be? Well, not of an overweight, follicly and dentally challenged recycling operative, but it irked her at times that she and Michael didn't seem to do that sort of thing anymore. Resignation and limited conversation were all part of the natural declension of a marriage. It had been nine years this year, but then she had no problem talking for hours with Jeff, and she wondered why that was. Familiarity breeds complacency, which inevitably begets boredom, and that quickly segues into contempt and apathy. Somewhat bizarrely, you eventually wind up despising somebody you once loved passionately. Well, that was what she had read somewhere. Maybe that was the problem, reading too much. But then, on that basis, all long-term marriages were doomed before they started. That was her thought for the day.

Occasionally, if she found herself in a mischievous frame of mind - Lauren would consider replying to Michael's opening gambit with a dry riposte. 'Someone did squeeze my arse rather affectionately at Clapham Junction and asked if I fancied a fuck in the bog to pass the time.' (*This appeared to be a recurring theme, and Lauren did wonder whether she was developing some sort of weird obsession about rough sex in confined spaces.*) 'But I told him I was a bit tired, so could we leave it for another day?' But she decided against it as it would only have set him off for the night, and she was not in the mood.

The tiny fissure that had opened between them a year before, when he was made redundant, was growing a little wider each day. And a little angrier - like a stubborn sore that wouldn't heal.

Lauren was conscious of the invisible delineation that had slowly manifested - but she had also convinced herself that it was all part of the natural progression/regression in marriage... She was never sure which noun to describe how she felt. She told herself it was probably the same for everybody else but wasn't entirely convinced.

'Hectic as always. How was yours? Any joy on the interview front?' is what she eventually settled on. It was just easier that way. She was referring to the interview he had attended the week before, but the letter he received that morning had not brought good news.

'No luck, sad to say. Same old problem – decided not to take anybody on after all, due to unexpected cutbacks...' Michael sounded more disheartened than usual, maybe because the reply didn't have the ring of natural candour about it. It read as if even they had become bored with interviewing people. But then maybe he was just interpreting it that way – he couldn't be sure. He was only on a nodding acquaintance with sincerity.

Lauren felt sorry for him. She knew constant rejection could be profoundly demoralising. Ultimately morphing into a vicious self-destructive circle. She had seen it happen before, at work, but what could she say? Lauren wanted to console him but knew that would only make him feel worse than he already did. So hard as it was for her to do and say nothing, she continued to do so, trying not to react adversely, responding as if the rejection letter was of no consequence.

She would empathise - of course she would. And she would offer measured reassurances. There was a line over which Lauren never usually stepped, but the line had become a gap growing wider every day, slowly turning into a chasm. One day she would have to decide which side she wanted to be on when it became too wide to jump over anymore. Michael was trying hard to find employment. But the scornful gargoyle of self-pity, standing imperiously on the other side of the line - now laughed at his downfall. It was also beginning to play a more significant role in their relationship and how she felt about him. Once the viral infection of pity and disdain took hold, there was little chance of shaking it free. The hideous effigy of rejection grew uglier and larger each day. Incongruously, so was Michael's waistline. A peculiar metaphysical juxtaposition was happening before her eyes.

She had experienced this apathetic mindset before at the office with underperforming staff. Invariably it would always take the same form. Progressively morphing into a suffocating sense of derision and corrosive disdain. Eventually culminating into a mendacious self-loathing for not being what they wanted to be and not becoming what they had hoped to become. It happened slowly. So slowly, at first, almost nobody would be aware it was happening. That was the nature of the beast. Then one day, she would notice something almost imperceptible was taking place. That would be the first stage of failure in social communication. Lauren was constantly vigilant, always looking for these miniscule tell-tale changes in other people. Now, she was beginning to see these self-same changes in Michael.

The brief, tumultuous, torrid affair with Jeff had all too quickly and a little disappointingly come to a premature end. The inevitable conclusion had not really affected or changed how she thought about him, or Michael, come to that. She had entered the relationship with a philosophical mindset preprogrammed for inevitable disenchantment. She had not been disappointed or surprised. She still cared for Jeff and Michael, but was she really in love with either of them, she wondered? Eventually, concluding she was not. Jeff had been sex, nothing more, another miserable attempt to grasp hold of an illusion, always just out of reach.

She loved Michael, but their relationship was slowly, infinitesimally segueing into something completely different, less intense. She knew she needed something more to sustain her soul. She loved him but was no longer in love, a subtle yet profound difference.

The one good thing about her dalliance, her very own Liaisons Dangereuses experience, as she liked to think of it – she loved the film and had watched it many times – was that it rejuvenated her flagging spirits on grey days. It allowed her to be able to stand back and reflect objectively on how things really were. She could now look at them both in a way she could not have done previously. Had she not immersed herself in the tempestuously rapacious but disastrous affair.

Jeff was a dilettante lothario. And being perfectly aware of that shortcoming, she had carefully and meticulously factored his fickle and mildly ambivalent nature into all her decisions.

Yes, it had hurt a little to be discarded after use, but they were still good friends, and she managed to secure the new post in Paris, so not all bad. In fact, Lauren thought she had come out of it rather well. That was until a tiny problem arose, an issue that she would have to confront sooner rather than later.

CHAPTER 26

The Synchronicity of Life.

It was now five months since Leja had become pregnant. However, there was still little, if any, visible evidence of the forthcoming event. It was inevitable with her being so naturally thin that she would show some signs early on. Even a tiny distending belly looks out of place on a woman with a stomach as flat as an ironing board. So far, it had not been particularly noticeable, apart from her breasts and bum, which had conspicuously increased in size.

Nevertheless, Michael knew he would have to broach the delicate issue with Lauren and had decided to do so that night. Best to do it before she noticed something and made her own comment.

'G and T, darling?' asked Michael as Lauren sat down in the lounge.

'Yes, please, but I'll have it with my dinner if you don't mind. Only a small gin and tonic, lots of tonic, please.' Michael poured a small gin with lots of tonic and some ice and placed it on the dining table, then poured himself a glass of wine and took a large swig.

'Dinner will be about five minutes if that's not too quick?' said Michael.

'That's fine. I'm starving. Haven't had very much at all today.'

Lauren wandered into the kitchen - sat down at the stripped pine Paris grey painted table they had found in an antique shop in Godalming High Street in 2003 - and sipped her drink.

Michael brought the first course over, sat down and smiled. He lifted his glass. 'Cheers, darling.' They touched glasses as they always did at dinner and began to eat.

'So, how was your day,' asked Michael?

'So-so,' replied Lauren meditatively.

'So-so, the work's not getting you down, is it,' asked Michael appearing a little concerned?

'No, work is fine. I was just thinking, I haven't seen Katie for nearly six weeks, not since the school holidays started, and I wondered how her new baby was. I miss seeing them all in the morning.'

'I would imagine they're fine. You'll see her again once school starts.'

'Yes, yes, you're right, I will.'

'Oh, by the way, talking about babies, Leja is pregnant.' Michael thought he should pitch straight in, not wishing to delay things any longer than was necessary. Leja had spoken to Michael earlier in the day and expressed serious concerns over the possible repercussions of announcing her condition. She thought it might be best for Michael to deal with the issue alone. Two onto one in a discussion of this nature might appear to Lauren as if she were being ambushed.

'Oh!' replied Lauren sounding a little surprised, not expecting something like that to have cropped up as a topic of conversation during dinner. 'I thought she'd broken up with...' She scrambled around in her head for his name, desperately searching for Polish names that might fit the bill, but nothing sprang to mind. She had met him once but had found him to be a singly unimpressive example, and he had left no lasting impression on her.

'Walter. His name is Walter, and yes, they have,' said Michael.

'Ah, that's right. That's why I couldn't remember it. Odd name that, for a Pole, doesn't sound very....' *Probably why it didn't immediately spring to mind*, she thought. Not an unreasonable explanation in the circumstances.

'Polish?' suggested Michael, with a blank expression.

'No,' said Lauren looking surprised. 'No, it doesn't, does it? So, what is she going to do about it? I presume she wants to leave, which will be a shame.'

Maybe this won't be so bad after all, thought Michael. 'Well, no, just the opposite, in fact.'

'How so?' queried Lauren, scrunching up her eyebrows.

'She has asked me to ask you whether she could stay on here... after the baby is born. She feels terrible about letting us down.'

'She's going to have it here?' asked Lauren, now sounding even more surprised but tempered with a hint of disparagement. Which was a little uncharacteristic for Lauren. Working in the city had made her resilient to game-changing surprises. But her elevation to running the Paris office with the additional pressure that engendered was making her less tolerant. Especially, of anybody or anything that upset the perfect momentum and trajectory of her career.

'Yes, she would like to carry on working here.'

'With a baby? But how will she...? I suppose... yes, it could work.' Lauren was seeing potential problems but almost simultaneously solving them in her head. Anyway, she also had her own problem to discuss. That was the way her analytical mind worked these days. Thinking on her feet (although she was sitting down at the time) was one of her stronger traits. It was the one which gave her the edge in the office.

'Why does she want to stay here?' queried Lauren, taking another small sip of her G and T. 'Doesn't she want to go home to be with her mother?'

'In Lithuania?' asked Michael with a hint of sarcasm.

'Yes,' replied Lauren, not biting.

'No, she said she would prefer to have it here. It's cheaper; in fact, it's free. And she is very happy working here and loves the job and looking after Daisy. And maybe with another baby, it would be good for Daisy to have some company?' That was a sneaky one to slip in because Lauren had mentioned on several occasions that it would be nice to have another child in the house and that it would be good for Daisy to have a brother or sister one day. *But maybe he should stop there; he didn't need to oversell it.*

'Em,' mumbled Lauren, quietly under her breath, weighing up the pros and cons.

'Your work commitments with what you have promised Jeff effectively prevent you from having another baby for a few years. So this situation could, in a manner of speaking, solve a couple of problems. In fact, it would be solving more than a couple?' *That was a brilliant bit of joined-up thinking,* thought Michael. He hadn't completely lost the ability to negotiate, not quite. 'There's plenty of room for a cot in the spare room next to Leja's bedroom, that's still in her part of the house, so we wouldn't even notice her most of the time. It means we wouldn't have to start looking for a nanny, housekeeper or cook immediately.' He was making the best case he could. The alternative didn't bear thinking about. This was the perfect moment to consolidate his position.

'Yes, I can see the benefits,' replied Lauren warily. She was deliberating over the proposal, trying to identify potential problems. But there did not appear to be any. As far as Lauren could see. Apart from the fact that she was also pregnant. But then she had chosen not to mention that development to Michael…. just yet.

'So, what about this Walter character? Is he not going to be a problem? He is bound to want to see his child?'

'Are well, there's the anomaly. I don't think he will be popping around because he is not actually the father.'

'Not the father, so, who is?' replied Lauren, delicately holding up her glass and peering through it as if gazing into another world and thinking about other matters.

'It's not you, for Christ's sake, is it?' she suddenly exclaimed.

Michael felt his testicles shrink as the accusation hit home. He clenched his buttocks tightly together and, without hesitation, continued drinking his soup. 'No, darling, it's not me. I have more pressing matters to contend with than shagging the staff. It's somebody she met at the pub. I understand. A one-night stand from what I could make out.' He sounded oddly vague about the circumstances.

'Is that what Leja told you?'

'Yes, in between other things.'

'Other things?' replied Lauren curiously.

'Well, she was obviously a little concerned about her position here. It all started off as a what-if scenario. But she let out the rest once I had assured her I didn't think you would have any objections.

'I see… I'm still surprised Leja didn't take me into her confidence first.'

'You weren't here, so I suppose it seemed the easiest route for her to tell me. I am here most of the time. She was very reluctant to talk to you first,' Michael added, flashing a ghastly expression of dread and apprehension. 'I think she finds you a little intimidating at times.'

'Oh. So Leja thinks I'm some sort of ogre now.'

'No, nothing like that. It's just that you work, and you run a tight ship. We are all dependent on you, so to some degree, we are all secondary to your needs.'

'Em,' said Lauren, quietly mulling over Michael's oddly sycophantic rationalisation. 'Oh well, what's done is done. I'll have a word with her tomorrow to sort things out.'

'You won't be too hard on her, will you? She's feeling very vulnerable right now.' Michael appeared uncharacteristically concerned about Leja's welfare, surprising Lauren a little.

'Of course not. Who do you think I am, some sort of heartless old harridan? I just want to have a friendly girl-to-girl chat with her, that's all... just so we both understand the guidelines.

'Good,' said Michael. 'That sounds good.' But he wasn't sure how Leja would stand up under close interrogation. That still worried him a little.. no, a lot.

'Actually... I'm surprised you are taking it so well,' enquired Lauren. 'I would have thought one of the servant girls becoming pregnant would have warranted instant dismissal.' It was clearly a satirical aside, but Michael was still slightly stunned by her cutting, below-stairs condemnation. Even a little hurt.

'That's not fair. I'm not that much of an ogre,' he swiftly countered.

'It was only a joke,' Lauren quickly responded. 'I hardly thought you would throw her onto the streets with her bags and baby in arms like some wretched Dickens waif.

'Oh, right, I see,' replied Michael apologetically. But it left Lauren quietly bemused at his response to the light-hearted slight on his sensibilities. 'It's lamb casserole for mains. I hope that's okay?'

'Should be lovely. Leja always makes a nice stew.'

'Another gin, or would you like some wine?' asked Michael, now more relaxed as the problem he thought might materialise appeared to be slowly receding from view.... for now.

'Rosé okay?'

'Lovely, just what I need to take this all in.'

Michael started to pour Lauren a glass, but Lauren abruptly put her hand over the glass after a few seconds. 'That'll be fine. I'm not all that thirsty tonight, actually.'

Michael continued topping up his glass and then cautiously proposed another toast. He was pushing his luck, and he knew it, but what the hell, he thought, life is life, in for a penny...

'To Leja and her bump,' said Michael.

Lauren felt an odd feeling wave through her body. She didn't know what it was and put it down to the revelation about Leja or possibly her slight problem but then thought no more about it.

'Leja's bump. Hey, wait a minute!' Exclaimed Lauren, now suddenly looking serious. Michael's heart skipped two beats...' *What did I get wrong? He thought. What the fuck did I say to give the game away?* Various possibilities raced through his mind, and just as he was about to splutter something...

'We can't toast Leja and her bump when she's not here,' exclaimed Lauren. 'Go and get her.'

Michael let out a short breath, smiled, stood up and swiftly strolled off to Leja's living room area with a sense of glowing relief. He gently knocked on her sitting-room door and walked in. He should have remembered to wait. Familiarity had got the better of him once again. It could have been a dangerous mistake.

'Leja!' he shouted.

Leja appeared in just her knickers and stood staring at him. 'Yes, master?' she whispered salaciously while slowly licking her lips. Michael was suddenly urged to do something, but it would have to wait. This was hardly the right moment, and anyway, his testicles had not completely recovered yet.

'Lauren and I have discussed the situation, and we both agree that it might be best for all if you stayed here and had the baby.' Leja smiled and provocatively played with her nipples just to tease him... Michael went quiet for a few moments, 'it would suit us perfectly,' he added as an afterthought. The interlude spoke volumes.

He spoke in an exaggerated, oddly stilted tone to ensure Lauren could clearly hear his every word.

I bet it would, thought Leja. She turned around, bent over, and started playing with her bum with both hands while wiggling her arse promiscuously from side to side. Michael was having a real problem containing his urges.

Leja turned back to face Michael again and smiled mischievously.

'We were just having a drink to celebrate your bump. So if you would like to come through in a few minutes,' he lowered his voice to a whisper, 'when you're dressed.' He raised his voice again to the exaggerated level and continued, 'we would like to toast you and your baby. Okay?'

'Our baby,' mouthed Leja slowly. Michael winced.

'Yes, that would be lovely,' replied Leja, now leaning back against the door jamb and gently rolling her nipples between finger and thumb again while smiling provocatively. This firmly placed Michael in an extremely uncomfortable place. He smiled but appeared distressed and left quickly to return to the kitchen and carry on with his dinner, looking much paler than when he had left.

'You are a bit stuffy at times, Michael,' said Lauren.

'What?' said Michael, sounding surprised.

Lauren smiled. 'Stuffy, like so reserved. You should let yourself go sometimes.'

'Oh, I see. Yes, maybe you're right. I will.' He smiled – his masquerade intact. 'I will definitely make an effort.'

A few minutes later, Leja appeared in the kitchen wearing heavily distressed blue jeans, a loose-fitting white chiffon blouse and smiling very sweetly.

'I really want to thank you both, especially you, Lauren. It is so kind what you saying, and I am incredibly happy.' She glanced briefly but intently at Michael and smiled.

Michael gave Leja a glass of the rosé. 'Is it okay to drink?' he asked, suddenly realising that maybe it wasn't.

'It is fine just a little, but soon, I stop altogether... for the baby, alcohol is bad...It can make the baby very stupid, I think.' Lauren suddenly felt a little warm.

Lauren and Michael both smiled in supportive admiration of her abstemious declaration. Although they were a little bemused by her last remark, which Lauren thought she must have misread in a magazine.

'I hope not,' said Lauren, 'otherwise London is going to be overrun by morons running banks before long.' Michael wasn't sure how to react to that observation and glanced at Lauren with a surprised expression.

'Not you, darling. I'm sure your mother never drank.'

Michael still said nothing and just took another sip of his rosé.

'So, how far gone are you?' asked Lauren.

'Nearly five months.'

'Five months!' replied Lauren, sounding surprised. 'Oh!'

'Yes, I am sorry I did not tell you early, but....'

'That's not a problem. It's your body, your business, but I must say you are carrying it well. I would never have guessed.'

Leja smiled. Michael appeared neutral on the revelation and just smiled placidly, saying nothing.

'Would you like to join us for dinner?' asked Lauren.

'No, it is okay, thank you. I had mine earlier.' She smiled and wandered slowly back to her bedroom.

'That's good, then,' replied Michael jubilantly, having successfully crossed the first Rubicon of the many Rubicons that lay ahead.

'Yes, it is,' replied Lauren a little introspectively. 'I am so pleased for her, but I have something of my own we need to talk about.'

'Shall I clear the bowls and fetch the casserole?' suggested Michael. 'We can chat over dinner.' He was so pleased with how the Leja situation had been so painlessly resolved that he hadn't noticed the slight change in Lauren's demeanour.

Michael placed the casserole dish on the table and spooned some lamb stew onto the two plates before sitting down.

'Well...' said Lauren, taking a tiny sip of her wine. 'This pregnancy thing seems to be a little contagious.'

'How do you mean? Don't tell me your mother is pregnant.' He could afford to be mildly irreverent, having recouped some of his wavering confidence. He had successfully crossed what could loosely be termed his personal Rubicon with relative finesse. However, what the future held was now, irreversibly, in the lap of the gods.

'Well, not quite,' replied Lauren shyly, slightly embarrassed.

'Not quite,' enquired Michael, now looking a little intrigued? He swallowed a piece of half-chewed potato and sipped his wine. 'Go on...'

'It's me! I am pregnant too. I wanted to mention it earlier but didn't want to steal Leja's thunder. I'm having a baby – we're having another child.'

Michael slowly placed his knife and fork on the table and leaned back in his chair. 'What?' He exclaimed. It was hard to gauge precisely how he felt or looked, for that matter. A chaotic amalgam of blank disbelief – whirling confusion, panic, and a sudden interest in the peculiar phenomenon of the cosmic synchronicity of life. Snowdrops appear at the same time each year. The full moon appears every twenty-eight days. And he had managed to inseminate two women almost simultaneously...

'We're having another baby!' There, she'd said it out aloud again. It was now common knowledge, or at least it was to the two of them. She was glad she had told him. *That was the easy bit over. Now it gets a little trickier*, she thought.

'But how... when... I thought that...' It was all a little confusing, and Michael wasn't sure what were the right questions to ask. Many a moment of jubilation is shattered by a poorly chosen comment. 'Is it mine?' being the all-time jackpot party-pooper...

Michael reverted to something safe and neutral... He had the fleetness of mind to realise that now was not the time for a crass interjection.

'So how far gone are you?' he asked, quickly followed by, 'I think it is absolutely marvellous,' which was accompanied by an expression of dumbfounded disbelief.

'Well, I think I'm about six weeks gone, so it should be February or March.'

'That's...' he thought for a minute, then suddenly realised the full ramifications of what she had just said. He was going to be a father again... twice. One would be popping out in December, and one around March... 'Amazing, absolutely bloody amazing. I don't know what to say.' He really didn't know what to say. He was lost for words, and then, just for a fleeting moment, he tried to recall when they had last had sex. It was some time ago – about two months, in fact – so that would be about right. *Christ,* he thought to himself, I must be incredibly virile in what could only be described as a moment of severely constrained elation.

'Say you're pleased,' asked Lauren, looking at him pleadingly? This was not exactly what she had planned or even considered. She hoped Michael would be happy about it despite their precarious employment situation. The situation would obviously be further affected by her being off work for a few months.

'Of course, I am pleased. I just thought that with what you said about Jeff and the new Paris contract, it would be three or four years before we would get around to it again, but this is just fantastic. I am really incredibly happy for you… for us.'

'I'm so glad. I didn't know how you would react,' replied Lauren, relieved.

'How would you expect me to react?' replied Michael. 'Ecstatic, that's how.' He leaned over the table to kiss her. As he did, just for a second, Lauren had a flashback to another kiss over another table. One which had caused a lot of confusion and chaos and set her on a journey she never thought she would ever take again.

CHAPTER 27

The Sheikh of Baddesley-Minton?

Early October 2009

Lauren slipped her key into the lock and opened the front door. She stepped in with her laptop and document case, gently kicking her foot back to close the door. She parked her two bags by the umbrella stand, dropped her coat on the ~~bannister~~bannister and kicked her shoes off before entering the lounge. It was past eight o'clock, and she had had a hectic day. The expression on her face said everything. The log fire in the inglenook was roaring away, its welcoming glow emanating a wondrously cosy feeling into the room. This is what she really looked forward to. Arriving home, seeing Michael and Daisy, and relaxing in front of the open fire.

Already the hustle of the day was beginning to fade away, rapidly becoming a distant memory. She never really managed to switch off on the train nor in the car on the drive home from the station, but as soon as she was through the front door - that was it. She was finished for the day. She collapsed on the sofa or, more accurately, gently lowered herself down. The bump had been a little troublesome today, and she did not want baby T to be aroused. Michael and Lauren had already chosen the two names, Tasha for a girl – Thornton if a boy.

'Hi darling,' shouted Michael from the kitchen, hearing Lauren arrive. 'Just warming up dinner. It won't be too long.'

Lauren looked wistfully around the lounge and watched the reflection of the flames on the wainscotting. It brought the oak panels alive, the silver streaks of the medullary rays dancing quietly to the flickering flames. A crackle from the fire broke the silence as a tiny splinter flew up and just as quickly died. *A bit like life in a way,* she thought, *all over in a flash, compared with eternity.* She experienced these odd moments of quiet metaphysical reflection from time to time. Then, for no reason, her mind returned to the incident earlier in the day when she saw Katie with her family walking over Shelbury Bridge. She was carrying her new baby in the same sort of jockey seat arrangement that she had used more than two years previously to carry Trinity Farrier. The baby that had suddenly died. Strangely, she had also been wearing the same red and white polka-dot dress that she had worn on one occasion back then, something that Daisy had noticed and commented on. But it was July back then, while today was the middle of October, and it was cold and not ideal weather for a summer dress. As before, one of the twins walked beside her, holding her hand; the other was presumably in the buggy. The walking twin was wearing a dress identical to Katie's. A near-perfect mini version of her mother, but without quite so much hair. Poppy was trailing a few steps behind, holding the lead for Alfie, tumbling along, last of all. The strange thing was Poppy appeared a little younger than Lauren remembered. The whole thing didn't seem quite right the more she thought about it, but then it had only been for a few moments, so maybe she was simply confused. But still, there was something about it that seemed unreal. She thought no more about the incident and turned to Michael.

'I'm glad that week's over. I'm looking forward to a weekend of doing nothing and putting my feet up.'

Michael came in from the kitchen and walked behind the sofa towards the drink cabinet, kissing Lauren on the head as he passed. 'Well, there's plenty of that to do. I am making a drink for dinner. Would you like something?'

'Let me think about that.'

'Fair enough.' Michael poured himself a large gin, topped it with tonic, and took a sip.

'Where's Leja?' asked Lauren.

'She's had a dreadful day. The baby is giving her hell. I think it's trying to break out a few months early.'

'Seems weird,' remarked Lauren looking whimsically at the ceiling.

'What?'

'Well, me out at work all day working with my bump, and our home help is here all day with her bump, sitting on her arse doing nothing, and you're left doing the cooking. We've definitely got something wrong somewhere.' She muttered something else, but it was incomprehensible.

'I said you should have given up work earlier, and anyway, we did say she could stay with her baby. And she does do some housework and washing during the day.'

'Yes, yes, I know – just being a bit baby bitchy,' replied Lauren apologetically. 'It's my hormones – I blame them.'

'Poor old hormones get nailed for everything,' replied Michael. Lauren smiled.

'I couldn't really,'

'Couldn't what?

'Just give up work, not now anyway. I made a commitment when Jeff gave me the Paris promotion, and that was only five months ago. So it was pretty decent of him to put up with me taking six months out.' *It's the least he could do as I'm probably carrying his baby,* thought Lauren, but she hadn't mentioned that to Jeff. She felt that was best under the circumstances... for now.

'Yes, that was pretty decent, I suppose. I would have sacked you if you'd been working for me.' Michael had some extraordinarily chauvinistic views on women in the workplace. Fortunately, they did not extend to his wife or their au pair. They were the exceptions; there were always exceptions.

'That is profoundly sexist and a bit misogynistic, don't you think?' Replied Lauren; *probably one reason they let you go first;* she quietly mused. *Possibly one of the reasons you cannot find another job.* She added this as a rider to her earlier thought, but only in her head. She was beginning to see Michael in a different light these days.

'Only joking,' replied Michael, now back in the kitchen.

Were you, wondered Lauren. 'Anyway, I have agreed to work another three months up to the end of January, that's my lot. I definitely don't fancy trekking across London in darkest winter with a passenger onboard.' She smoothed her tummy, which had hardly changed at all.

'So, Jeff hasn't made too much fuss about the baby?'

'No, not really. As long as I get back by June, he'll be okay, and I have said I would do some work at home, but only an hour or two each day, at most.'

'I don't mind helping around the house,' said Michael. 'I don't have anything else on right now, but hopefully, that won't last much longer. Once Leja's baby is born, we will be halfway back to normal... It will make a change, doing this, and it's good to see things from another perspective occasionally, but I must get back to work soon.' He almost appeared to be enjoying the temporary domestic arrangement. With two pregnant women in the house, the mornings were occasionally entertaining. At times, Michael fantasised about being a far eastern sheikh with his wife and Leja, his number one concubine, in tow, but that was not exactly how they saw it. And he was not having much sex with either of them now. So, *incredibly crap timing on that one*, Michael mused. Especially as he was lumbered with some of the cooking. So, the sheikh-harem-concubine fantasy he had created in his head looked less attractive by the day.

But tomorrow was Saturday, so there was no school run, which was some relief from the early morning chaos. Michael still wasn't driving Daisy to school; it was pointless, as Lauren was going the same way to work. But it did make him feel a little guilty waving his four-month-pregnant wife and his daughter off each morning and then shutting the door and slipping into Leja's warm bed for a few hours. Mind you, even that hadn't been quite the case recently. Over the past few weeks, Leja had tended to be a little grumpy in the mornings. She displayed distinct signs of being less than interested in fornication in any format whenever he suggested it. But at seven months pregnant, I suppose that was to be expected, he kept telling himself.

'I would love a cup of tea when you are ready,' said Lauren, eventually deciding.

'Right, two minutes,' replied Michael.

Later, they sat at the kitchen table, had dinner, watched a little television in the lounge, and then went to bed.

The following day.

'Could you make me a cup of tea, darling,' asked Lauren. She was drinking a lot of tea these days.

'No problem,' replied Michael looking at his watch. It was seven-thirty and still dark outside. He slipped out of bed, put on his slippers and dressing gown, and approached the bedroom door.

'Could you make one for Leja as well?' added Lauren. 'She'll need one if she's had a night like mine.'

'No problem,' replied Michael. He went downstairs to the kitchen and put the kettle on before wandering into Leja's

210

bedroom. Michael knocked gently on her door before opening it. The room was still dark as he slowly edged towards the bed to see if Leja was awake.

'Boo!' shouted Leja.

'Ahhh!' exclaimed Michael, jumping up.

Leja was already up and flicked on the light switch by the door to reveal she was standing behind him wearing just a flimsy pair of tiny lace panties. They were wholly inadequate for the purpose intended. Obviously designed with some sensual agenda in mind, but not for someone seven months pregnant. It just didn't work for Michael.

'I heard you come downstairs and thought I would surprise you... Did I,' Leja asked coquettishly?

'Yes, you did. I nearly shat myself.'

'I was going to come into kitchen to make tea.'

'Oh, that would have been wonderful. Especially if Lauren had also come down and seen you prancing around with your tits flying all over the shop. Would have painted a delightful picture of what goes on during the week.'

'I don't think about that,' said Leja sheepishly.

'No, you don't – didn't,' replied Michael with a very stern expression.

'Is this not funny,' she asked with an elfin-like expression of naughtiness?

'No, it is not.

'My nerves are shot to pieces with two pregnant women in the house.'

'So why you sneak round in dark. I thought you want my body?' She touched her hands lightly on her head and waggled her breasts at him. 'You like lick my nipple?'

'You haven't been in the mood much lately,' replied Michael. 'I thought you would still be asleep.'

'No, I not sleep, I need you, I need bang fuck please.' She smiled.

Michael looked at Leja cavorting in front of him and tried not to be distracted, but he had become transfixed by her ever-changing body shape. Her breasts held a particular fascination for him. They had increased in volume quite dramatically over the last couple of months, far more so than Lauren's, and they still vehemently defied the laws of gravity. He found himself making bizarre comparisons between the two - which he despised himself for doing. But in his enforced confinement, it was one of the few pleasures still available to him.

'I popped in to see if you wanted tea.'

'Yes, please, that would be nice, but first, I would like to have sex as we haven't done bang fuck for nearly three weeks.'

'Well, that's not for want of trying,' replied Michael curtly.

'I know it is grumpy me, but I feel better now and very horny.'

He looked at her now distended abdomen, noticing her inverted belly button protruding like a third nipple. But without the large mahogany brown areola, which was clearly evident around her natural nipples. They had darkened quite noticeably over the past few months. He presumed that it must have been an Eastern European thing.

For seven months pregnant, her body still looked remarkably appealing. In fact, far more so than Michael had expected. Conversely, Lauren had become quite large this time, much more so than when carrying Daisy. She had also become very grumpy and irritable. This was unusual and probably due, in part, to the additional pressure of work and because she was unable to ever get completely comfortable in bed. That was Michael's best guess. At times, she even appeared to resent this sequestration of her body, as if it had not been her choice, but it had.

Leja had retained her carefree exuberance and lust for sexual activity, albeit slightly less inventive than usual. In contrast, it had waned almost to the point of extinction as far as Lauren was concerned. So, things had not worked out too badly, sex-wise. Although a little more stressful, logistically speaking, from time to time. It never occurred to Michael just how shallow a person he had become. Only a nonpartisan observer could see the change – or Lauren if she knew the truth. But then, she wasn't exactly Caesar's wife either.

'We can't right now, for Christ's sake,' replied Michael. 'Lauren's upstairs waiting for her cup of tea.'

'It only needs to be quickie,' replied Leja demurely, trying her absolute best to accommodate the demands on his precious time.

How can I resist? He thought. Daisy wouldn't surface till about ten. Nothing would wake her up earlier, and Lauren was still trying to get back to sleep.

'Okay, you win, on the bed,' he manfully instructed, 'but we must not make a noise. The house is really quiet right now. You can hear every sound.

Leja quickly removed her tiny knickers and jumped on the bed, waving her bum at Michael while whispering, 'Come and get me, little English boy.' She always called him her little "English boy," which he believed was due to him being English and relatively youthful for his age. In reality, it was because he had a small penis compared to her previous lovers in Lithuania and even her Polish ex-boyfriend. But she didn't want to mention this shortcoming as she knew it would probably upset him and give him sleepless nights and possibly an inferiority complex. She had become aware that Englishmen were surprisingly sensitive about the dimensions of their genitalia.

Michael completed the deed in under five minutes, a record for him, and slowly withdrew his penis while holding on to her hips. They had managed to reach orgasm simultaneously without any of the usual screaming and shouting, which, strangely, he missed, but under the circumstances, was an absolute imperative. He would have had a problem explaining a noise to Lauren (Like two Barbary apes fighting over a banana in their kitchen). Especially when they had no pets except for Daisy's hamster. That made no noise at all, apart from an occasional gentle squeal. Leja did not do soft squeals.

There had been some low-level moaning from them both, but nothing loud enough to reverberate around the house and cause a disturbance. In fact, Michael found it strangely exhilarating having to restrain himself from shouting. He often bellowed out all sorts of unusual things during intercourse. Cricketer's names and their best seasons were a particular favourite: 'Gary Sobers, '73... Amazing! Before plunging a little deeper - Brian Lara 92-93 against the bloody Aussies... Yes!' and occasionally, at the seminal moment, 'Ian Botham, '81... Wow!' just before tightly squeezing her breasts. Leja never entirely understood what Michael was shouting about but presumed it was a traditional and quintessentially British thing. For that reason, she would smile and try her best to look suitably excited by his exultations, although she didn't understand.

After a minute or so, Michael let go of Leja, and she collapsed onto the bed and turned over to face Michael, still standing at the end.

'Was it good for you?' she asked, smiling. She knew it was but asked anyway. She knew men liked to have their egos occasionally massaged and their penises. 'It was lovely for me,' she added wistfully.

'Yes, it was wonderful. It is always wonderful making love to you, Leja,' replied Michael politely while hurriedly pulling up his pyjamas.

Making love, thought Leja. I thought it was just a quick fuck, whatever... I wonder why he suffixed the appraisal with my name. She wondered if he had forgotten who she was because he could not see my face. Sounded very formal, just a teeny-weeny bit like something Simon Cowell might say on 'Britain's Got Talent' after watching a performing dog act.

'Yes, I love making the love to you too. It was a very....' she was desperately searching for the right words. Anything other than 'fulfilling fuck,' the assonance she knew would instantly dissolve her into laughter and spoil the moment. She eventually settled on 'intense and deeply meaningful moment,' and Michael seemed touched by that. *But then that didn't take a great deal*, she pondered. *A trifle cynical, possibly, but what the hell?*

'So, Leja, would you like a cup of tea?' repeated Michael after the short delay.

Leja had slipped under the bedcovers but poked her head back out to answer. 'Yes, please.'

'Right, I'll go and sort that out.' He wandered off, and Leja pulled the duvet back over her head to contemplate life so far.

Ten minutes later, he returned and placed the cup of tea by Leja's bed, but she had fallen asleep.

Poor thing thought Michael. I must have completely exhausted her. I must be a little gentler in the future. These Lithuanian girls have probably never had a real man, and I can be a bit of a brute. Then he quietly closed the door behind him just as Leja farted a perfect A flat. He smiled affectionately, then made his way back upstairs.

'You were a long time, darling,' said Lauren, sitting up.

'Yes, I'm sorry, got side-tracked by a noise outside, so I thought I'd better investigate, but it was nothing.' He got back into bed and passed a cup of tea to Lauren.

'Did you not hear that distant bumping noise?' asked Lauren idly

'Bumping noise?' repeated Michael with a blank expression. 'What kind of bumping noise?' he asked quizzically, giving his best impression of somebody who had not heard anything.

'Sort of like the noise the bath tap makes when there's air stuck in the pipes, Bump-bump-bump-bump-bump-bump-bump-bump... and then it sped up for a few seconds before it stopped suddenly.'

'Must be the central heating warming up,' suggested Michael.'

'Possibly,' said Lauren, deep in thought. 'It reminded me of something, but I can't think what.'

'Biscuit?' suggested Michael.

'No thanks, this is fine.' Lauren finished her tea and then laid back down to go to sleep.

Michael remained sitting up, wondering how she had managed to hear them when they had made such an effort to be quiet. He made a mental note not to have further physical contact with Leja while Lauren was in the house. His only problem might be convincing Leja to agree.

Two months later, in early December, Michael drove Leja home from the hospital with baby Joshua. This was the name he and Leja had agreed upon during one of their less frenetic love-making sessions. His first son, albeit by way of a circuitous route and an unusual domestic arrangement. Deep down, he knew he would have a fundamental problem, not forming an attachment to his first son. He suffered many sleepless nights deliberating over the conundrum. If Leja decided to leave, he could lose his son forever, but if he stayed and Lauren found out, he could lose her, Daisy, and probably the house... Problems, problems, always problems.

CHAPTER 28

Angels with Black Wings.

'One of my friends has asked me if I would like to go for a sleepover this weekend. Would that be okay?' Daisy did not bother raising her head when she asked the question. She was utterly absorbed filling in the wrong colours on one of the pages of her colouring book.

'Which friend?' asked Lauren, sitting opposite Daisy and doing some work on her laptop. 'And why are you colouring in the wrong colours? Angels do not have black wings.'

'Mine do. I'm bored.'

'I can see that; they should be white, though.'

Daisy continued colouring in the black wings. 'They're black angels.'

'Oh, I see. I thought all angels were white.'

'Not necessarily,' replied Daisy, glancing up at Lauren, wondering if that could be misconstrued as a racially controversial comment. Daisy had heard about discrimination at school but did not completely understand what it meant. She knew it concerned people with a different skin colour than her... like her angels, but that was it.

'Oh,' said Lauren thoughtfully.

'So, can I go?' repeated Daisy, discounting Lauren's suggestion on the colour of the angel's wings.

'Where,' asked Lauren, who was partially distracted by what she was typing?

'Poppy's!' replied Daisy, who was now becoming a little annoyed by her mother's obfuscation.

'I thought you said...' She finished typing and sat back in her chair, pleased with herself. She rolled her fingertips on the table several times, obviously pondering over something she had written, then looked up at Daisy. 'I thought you said you weren't in her class any longer.'

'I'm not, but we are still friends. She did come over here in the summer.'

'Did she?'

216

'Yes, she came to my birthday party.'

'Oh, yes, I do remember now. A nice girl, tall, long hair?'

'Yes,' replied Daisy, wondering why there were so many questions.

'So, can I go… please?'

'I will have to think about it.'

'They are really nice people. I've met her dad at school loads of times. He's a nice person.'

'He's the potter, isn't he,' asked Lauren?

'Yes,' replied Daisy. 'That's right, and you know Katie.'

Daisy, eloquent and articulate as always – when necessary – was displaying a remarkably intuitive and well-constructed petition, but then she always did whenever she wanted something.

'I still only know her by sight,' replied Lauren. 'I've never actually met her.'

'Well, this is your chance. You always said you would like to meet her.'

'Yes, well…' Lauren's attention returned to her laptop. She continued typing while quietly pondering over Daisy's remarkable ability to recall brief, almost indiscernible extracts from vague conversations they had held months ago. Lauren had mistakenly assumed. Daisy had not been listening, but apparently, she had. More importantly, she still had mixed feelings about whether meeting Katie would be wise. It could profoundly change the spiritual relationship that existed between them. Yes, it was unusual, as they had never spoken. But they had somehow transcended the conventional boundaries and parameters that governed most relationships. For her, it seemed to work. That was all that really mattered.

'Poppy came here for my birthday party, and her parents don't know you….' She let that statement hang in the air for a moment. 'What more do you need to know?' Daisy was becoming a little impatient, not even bothering to lift her head from what she was doing when she spoke. It was one of those peculiar conversations conducted without ever making visual contact.

While you are looking at the menu in a restaurant, the waitress is looking at her order pad. Both totally disengaged, preoccupied with what they were doing, but just managing to make audio contact. The girl at Tesco's checkout desk is deeply ensconced in scanning your shopping. (not that Lauren knew where the local Tesco was, her mother Rosemary having indelibly transcribed the letters M&S on her brain at birth).

'Well, a little more than we know right now,' replied Lauren abruptly.

'Poppy is one of my best friends,' mumbled Daisy.

'I'll speak to Daddy about it,' said Lauren, conceding that that wasn't a valid reason to object.

'You do see them on the bridge.'

'Not recently, I haven't, not since I've been working shorter weeks.'

Daisy grunted something inaudible, not looking up from what she was doing.

'Anyway, seeing them does not actually mean we know them. It just means we are aware of their existence.'

'I know them. Well, I know Poppy and Mr Farrier.'

'But we don't,' said Lauren sharply, but she quickly apologised. 'I'm sorry, I didn't mean it like that.'

Daisy mumbled something else incomprehensible.

Lauren again lifted her eyes off the keyboard and looked at Daisy. 'I just want to check it with Daddy, that's all. One of us will have to drive you across so Daddy or I can meet them, so everything will be okay. Don't worry.'

The conversation went quiet for about thirty seconds while Daisy continued colouring the angel's black wings. Lauren finished what she was doing on the computer.

'I presume it is tomorrow night?' asked Lauren, now virtually surrendering to Daisy's request.

'Yes, about six o'clock.' Her eyes lit up.

'Well, Daddy will probably have to take you because I may be home late tomorrow. He'll be back in a minute. I'll ask him when he gets in.'

Daisy continued colouring her picture, still applying the wrong colours to other parts of the angel.

'Thank you, Mummy,' she whispered after a few minutes. She had obviously reviewed the whole conversation and was now satisfied with the outcome.

'That's okay, but I still think those angels' wings should be a different colour, not black.'

Daisy did not answer.

Friday evening: Daisy's sleepover.

Lauren arrived home early on Friday, having thought about who would take Daisy to Poppy's house and decided she would take her after all. She wanted to meet Katie. It was about time. Michael and Daisy were sitting in the lounge, Michael reading the newspaper - Daisy watching television.

'Have you packed your bag?' asked Lauren as she walked into the kitchen.

'Yes, toothbrush, PJs, clean knickers. Leja has checked to make sure I haven't forgotten anything, and I have some treats.'

'Treats,' enquired Lauren curiously?

'Daddy bought me some chocolates.'

'Did he?'

Leja wandered through into the kitchen. 'Hello, Mrs Penfold, did you have good day?'

'Not too bad. How was yours, and how is baby Joshy?'

'He's getting better. I am sorry if he wakes in night,' she started making up a milk bottle.

'We can't hear him, so that's not a problem,' reassured Lauren.

'Good,' said Leja. She finished preparing the milk and wandered back to her room.

'What time have you arranged to be there, Daisy?' asked Lauren.

'I said somebody would drop me off at about six o'clock.'

'Right, well, you had better get everything in my car. We'll leave in a few minutes, then I can settle down for the night with baby T.' Lauren slowly ran her hands over her bump. She still referred to her unborn baby by the initial letter they had given it in the beginning, although they now knew he was a boy. It seemed odd to refer to the bump by a proper name.

Daisy rushed upstairs to get her travel bag.

'I'll be back in about half an hour,' said Lauren walking back into the lounge and tapping Michael on the head while he continued reading the newspaper.

'Are you sure you don't want me to run Daisy over to the Farriers?' asked Michael.

'No, no, it's fine. I want to meet Poppy's mum anyway. Having seen her crossing Shelbury Bridge regularly for the last two and a half years, I think it's about time I spoke to her. She has probably been wondering who the loony in the car is, who gawps at her most days anyway. It will give me a chance to explain my behaviour.'

'I'm sure you don't gawp,' replied Michael.

'That's what it feels like sometimes.'

'What time do you want dinner? asked Michael looking up. 'When you get back or later?'

'Later will be fine.'

Daisy reappeared in the lounge. 'Bags in the car.'

'Right, we'll be off,' said Lauren.

'See you when you get back,' replied Michael, waving his hand.

Lauren and Daisy drove off to Poppy's. Michael went to the drinks cabinet, poured himself a small whiskey, flicked off the television, and started rereading the newspaper.

After a few minutes, Leja wandered in from the kitchen, walked over to the sofa and stood behind Michael, running her hands through his hair - gently scraping her nails across his scalp. She knew that drove him mad.

'Hi Leja,' said Michael casually, trying not to pay too much attention. Leja loved to play these dangerous games when Lauren wasn't there. She knew it unnerved him, putting him on edge. But the element of risk adrenalised his body; it made him feel alive, and the feeling was too strong to resist. His mind was firm, resolute, and could hold out against her advances, but sooner or later, his body would weaken and eventually surrender.

There was a time when Michael would experience this exultant, almost glorious feeling just by making a small killing in the city. But those days were long gone and unlikely to return any time soon, so he took what pleasure he could, when he could, to satisfy his desire.

'I notice the house is empty,' said Leja

Michael smiled. He knew where this was going.

'Lauren will only be gone for half an hour,' he said. 'We don't have time to do anything.'

But he wasn't allowing for Leja's tenacious nature.

'How long do we need,' asked Leja, slipping her hands slowly down his chest inside his shirt and playing with his nipples? She knew that drove him mad and that he would not be able to resist her for long.

'But what about Joshy?' replied Michael.

'He's asleep. I've just given him a bottle.'

'So, how is the little lad?'

'Our son. You mean, how is our son,' said Leja.

Michael smiled at the thought. 'Yes, our son.' The reality of the bizarre situation sent a searing pang of anguish through his body.

'He's fine, and we won't wake him if you're quiet.'

Michael put his newspaper down and put his arms up to catch hold of Leja, and realised she was naked,

'Ah!' exclaimed Michael. 'That's very naughty. For God's sake, we could be interrupted at any moment... by the neighbours or the postman. He delivers about now, sometimes with parcels, and this would take some serious explaining....'

'The Postman,' repeated Leja laughing. 'Umm, I've never been *interrupted* by a postman.' She wiggled her arse. 'I bet he delivers every little package in his little sack. He can post anything large into my little slot,' mumbled Leja.

Michael couldn't help but be turned on by her comments.

'They don't use sacks anymore; it damages their backs. They use little trolleys now.' He was trying to slow Leja down.

'That is good. I wouldn't like to think of him straining himself.'

'Joshua might wake,' suggested Michael. His brain was struggling for reasons not to give in to her demands.

'Well, we had better be fast and get on with it while we have five minutes to spare,' replied Leja indifferently to his apparent concerns. Leja wanted sex on her terms, and she wanted it now. Michael gently pulled her over the back of the sofa in a somewhat ungainly manoeuvre before kissing her and fondling her arse and breasts. Meanwhile, Leja hurriedly unbuckled his belt, endeavouring to pull his trousers and underpants down. It was all a little haphazard and disconcerting for Michael, being physically manipulated by a woman half his size but still a bit too tame for Leja. With her on top, now controlling events, Leja competently guided Michael's penis into her body, where it remained locked. They began, albeit a little unsteadily at first, to perform an erratically sexual act or, more precisely, a bang- fuck. (*To use Leja's terminology*). It lacked the emotional dimension that Michael liked to think he brought to these moments. But then, he was prone to self-delusion occasionally.

Leja suddenly morphed into Diane the Valkyrie riding her stallion into battle with Michael as her stallion. She was now throwing herself wholeheartedly into a sort of Bronco Billy routine. His trousers and underpants dangled precariously at the end of his legs, caught up around his shoes. He had not been able to remove them, and they now swung indolently over the end of the sofa. It all made for a less-than-beguiling sight. The image of which would have undoubtedly put a severe damper on their enthusiastic ardour had they seen it from a neutral position. It would also have caused great amusement and considerable consternation to anybody walking in on the proceedings; fortunately, nobody did.

They eventually finished what they had started, for which Michael was eternally grateful. He had harboured fearful feelings of vulnerability having sex in the middle of the lounge precariously balanced on his favourite sofa. He would never feel quite the same again when sitting on the couch with Lauren. He was more used to sex being less hurried, with a little more privacy and in a bed. Semi-alfresco coitus was not really his cup of tea. The imminent threat of being caught *in flagrante delicto* was even more troubling.

Leja idly wandered towards the kitchen, looking for a piece of kitchen roll, having completed the deed and dismounted. She did not appear to have a care in the world, which she didn't in some respects. Michael looked at her body, which had recovered amazingly after the birth. She had almost regained her original figure apart from her breasts, which were still significantly more prominent. He credited this enhancement to her breastfeeding Joshua.

'Now, wasn't that nice?' exclaimed Leja loudly from the kitchen. 'Did you like spontaneity? I think that is what you say.'

'Yes, yes, it was, and it is, thanks.' Michael was still feeling a little flustered. His newspaper had been seriously ruffled during the altercation, and he was now endeavouring to put it back into some resemblance of order. He pondered briefly why Leja had adopted a more aggressive role in their lovemaking. Even more so than before she became pregnant with Joshua. Maybe, having a baby had ignited new energy in her body and made her more assertive. He wondered with some trepidation what else might be in store for the future. Then he remembered that he was happily married with a daughter, well, a daughter, and now a son, technically speaking. That was when he realised what an absolute shambles his life had become.

'That is our first make fucking for nearly three months,' said Leja wistfully. 'Am I still good bonking?' She posed vampishly in the doorway to the kitchen in just her knickers, leaning on the frame with one hand raised aimlessly above her head and the other gripping the door frame.

'Of course, you are,' replied Michael supportively, turning to look at her. Her odd terminology never failed to amuse him.

'I thought maybe I lose knack after having baby.' It was a plaintive, heartfelt enquiry filled with genuine anxiety and a tangible sense of apprehension. Michael realised that this confident, gregarious, and sensually provocative woman now standing virtually naked before him - the woman with whom he had been having a torrid affair for nearly a year, was still very vulnerable and susceptible. Even she was not immune to the vagaries of self-doubt, insecurity and the uncertainties that befell most pregnant women at some stage. She, too, needed and deserved some reassurance and comfort.

'You are an incredible woman, Leja. You are gorgeous, and you have an amazing body, and no, you haven't lost the knack, and one day you will make some fortunate man an amazing wife.' He smiled faintly condescendingly but not so she would notice.

Well, that was probably about as near as you will ever get to sincerity, thought Leja, so that will have to do for now. 'Thank you, Michael,' she replied before disappearing into the kitchen.

'What time would you like me to prepare dinner,' said Leja, popping her head back around the kitchen door? She was still half-naked.

'Shouldn't you put something on first?' asked Michael, glancing over. 'It could be a little dangerous.'

'No, I don't think so. Cooking without clothes is so... liberating. I feel I am in touch with food.'

Odd pictures appeared in Michael's head for a moment. He wasn't sure about the 'in touch with food' bit. 'I still think you should put some clothes on, just in case.'

'Okay, my little tiger, just for you.' She wandered out of the kitchen, across the lounge and back to her rooms. Michael expressed a sigh of relief and carried on reading the paper. Leja reappeared a few minutes later. Now wearing some Christmas tinsel on her head, a black G-string, high heels and some dangly earrings, which she flicked gently as she passed through the lounge en route to the kitchen.

'Happy Christmas, Michael,' she mumbled as she strolled past him - waggling her arse.

Michael glanced up at her, shook his head in despair and resumed reading the paper.

CHAPTER 29

Nice Jumper!
December 2009

I pressed the bell on the Farriers' front door. It was one of those old clockwork contraptions you must wind up daily. It produced a loud reverberating ringing sound. The whole door seemed to be rumbling in perfect syncopation. At that precise moment, it reminded me of a band of frantic dwarves bashing away on ridiculously small anvils in the Disney film *Snow White*. For a few seconds, I wondered who would have been responsible for winding the bell each day. Looking back much later, I realise it was a ridiculously incongruous thing to think about at that moment. But then, that is the way my mind works at times. Especially when I am simultaneously feeling nervous and exhilarated.

As I stood there waiting for the door to open, still mulling over the bell quandary – I became aware of a curious apprehension the like of which I had not experienced before. There was no rational explanation for why I should feel this slight uneasiness. It wasn't as if I had suddenly been gripped by an ominous sense of foreboding or concern; it was more a sense of mysterious expectation.

I attributed this sensation partly to not eating much during the day and partly to my bump. It had been irritably mobile for most of the day. Displaying its displeasure at being hunched up while I was driving and was now endeavouring to convey the message that it was hungry. *When is my food coming*? I could almost hear it mumbling. I would be having dinner as soon as I returned home. Hopefully, that would alleviate part of the odd sensation I was experiencing, if not all.

The front door slowly opened squeakily at first; it was one of those old, heavy, Gothic-arched oak doors with black iron bolt heads. Poppy rushed out and cuddled Daisy. 'I am so glad you came. I love you so much,' she exclaimed animatedly, then she glanced up at me and smiled precociously. 'Hello, Lauren.'

Initially, I was surprised but assumed that Daisy must have already told her my name.

'Hello,' I replied. 'You must be Poppy.'

Daisy said nothing. She didn't react well to overly affectionate greetings; she never had. The door opened further to reveal John wearing a perfectly matched rich cream-coloured jumper with dark-brown cord trousers. I have no idea why I noticed that, but I did. John gave me a lovely welcoming smile - and for a split second, I experienced a strange sensation I had never felt before.

'Nice jumper goes well with the trousers.' The words were out of my mouth before I realised how crass they sounded. I don't know why my first impression of John seemed to be based on half-decent colour coordination. That was ridiculous. I could hear my brain saying, *get a grip. What are you on?* But it was probably because that was what I did – make things appear accessible and desirable and lovely.

'Hi, Poppy,' said Daisy in a demure tone before glancing up at John. 'Hello, Mr Farrier. Thank you for inviting me.'

'It's our pleasure,' replied John. He smiled at me a little oddly. 'Hello. I'm ~~John, and~~John, and thank you for the compliment.'

I was a little confused for a moment before realising I had actually spoken the words that were in my head. It had not been my intention. I smiled and tried to move on, making a mental note to think a little more before saying anything else. Daisy also gave me a funny look, so I knew what I said must have sounded strange. I was usually at ease in this kind of situation, but not today. The lump gently kicked me, making its own comment. *Great,* I thought, *even my foetus has an opinion on my blundering sartorial analysis. Or was it a severe case of early-onset baby brain?* I wondered.

'Hello, I'm Daisy's mum, Lauren, but you probably already know that.'

John smiled. 'Would you like to come in? You probably want to check me out to make sure Daisy will be safe.' It was a little blunt and unexpected, but yes, that was why I had come, so I wasn't going to deny it.

'Thank you, but I'm sure she will be perfectly safe in your home. Daisy has already told me so much about you....'

John looked at me, a little intrigued. 'Has she? I didn't think there was much to tell.' John ushered me into the lounge; Daisy and Poppy disappeared into another part of the house, leaving us alone.

I looked around the room. It was old-world cottage style, with oak beams across the ceiling and vertical beams set into the bare brick walls. It was of a similar age to our house but had not been modernised. There were quite a few family photographs scattered around the room, some on a miniature grand piano, some on an antique French dresser - the kind with the ornate pillars at the front supporting the top cupboard - and some others on the window seats. On the walls were larger photographs and drawings in gilt frames of someone I immediately recognised as Katie.

'It's a lovely room, very cosy.' I walked around, looking at the photographs.

'Yes, yes, it is, *we loved it*. I am extremely fortunate; I grew up here and then inherited the house after my father died.'

'I am sorry, I didn't realise....'

'No, that was over ten years ago, not recently.'

In each corner, on a small table, sat a tall, highly polished black vase with what at first appeared to be a very ornate gold filigree pattern. The jars seemed almost translucent, but they were not glass. They were unlike anything I had ever seen before.

Simple candle-style wall lights lit the room; the ceilings were too low for chandeliers. The floor was polished umber flagstones; the colour reminded me of a holiday villa we had hired in Tuscany a couple of years ago. In the middle of the floor, a large rug covered the central part of the room. I knew a little about high-quality Asian-African carpets, something I picked up from Rosemary and her experience working in a friend's antique shop in Lavendon. This was a very high-quality Moroccan carpet. I knew that much.

'Beautiful carpet, quite exquisite,' I remarked. 'Looks around a thousand knots.' *The carpet must be safe territory, I thought. Please don't mention that it goes well with his jumper...* I repeated the last phrase to myself to ensure I didn't.

John looked surprised and smiled.

'Well, you know your carpets.'

'Not really. My mother taught me just enough to give the appearance of someone scraping by with plausible knowledge on the subject. But it's just bluff, really – I am sorry.'

John laughed. 'Nothing to apologise for. Your mother is very discerning, and she sounds very wise.

'Yes, yes, she is, and formidable at times.' I suddenly felt more at ease in his company.

'We bought it in Casablanca, would you believe, from a man who insisted we call him Rick when he obviously wasn't a Rick. He said he had always been fascinated by the film, so he called his shop 'Rick's.' Odd sort of character, but we both liked him. He told us a delightful story. It was just a sales patter, we knew that... but then they always do that, don't they? Cast an illusion to capture the moment and entice you to buy; you just can't walk away after that.

'He said it was an extraordinary carpet with special powers. If we both walked over it in our bare feet, once a day, every day, holding hands, we would always be in love. So we did, for years, and it worked...' John's voice trailed off for a few moments oddly... 'So, we spent an exorbitant amount of money buying the carpet and bringing it back to England, but it was worth it. We were on honeymoon, so...' He paused again momentarily. 'And Katie loved it.'

'It's beautiful.' I repeated a trite lamely. I could not think of anything to say after he had recalled the story. It was obviously something very special to them, probably a story he had not told many others. It was something the two of them probably kept to themselves, a private ritual until this moment, and yet, oddly, he had told me. Someone, who was virtually a stranger, and now I felt like an interloper, invading his private thoughts. It was an intrusion into his inviolate memory, and I felt I shouldn't be a part of it. I knew he wouldn't see it like that, but that was how I felt.

'The black vases are fascinating....' I wasn't sure which objects to mention and which to avoid. Anything in the room could have sentimental attachment, but the vases looked like a good bet as neutral territory.

'It's Shelbury Bridge,' said John. 'I tried to capture the legend of the curse. It's a common theme throughout a lot of my work. The customers in the shop seemed to like it.'

I glanced at John. 'The legend of the curse? I've never heard of any local legend.'

John smiled. 'Ah, you haven't lived here long, so you probably wouldn't have heard the tale.' He spoke as if he were a storyteller.

I was strangely captivated by something I knew nothing about, but somehow, I knew it would impact my life. 'So, what is this legend,' I asked? I was intrigued, not so much by what he said but by how he had shrouded the story in a gossamer haze of fairy tale enchantment.

'Have another look at the vases,' suggested John, smiling.

I walked back over to the largest of the vases to have a closer look; in fact, it was nearer the size of a water carrier's urn. This time I realised that the ornate gold fretwork pattern surrounding the vase was, in fact, a drawing of a bridge not unlike Shelbury Bridge. In the middle of it stood a boy and a girl holding hands and gazing down at a raging river below. The girl appeared impoverished, her dress was threadbare, and she had no shoes. The boy was different; he was well dressed in fine clothes and wore shiny buckled shoes. A small handcart was being pulled onto the bridge by an old man on one side. A well-dressed gentleman sat on a beautiful-looking stallion on the other. The drawing seemed to relate to a period around the eighteen-hundreds.

'What is the story?' I asked.

John smiled, 'It was back in 1732 when Jennifer Hawley met her fate. She was old and confused, and the good folk in Lavendon accused her of using witchcraft to turn her daughter into a pony for the devil. The simple fact that Jennifer's daughter had a deformed hand may have been the only reason the villagers accused her of the crime. Jennifer and her daughter were imprisoned in Lavendon jail, where they were both tried and found guilty of witchcraft. They were sentenced to death, but the daughter managed to escape. Jennifer was not so fortunate. The day after sentencing, she was stripped and rolled in tar. She was then hauled over Shelbury bridge to Baddesley-Minton, where she was tied to a stake and burnt to death. Her remains were thrown from the bridge into the river. But, before she died, she cursed the two villages. *If a man from one village and a woman from the other were to fall in love and marry, they would never have children, and their passion would wither and die.* Oddly enough, there were no marriages between the residents of the two villages for the next hundred years.'

Then one day around 1850, two star-crossed lovers, the two you can see on the vase, decided they wanted to be married and have children.'

'And one was from Lavendon, the other Baddesley- Minton?' I suggested.

'Yes, that's right.' John smiled again. He seemed to like retelling this tale. 'But they were afraid that if they did marry, they would fall out of love and never have children as the curse predicted. So they had to decide whether to stay together and take a chance or part forever. And that is the legend of the curse of Shelbury Bridge.' John waited for a few moments before continuing, 'So, what did they do?' he asked with an odd look in his eye.

'I don't know. I would probably get married and take a chance.'

'Ah, a true romantic,' replied John, smiling.

'Love is all there is - that's all that really matters,' I replied, surprising myself. It sounded almost poetic, if a little cheesy. Maybe it was a line from a Bob Dylan song. I wasn't sure where that had come from.

'But they didn't,' said John.

'Oh, they parted?' I was a little surprised at my own suggestion. It just didn't seem right.

'No, no, they didn't do that either. The two lovers jumped from the bridge holding hands and drowned in the raging river so they could be together forever.

'Oh.' I was slightly surprised by the ending; it wasn't what I had expected.

'But the curse on the bridge was lifted from that day.'

'So not all bad news?' I suggested cautiously...

'Absolutely not. Now all the poor maidens of Baddesley-Minton run over the bridge to Lavendon or possibly Godalming to find rich husbands as soon as possible.' John smiled at me with just a tiny hint of irony. I don't think he took the story too seriously.

'That's still an incredibly sad story.'

'But does it make sense?' asked John curiously.

'Yes, I think it does. I understand,' I replied, smiling and picking up a photograph of John and Katie. I couldn't help but gaze at Katie; she seemed to be smiling back at me. *Obviously, a very gifted photographer* was my first thought.

'As I said, the true romantic,' whispered John.

John gestured to a sofa, and I sat down, still clinging to the photograph, which I found myself strangely drawn to for some reason. Something about it intrigued me, but I did not know what exactly.

'Your wife is stunningly beautiful.'

'Thank you,' replied John quietly.

'I often saw her and your family when I drove Daisy to school – she may have mentioned me. I normally passed her as I crossed Shelbury Bridge, but Michael has started taking her to school since I started maternity leave – waiting for my bump to arrive. So, I don't see her anymore.' I rambled on a bit, talking in short staccato phrases, desperately trying to fill the airless spaces with a rhythmic articulation – but it wasn't working.

John's expression began slowly changing as I spoke. He appeared to become strangely and inexplicably saddened by what I was saying. My words seemed to be having completely the wrong effect on him. Then I remembered what Daisy said about Katie losing Trinity two years ago. I realised I may have been unintentionally tactless, yet, for some reason, I knew that was not it. That was not what had caused the change in his demeanour.

This was not going quite as I had expected. I seemed to be missing something, but I couldn't figure out what. I thought that maybe I should leave now before I said anything else out of place. Flight or fight and all that stuff started whizzing about in my brain, but it wasn't relevant to my situation.

'Yes, she loved walking the children to school over the bridge. It's very picturesque, especially in summer.' John sounded quite wistful yet perfectly comfortable with my slightly inane ramblings, so maybe, I had completely misread the situation after all.

'The whole area is an inspiration for much of my work, especially the bridge.'

'I imagine Katie is as well,' I added, glancing around at the many photographs of her on the walls. 'She's very stunning.'

'Yes...' replied John. He was going to say something else but changed his mind, and the moment passed. 'Yes, she was, very much so.'

'I'm actually a little jealous of her....' I didn't mean to just blurt that out, either. It sounded a bit crass again and a little weird, having just met John, but somehow it slipped past my lips before I could do anything about it. My mind was not working properly today for some reason.

'Jealous!' exclaimed John. 'But why? He appeared surprised, oddly and slightly confused by my declaration but not offended.

'Well, not actually jealous, that's the wrong word. Envious... that's the word.'

'But why so? I don't understand.' John still looked confused.

'She always seems so serene – unflustered and untouched by the world and all the chaos. Every time I see her, she always has this calming effect on me, which could last all day. And believe me, sometimes, I needed that. Sometimes I actually wished I had her life and not mine.'

'She was like that,' said John, 'but that's a terribly sad thing to say. I...'

'Don't get me wrong!' I exclaimed... John was now looking even more puzzled as I interrupted him. It was a bad habit I had picked up in board meetings. I was trying to get out of it, but not today.

'I love my husband, I love Daisy, where we live, and what I do, but something is missing from my life. For some reason, whenever I saw Katie, I knew she had found it... whatever it was, and I wish....'

I replaced the photograph on the side table but couldn't take my eyes off it. 'My world is so hurried... so intense... so...' I glanced up at John and then back to the photograph as I began to experience an unusual corporeal, almost metaphysical sensuality coursing through my body. It seemed to emanate from Katie's eyes, reaching out to me, trying to say something.

'I'm sorry, I'm beginning to sound a bit like an extremely thankless woman.' I smiled at John and glanced back at the photograph again. I was about to continue when I noticed John's face suddenly change. It was now almost expressionless, and the colour seemed to be slowly draining away. He sat down in the armchair facing me, looking strangely intense.

'So, tell me,' he asked quietly. 'When did you say you last saw Katie?'

'Oh, I haven't seen her since....' I half expected her to suddenly appear in the room and we would finally meet, but she didn't. I looked upwards, scrabbling around in my memory. 'I stopped going in every day around the end of November. So it was probably just before, maybe the last week in November. Yes, that sounds about right. It's the bump - it's taking control.' I pointed at my bump. 'It's a little bit precarious behind the steering wheel anyway, so Michael or Leja drive Daisy to school now. I just do the odd thing around the village. But why do you ask?' I was beginning to sense something wasn't quite right.

'Late November, you say,' queried John? His expression had now segued from confusion to incomprehension and disbelief. His mouth opened a little as if he were about to say something, but no words came out. After a few moments, he spoke almost in a whisper, 'Are you certain?'

'Yes, why? Have I got something wrong?' At that moment, I hastily backtracked, running back over everything we had spoken about in the past few minutes. That was when I realised he had placed Katie in the past tense with some of his replies. I had just assumed it was a slip of the tongue and had not taken any notice. But if he had not made a slip, that did not make any sense unless she had left him. Or she wasn't beautiful any longer, which made even less sense. 'Look, I am sorry if I've said something out of place, but whatever it was, I meant no harm.' All sorts of possibilities now began running around in my head.

John still looked stunned, as if he had lost the power of speech. His mouth was half-open, and his lips moved, but no words came out. He moved from the armchair to the sofa, but didn't take his eyes away from mine and then, very softly, said the words that would change my life forever...

'Katie died... nearly six months ago, on July the third, from cancer.'

I was suddenly overwhelmed, lost in a tsunami of absolute confusion. Desperately, I tried to reposition what I had just heard into the chronology of what I had done over the last six months. It was like rearranging a massive jigsaw puzzle with all the same pieces and somehow having to come up with an entirely different picture, but one that made perfect sense... This didn't. I was having a real problem processing the information – nothing fitted, and nothing had meaning. Yet, somehow, I knew I must make it fit. I gasped for air, suddenly realising I had forgotten to breathe.

What did I really know? I began asking myself. I had driven to work each day and had taken Daisy with me. We had passed over Shelbury Bridge daily, and at least twice a week, we had seen a lady... Katie, with her family walking over the same bridge to school, but John was now telling me that Katie had died six months previously. That was a certainty, or was it?

This was ridiculous. The whole scenario was preposterous, and for a moment, I began to wonder... I even considered whether my pregnancy's advanced condition and the related hormonal changes I was experiencing could have created some neurological disorder in my brain. But then I reasoned that I hadn't been pregnant for two and a half years – it had just been seven months, although, at times, it felt like a lot longer. I had first seen Katie long before I became pregnant. I hadn't been hallucinating then - that was the reality, I think. So why would reality segue into fantasy just because I had fallen pregnant? Daisy had seen Katie too, so I couldn't be mad (which did briefly cross my mind), but I wasn't a hundred per cent confident about that anymore. I wasn't sure of anything. Self-doubt had taken control, and that was the only way this could make any kind of sense – by disbelieving and doubting everything.

'Dead? Katie's dead? But...I am so sorry, so deeply sorry, but I didn't know – I don't understand....'

John interrupted. 'You said you see her, and you wanted her life?'

It sounded sinister and disturbing when John repeated the words back to me, but I had not intended it to sound like that.

'No, not like that. I just loved the life she seemed to have. It just seemed so perfect, but that was all wrong. Daisy and I saw somebody who was obviously Katie almost weekly for the last two and a half years. But I – we - must have made a terrible mistake over the last six months. We must have confused her with somebody else.'

John didn't appear as distressed as I would have expected him to be under the circumstances. He just seemed confused, but then so was I.

'Can you tell me exactly what you saw?' he asked, almost in a whisper. I was having a problem staying focused on John's face. I had never experienced such profound sorrow at such close quarters before. It was as if his eye sockets were turning into hollow voids.

'I saw somebody... pushing a buggy with, I think, twins, and behind her was Poppy, normally. Daisy knows Poppy by sight, I don't, so I had no reason to doubt what she was telling me and....' I stopped momentarily, hesitating to mention the baby that Katie had carried to school. The baby, whom she suddenly didn't bring any more. – But I couldn't stop now; something drove me on to tell it all, in its entirety, as I had seen it. 'About two and a half years ago, when I first noticed Katie, she was carrying a baby in one of those papoose carriers on her chest...' I could see tears begin to trickle down his cheek, and I didn't know what to do. So I moved a little closer and put my arm around him to try and comfort him for the pain I knew he must be suffering. Which I had unknowingly visited upon him and for which I alone was responsible.

'I am sorry. That shouldn't have happened. Please go on,' said John. *Why was he apologising?* I thought. *What has he done? It was me who should be apologising.*

'Well, there isn't much more to say, really. There was a dog, an Afghan hound, I think it was called... Alfie.'

'Yes, that's right, Alfie. That was Katie's. Well, the family's, really, but he was very attached to her.'

As if on cue, the dog I had seen so many times on the bridge wandered into the lounge and lazily shook its head. He had obviously been sleeping.

'Katie loved Alfie. We all do,' said John. Alfie wandered over and nuzzled his head on my lap as if I were an old friend.

'He likes you,' said John, sounding a little surprised. 'That is very unusual. He hasn't taken to any strangers since Katie....'

'I don't understand,' I mumbled. 'I just don't understand what has happened... happening,'

'Neither do I, but I believe every word you have told me. I don't doubt that, not for one moment, but there must be some simple explanation. I just have no idea what it is.' John instinctively put his arms out to embrace me, two kindred spirits searching for consolation. We held each other for a few moments before parting. I felt an inner warmth I had not experienced for a long time.

'I think I should be going now,' I whispered. I was feeling uncomfortably comfortable in John's arms. I was also becoming a little concerned over what Daisy would think if she were to walk in and see us embracing when we had only just met. It would take some explaining.

'Yes, yes, of course,' replied John. 'I am sorry. I have held you up. Your husband will be wondering what I've done with you. Probably thinks the nutty potter has stolen you away from him to keep for himself.' He smiled self-deprecatingly as if nothing was further from his mind - but I experienced another odd moment of confusion before getting up. The throwaway line had somehow encapsulated a subtle undertone of desire, a sense of yearning for something...

'The nutty potter?' I queried. I couldn't help but smile at the self-deprecating sobriquet he had used.

'I'm sorry. I thought you would have known,' said John.

'Known what?'

'That's my nickname – at school – so Poppy tells me.'

'Oh, I see.' I must have looked slightly intrigued and amused by the unusual epithet. It lightened the mood just a bit for a few moments.

I ran the phrase over in my mind several times to see how it sounded.

'I should explain,' said John. 'When I give one of my pottery demonstrations at the school, I try to keep it interesting by telling them stories about the history of pottery. Some of those are connected to some of the old Egyptian gods. My favourite one is Khnum, the god of the River Nile. He made babies with clay from the banks of the Nile and then placed them into their mother's wombs... he was known as the Divine Potter, you see.' John smiled. 'Anyway, one of the class, I can't remember who, no! Actually, I think I can. I believe it was Daisy, oddly enough. She promptly corrected my anatomical improbability. And ever since then, I understand they refer to me as the...

"The nutty potter," I offered.

"Yes, but I believe it is with affection. At least, I hope so.'

'It's not a bad nickname,' I suggested. 'It could have been worse, a lot worse... with children.'

'I guess it could have, but I don't mind. In fact, I find it rather endearing in an odd sort of way.' John smiled again.

'Do you want to say goodbye to Daisy?'

'Yes, yes, I would. Thank you.'

'I'll go and find her.' He stood and left the room, leaving me alone to tidy up my mascara.

After I had sorted myself out, I stood up and wandered slowly around the room, taking in some deep breaths, and then I started to look at all the other framed photographs. It was then I noticed something peculiar about them. In each photo of Katie and John, John appeared to be looking directly at the camera - as most people do in a photograph. But Katie seemed to be focusing on something else altogether. Something just slightly off-centre. It gave the illusion of the tiniest detachment from reality. As if she were staring abstractedly at somewhere or something in the middle distance just behind the photographer. Something nobody else could see or hadn't noticed. Then I realised what Katie was looking at: it was me.

At first, I thought it must just be an optical illusion or some sort of trick of the light, possibly the result of an instruction by the photographer. But as I moved from photograph to photograph, the same optical allusion recurred, each becoming more apparent. As the pictures must have been taken by different photographers over many years, this uncanny characteristic could not easily be attributed to just one person's suggestion. It was as if Katie was trying to convey something of immense importance to me by some sort of subliminal reimagining of the photographs. It felt like she was sending me a message, but I could not imagine what the message was.

It did not make any sense at all. Maybe, I was simply being overwhelmed by everything. Inexcusably allowing myself to be swept up in the emotion of my feelings. The photographs had been taken long before either of us was aware of the other's existence, so Katie could not possibly be looking at me. I must, therefore, be completely misreading the moment, and yet... she was;was somehow, I knew she was. This much was incontrovertible.

Daisy came rushing into the room and threw her arms around me. 'Thank you for letting me stay, Mummy. This will be such great fun.'

'It's only a couple of days, Daisy. I must pick you up on Sunday, ready for school on Monday.'

'Yes, I know, but...' Poppy came into the room and smiled at me again.

'Hello, Mrs Penfold. I am sorry I called you Lauren earlier. That was very impolite of me before we were properly introduced.'

'Hello, Poppy,' I replied. 'Don't be silly. Please call me Lauren. It's lovely to meet you properly, at last; we've seen you so many times on our way to school passing over Shelbury Bridge its....' Without even completing the sentence, I stopped, realising that it directly contradicted what John and I had been discussing only moments earlier. I still hadn't quite come to terms with that revelation. I glanced at John, who had adopted an expression I could only describe as tranquil bewilderment. He was obviously following the drift of the conversation but also confused by what I had told him earlier - and by my innocent reference to the sightings on Shelbury Bridge. For a moment, I thought he might take umbrage, but he did not. We were both in a quandary, but I knew he understood I had not said it to cause distress.

'Shelbury Bridge?' enquired Poppy, appearing a little mystified. 'We haven't walked over the bridge for ages, not since...' Her expression suddenly changed as she momentarily glanced towards her father. As if seeking guidance or visual absolution for almost uttering the words she was trying so hard not to say. 'So, Dad drives us in most days – through the forest. That doesn't go over the bridge.' She smiled briefly, relieved she had managed to negotiate her way out of the awkward moment but still appeared confused by my comment. She started to wander off before turning back to me with one last quizzical glance.

'You did see me at Daisy's birthday... I came over to your house for the barbecue. That must be what you remembered, but that was back in the summer.' Poppy smiled and turned again to wander off back in the direction from where she had just come.

I would have loved that explanation to have answered all my questions, but it wasn't even close.

'Are you coming, Daisy?' Poppy enquired as she walked away.

'Yes,' replied Daisy, hurriedly kissing me and then running after Poppy.

I looked at John again, further confused by what Poppy had just said. 'I still don't understand who I saw each day... if you were driving Poppy to school.'

'I can't explain it either,' said John. 'All I can tell you is, I have a lady who comes in each day to look after Louise while I'm driving the children to school... on the back road. It doesn't go anywhere near the bridge. She also looks after Louise while I work in the pottery.'

'Louise?' I enquired, a little surprised.

'Yes, our baby daughter.'

'That's my mother's middle name,' I replied, realising immediately how trite that sounded in the context of the conversation we had just had. 'I am sorry that sounded a bit crass. I'm having a very unusual day.'

John nodded as if to say, *please don't apologise – I understand*. 'It was Katie's idea. She chose the name. It was one of the last things she did before....'

'I'm sorry. I didn't mean to upset you again. It just seems like I'm saying all the wrong things today.'

'No, you're not - not at all,' reassured John.

'So how old is Louise?'

'Eight months. She was born two months premature – by emergency Caesarean section. Katie's cancer was spreading fast and moving aggressively toward her womb.' John paused for a moment gathering his thoughts before he continued. 'We lost Trinity in 2007 because of the after-effects of the chemo Katie received for breast cancer while she was still pregnant. The doctors said the chemotherapy would not harm the unborn child, but something unexpected happened. Trinity died a couple of months after she was born – the drugs had lowered her natural resistance to infection to a fatal level. She could have died from a simple cold; she was so vulnerable. After that episode, Katie refused all treatment when the cancer returned during her last pregnancy - until after Louise was born. But by then, the cancer was too far advanced… They couldn't save her. We did talk about it for a long time, but Katie was very stubborn. That was what she wanted, and nothing could dissuade her otherwise. As Katie was dying, she told me that everything would be all right eventually and that she had made an arrangement, but I never knew what she meant by that.'

I felt a horrible, sickly lump well up in my throat, accompanied by that horribly gastric taste you encounter just after vomiting. I just wanted to cry my heart out, I wanted to be sick, I wanted to say something good, I wanted this all to end, but it wouldn't, not yet. I wanted to hold John to comfort him, and I wanted to be held and be comforted, and I wanted the ground to swallow me, but it wasn't going to happen.

I began to conjure up horrible thoughts and visions of this cancer growing relentlessly, remorselessly towards Katie's unborn child, with only one dark, malevolent intention. Horrific images began to whirl around in my head, sending ice-cold shivers down my spine. I could see tiny little gossamer threads of death spiralling out in all directions from the tumour in search of virgin territory to invade, overcome, and consume. I had never had thoughts like this before and prayed to God that I would never have them again.

'I am so lost, John, so utterly bewildered and confused. I don't know what is happening or what to say or do. I feel so completely helpless and powerless. I always thought my life meant something, that it was going somewhere, that I was working to make us the life we wanted, and we would be happy, but we aren't, not really. And then, one day, the very first day, I saw Katie walking across that bridge. I knew instantly that my life was pointless and selfish and that it was all about material things apart from Daisy and Michael. Katie's life seemed so fulfilled, accomplished, and peaceful, and I wanted what she had and….'

I could hear myself mumbling, and I could feel my lips trembling. I was fighting to hold back the tears, tears that would have so easily helped me vent my feelings, but that would have been inappropriate. I had not suffered the loss: I was not the one in pain. This was not about me for once, this was about somebody else, but I felt a mess.

John moved closer to where I was sitting again, pulled me in close and held me for a while.

'I don't know what is going on, either. We will just have to deal with it together - when we find out what is happening. I am sure it will all be all right in the end.' They were reassuring words, and I took great comfort from them.

After a minute or so, we parted. 'I had better get going. My dinner will be ready, and I have some work to do tonight.' I smiled at John through smeared eyes. It seemed such an oddly incongruous thing to say. So pragmatic, so ordinary, which in a way, was a welcome relief to both of us after the traumatic, mind-challenging minutes we had just shared. I stood up and straightened my clothes.

'Absolutely. Nothing worse than being late for dinner,' said John stoically as he came to his feet.

'No,' I replied in a whisper.

'No,' repeated John, walking me to the front door.

'I must look a complete mess, and I apologise for upsetting you. I really didn't mean to....'

John leaned over and kissed me, his hands gently holding the back of my head, and at that moment, I knew exactly what Katie had found and what I was looking for. I wanted to carry on and kiss him forever and make love to him there and then, but I knew that was not going to happen and probably never would. Especially not today, as I had a huge lump just below my boobs that would have made things a little ungainly and highly problematic. Then I suddenly remembered that I was this size and shape because I had conceived my baby with another man, not my husband. My morality compass was seriously malfunctioning.

'You don't look a mess at all,' said John as our lips parted, '...you are a stunningly beautiful woman.'

I was a little confused, 'Why did you kiss me?' I blurted out.

'I felt compelled to.'

'But why?' I wasn't annoyed with him or anything like that. I just didn't understand.

'You have had a shock, we both have and in your condition, I thought I should do something to settle you down before you drive back. I wouldn't want you to have your baby in the car on the way home. I thought if I kissed you, it would put your mind at ease.'

'That's a really great line,' I replied, smiling.

'It's the best I can come up with, but I'm glad I did.'

'So am I,' I replied, 'so am I.'

'I am sure if we both think about what just happened for a few days, we will come up with a straightforward explanation and laugh about it.'

'Yes, I think you are probably right,' I replied, but with little conviction.

'I'll see you Sunday, teatime, then?' asked John.

'Sunday?' I inquired curiously.

'To pick up Daisy?' he hinted.

'Oh, yes, of course. I completely forgot.' I smiled and left, and John slowly closed the door as I walked back to my car.

On the way home, I thought about what we had said, but I thought a lot more about the kiss. I had not been kissed like that in a long time. In fact, I couldn't ever recall being kissed in a way that affected me the way that kiss had. It was probably down to my hormones; they were all over the place. I don't know. Nothing seemed any clearer, and I could not see any way that it could be. For a few seconds, my mind flashed back to that day on the bridge when I had seen Katie and heard the words, "*be happy with my life.*" The words kept running around in my head.

I arrived home and sat down for dinner with Michael, who appeared a little sheepish and uncharacteristically attentive.

'So, what are they like?' he asked.

'The Farriers?'

'Yes, of course.'

'To be honest, I don't really know.'

'You don't know, and you left Daisy there?'

'Katie's dead!' I was still feeling a little stunned by the events of the past hour and hadn't really had a chance to configure the words less bluntly. They just seemed to fall out of my mouth.

Michael gulped the gin he had just sipped. 'Dead! What do you mean, dead?' Realising at once what a ridiculous question that was, he apologised immediately. 'I'm sorry. What I meant was how, when?'

'Six months ago - cancer.'

'So how is what's his name?'

'John... that's Poppy's father's name, John,' I replied abruptly. For some inexplicable or possibly not-so-inexplicable reason, I felt a little exasperated. How could he not remember the name of the man who had been tutoring our daughter in pottery? Somebody Daisy had spoken about on various occasions, and the same person now looking after our daughter over the weekend.

'Yes, John. How is he doing?' *Another ridiculous question,* thought Michael. *I really do need some joined-up thinking here.* 'Is there anything we can do to help?'

'Not really. John is coming to terms with it as best as he can. It was expected, but nevertheless still devastating for him.' I wondered wistfully just how he must be feeling at that moment.

'Oh, I see,' said Michael. 'But... if she died six months ago...' Michael paused, cautiously deliberating on how exactly he should phrase his next question. He desperately wanted to avoid falling through another gaping trapdoor. 'How...' he paused for a second time, just to be certain how he should continue, still very uneasy about the central issue. 'How did you see her crossing Shelbury Bridge over the past six months if...?'

'Well, that's the thing. We did see her, but then we didn't.' I must have taken on a vaguely glazed expression as if I knew precisely what I was saying but not why I was saying it. I could see that Michael was struggling to understand.

'What?' replied Michael, desperately trying to get back on the same page as me.

'Well, we, that is Daisy and me, saw her and her family, I'm certain of that, but they never walked over Shelbury Bridge... Apparently, John has driven Poppy and the twins to school using the back road through the woods every day since Katie died in July... And that was nearly six months ago.'

'So, who did you see?'

'I don't know. Some sort of hallucination or an illusion... I really don't know.'

CHAPTER 30

Stuck like Glue.

Sunday evening, December 2009

I lowered the book I was reading, glanced at my watch, and then at Michael, who was half asleep listening to something on his iPod.

'I'm just going to pick up Daisy.' But Michael did not hear me, so I threw a cushion over to his armchair, which startled him momentarily.

'Ah! What was that!' he exclaimed, jerking in his chair and pulling off his earphones.

'I said, I am just going to pick Daisy up. I couldn't get your attention.'

'Oh, right. Are you sure? It is very dark and miserable out there. You should rest – I'll go.'

'You been drinking,' I replied abruptly, 'and I haven't.'

'Only a few glasses of wine,' replied Michael indignantly, as if that didn't count. The three-quarters-empty bottle of wine stood next to his glass.

'I think more than a few – it's still illegal, you know, and you will have Daisy in the car… I'll go.'

'It's Sunday, for Christ's sake. There's never any police around here on Sundays or any day for that matter.'

I looked at him, stunned with disbelief. 'You can't honestly believe you could safely navigate the back roads in the dark – half pissed! If you want to kill yourself and go to hell, fair enough, but I don't want you taking our daughter with you. And what do you think the Farriers would think? You turning up…' I didn't finish. I didn't need to.

Michael shrugged his shoulders childishly. He hated being chastised over his drinking, or 'bibulous merriment' as he liked to refer to it. A disingenuous euphemism he had picked up from one of his colleagues at work. That was when Michael had a job, of course – but he knew I was right.

'I'm Sorry, I forgot. I could pick Daisy up in the morning. I'm sure the Farriers won't mind her sleeping over for one more night. I could phone them.'

'Farrier!' I corrected quietly.

'Sorry?' said Michael, slurring a little and sounding confused.

'Katie is dead, so there is only the one Farrier senior: John.'

'And all the children,' replied Michael, after a long pause, sounding astonishingly puerile. 'That's Farriers, isn't it?' he accentuated the 's' at the end as if that made a significant difference. There is nothing I could think of that is more reprehensible than an obstreperous inebriate. Not at this particular moment, anyway. I hated him when he was like this.

'Yes, okay - Farriers,' I conceded with a glare of indignation that could have burnt a hole through ice.

'Anyway, Daisy has school in the morning, and I agreed to pick her up tonight. I'm sure John has enough to do with his four children in the morning without another disruption. So, I will fetch Daisy.'

Michael grunted something.

I slipped my coat on and left without saying goodbye.

Michael put his earphones back on and topped up his glass, balanced precariously on the edge of the table next to his chair. He took another long sip, closed his eyes, and slowly drifted back into the mellifluous oblivion of whatever he was listening to.

I drove slowly up the winding drive towards John's house as no lights were visible except for a single outside lamp on the porch, and there was no moon.

'I think that's your mum arriving, Daisy,' said Poppy, jumping up and peering out of the window of the bedroom they had been sharing.

'That's a shame,' said Daisy.

'Why?' asked Poppy.

'I like it here; you are all so like a family.'

'A family?' repeated Poppy curiously. 'But you have a family; you have a mum. I don't anymore. You are luckier than me.'

They both fell back onto Poppy's bed and gazed at the ceiling.

'I know you don't have a mum, but you are so happy, and your dad is so....'

'Nice?' offered Poppy a little whimsically.

'No, not nice. I don't mean your dad isn't nice; he is, but there is something more than that... there is something else here. I can feel it... something in the air. It seems to be in everything you all do and say. It's just different, I don't know what it is, but I like it.'

'That was Mum,' said Poppy.

'Your mum,' asked Daisy curiously?

'Yes, that's what she did; maybe that's what all mothers do. They bring everything together and make it stick.'

'Like glue?'

Poppy laughed. 'Like glue,' she repeated wistfully. 'Yes, like glue. Mum was the glue that held us all together.'

'But now she's gone, will you become unstuck? Will this all change?'

'No... nothing will ever change. My mum was super glue. We are all stuck together forever.'

'Forever,' said Daisy with a smile?

'Yes, forever.'

'I wish I were stuck in your glue,...' said Daisy.

They smiled at each other and hugged. 'Can we be friends forever,' asked Daisy?

'Of course,' replied Poppy firmly, 'and one day, you may even feel a little bit sticky too.' Daisy smiled and carried on looking at the ceiling.

I pushed the old wind-up bell and waited for the door to open, half expecting an elf to answer it as I had the first time I rang it on Friday. An elf didn't open the door - it was John.

'Hello, John.' I didn't mention what he was wearing this time.

John smiled, and speaking quietly, he replied, 'Hello Lauren, it's good to see you - come on through.' He closed the front door behind me, and I followed him into the lounge. The blazing fire in the hearth threw dancing shadows around the room, making it warm and welcoming. The place exuded a strange amity that I could not easily explain. If pushed, I would probably describe it as ethereal tranquillity, something I found very little of at home these days.

'Would you like to stay for a few minutes? I could make you a cup of tea while Daisy gets ready. She's probably still packing her bag.'

'Yes, that would be lovely, but can I ….'

'It's through there,' John interjected, pointing towards the downstairs cloakroom.

'Can I take your coat?'

I smiled, looking a little surprised. John had pre-empted me by a few seconds as if he knew precisely what I was going to ask.

'How did you…?'

'Katie always had to use the bathroom immediately after a drive when she was pregnant, especially when it was getting close to her time, as you must be. She said she had the bladder the size of a plum when she was carrying.'

'Oh, I see.' I handed my coat to John, smiled again, and turned to go to the cloakroom.

I wandered back across the lounge towards the kitchen, where I could see John making the tea.' 'It's very tranquil here.'

'It is now; they've all gone to bed except for Daisy and Poppy. Not so a few hours ago, though. It sounded like carnival day in Rio.'

For some reason, ~~that~~which made me smile - it conjured up strange visions in my head. 'Really?'

'No, not really, I love it. The sound of the children running around creating chaos and being happy – it's what Katie would have wanted.' John came from the kitchen with a tea tray and placed it on the table in front of the sofa. 'Please sit down.' I sat down on the sofa at the other end.

'How do you like it?' asked John.

'White, no sugar, thank you.'

'Look, I need to clear the air…' said John, 'I must apologise for the other night. I shouldn't have kissed you. I took advantage of an emotionally charged moment, and I shouldn't have… I really don't want that moment to spoil our relationship.'

'You aren't spoiling anything, and you didn't take advantage of me. I'm a big girl now.' We both smiled at the unintended pun.

'Good, good, I'm so glad. Poppy and Daisy get along so well, and I would hate to think I had done anything that might jeopardise their friendship in any way.'

247

'You haven't,' I replied... 'you really haven't,' I repeated under my breath. I wanted to reach across the small divide between us, touch John's face, and feel his lips on mine again, but I knew that couldn't happen. I wondered why I felt like this; all this confusion played havoc with my senses. A tiny smile flashed across my face for no reason.

'You're smiling, so presumably, you don't think too badly of me?' said John.

'I don't, not at all,' I replied. 'Look, I understand you are grieving for Katie right now, and I am pregnant, so we both have a lot of emotions we have to deal with right now. Coming here and meeting you like this is bound to cause some confusion, and everything is going to get a little muddled. We are both looking for reassurances about different things, so we are naturally vulnerable to external sensitivities. That is why what happened, happened, ships in the night and all that....'

I had given John the perfect escape route; all he had to do was agree with me, and it would have finished there and then, but he didn't take it. 'Listen to me, I am beginning to sound like some agony aunt out of the Mail; I do go on a bit at times, please forgive me.' We both smiled at my admission.

'Nothing to forgive,' replied John. He poured two cups of tea and passed one to me.

'Can I tell you something, Lauren? Something I have not spoken about to another living soul, something that Katie and I talked about....'

'Do you really want to tell me? I'm virtually a stranger; should you confide in me, I feel like I'm intruding into....'

'No, you're not intruding. I feel I can. I want to... this is what Katie wanted.'

I sipped my tea and looked at John, surrendering to his request.

'Before she died, we made a pact. Katie told me I must not grieve, well, not for too long. She put a time limit on it... Three months. She said that would be perfectly respectable under the circumstances. She didn't want me moping around the house for years, slowly turning into a turnip.'

'A turnip?' I exclaimed, thinking I had misheard John.

'Yes, a turnip. Katie meant a hermit, but she thought turnip sounded better – that was Katie.' We both laughed. The admission brought a welcome lightness to the moment and another poignant insight into a remarkable woman I would never get to know.

But I couldn't keep it up for long. The thought of the unimaginable pain Katie must have gone through. Knowing that she was about to lose everything she held dear was starkly juxtaposed with the ridiculous levity and flippancy of the moment. This was too much to absorb. The tears welled in my eyes and began running down my cheeks. I was laughing, and I was crying, and I was very confused. How could I ever consider that a man like John, who had a wife like that, would ever want to have anything to do with a woman like me. Someone who had cheated on her husband, was pregnant by her boss and had now kissed another man, John, passionately only two days before?

'Hey, there's no need for that. I've come to terms with it now. We all have.' John moved across the sofa to comfort me.

'But how? I don't understand how you can?'

'Because she insisted. She sat us all down a few days after Louise was born and told us what would happen and how we would deal with it. And when the children had gone to bed, she told me something else.'

I wiped the tears away with my handkerchief, which I always kept close at hand these days, and tried to compose myself. John was obviously saddened at having to recall the conversation they had had. But at the same time, the joy of the times they had spent together just outweighed the sorrow – and it showed.

'She told me she would help me to find somebody else, somebody who would take her place and help to glue us all back together again.'

I looked into John's eyes and saw the humility and stillness that made him what he was. But I still didn't quite understand what he was saying.

'But how? How could she do that if she was….'

'She said it would take a little time, but she had found someone, and soon she would let me know.'

Daisy bounded into the room, followed by Poppy. 'Hi, Mum, I'm ready.'

'Hi, darling.' Daisy threw her arms around me and kissed me.

'I have had a lovely time and would love to come over again. It's so nice.'

'We will have to see. I'm sure Mr Farrier is terribly busy.'

John looked at Lauren and mouthed, 'any time.' I struggled to get to my feet; the couch was lower than at home. John's arms shot across to help me, and his touch made me feel good. 'Thank you. It can be a bit of a struggle at times with junior.'

'I understand.'

We both walked to the door, and Daisy opened it and ran out to the car. Poppy waved and turned to me.

'Goodbye, Mrs Penfold. Thank you for letting Daisy come over. We had great fun.'

'I thought I was Lauren now?'

'Is that okay?' asked Poppy, glancing up at her father.

'Of course, it is,' replied John.

'Goodbye, Lauren,' said Poppy. 'See you soon.' She skipped back across the lounge and up the staircase.

'Will I see you again?' asked John quietly.

I didn't answer but cautiously stepped back from the door, so Poppy couldn't see me from the car - I pulled John close, wrapped my arms around him and kissed him. I had been waiting to do that for two days, and as I did, I felt the same feelings again, which I hadn't felt for so long. I could sense that John didn't want to let me go, but he did – eventually. I turned around and started waddling back towards the car but then felt this overwhelming compulsion to turn and walk back to where John was standing. John was now looking a little confused.

'You can see me every day if you want to... when we wake up together.'

John didn't know what to say; he seemed to have lost the ability to speak.

'I'll ring you in a couple of days... we can talk.'

'Please,' replied John smiling.

I turned to leave, but this time with a new emotion to consider, along with all the other emotions swimming around my head. I also wanted to skip back to the car, but that would have been utterly ridiculous for several reasons...

CHAPTER 31

The Final Redemption.
April 2010

Leja was up early as Joshua had been crying most of the night, and Michael had gone upstairs into the spare bedroom to get some sleep.

He ambled downstairs into the kitchen, where Leja was making some milk up for Joshua while nibbling on a piece of toast.

'Morning, Michael. Would you like coffee?'

'Yes, that would be nice. I will skip breakfast, though. Get something at the office. I need to show willing as I'm the new boy.' He grinned at the thought.

It seemed odd that Lauren was no longer there; whatever they had, it was gone now. Lauren had been replaced by the soulless entity that was Leja, the woman he had started an affair with while his pregnant wife was out working. She was pleasant enough, very amiable, and Michael still had innovative sex with her occasionally, whenever time allowed. Depending on his state of mind when he arrived home from the office. But he had now started drinking again on the train home. It dulled his senses just enough to allow him to forget what he had once had. And had let slip away through carelessness, lack of attention and plain stupidity.

More alarmingly, and for some indiscernible reason, he had now developed an erectile dysfunction problem. So, he was worse off now in the sexual gratification department than before the separation. Maybe it was his age, he thought, past his prime at nearly forty, or was it something psychological. *Who knows?* He mused quietly to himself in his study from time to time.

He sat down at the kitchen table, sipped his coffee, and made a mental note to go and see a shrink in the city when he had a chance; that would sort the problem out.

However, he did wonder how he had managed to artfully navigate the short distance from feast to famine so quickly, hardly noticing the transition at first.

Daisy staying over was part of the separation arrangement. But she had never quite taken to Leja's sudden unexpected elevation to stepmother-in-waiting. Which was precisely how she now regularly referred to her, much to Leja's irritation.

They had been friends once, but their friendship had faded like winter's early morning mist over Shelbury Bridge. Any respect that Daisy may have had for her had gone. It went when it became apparent that she had been instrumental in changing forever the family unit that Daisy understood and had once enjoyed. This aspect of the new parental arrangement was not to Daisy's liking, not one bit. As far as she was concerned, it was a derisive and divisive attempt to inveigle and corrupt her conventional sensibilities. She refused to allow this parody of a relationship to change or affect her opinion. Fortunately, the situation at John's house was completely different and far more to her liking.

Leja had also not fully embraced the clichéd stereotypical mantle of "the other woman." She was far smarter than that. She was a bright new variation on an ancient theme. These days, lithe Lithuanian au pairs invariably marry their employers and not always the husband. *A lesson for us all,* thought Michael. That was the morality tale he expounded at every opportunity, but only to female co-workers. He felt he could ingratiate himself with them by explaining the downfalls of infidelity - and how stupid he had been. But his self-effacing confessional façade lacked integrity and verity, the most fragile elements of any relationship. They considered him a weak, gullible, feckless fool lacking moral fibre. Someone who couldn't keep his dick in his trousers elicited little sympathy from them. The servant had become the master and was now assailed continuously by the hubris of this oxymoronic relationship.

He tended not to discuss the change in his marital status with male colleagues. It would only invite further scorn, derision, and embarrassment. Most of them had Eastern European au pairs who they were probably shagging. Hopefully, with more decorum and discretion than he had exercised.

'Is Daisy up yet,' asked Michael, casually munching on the piece of toast that Leja had been nibbling? She flashed Michael a look of disdain as if he had stolen something of immense value from her. The Baltic bear was beginning to show its teeth.

'Would you like toast?' she asked brusquely.

'No thanks, I'm not hungry right now,' mumbled Michael. Leja looked at him oddly. The concept of laboured irony was something she still didn't fully understand.

'I think I heard her moving around just now,' said Leja.

'What?' asked Michael.

'Daisy. I think I heard her moving upstairs.'

'Right, okay. I'll give her a call.' Michael crossed the lounge to the staircase. 'Daisy, are you up yet? Breakfast is ready, and we're off in ten minutes.'

'Coming, Dad,' came the disembodied reply from somewhere in the distance.

'She's coming,' said Michael, stepping back into the kitchen and sitting down to finish his coffee.

'I will make her toast today, yes?'

'Yes, that should be fine.' Leja flashed Michael an odd expression. Seldom did she get it entirely right.

Daisy suddenly appeared in the kitchen. 'Hello, I'm here and ready.' She dropped her weekend bag on the floor. 'I'll take my washing home for Mummy to do.' She smiled at Leja – it spoke volumes.

'Okay, that is good. Would you like toast and jam,' asked Leja?

'No,' replied Daisy a little abruptly. 'I will have porridge, please.'

'Okay,' said Leja, flashing another wincing expression at Michael. 'Two minutes.'

Michael got up from the table, unplugged his iPhone, which had been charging on the worktop, and slipped it into his jacket pocket. He checked some details on his laptop, closed the lid and picked up his overcoat and scarf.

'Right, I will see you and little Joshy tonight,' said Michael, placing a peck on Leja's cheek.

'Tonight, I make special Lithuanian dish for supper. Cepelinai and zrazai,' said Leja.

'Em, sounds delicious,' remarked Michael a little cagily.

'See you in two weeks, my favourite stepmother-in-waiting,' said Daisy mischievously, air-kissing Leja as she made her way to the front door.

'Goodbye, Daisy, we had wonderful time, yes?' asked Leja. It was an odd heartfelt question, and Daisy could see that Leja was trying her best to make everything work. They had been good friends once before everything had changed, and she knew it couldn't all be Leja's fault.

'Yes, we did. See you in two weeks.' Recanting a little from her prior standoffishness, Daisy walked back over to Leja and hugged her. Michael smiled at Leja, happy that they appeared to be getting on a little better, and then they left. Leja looked a little surprised and stood for a moment in the empty kitchen pondering...

Daisy threw her overnight bag into the boot, jumped into the back seat behind Michael and did up her seat belt.

Michael drove cautiously up the drive. There had been a heavy frost overnight, and ice had formed on the puddles in the shingle. April was late for a frost, but winter had come late this year. Out on the main road, he turned left and headed for Lavendon. After about five minutes, Shelbury Bridge came into view. As always, the valley to the left down to the river, wondrously picturesque in its early morning glory, took his breath away for a few seconds. Then, just as they approached the bridge, Daisy gazed at what she saw on the pathway on the other side.

'Look, Dad... there's Poppy and Jamie and Ka....'

She stopped talking for a moment. Michael was now also looking across to where the family were walking, but it wasn't Katie. It couldn't be. It was Lauren.

'I'm sorry, Daddy, I made a mistake. Can you stop, please?'

'What?' said Michael. 'Stop? Why?'

'Stop the car, please, Dad.'

'But why?'

'I want to get out, Dad. I want to be with Mum and my family.'

Michael pulled the car up just at the start of the bridge. Daisy jumped out and came around to the front window, which Michael had lowered.

'I love you, Dad. You are lovely, but I have to be with....'

'I understand… I understand. Off you go.' Daisy checked both ways and crossed the road, running over to Lauren. Michael felt a gut-wrenching sensation in his stomach.

'Hello Mum, hi Poppy, hi you two.' Jamie and Julia hugged Daisy, Poppy grabbed her hand, and they reformed into an orderly queue. Lauren was upfront, holding Jamie and Julia's hands, followed by Poppy and Daisy, now chattering away. Last of all was Alfie, looking a little older these days and walking a little less vigorously than he used to, but still connected to Poppy by the lead she was holding. Everybody was smiling, talking, and happy, especially Lauren. She was more content now than she had been for a long time. She now left Louise and Thornton at home with John; he liked looking after them in the mornings while Lauren walked the children to school.

As Michael slowly passed this nomadic caravan, he shouted across the road to Lauren, 'I'll drop Daisy's bag off tonight. Is that okay?'

'That will be fine. Are you okay,' asked Lauren?

'Fine, absolutely fine,' replied Michael, smiling.

'Good. I'm glad… I'm so glad.' She smiled and then carried on walking.

Michael smiled to himself and pressed the button to wind the window up, but he wasn't fine, not at all, and would probably never be completely fine again. He drove on to the railway station and boarded the train to London. But life would never be the same. He would drive to the station on that same route each day for the next ten years. Some days he would pass the lady on the bridge that used to be his wife, and each time he would wonder why she no longer was and why she was now married to somebody else. But he would never understand. How could he?

LAUREN'S PROLOGUE

March 2012

As for me? Well, Thornton Penfold was born on the third of March 2010, and I left Michael three weeks later after I told him I had been unfaithful and Jeff was Thornton's father. He did not understand why I was leaving, and being perfectly honest, I didn't either. I just felt I had to go. Michael was puzzlingly forgiving about my affair with Jeff and having his baby, but still, I left. He still didn't mention his relationship with Leja then; that surprise came later.

I pitched up at John's house with Daisy and Thornton, making a passable impression of a fallen woman from a Dickens novel. When he opened the door, he did not utter a word; he didn't have to. He just pushed the door a little wider and beckoned us in. As I passed him, I looked up, and he smiled, and I knew instantly that I had made the right decision. He kissed me hello, then casually walked past me to the car to bring in our suitcases as if everything were as expected, but then it was. We were home at last.

About a year after that, around July 2011, while shopping in Tesco's in Godalming, I ran into Leja's Ex, Walter - the plumber.

'Hi Walter, how have you been? I thought you had moved to London.'

Walter didn't recognise me straight away. 'It's Lauren, Lauren Penfold. Don't you remember me? Leja used to be our au pair before….'

'Ah yes, I remember now. I should not forget such a lovely lady,' he replied apologetically, giving me a wonderful smile; he had beautiful teeth. *You're an old smoothie,* I thought to myself. Maybe Leja was right to dump you after all.

'So, have you seen Leja lately?' I asked in all innocence.

Walter looked at me a little oddly at first. For a moment, I thought a fly had landed on my nose, and I quickly tried to focus on the tip, but there was no fly. I glanced back at Walter.

'Leja dumped me for another man and have his baby.'

Well, yours, I thought, was my first reaction.

'She told me she was having affair with a married man, and they would soon be married after he get divorce.'

Ahh… The penny dropped. Well, not so much a penny, more like a large bag of wet cement. Prat. What a bloody stupid prat, I thought.

'Who was he? Do you know?' I asked idly. As if I needed to.

Walter went blank on me again; the Polish have a habit of doing that when confused.

'Leja tell me it is Michael… your husband. Are you still married?' I could not believe he had just asked me that. Homer Simpson's classic exclamation sprang to mind. Derrrrrrr!

Walter looked genuinely concerned, slowly realising he might have let the cat out of the bag. 'I am sorry if I give you surprise.'

'No, of course not, nothing to apologise for. I left Michael two years ago, but for another reason.'

'Oh, that is good. So, are they still together?'

'Oh, yes, they are.' *For better or worse*, I mumbled under my breath.

He looked down at the double buggy I was pushing. 'These are new, yes?

'Louise and Thornton? Yes, they are. The other four are at school.'

'Six children! That is wonderful, but how do you cope?'

'I just do. It's what I've always wanted.'

'I see,' he replied, but I don't think he did.

'I thought you only had one daughter when I was with Leja?'

'That's right.'

'So how…' he was going to ask me something deep and meaningful, but he changed his mind. I could see his brain whirling around in tumultuous confusion.

'It's complicated,' I said, smiling.

Walter glanced at his phone. He had just received a text at the most opportune moment. This enabled him to extricate himself from this peculiar and somewhat uncomfortable conversation.

'I must be going. I have emergency… Big leak in anti-natal clinic.' I didn't dare ask.

He was gone, and I was left there deliberating over a monumental event in my earlier life that I hadn't known anything about twenty minutes earlier.

"Bastard!" I muttered as I walked away. Well, not actually muttered, not going by my fellow shoppers' reaction in Tesco's. Any tiny embers of guilt I may have harboured about leaving Michael were totally extinguished at that moment. My decision had been entirely justified. "The bastard!" I repeated, "The absolute bastard."

Still, I didn't love him anymore, so did it really matter? I did have my Parisian fling with Jeff and have his baby, so all's fair in love and war, I suppose. Talking about Jeff, well, that was a bit of a surprise too. It turned out that he and Zefe were now affectionately known as Jefe and Zefe (I am not making this up, God's honest). Anyway, Zefe sold Zeferelli's in Highgate, and Jefe retired from Barrington Marsh Associates with his pot of gold. They opened Zeferelli's Café together in the Piazza San Marco in Venice. It turned out that Zefe did have a bit of Italian in him, along with quite a few other nationalities. Anyway, they were now happily living together; well, they were the last I heard. I was right all along about Zefe, but a little surprised about Jeff, but then, maybe not. Did I ever mention Thornton to Jeff? Well, that's for another day, another book.

I fondly remembered my lunch dates at Zeferelli's with Jeff and our trip to Paris, but that was another life for me and definitely a different experience for Jeff.

Michael managed to get a decent job just after I left, back in the city. He was now happily ensconced with son Joshy, the lovely Leja and occasionally Daisy when she stayed over. But she only did so out of spite. She had overheard Michael talking one night about his inability to make love to Leja whenever Daisy stayed at weekends. And as they apparently never managed it during the week, Michael being too tired by the time he got home. Eleven-year-old Daisy now had virtual control over her father's sex life. Something which she found highly amusing, even more so since she found out he was Joshy's father, which obviously, I had to tell her as soon as I had found out. Poor Michael. I feel so sorry for him at times. Not really – just joking.

As for John, well, I explained Jeff's situation, but it did not make any difference. I had had a fling because I was unhappy, so what. That was all he ever said about it, apart that is from something he muttered just once: 'It takes two minutes to father a child, but a lifetime to become a father.' I know, a bit car bumper stickerish, but it stuck in my mind then and would stay in my mind for the rest of our lives together.

Finally, there is Katie, the woman I never met and the woman whose place I took. But she chose me; she wanted it to be me, the person to continue her life and be the mother to her children because she could not be there any longer. Wherever you are, Katie... Thank you. Thank you for choosing me. I love you, though I will never know you. You have made my life complete, and hopefully, somehow, someday, I will return the favour.

Did I return to Barrington Marsh Associates and continue with that fantastic job they had given me? Please tell me you have been paying attention.

No, I did not. I took back control of my life, and that is how it will stay.

The End.

I would like to thank you for reading my story. I would also like to make a special dedication to Rachael, a lady I have never met. But whose words touched my heart and inspired me to write Be Happy with my Life after reading her Facebook posting.

RACHAEL'S FACEBOOK POSTING (AROUND 2016)

I used to be a full-time working mum. Every morning for the past 10 years, I have driven from Torquay over the Shaldon bridge on my way to work... and most days, I've driven past a beautiful lady with crazy blonde curly hair... she started out 10 years ago, walking her eldest baby to the primary school with her younger ones carried on her chest and in double buggies while walking her beautiful puppy retriever.

Every morning I would watch her, in awe at how organised she was, how she could possibly manage and how happy her babies looked. I would then continue the rest of my journey to work with a lump in my throat that someone else was doing all those things with my babies because I felt I needed to be at work.

This lady made me realise that actually, I should work a little less and learn to manage a little more...

So, as I drove past you this morning and I saw you kissing your daughter on the forehead, who once I saw as a tiny baby and is now a little lady... and your dog was walking at a much slower pace beside you now he's so much older. I imagine all your other children have now grown up and go to secondary school and walk themselves to school... I just wanted to post on here, in the hope somehow it will reach you, to say thank you. Because of you, I have now reduced my working hours... so I can spend some mornings at home doing the crazy school runs with all my babies; I make sure I go and fight back the tears watching all their school plays & bake (mainly inedible) cakes for the fetes... and I love all of it!

It's amazing that seeing a 30-second glimpse of someone else's life once a day can make yours so much more enjoyable xx (sic)

If you did enjoy this book, why not try the fifth in the Story Teller Pentalogy. Each tale explores a relationship and how it can change.

CHAPTER 1. THE KILLING PLAN.

Part I

2023. For reasons never clearly explained at the inquest, the car in which they were travelling untethered itself from the left-hand carriageway matrix, crossed the electronic central reservation and re-tethered itself to the right-hand carriageway oncoming vehicle matrix. Strangely, no alarms sounded. The sixty-ton SCOMTEL freightliner practically obliterated the vehicle. Rendering it utterly unrecognisable after nine sets of giant wheels had passed over it. Eventually, the freightliner pulled to a halt approximately two hundred yards past the point of collision. At first, the police did not believe the wreckage was a car at all but simply something that had fallen from the back of a lorry. However, closer inspection of the debris – coupled with the frantic emergency telephone call from the driver of the freightliner – indicated that something far worse had occurred.

The ferocity of the impact had left no part of the flattened vehicular collage thicker than the width of a finger. This meant there was insufficient body mass to immediately confirm the involvement of people. The tech team could only find scraps of body tissue, blood residue and some tiny fragments of bone. Most of the blood had soaked into the road by the time the emergency services arrived. This could easily have been attributed to a hedgehog or a badger, but it was enough for the forensic team to later confirm from DNA analysis that two people had been involved and who they were. The only item from the car that appeared undamaged by the impact was the tiny plutomarium isotope from the vehicle's power system. Somewhat conspicuously, this was lying in a small pool of quietly bubbling mahogany brown liquid. It glowed with a shimmering shade of pink, a chemical reaction usually triggered by the presence of saltwater.

The road was closed for two days while the forensic investigation team tried to discover how a vehicle could break free of the AMGS (Atlas Matrix Guidance System) and then reattach itself on the wrong side of the road. The many failsafe procedures built into the road and the computerised guidance system integrated into every Protton vehicle's electronic brain made it technically impossible. Nevertheless, it had happened. It was eventually determined at the inquest that it was probably due to an anti-transient system malfunction of an unspecified nature, whatever that was supposed to mean.

Catherine
Part 2

It was a late summer's day in 2009. Still warm but soft, delinquent breezes had begun to blow, heralding nature's autumnal transition. A time when unforgiving temperaments had mellowed and were starting to prepare for the equinox that would eventually sweep them, imperceptibly, into the cold depths of winter. However, before those

261

darker days arrived, there would be a period of graceful light and long shadows. Hopefully, these would soften the sharp edges of the harsh reality that was to follow.

The first golden leaves were beginning to fall. Each caught up in a spiralling vortex as if waltzing to Strauss at a Venetian ball in the Doges' Palace before breaking free and wistfully pirouetting to Mother Earth. Occasionally, one or two would find a final breath of wind. And for a few moments, in silent desperation, they would swirl upwards one last time to dance around the gates of Downing Street. Amid the hustle and bustle of daily life, each leaf seemed to believe it was an integral and indispensable part of the proceedings before it quietly surrendered to the inevitable and eventually settled down onto the cold grey pavement. Finally, it was preparing to shrivel away and turn to dust or be swept away by the council street cleaners.

Sergeant Mackenzie Parish, as he was then, first noticed Catherine on one of these days – their lives would always be marked by such moments. She was part of a delegation of trainee doctors visiting Number Ten to present a petition. They objected to the excessive hours they were forced to work in hospitals during their final years at medical school. They believed this practice jeopardised the fundamental integrity of the job for which they were being trained. Catherine had only been at medical school for just over a year but still felt passionately enough about their grievance to join the committee that had prepared the petition. The fact that she was stunningly beautiful had not been wholly lost on the other committee members. To some degree, they were guilty of co-opting her into assisting them on the established marketing tenet that the media were always slightly more responsive to and supportive of a cause with a visually attractive and articulate spokesperson – and a justifiable complaint. A patronisingly sexist ploy to present an argument, possibly. But doctors live in a world of pragmatism - not a make-believe Disneyland where dreams come true and there is always a happy ending. They needed all the media attention they could muster, and Catherine was the means to that end.

Parish was there on routine security duty when he first noticed her in the crowd of interns chanting and waving placards. She was hard not to see. She also happened to be holding the petition, patiently waiting her turn to present it to the aide who eventually came out from Number Ten and up to the railings that now barricaded both ends of Downing Street. The days of handing over a petition, with all the attendant kudos of a photograph in front of the famous black door, were long gone. Catherine had read somewhere that the colour you painted your front door indicated something about you. Black, oddly, was considered to convey the message, 'Stay away! We don't appreciate visitors – Private.'

On the other hand, Red meant you were probably a liberal-minded extrovert, an exhibitionist, al-fresco sex sort of person. Green suggested a traditionalist, staid, conformist; white, organised, religious, neat, clean, and so on. It was all vacuous rubbish, of course, but it filled a couple of pages in a Sunday colour supplement once a year.

Although she was some ten yards away, her zeal and animated desire to make her point were plain to see. It was this burning desire that first captured Parish's attention. Charming itself into his imagination where it ran wild. When their eyes met, it was just one fleeting glance, but in that split second, he could see the fiery passion in her soul. Something that had been missing from his life for a very long time.

Catherine turned back to speak to the aide from Number Ten, and the moment was gone. She handed over the petition, thanked him with a smile, and press photos were taken. Garrulously walking away with her friends, momentarily exhilarated at having succeeded in her mission, she turned back – the frenzy of the previous moment's elation now abated – and gazed at Parish for the second time. The apocryphal tales of love, at first sight were never further from either of their minds. But in that one fantastic moment, any preconceived cynicism was shattered like an enormous explosion in the brain. She turned around and made her way slowly back through the jostling crowd toward where he stood. It felt like one of those stupid slow-motion moments in a film when the camera was over-cranked and re-run at normal speed. He continued to gaze at her as a stunned gazelle mesmerised in the glare of headlights. The traffic's commotion and noise became muffled and grey and began to fade from his consciousness. He felt his heart pound in his chest as if it were about to burst. This wasn't really happening, he thought. I've been watching too many romcoms. Maybe I should get out more and socialise with ordinary people. All these thoughts raced through his mind when she suddenly stood before him, gazing up interrogatively, without a splinter of shyness.

'I'm Catherine,' she spoke quietly and smiled disarmingly. 'Would you like to come for a drink? We're celebrating.' The lilting quality of her voice seemed to hang listlessly in the air.

I didn't answer immediately. I needed to make sure I hadn't imagined it. My throat had chosen this particular moment to dry up for some inexplicable reason, so I couldn't respond, even if I had wanted to. After a few moments, sufficient moisture returned to my throat, and I was able to reply to what was now a somewhat perplexed Catherine.

'Eh, yes,' I eventually spluttered out, 'but I'm on duty right now. Could it be tonight? I'm off at six.' I suddenly felt like a little boy back at school, explaining to a potential date that I had to stay behind in detention and couldn't walk her home. It all sounded so embarrassingly feeble, and we both knew it.

'Oh! You're a police officer!' she replied coyly. 'I didn't realise.'

'Eh, yes,' I replied a little cautiously. I think my eyes instinctively opened a little wider despite the sunlight. They tended to do that under certain circumstances, this being one of them. Probably has something to do with the brain suddenly demanding more visual information to fully assess how that admission affected someone's demeanour. Body language, expression, eyes...

'Is that a problem?' I asked, suddenly aware of a hint of intractability in her voice. I was unaccustomed to being asked out by an attractive woman, especially one I had never met before. Her precocious suggestion had caught me completely off guard. Catherine had also detected the thin martyred air of remorseful anguish in the tenor of my voice (which she later told me she found quite endearing) as if this liaison might suddenly end because of who I was, and all would be lost. Like most women, she was hard-wired with the mysterious ability to extrapolate a meaningful inference from the tiniest gesture or inflection - as far as men were concerned.

'No, not at all, I just didn't realise,' replied Catherine reassuringly. The words were enough to staunch any further loss of confidence I might have felt, and I think she knew that. I had half expected some dry political comment, conditioned as we were to be taunted with all manner of cleverly constructed, politically biased epigrams at these assemblies - but none was forthcoming. 'Aren't you going to arrest me then,' she asked playfully? Her face lit up with contained pleasure as she swivelled playfully on her high heels, her eyes never losing contact with mine.

'Why should I arrest you? I asked. Surprised at the question and unsure how I should reply. 'Have you done something wrong?'

'No,' she replied, 'but I'm sure you could think of something... if you really wanted to.' I smiled; unbelievably, I knew I was already falling in love. We stood there silently for a moment - just looking at each other as if unsure of what should happen next.

'Pen!' she suddenly spluttered, holding out her hand and waving it around jauntily.

I rummaged desperately through my pockets and eventually found a pencil, which I held up, maybe a little over-jubilantly. Catherine smiled kindly, trying not to laugh, took it and scribbled down her telephone number on a scrap of paper she had produced from her jean pocket and handed them back to me. 'Call me when you are...' Catherine paused for what seemed like an interminable amount of time, carefully considering which word to use to close the instruction before eventually settling on 'available.' She uttered the word slowly, letting it drift out of her mouth on a small breath of air - with all the hidden agenda she could marshal into four tiny syllables without sounding slightly demented. Then she smiled again.

I was initially slightly surprised at her manner, but then again, I was not. This was who she was. Catherine reached up on her toes and kissed me gently on the cheek, 'there you go.' Then she turned on her heels and sashayed her way back to her friends, waving goodbye with her hand above her head as she disappeared into the crowd. I didn't move; I couldn't. Somehow, I knew I must remember this moment. Commit every detail to memory, every word, every gesture, and every inflection, for it would never happen again. I called her at six-thirty that night, and we arranged to meet up at a pub near Trafalgar Square, and our life began.

Jade
Part 3

2023. Jade had been staying at a friend's house on the other side of Providence near Harlow for a couple of days. Catherine had agreed to pick her up that night as Parish was working late, and she had a few things to do on the way. It was nearly nine o'clock, and darkness had descended when Catherine arrived at Tasha's home.

She was going to toot the horn to alert Jade she had arrived. It was cold outside, and she was warm and cosy inside the car and didn't relish the thought of getting out into the freezing wind, even if only for a few minutes. But noticing how quiet it looked – it was an attractive neighbourhood, with pretty, tall, narrow townhouses and ornate lampposts. The residents would probably not appreciate their peace and tranquillity being rudely interrupted by some inconsiderate stranger sounding a car horn in the street while they were all quietly dozing in front of their holavisions. She reconsidered her decision, slid out of the car, gathered her coat tightly around her to fend off the biting wind, and quickly made the short journey to the front door and rang the bell.

Jade answered the door with a smile - already wearing her coat, scarf, and pink woolly hat. 'Hi, Mum.' She kissed Catherine on the cheek. 'I'm packed and ready to go.' She pointed to her small rucksack by the door. She knew she was not the best timekeeper in the world - but she had obviously made an effort to be ready on time today. It would be a long drive home in the dark.

'Bye, Tash. See yer later,' Jade shouted up the staircase. 'Thanks for everything.'

'Bye, Jade. See you Monday,' came the disembodied reply. Jade smiled, picked up her rucksack and slammed the front door behind her. The wintry night air seemed to have no effect on her.

'Tash is having a bubble bath,' muttered Jade as they walked down the path. 'She'll be hours. She likes to put all those little pink candles around the room, burn incense and play whale music while soaking. I had one earlier... it's very soothing, music, candles and everything....'

'Sounds lovely,' said Catherine, but she did wonder about the whale music. 'I think maybe I'll have a bath when we get back.'

Jade threw her rucksack into the back of the car and flopped down next to Catherine.

'The bath has made me a bit tired, Mum. Is it okay if I go to sleep?'

'Of course, it is. I'll join you in a few minutes anyway,' replied Catherine. Jade pressed a button to lower the back of her seat into the sleeping position and closed her eyes, and Catherine drove away.

Catherine didn't enjoy driving long hours at night, so she, too, would sleep once the car was locked onto the AMGS network. There was nothing further for her to do until they arrived home. She looked across at Jade, now snuggled up into a ball. Already blissfully asleep, her face a serenely calm marble sculpture peeking out from her hood, flawless and untainted by the ravages of time, obligation, or responsibility, with no concept of what fate might await her. The triumphs that she might reach out to touch - the disappointment when they recede just beyond her grasp. You never know what might lie ahead in the years to come. Oh, to be young again. Oh, to be you, thought Catherine. Not a care in the world – a free spirit without... without what, she pondered? I have Parish, I have you, and I have a career. What more could there be? She admonished herself for one fleeting moment of selfish ingratitude - then wondered from where she had conjured those thoughts. Instead, she pushed the corrosive line of harmful indulgence from her mind and deliberated over the unmistakable similarity between father and daughter. It was still a remarkable aspect of human design to assiduously carry forward small, unique traits from parent to child. The same features would always endear and cement families. Nearly everything would change throughout their lives, but certain things would forever remain the same.

Maybe it was time to have another baby. Maybe her hormones were playing games with her mind; she was not getting any younger. Jade would be off to university soon, and then she and Parish would be alone again. Was it wrong to have another baby to alleviate the pain they would feel when Jade had gone? I will mention it to Parish tomorrow; yes, I will do that. She made another mental note to broach the subject over dinner the following evening and tried to settle down to sleep. But sleep wouldn't come.

Her mind flashed back to the day they first met. She smiled, thinking of the first few weeks of their relationship. Chaotic rotas to juggle just so they could be together. Intense candlelit meals in a quiet bistro or restaurant when neither was hungry. The food was played with but seldom eaten. Sometimes, the waiters would ask if something was wrong with it - but there never was. They were just too immersed in each other to eat. Too involved with each other, talking about anything and everything. And then there were the long nights of lovemaking at Parish's flat. Catherine lived in a shared house with three other girls, which was not ideal for what they had in mind. Sometimes, in the mornings, they would have exotic feasts, figs, guava fruit and eggs benedict or smoked salmon, wild strawberries, and pink champagne. A little decadent, maybe, but an essential respite to allow them to regenerate and replenish their exhausted bodies and prepare them for the labours of the days ahead.

Those deliriously irrational days and nights stretched into weeks and months, then years - but the passion of their frenzied existence had now slowed a little since Jade was born. The three of them had eased into a gently quixotic intermezzo - a pause before the raging storm.

The Killing Plan.

If you enjoyed this book, why not try the first book in the Story Teller Pentology. Each tale explores a different kind of relationship and how it can change. Death of a Sparrow.

Chapter one follows......

CHAPTER 1. DEATH OF A SPARROW.

Marissa's story.

Many things happen that make sense, but so many more do not. I have tried to unscramble one from the other. But as time passed, a mist of uncertainty, confusion and doubt descended over what happened on that first day and all the days that followed. I could blame this on a declining memory, but that would be disingenuous - to you as the reader and to me as the writer. The proverb goes, *Reason will prevail when tension is becalmed,* and I believe the tension was stilled for a few brief moments. And in those few moments, reason determined the destiny of the world. I have no desire to tell an untruth or to mislead, but I may. If I do, please forgive me, for it will not be by intent.

This is my story of what happened on the eight days of Hanukkah in 1943.

The Second Night of Hanukkah 1943.

Nica was clearly not happy. His glazed expression a curious montage of disheartenment, confusion and, to a lesser degree, resigned acceptance. Each emotion pulling him in a different direction. Each vying for overall control, endeavouring to assert itself as the dominant force to be reckoned with. He was clearly in a bit of a muddle.

At times he could also be infuriating and stupid and many other things, but I could trust him, and in a way, I loved him. He was honest, tolerable (most of the time), and amiable. I would probably marry him one day when we were old enough. If nobody more suitable came along and the Germans hadn't shot him in the meantime. But of course, he didn't know that - not back then, but then neither did I... not really.

Those who did know him - knew him well, that is, would have understood him. They could read his face and, with a reasonable degree of certainty, determine where his mind was at, but not today. Considering the incalculable number of subtle variants of mannerisms, demeanour and emotion in play, it would have been virtually impossible.

He was struggling with one of the two suitcases he was carrying across the platform. That was obvious. I later discovered that he had no problem with his own case, just the one belonging to his sister, Tania.

For a brief moment, Nica wondered why he was carrying it at all. Tania's case was obviously much heavier than his, and this annoyed him intensely. But his father had asked him to carry it, and he had respectfully agreed. Nica seldom argued or disagreed with his father's requests; there was never any point. His father knew many things that he did not, and he understood that his own desire to learn was perfectly matched by his father's desire to teach him all he knew.

A delicate sense of equilibrium existed between them, which would remain for the foreseeable future. To this much, he was resigned. One day, however, he would become as knowledgeable as his father, possibly more so and then no longer would the equilibrium be maintained. He would then not just be a son but a man in his own right. He would then make his own decisions but until that time....

Shuffling across the station platform in the howling wind and snow, dragging two suitcases was not exactly how Nica had imagined spending the first day of Hanukkah. But then much had happened over the last few days that would change how he might celebrate the festival of Light in the future - and how he would remember Hanukkah 1943. It would be indelibly transcribed into his brain for the rest of his life, however long or short.

For a moment, he wondered what Tania could have packed that made her case so much heavier than his. Standing at the steps to the carriage, he took a deep breath. Then he hoisted the two cases, one at a time, onto the small backplate platform before quickly clambering up behind them. His father had taught him to always take a deep breath before engaging in any activity requiring a sudden energy spurt.

Nica and Tania were only allowed one small suitcase each for the journey. Their parents, Dr Franz and Mary Schiller, had carefully packed them the night before with essential clothing, a few personal items, a little food, and in Tania's case, half a dozen house bricks, just in case... That was the best explanation Nica could come up with.

Standing on the tiny backplate, he hesitated momentarily and glanced back at the ocean of bewildered faces. The unmistakable haze of desolation and sadness rose from the crowd like the steam from a freshly cooked bread pudding. He could feel it, almost touch it, as it penetrated every pore of his body. Overwhelmed by this episodic wave of sorrow and anguish – he was drowning - he might never breathe again...

He half hoped, in desperation, to see at least one familiar face amongst the hundreds of confused faces waiting to board the train, but he did not. He saw uncertainty and puzzlement in each tiny pink moon, obediently shuffling forward. He knew this was to be expected, for he, too, felt the same. What he had not expected to see, suffused amidst these unsolicited sensations, was the tiny glimmer of hope, but this was, by far, the frailest sense.

The blizzard, which had been blowing relentlessly since early morning, now shrouded and transformed every huddled body into a blanket of undulating white velvet. It effectively obliterated any possibility of meaningful recognition. All the frenetic energy of the swirling snowflakes, each contemptuously gyrating in a tiny vortex of ecstasy. Each diametrically opposed to the almost motionless lines of children waiting patiently to board the train.

'Hurry up!' somebody half-heartedly shouted. 'I'm freezing my bollicks off out here,' but Nica did not reply, for he did not hear the plea. His mind was elsewhere as he shook the snow from his coat and entered the carriage. Tania, who was following just behind, still appeared to be half asleep - utterly unaware of what was happening around her or even where she was, for that matter.

This was not like Tania; she had always been the curious one. The one who asked too many questions, the one with such acute peripheral awareness that, at times, she knew precisely what was happening behind her head as well as in front of it. Today, however, she was aware of nothing. She was still confused by the sense of wretchedness that had totally overwhelmed her the previous night when her parents had explained what would happen the following day. The words bounced around the kitchen, desperately looking for somewhere to land before her brain conceded to the inevitable and allowed them to enter. Still, they made no sense.

Before passing through the station's final barrier, their parents kissed them both. They held them tightly - bidding them farewell and a "Happy Hanukkah." Happy Hanukkah! It sounded strange – meaningless and absurd – without purpose. Tania wondered how they could wish them happiness when they were being made to leave their home and everything they had ever known. They were going to a place they had never been before to live with people they did not know – and they had no idea when, if ever, they would see their parents again.

Nica tried to open the door to the carriage but couldn't - the handle was frozen and very stiff. He wrenched it a second time, and it opened. He glanced at Tania and smiled.

Inside the carriage, he saw the other children scurrying around, lifting bags onto racks, and deciding whether to sit by the window or gangway. He started to edge his way through the chaos and confusion, closely followed by Tania, slowly making their way down the centre aisle. Eventually, he found a four-seater section near the interconnecting door at the end of the carriage. There were three spare spaces. One of his friends, Janez, was already sitting in the fourth space reading a book. Nica hoisted the two suitcases onto the overhead storage rack, struggling a little with Tania's, before eventually dropping down onto the wooden bench and sliding up to the window. Tania sat down beside him, facing Janez.

'What did you pack in your case?' asked Nica, turning briefly to Tania with a sarcastic smirk, 'half a ton of coal?'

'No, just some essentials, thank you,' muttered Tania with rueful indifference. This was oddly out of character - she was usually more forthright. Her reply, bordering on the edge of courteousness, was strangely unnerving for Nica.

Nica shrugged with a hint of curiosity. He was not entirely satisfied with Tania's answer - but felt disinclined to interrogate her further; it wasn't that important. He thought that was the best course of action in the circumstances.

Janez looked up at them, casually acknowledging their arrival with a quick smile. He glanced at the large ushanka hat that Nica was wearing but made no comment. 'Thought you two weren't coming?' He flashed them an inquisitorial expression.

'Wouldn't miss it for the world - I love a day out,' mused Tania.

'Well, we did think about not bothering, but the krauts insisted,' replied Nica, with a derisory air of defiant arrogance.

'Did you get breakfast before you left home?' asked Janez.

'Yes,' replied Nica, 'why?'

'I don't think they will be giving us anything, I did ask – out of curiosity, but the shitlicker just grunted.'

'The shit-lickers wouldn't give you the drippings from their arses,' added Nica with a sneer.

Hungarian soldiers were called many things by Slovenians after the German invasion. But shit-lickers was by far their favourite term of abuse. The Slavic attitude towards their former neighbours changed dramatically after the extreme north-eastern zone of Slovenia, Prekmurje, was transferred to Hungary in April 1941. This was by way of an axis power arrangement when Germany dismembered Slovenia. The rest of the country was divided between Austria and Italy. The northeastern zone was controlled by Hungarian soldiers but with German officers. The Germans didn't trust their new allies that much.

'Aaaah,' squelched Tania, screwing her face up in disgust and sticking her tongue out as if she were about to vomit. 'I wish you wouldn't use that word,' glaring at her brother with half-closed eyes. He knew she hated it when he cursed publicly, but he did it anyway. She thought it demeaning and common and hated being associated with him when he was like this. He would never have used the word in front of his parents.

'What word?' replied Nica, feigning puzzlement.

'You know what word. That word... it's disgusting. Father would chastise you if he heard you, and the soldiers will shoot you dead in a heartbeat if they hear it.'

'Father's not here, so he can't say anything - and the shit-lickers are stupid and deaf,' snapped Nica. His expression didn't change this time, but a noticeable hint of resentment and contempt hovered in his tone. It was as if he held his father responsible for him being where he was today.

'No, but I am here, and I did, so I must act in loco parentis, so to speak, and monitor your language,' replied Tania in a moralizing tone. Nica shrugged disagreeably at Tania's presumptive assertion.

'Must you, really?' he replied impertinently with a curt shake of his head.

'Yes!' replied Tania adopting a strange matriarchal glaze.

Nica gave in, as he always did with Tania. He thought he would have a stab at sarcasm instead. 'I guess it beats sitting around a cosy roaring fire, eating hot chestnuts, drinking mulled wine, and singing happy Hanukkah songs. Yes, I definitely prefer to be starving on a train while freezing off my testicalia.'

'Aaaaaah,' murmured Tania, even louder than before. She also hated hearing any words related to male genitalia. Unfortunately, Nica had an encyclopaedic knowledge of the subject, having read the relevant section in every one of his father's reference books, and there were many. Tania mumbled, 'I don't feel well,' then she shut her eyes and pretended to sleep.

'What's loco parentis?' asked Janez, a little puzzled.

With a curious expression, Tania half opened her eyes. With a hint of a smirk, she explained, 'It means I am acting as Nica's parents while our real parents aren't here.' She smirked at Nica.

'So you are in charge of Nica?' inquired Janez, obviously baiting their conversation.

'Yes, because I am the sensible one.'

'In your dreams,' interrupted Nica grinning at Tania.

'I have to be in charge to ensure you keep your mouth clean,' replied Tania with a scowling expression. 'It's like a toilet sometimes.'

Nica didn't reply, and Tania shut her eyes again. Momentarily she reopened them.

'Is that even a word?'

'What word?' replied Nica, Goading Tania to utter another word she found repulsive.

'You know what word,' replied Tania, realizing she had backed herself into a corner again.

'The horrible word you just said.'

'TES-TI-CAL-I-A, you mean?' He pronounced it very slowly, over-emphasising the five syllables.

'Yes.'

'Well, it is a proper word. I found it in a book,' replied Nica proudly.

'Did you,' replied Tania condescendingly. She fervently believed that he only read books simply to discover unpleasant words to taunt her with.

'Yes.'

'Right.' Tania shut her eyes again and stuck her fingers in her ears.

Janez grinned at Nica's spat with Tania. It amused him. 'Where's Marissa?' he asked.

'Don't know, haven't seen her,' replied Nica. 'I glanced around the platform before boarding, but it was pandemonium. I couldn't see anybody clearly. Thought she might already be here with you.'

Janez shook his head. 'I kept a place for her,' he nodded to the empty space where he had left his suitcase, 'but I haven't seen her.'

It went quiet for a while as they gazed out of the carriage window, looking at the other children on the platform, still waiting to board the train.

'Do I look stupid in this?' asked Nica, gingerly peeking out from under the curiously large brown Ushanka hat he was wearing. It had large dangly flaps hanging down on both sides to cover his ears, obviously to stop them from freezing. But it also gave him the appearance of a dangerously oversized demented hare.

'Do you really want me to answer that?' chipped in Tania, opening one eye - desperately trying not to laugh.

The hat was far too big for him; it almost covered his eyes, but it kept his head warm – and that was all that really mattered.

It had been his father's till today, but Franz had placed it on Nica's head at the railway station just before he and his sister passed through the final barrier. Now it was his.

'Not at all,' replied Janez, smiling at Tania's reply. He enjoyed watching them bicker. 'I did wonder about the size, though.'

Nica glared at Tania. 'Ah, you're back with us again; I was getting worried about you, and I asked Janez for his opinion, not yours.'

'Were you?' asked Tania, smirking.

'Yes.'

'Well, I thought I would stick my nose in anyway.'

'I thought you weren't well?' asked Nica.

'It's only some of the words you use that make me sick, but I'm feeling a little better now, thank you,' said Tania with another squinty smirk.

'I can tell,' mumbled Nica.

'But I'm still a bit sad,' said Tania.

'We're all sad, but we must put up with it for now and put on a brave face.'

'Yes, I know,' said Tania, 'but...'

'It's a lovely ushanka, interrupted Janez without any hint of sarcasm. 'Is your head hot?'

Tania glanced at Janez in disbelief - stunned by the banality of the question.

'It's actually just right... It was my dad's. That's why it's too big,' replied Nica.

'I sort of guessed it wasn't yours,' replied Janez with a tiny smirk before returning to his book.

'Don't lose the ushanka!' His father, Franz, had plaintively shouted just as Nica and Tania stepped into the carriage. But his plea had been drowned out by the howling winds whipping through the station and the heavy muttering of parental uncertainty filling the air. Nica never considered that those few innocuous words might be the last he would ever hear from his father.

Three slender threads of commonality connected Dr Franz Schiller and his wife, Mary, with the other parents left standing on the platform. The first was a small yellow cloth badge in the shape of the Star of David, preeminent on every coat breast embroidered with the word žid.

The second was a visceral sense of confusion and trepidation, suffocating the air like a heavy mist of warm treacle. Conversely, the more prosaic ice-cold driving winds and snow cut through the atmosphere like a warm knife slicing through butter. The third was that only children were boarding the train, their

children. In a trance-like state, Mary watched as each child stepped regimentally into their chosen carriage in a strangely mechanical manner. It reminded her of clockwork soldiers she had once seen in a toyshop window in Lendava before the war. The shop wasn't there anymore. There was no longer a demand, or the money for frivolous expenditure on children's toys - especially those with military connotations.

For no particular reason, the children had, without prior instruction, formed themselves into four orderly queues and were waiting to board their selected carriage. Slowly they were devoured as tiny morsels of nourishment for this metal monster. But the monster's appetite would never be satisfied until it had consumed every last vestige of innocence.

Herded like cattle behind the ominously tall, rusty grey metal barriers, the corralled parents painted an inglorious picture of enforced incarceration. The Hungarian guards erected the barricades to prevent last-minute fraternisation or emotional outbursts between parent and child. Anything that could cause a delay in the loading process was to be avoided at any cost. At this, the final moment of parting, denial of compassion, the last remnant of humanity - the unconscionable act of a thief in the night stealing time - inflicting heartache.

But it mattered not, for the parents and the children had already said their goodbyes.

Frail and withered by years of war, Mary had to endure the final attrition - losing her children, probably forever. She knew she would not see another summer, only the glorious apricity of one more winter before her days were done. Her spindly blue fingers, skin like gossamer, tightly grasped the wire barrier. She hoped for one last glimpse of Tania and Nica before they boarded the train, but they were lost in the crowd. Mary wept quietly, unobtrusively. That was her way, not for her the vacuous piety of grief; there was no reverence that could be shared; it was hers and hers alone. Franz kept his feelings in check, as he always did. Of course, he loved his children as much as Mary and would miss them just as much after they were gone, but he did not show it – he would not show it, not yet. There would be time enough later for sorrow and remorse, but not now; that was his way. He was powerless to change anything, and hopefully, Mary would understand.

The night before; was the first night of Hanukkah, and they had recited the three Maariv prayers together. Nica had lit the Shammash and the first candle, a custom he looked forward to each year since his Bar mitzvah. He would not be lighting any more candles at home this year. After prayers, they sat in the kitchen to eat fried potato pancakes. Franz explained to Nica and Tania that they would be going on a long journey the following day. They even managed to laugh a little. Hanukkah was always a joyful time. But in their minds, they all wondered when and if they would ever celebrate as a family again. And what the circumstances might be….

Tomorrow they would travel on a train with hundreds of other children to their new home. But Franz and Mary would not be going with them. They had never been separated before.

'So tell me, father,' said Nica, 'Where are we going?'

'You are being evacuated to Switzerland for your own safety.'

'But why Switzerland?' asked Tania curiously.

'Because that is where they are taking you.' Tania wondered who the "they" were but said nothing. She knew her parents would not send them anywhere if it was not necessary. Let alone on a journey to a different country where they were uncertain of the destination and who would be there to meet them.

'Switzerland is a good place,' replied Franz reassuringly. 'It is a neutral country not involved in the war, so you will be better off there than here. So tonight, after supper, you must prepare for the journey. It should take about two to three days to get there, but once you arrive at your new home, you will be safe until you return to us after the war is over.

Tania and Nica couldn't see any sense in being separated from their parents, but their concerns had been partially alleviated by their parent's reassurances that they would soon be reunited.

Death of a Sparrow.

Please email me to let me know if you liked this book.
summersetdowns@hotmail.com

Printed in Great Britain
by Amazon

21028643R00164